LIVINGSTON UNFOUND

MARA BENETTI

The Book Guild Ltd

First published in Great Britain in 2021 by
The Book Guild Ltd
9 Priory Business Park
Wistow Road, Kibworth
Leicestershire, LE8 0RX
Freephone: 0800 999 2982
www.bookguild.co.uk
Email: info@bookguild.co.uk
Twitter: @bookguild

Typeset in 11pt Minion Pro

Printed and bound in the UK by TJ Books LTD, Padstow, Cornwall

ISBN 978 1913913 267

British Library Cataloguing in Publication Data.
A catalogue record for this book is available from the British Library.

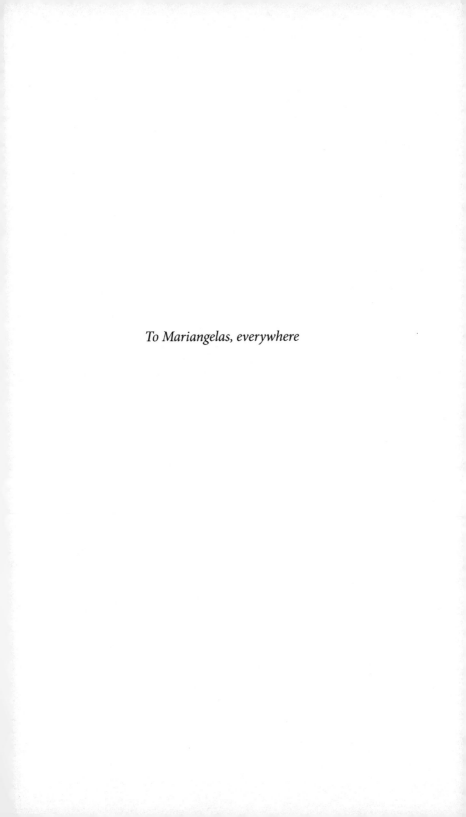

To Mariangelas, everywhere

FOREWORD

The story of *Livingston Unfound* is based on a diary I kept in the mid-eighties. Having recently graduated in Latin American studies from Essex University, just like the protagonist, Monica, I spent two years travelling in Central America.

The period turned out to be one of the most significant of my life, and one which I've kept revisiting during the last three decades.

It may be hard to imagine how different the world was then, so, for the benefit of readers unfamiliar with the history of those years, I have included a short reference section at the end of this foreword.

The eighties were the tail end of a period of hope, radical ideas and desire for change that had its peak in the sixties and seventies and saw the rise of countless anti-establishment movements and anti-colonialist protests around the world.

This period was particularly turbulent and momentous in Latin America, where many dictatorships were being challenged and the oppressed were fighting for long overdue political change.

Inspired by left-wing leaders like Fidel Castro and Che Guevara, many young people from the West flocked to Cuba and Nicaragua. They wanted to support the new revolutionary governments and the more equitable economies that were being established there. In the mid-eighties, I belonged, just like Monica, to the rearguard of that generation.

Despite the exceptional vibrancy of those years, *Livingston Unfound* is not, however, an account of the political events occurring in Central America at that time. It is the journey of a woman travelling on her own, taking risks and facing dangers, choosing friends and lovers across cultural boundaries and, above all, struggling to come to terms with the inevitable conflicts and contradictions that come with being a relatively affluent foreigner in a land of poverty and repression. Like a mirror held up to her, the journey she sets out on forces her to acknowledge her privilege, while she strives to see the world with new eyes.

Monica's story raises some of the fundamental questions travellers often ask themselves. What is the best way to explore a place, to absorb it and understand it? How can one fit in? How should one deal with the many differences separating one's own experience from that of others?

What follows is an autofiction. That is to say that, while much of *Livingston Unfound* has been fictionalised for the purpose of constructing a narrative, most of it is true to the spirit of my experiences in Guatemala, in general, and Labuga, in particular.

Many Livingstonians, as well as some of the people who lived in the village at the time, may recognise themselves in the characters of the story. In order to disguise their identities, I have changed their names. At the same time, as a writer, I must try to be faithful to the times and the situations – even where those situations flatter no one, including the author.

*

SOME NOTES ON THE POLITICAL BACKGROUND TO THE STORY

NICARAGUA – After the Frente Sandinista de Liberacion Nacional (FSLN) overthrew the Somoza regime in 1979, a period of restructuring followed in all sectors of the country's economy, directing it towards a mixed system of state interventionism and entrepreneurial capitalism. When, at the end of this emergency period, Daniel Ortega was sworn in as the democratically elected president of the new government, the USA imposed an economic embargo on the country, and backed the *Contras*, a rightist counter-revolutionary group, with weapons and military training. The USA also discontinued the Peace Corps aid programme in Nicaragua, while doubling the number of its volunteers in the neighbouring countries, raising suspicions that some of them might be CIA agents.

CUBA – The Cuban Revolution ousted the military dictatorship of Fulgencio Batista on the 31st of December 1958, replacing his government with a socialist state. This had powerful domestic and international repercussions, as the nationalisation of the economy initiated by Fidel Castro led not only to a USA economic embargo and the interruption of diplomatic relations between the two countries, but also to the establishment of close military and economic ties between Cuba and the Soviet Union, an alliance that lasted until the Soviet Union's collapse in 1991.

In the conviction that the only remedy against imperialism, colonialism and monopoly capitalism was world revolution and proletarian internationalism, Castro's government heralded an era of Cuban intervention in several foreign military conflicts, including the Angolan Civil War and the Nicaraguan Revolution.

A crucial role was played by Ernesto "Che" Guevara, a former commander in the Cuban Revolution. Although at first invited to cover a number of important positions in the new government, in 1965 "El Che" left Cuba to foment the revolution abroad, first unsuccessfully in Congo, and then in Bolivia, where in 1967 he was captured in an ambush by CIA-assisted Bolivian forces and summarily executed.

Che Guevara's single-mindedness and his unrelenting dedication to the struggle for freedom and justice have made him a countercultural symbol of rebellion. He was the quintessence of the "new man", driven by moral rather than material incentives. To this day, the famous photograph of him looking into the distance appears on countless T-shirts and students' walls.

GUATEMALA – Between 1960 and 1996, the Guatemalan government, right-wing paramilitary organisations and left-wing insurgents were all engaged in the Guatemalan Civil War. The indigenous population suffered the most as a result of this war. In the late nineties, the Truth Commission estimated that more than 200,000 people were killed during those years, the vast majority indigenous civilians, and 93% of the killings were attributed to the military. The commission determined that in several instances the government was responsible for acts of genocide. Within the conflict, government forces were supported by the USA, whereas Cuba sided with the insurgents.

In the West, awareness of the ethnic dimension to the conflict increased with the publication in 1983 of *I, Rigoberta Menchú*, a memoir by a leading Mayan activist, who, in 1992, was awarded the Nobel Peace Prize on account of her work for social justice.

For nearly two decades, the government was controlled by the army. Then, in 1985, Vinicio Cerezo, a civilian politician of the Christian Democracy Party, won the elections with almost 70% of the votes.

Although Cerezo's government saw a marked decrease in political violence, it was strongly criticised for its reluctance to investigate and prosecute cases of human rights violations.

It took another decade for peace negotiations to be concluded. In December 1996, the government signed a peace agreement with the opposing forces and thus ended the thirty-six-year internal conflict.

UK – Latin American studies as a discipline emerged in the UK in the mid-1960s in the wake of the Cuban Revolution. The UK's first department of Latin American studies was established at Essex

University in 1968. After the 1973 coup in Chile, led by General Pinochet against Allende, the British government gave asylum to 2,500 Chilean refugees, and many universities saw an increase in the number of students enrolling in their Latin American studies departments.

In the early eighties, the Nicaraguan Solidarity Campaign began to organise and send work brigades to Nicaragua to help with the projects the Sandinista government was promoting in the poorest areas of Nicaragua.

USA – The USA have always considered Central America their own "backyard" and have always exerted a tight control over its politics. In the mid-eighties, the Sandinistas were the latest enemy and, in order to create a continuous state of alert in the country, thereby eroding grassroots support for the Sandinistas, the USA backed the Contras in their sabotage operations against many of the schools, health centres and cooperatives set up by the new government.

In the mid-eighties, the US Embassy in Managua was weekly picketed by dissenting American and non-American protesters.

PART ONE

CHAPTER ONE

ON THE WAY TO PANA

The Blue Bird bus was packed tight with passengers – row upon row of small Mayan men clad in Western clothes, with large cowboy hats thrust low over their faces, their heads bobbing up and down, or side to side with each jolt and road bump. I looked at them dozing away in the sweltering heat of the afternoon, arms, legs, heads hanging loose, surrendered.

I was squeezed in at the back with a handful of other women. They sat still and composed, while I shifted from one buttock to the other – how could they not feel the hard metal seats? Beads of sweat clinging to my brow, I counted the hours that separated us from our destination. Time crawled by, but there was no way of getting anywhere quickly in Guatemala. The country was incredibly beautiful. It had it all: mountains, lakes, traditions, mystery, but the state of transport was abysmal. Take the bus I was travelling on; it had no suspension to speak of. As we juddered along the gravel, I could feel each bump bruising my behind. And yet, look at everyone sleeping – no one else seemed to mind the discomfort.

The driver took a bend and the bus swerved, jolting me out of my seat. As the road straightened, we came to an abrupt halt. All around, heads jerked into wary wakefulness. I peered through the thick film of dust that covered the window but couldn't see a thing.

With a rattling clunk, the bus door opened and a soldier in combats climbed on board. Waving his gun, he barked a few brief words at the driver.

'*Sí, señor, por supuesto. Con mucho gusto, señor!*' the latter replied, jumping to attention.

The soldier gave the man a surly look, flapped his knotty, sun-browned hand impatiently, and left.

'*Ándale!* Get out! *Todos!*' the driver shouted to all of us and, as if eager to please, he stood there by the door, making sure no one stayed behind.

I followed everyone along the aisle. In silence, eyes darting from side to side and out of the windows, people shuffled in between the seats, then down the steps and into the open. The young woman ahead of me stumbled over her long Mayan skirt as she alighted. To steady herself, she seized my hand. Hers was cold and sweaty, just like mine. I felt my heart pounding through my ribcage as I jumped the last step onto the ground.

Outside, a long line of men, my fellow travellers, stood hands up and legs rigidly apart, faces pressed hard against the hot metal of the near side of the bus. A patrol of four or five soldiers, all of them Mayan, frisked the men meticulously, impassively, guns at the ready.

Together with the other women and the girl who a moment ago had grabbed my hand, I was directed to the front of the bus and made to stand in a line by the headlights, from where the men couldn't be seen. I tried to catch someone's eye, but everyone faced front, in silence, giving nothing away.

The line moved slowly forward and, finally, when my turn came, there, right in front of me, stood an officer, or what to me looked like an officer, to judge by his more expensive uniform and

4

the insignia on his left breast pocket. He gestured brusquely to step closer.

'*Papeles!*' he snapped.

With shaky hands, I fumbled inside my waist pouch, and, in the end, I managed to produce my passport and handed it over to him.

He leafed through it, pausing occasionally to examine some detail or other. Then he looked up and stared at me.

'*Espere aquí,*' he ordered, and, holding my passport, he marched out of sight.

I stood there, a dull pain spreading from the back of my neck over my shoulders. No one spoke; all I could hear was the rustling of the women's feet behind me, and my own galloping heartbeat. Just below my left eye, I could feel the beginning of a nervous twitch.

What was the problem? Would I be taken away? And if I was, would any of my fellow travellers speak out, try to stop the soldiers? They were as terrified as I was. And my folks at home, my mother, would she ever hear about it?

I recalled the conversation I'd had on the phone with her a couple of days earlier.

'Guatemala!' she'd shouted down the line when she heard where I was ringing from. 'Isn't that where people disappear? Isn't that where they have death squads? My God, Monica, what are you doing there?'

I'd tried my best to reassure her. 'That's what the Western media say. It's just the usual scaremongering. Really, *mamma*, this place couldn't be more peaceful. It's so beautiful. People are so kind, so gentle...'

The officer returned at last.

'*Nombre y apellido!*' he shouted, waving my passport in the air.

Impossible to read from his expression what he was driving at.

'Monica Florimonte,' I said, forcing a smile out.

'*De dónde?*'

At every Central American border, I'd been asked the same question, most likely because my surname seemed to give the lie to the nationality of my passport.

'I'm British, but my parents are Italian. I was born in Italy. *Born in Treviso in 1956,* see?' I pointed to the first page.

He didn't look at the document, but stared at me long and hard, weighing up my answer. I knew what was coming next. He demanded to know where I'd been before coming to Guatemala.

I swallowed hard, trying to control my voice. 'In Nicaragua.' The man looked up. 'Teaching English for four months,' I added.

Nicaragua didn't seem to be the problem, though. But, earlier, where had I been earlier?

He held open the very last page of my passport, and there was the Cuban stamp. The simple mention of Cuba always raised eyebrows in Central America. Cuba, Fidel, Che, the Revolution; that was people's train of thought.

'What were you doing in Cuba?' He pressed on, the mouth of the rifle he held across his chest getting dangerously near. 'Who do you know there?'

I stood rooted to the spot, racking my brain for something to say that wouldn't arouse his suspicions. I'd visited schools and hospitals, I'd met journalists and writers; all contacts I'd been given by friends and friends of friends. I'd even tried, and failed, to get a job as a translator with *Granma*, the Communist paper. That wouldn't go down well.

'I travelled around,' I replied.

The officer stared gloomily at me, then at the stamp on the passport. '*Y ahora adónde?*'

'To Panajachel.'

'*Para qué?*'

'I've heard it's a nice place. The lake is *muy bonito.*' Did I sound convincing? It was nothing less than the truth, and yet I could hear my voice cracking.

The officer didn't say a word. With knitted eyebrows and a scowl on his face, he stared fixedly at me. He perused the passport once more at length. Then, his black, impassive eyes riveted on mine, he asked:

'*Turista?*'

'*Sí, sí.*' I nodded emphatically. '*Turista.*'

He looked at me again, taking in my leopard print trousers, my bright pink shirt, the long dreadlock dangling to the side of my left ear.

He turned to someone who stood somewhere behind the bus. '*Turista!*' he shouted. The other man shouted something indistinct back.

That seemed to settle it. With a dismissive flick of his hand, he returned my passport and signalled I was free to go. The next woman in line stepped forward, hardly a sound coming from anyone.

A little later – I was glad to see no one had been taken away – we were all back in our seats. Eyes averted, a blank expression on everyone's face, people sat in silence, completely still. Cold shivers ran down my spine.

A fine drizzle began to fall. With a crank of gears and a nervous backward glance, the driver started the engine.

As the bus finally pulled away, a tall man emerged from the makeshift garret, threw his half-smoked cigarette to the ground and stubbed it out with the sole of his boot. There he stood amid the diminutive, poorly rationed Mayan soldiers, a corn-fed khaki-clad Colossus in a green beret. An American, no doubt; one of the many US military advisors providing "technical assistance" to the local army. I knew about the counterinsurgency operations these special units had carried out since the sixties. I knew they were here to help the Guatemalan army wipe out any dissenting voice. I knew that without question they were murderers.

Shivering, I sat staring through the dust-covered window as the bus careered along the country road.

*

When the bus came to its final stop, my heart was still pounding.

Panajachel was far from the quiet Indian village by Lake Atitlán I'd imagined, but for once I welcomed the buzz of the tourists around me.

The place had everything a traveller could wish for – a couple of venues showing films in English, three bicycle-hire shops, dozens of travel agencies organising trips anywhere you'd care to go, and then maps, guidebooks, and even bus timetables. There were also scores of trendy cafés and restaurants of all kinds – from the fast food joint to the macrobiotic bistro – and all of them packed.

As I walked along the main street looking for an affordable guesthouse, I could hear snatches of conversations in many languages. The Americans seemed to be by far the majority, but there were Europeans too, French, Italians, Germans, as well as a handful of Brazilians and other South Americans. But unlike the people I'd met and worked with in Nicaragua – all of them on a political mission, committed to the revolution and with no time for partying – these here were mostly jolly hippies blending in with the locals, and even outdoing them with the brightness of their clothes.

As for the Mayans, they were comparatively few. Staggering under impossibly heavy loads, they walked through the crowd peddling their handwoven fabrics.

'*Compre! Compre! Qué busca?*' they hollered relentlessly. '*Mire este huipil! Sólo veinticinco quetzals! Cuánto ofrece usted? Diga...*'

'*No, gracias!*' I kept on saying to the right and to the left, trying to disentangle myself from them.

I finally chose my *posada*. Called *The Lost Quetzal* after the nearly extinct national bird, it was priced just right for my dwindling finances. A young woman with a strong French accent asked me for my passport, then proceeded to inform me where in town I could find the best of everything.

I'd just landed in la-la land, it seemed.

In the days that followed, after months of *chuchito* lunches at market stalls, I allowed myself to reconnect with the familiar world of muesli breakfasts and chocolate croissants, and even indulged myself with long, steamy showers and perfumed gels.

But, as I lay on crisp cotton sheets sipping my morning *cappuccino*, I was haunted by the memory of the roadblock and the soldiers' menacing glares.

Of course, I knew about repression and about people disappearing. During the four years of my Latin American degree, I'd been lectured over and over about it. But this was different. This was the real thing, and not only had I never come so close to danger, but I'd never, ever thought anything of the kind could happen to me.

What irked me most was realising how scared I'd been, and how scared I still was. In my fear, I'd clutched at that word "*turista*" as desperately as a drowning person clutches at the first thing they lay hands on. 'Me, a tourist?' I'd usually scoff. 'No, not me. I'm much more than that,' I'd insist. 'I'm not just passing through, like most. I take things in, I get to know people, I get involved. Isn't that why I'm here, doing my bit to make the world a better place, well, Nicaragua at least?' But here in Guatemala, where the "revolution" wasn't going quite so well, at the first sign of trouble, I'd gone to pieces and taken refuge behind those hateful three syllables. '*Tu-ri-sta, sì, señor, soy turista,*' I'd replied, standing to attention.

And like all *turistas*, I was now in Panajachel. Whereas both in Cuba and Nicaragua, because of the US embargo, food was rationed and most shelves were bare, Panajachel was like a huge market where the old capitalist mantra ruled – "consume, consume, consume". And, as l found my way around, I realised that, almost down to the last shop, the economy was in the hands of foreigners. They owned the cafés, the bars, the hotels, and even most of the craft shops. They didn't make the crafts themselves, of course. They commissioned them from the Mayan artisans around the lake and then sold them at much inflated prices. The streets of Panjachel were crowded, chaotic, riotous. They brimmed full of *turistas*. The longer I stayed, the more alienated I felt.

When the hubbub became too overwhelming, I decided to spend as much time as possible out of town. I'd wake early and simply walk in whatever direction my feet chose for me.

One afternoon, I discovered a narrow path hidden behind the last few market stalls and, with barely a thought for where it might lead, I followed it up the hill. The ascent was steep and difficult, but as I reached the top, my desultory curiosity was rewarded. Stretching way into the distance was a magnificent plateau dotted with adobe hamlets poking through the swaying corn. All around was still, save for the buzz of insects, the occasional birdsong, the rustling of the corn. No footfalls but my own. On reaching the plateau, the path became wider, its final destination concealed amid the tall yellow stalks. Turning away from the blue expanse of the lake with the verdigris of the volcanoes towering over it, I followed the ample bends, drawn into the golden fields and the enveloping peace.

No further than a hundred yards ahead, the stillness was broken by the murmur of voices; a few more steps and there they were, two men talking in the shade of some trees. The one with his back to me was Mayan. From the woollen blanket wrapped around his waist, I knew – every village had its distinct pattern – that he was from Sololá, the main urban centre of Lake Atitlán. The other man wore similar clothes, except for his jeans, walking boots and the multi-coloured headband which kept his long dark brown hair off his forehead.

On seeing me approach, the Mayan man hurried across the fields on his bare brown feet and disappeared amid the yellow sea of corn.

'Hi, there!' the other guy yelled with a smile that brimmed over the frame of an ample *Zapata* moustache. 'Do you speak English?'

The American twang was unmistakable. I resignedly introduced myself.

He was Martin, from San Diego. It turned out that he'd walked the same path as me for much the same reasons.

'Oh, yeah, Panajachel!' The broad smile contracted. 'So many tourists! Guatemala at its worst, I guess. But that's where I go whenever I want to meet friends. Sooner or later, we all seem to converge there.'

'It must be the lure of the pancakes.'

He laughed, as if this attempt at small talk was the most accomplished of sallies. I read kindness in his light brown eyes and warmed to him.

There was something Latin about him. I told him.

'My dad is Cuban and my mom's Polish. That good old US of A melting pot…' he said.

We both turned and, in the most natural of ways, began to walk the path side by side. I took another glimpse at those light brown eyes, and suddenly I found myself telling him everything – the roadblock, the passport check, the driver standing to attention, the people scurrying off the bus…

'…and this American soldier! I've never actually seen one of those. Not in the flesh,' I finished.

'Yeah, those guys are all over the place and they're dangerous!' He was about to say something else but then took a step back. 'You're brave.' He hesitated. 'I mean, a woman travelling around this place, on her own…' He looked at me, testing my reaction, and then burst out: 'Jeez! That sounds patronising, but you know what I mean…'

I did know what he meant. At the roadblock, when we were separated from the men, I feared the worst. I remembered how scared I'd been, how my body had frozen. I froze again now as I recalled the episode. I wanted the feeling to disappear.

'Yes,' I said, 'but if I'd never taken the risk of going off the beaten track today, we'd never have met.'

He threw me a quizzical look, then laughed.

'You've got me.'

I liked him. He was different from any of the Americans I'd met before, and certainly he had little in common with those I'd seen in Panajachel. He seemed interesting and sincere, not bad-looking either.

'And you, Monica, what brings you here?'

'This place fascinates me. At university, I did Latin American studies. It was the big thing then. So much happening. Then, a few years after graduating, one day, finally, I felt it was time for me to come and see things with my own eyes.' I paused, struggling to express all my pent-up emotions, my good intentions, my dreams. 'I suppose I'm trying to find something worthwhile to do in this world.' The words spilled out, laying bare my naivety.

'Wow!' He gave me a smile of gentle mockery. 'And have you found it yet? This worthwhile thing?'

'Right now, I'm teaching English in Nicaragua. Officially, I'm here to renew my visa. Unofficially, I'm on holiday from my college. It's half-term. But… to tell you the truth, I'm not happy with my present job.'

'Why is that?' he said, surprised. 'It sounds pretty worthwhile to me.'

'I thought it would be, but it turns out I'm teaching English to a bunch of middle-class wannabe Spielbergs and Ridley Scotts so they can pitch their next big idea to the Hollywood moguls. Where are the ordinary Nicaraguans that need my help?'

He laughed and looked at me with sympathy. Then, still chatting, we walked together and caught the last bus back to Pana.

*

Back in the village, amid the usual comings and goings, we were met by the novelty of the night – an impromptu flea market that sprawled everywhere in sight.

A young crowd of long-haired barefoot foreigners, many of them wearing similar clothes to Martin's, had set out their wares on shawls and blankets draped along the pavements. As we walked by, they rattled off at us a multilingual litany of 'Hey, guys! *Compre! Collares, anillos, pulseras! C'est à bon marché! C'est une occasion! Tutto di qualità! Compre! Compre!*'

'I bet you this lot hasn't a clue about what's going on in Guatemala,' I said glumly to Martin as I stepped over piles of trinkets and gewgaws. 'Death squads, mutilated bodies, the military... what do they care? Give them a bit of trade, their daily *ganja*, that's all they want, they're satisfied... That's hippies for you, I guess.'

"C'mon, don't be so harsh. These guys are exploiting no one,' he protested. 'They just want to make ends meet while travelling. What's wrong with that?'

As I had with the word *turista* earlier on, I felt the need to distance myself from this crowd. I'd been called a hippy so many times in Nicaragua, and every time it felt like something diminishing, something very close to an insult.

But Martin was right. For all my face-saving protests, I had to agree that hippies hadn't done a thing to justify my rant.

'Look around,' he said, and threw out his arm, taking in the vendors with the brightness of their clothes and of their wares, and me with my leopard trousers, my dreadlock, my wristbands, and himself too, with his bandana and multi-coloured waistcoat. 'Tell me, are you and I so different from these people?'

Sure enough, we blended in completely. My indignation evaporated. I laughed along.

'Hey, brother!' Halfway down the street, a tall, lanky man surged forward, taking long strides towards us. 'How are you, man?'

'Hi, guys! Great to see you again!' Martin's effusive greeting extended to an attractive blonde woman who, a short distance away, sat crouched on the pavement, the folds of her skirt gathered around her. Holding in mid-air the ends of the straw basket she was braiding, she looked up, narrowed her eyes in recognition and then gave him the warmest of smiles.

Martin turned to me. 'Monica, meet Brad. And this is Breeze.'

'Hi there!' I waved, inwardly rolling my eyes. *Breeze...* Like that was a real name.

'Martin! Martin!' From behind the two, the ash blonde head of a little girl appeared. She rushed over, her slightly squinted azure look full of excitement.

'Hi, Ananda! I've missed you!' Martin bent over and hugged her. 'Aren't you all supposed to be over in Mexico this time of year?'

'Yep, we were about to leave, but then our VW clapped out. So here we are, chilling out in San Pedro.' Brad pointed past the stalls, over the strip of blue water, at some vague point the other side of the lake. 'We came here tonight to sell our stuff.'

'Business is good just now in Pana,' said *Breeze* while her nimble fingers moved on rapidly, twisting and folding several strands of straw simultaneously. 'And you, Martin, what brings you here?'

'I'm just passing by, really. I'm on my way to Mexico, but first I want to visit el Altiplano, the Highlands up in the north. Have you been?'

The two shook their heads, and Martin continued: 'I've heard so much about it. Everyone raves about the amazing costumes, the people, the traditions, the scenery. The best in Guatemala, they say. So, that's where I'm heading.'

'Hey, man, you can't go yet...' said Brad, taking Martin's arm in his. 'Just now when I saw you, I thought, *Here's my bro, my saviour, my only hope...* You can spare a morning to help me with the van, can't you?'

He turned to me.

'Did you know that Martin here is a wizard mechanic? He plays it down because he's modest. Guess that's not the kind of thing you'd brag about to impress a girl—' He threw Martin a sly grin.

'Why don't you come back with us tonight?' *Breeze* butted in, giving Martin the most seductive of smiles. 'I made a fantastic bean stew earlier. Come and eat with us. Stay the night and tomorrow you can help Brad with the van.'

'C'mon, Martin, come with us!' The little girl grabbed his hand.

'Okay, okay, no need to flatter me. All right, I'll come!' He finally surrendered.

I wasn't certain the invitation extended to me, but either way, right now, I needed to pick up my mail, and most of all I needed a shower.

'Monica, as you see, this young lady wants me.' Martin smiled at Ananda and then at me. 'But it'd be nice to meet up again. What about dinner tomorrow night? At the end of this road, there's just the place. Whadda ya say?'

'Sure!'

'Pancakes on me then!' He laughed. A big hug sealed our pact as we parted.

Back in my room at the Lost Quetzal, I dug out my old copy of the *Rough Guide* to Guatemala from my backpack. Then, snug up in bed, I read all there was to know about el Altiplano.

*

The Sunset Café was at the lake end of Calle Santander, one of the two main roads of Pana that run parallel to each other towards the lake. I walked the whole length of the street as the crimson sunset spilt out over the shimmering water and the surrounding hills.

Past the wooden fence, the café had an open area where people sat in small clusters eating as they admired the view.

I looked around the tables. At the far end, under an archway covered by the cascading blooms of a purple bougainvillea, I caught sight of a bright bandanna and a headful of brown hair. Martin sat facing away from me. Just then, he turned.

'Hey, Monica!' he called out. 'Come and join us.'

There was a woman sitting with him.

The guy certainly knew everyone.

Martin did the introductions and we shook hands.

Suzanne was strong and solid. She had the worn-out look of someone who'd been on the road for a long time, but her youthful smile cancelled out the initial impression of fatigue. Her handshake was firm and confident, her eyes large, unblinking.

She leant across to pick up the backpack slung on the chair next to her to make room for me.

'No, please, leave it,' I said to her. 'I'm fine here.' Grabbing a chair from a nearby table, I placed myself between her and Martin.

'Looks heavy,' I said, pointing to the bulging pack. 'You must have been on the road for a long time.' I braced myself for the usual one-upmanship travellers engage in whenever they meet.

'No, not really. I've been here for three months working in the same place. The day after tomorrow I'm flying home, so here I am in Pana, giving myself a treat.' She gestured at the feast of creamy pancakes and heaps of salad on the table in front of her.

'The lure of the pancakes, see?' Martin winked at me. Then, his voice became earnest. 'Suzanne here works for a human rights organisation with the families of the disappeared. Trade unionists, mainly, am I right?' he asked Suzanne.

'Trade unionists, yes, occasionally teachers, the odd journalist…' she said, 'mostly liaising between them and my organisation.'

'What's she isn't telling you,' Martin leaned across the table, 'is that she lives with these people at great risk to herself.'

'He thinks I'm *so* brave,' Suzanne waved her hand dismissively in his direction, 'but the risk to me is nothing compared to what these people face daily. They're the brave ones, not me.'

'Wow! I'm with Martin. You're brave,' I said to her. 'I couldn't do what you're doing.'

I thought of how paralysed with fear I'd been at the roadblock just after a few questions. And here was this woman – committed, strong-minded, unwavering, and, what's more, not in the least bit smug.

In theory, hers was the kind of work I thought I could see myself doing, that meaningful, worthwhile something.

She looked at us with her serene expression that made everything appear simple, as though it was the most natural thing to do.

Could I be as brave? I sat there in awe.

The sound of skipping steps came closer on the gravel. Two freckly little arms circled Martin's neck from behind the chair and, before he could turn around, two small hands covered his eyes.

'Who's this?' chanted a little girl's voice. 'Guess…'

'Umm... I wonder... Could it be a little devil I know, some mischievous little girl called Ananda? Yeah, I gotcha!' Martin laughed, and the girl spun around and threw herself onto his lap.

'Ananda, c'mon, leave Martin alone! Can't you see he's busy?' said *Breeze*. Tall and slim, in a peacock-coloured satin kaftan, she sauntered across to our table, the strings of glass beads around her neck catching the last of the sunlight. Close behind her came Brad in a black T-shirt and torn jeans.

'Hi, guys! Everything okay?' said Martin.

Jewellery jiggling with every step, Breeze walked up to him, bent over and planted a resounding kiss on each cheek.

'That's for doing such a wonderful job on our van! Thanks, babe! You're worth your weight in gold,' she said to him in a silky voice, dragging a chair from the empty table opposite and sitting herself alongside him.

'Yeah, man,' said Brad, patting Martin's back. 'Thanks to you, we're off tomorrow.'

Once we got through the introductions, the conversation buzzed. It was all about their plans, the route they'd be taking, the places they'd visit along the way, and the far-out people that just the three of them knew. I had little to say, so I sat back and observed everyone.

Breeze had eyes only for Martin. Flashing a smile at him, she piled up her long blonde hair on top of her head with both hands. She held the pose and looked around, as if to say, *Aren't I beautiful?* Then, like a consummate actress, she let it tumble down onto her shoulders in rebellious billows of gold.

Suzanne and I exchanged a knowing look.

Seemingly unaware of being the centre of so much attention, Martin talked on.

The other person oblivious to it all was Brad. He'd plonked himself on the furthest chair and rolled up a joint and was now looking vacantly at Ananda as she chased a brace of ducks and their ducklings across the yard.

I wasn't listening. Lost in my own memories, I thought of Richard, my ex, of our relationship, of the many affairs he'd had while going out with me. All that stuff about free love and open relationships! It all came back: the pain, the jealousy, the feeling of not being valued or loved enough. Until he'd found someone he liked more than me – an attractive blonde full of self-confidence, just like this… like this… *Breeze.*

'Hey, guys, let's go!' Breaking out of his slumber, Brad suddenly stood up. 'The ferry leaves in five minutes. Ananda, come!'

'See you guys!' said Breeze, stretching catlike as she rose from the chair. 'And, Martin, when you're in Mexico, come and see us. You know where to find us, don't you?' She bent over and gave him yet another resounding kiss.

'Yeah, man,' said Brad, still oblivious, or just not that bothered that his wife was all over another guy.

'Bye, Martin!' Ananda came rushing for a hug.

'We'll be waiting…' said Breeze, turning one last time with a lingering smile.

As soon as they were out of sight, Suzanne turned to Martin.

'It seems you've made a double hit there,' she teased him. 'Mother *and* daughter, not bad.'

'Yeah,' I said cautiously. 'Breeze seems to like you quite a bit…'

'She's like that with every other guy,' Martin said dismissively. Was he a bit rattled? 'It doesn't mean anything,' he continued, now with a warm, slightly shy smile. 'There's no harm in it, and there's a good woman beneath all that, a good mom too, and let's face it, I'm not exactly Robert Redford.'

'Oh, yeah…?' Suzanne raised her eyebrows in jest.

We all laughed.

The night had finally descended and now that the hippy family had gone, the three of us seemed more relaxed. We sat there chatting, not minding in the least that our food was taking so long.

From the far distance came the sound of gunshots. We looked at each other, alarmed.

'What's that?'

'Nothing good for sure,' said Suzanne. 'It comes from the other side of the lake, from one of the villages.'

We stared hard into the darkness, but there was only thick forest in front of us. It looked feral and threatening.

As we sat there chatting happily, horrible crimes were being committed; countless dangers lay in wait.

'Monica,' Martin broke the ominous silence. 'I've told you, right? On my way north, I want to go and see the Altiplano. And you're on holiday, aren't you? So, I was thinking, what about coming along with me?'

'You want to be my bodyguard?'

'I was hoping you'd be mine!' he quipped back.

It was settled right away. Martin and I made arrangements to set off together the following day.

At last, our order of pancakes arrived, together with two bowls of chicken stew and a tall pile of tortillas. I was famished and, as I tucked into the food, my mood began to improve. The others seemed happier too. Now, on every table, the flame of a candle cast a soft halo around each party, breaking up the terrace into intimate islands of light. We sat there well after the plates were cleared, chatting and joking. Our laughter drifted out over the darkening lake with its encircling silhouettes of mountains. Encouraged by everyone's cheerful mood and the intake of a few more beers, I forgot all about the soldiers, the roadblocks, my private jealousies and fears. Lulled by a new sense of peacefulness, I let go of my anxieties and allowed myself to enjoy the night.

CHAPTER TWO

THE ALTIPLANO

The following morning, we took the early bus to Huehuetenango, the obligatory departure point for most of the highland villages. Our destination was Todos Santos Cuchumatán, but our bus was nowhere in sight. We waited.

The station sprawled onto the nearby street market, with some of the ramshackle Blue Bird buses parked right by the side of the fruit and vegetable stalls. All around was the hustle and bustle of small clusters of Mayan people, each wearing its own distinctive *traje*.

Sitting on our rucksacks, we watched them rush past as they looked for a bus that would take them to their destination. All the women wore their traditional costume; the men sported a mishmash of indigenous *trajes* and western clothes, and the children scampered around in miniature replicas of their parents' clothing.

'See those women over there?' I said, pointing at a group wearing identical red blouses with a floral pattern around the neck. 'They are from Quetzaltenango, near the Mexican border. And those men on the left with the ugly trainers, can you see the birds and the foliage embroidered on their mid-calf trousers? They are from Santiago Atitlán.'

I didn't mean to show off, but the way Martin looked at me with a mixture of surprise and admiration encouraged me to carry on. 'You know, don't you, that the *traje* tells you which village people are from. Look at those patterns, aren't they beautiful? But the best thing about them is the stories they tell – about the origins and the myths of that community, about the Mayan universe and how people see the world... I think that's fascinating, don't you?'

'Wow! Monica, I didn't realise you knew all that. Where did you learn it?'

'Most probably in one of the few lectures I didn't bunk.'

Meanwhile, people flocked first in one direction, then in another, towards every new bus that drove into the station. Eventually, each group found the right bus, hoisted their huge bundles onto it, and left. Each and every group, except us.

We killed time munching on the sandwiches Martin had made that morning: fat bread buns stuffed with avocado slices, banana rounds and finely chopped garlic.

It was an odd combination, but such was my appetite I'd eat anything.

'This concoction of mine,' he boasted, 'is guaranteed to keep in check any bug, even the most vicious. And it doesn't taste bad either, eh?'

He sounded like an eager boy scout about to defy the wilderness, armed with his compass and a handful of clever tricks.

I looked at him. He was kitted out for the trip – Hi-Tec trainers on his feet, a Swiss Army knife dangling from his belt; he even showed me proudly the drinking water kit he carried. 'It'll come in handy on the marshes, you'll see,' he said. What marshes?

Next to him, I felt hopelessly ill prepared. My guidebook was five years old, and I had no proper walking boots. But, as I looked at all his paraphernalia, I couldn't hide a smile. Why bring along all these props and gadgets, when the idea surely was to experience life just like the locals?

A full two hours into our waiting, rumours began to spread that the Todos Santos bus had broken down along the way.

When we finally managed to locate the stationmaster in between clapped-out old coaches and rows of market stalls, he confirmed, 'The next bus will be in three days. Nothing till then.'

'Well, Monica,' Martin turned to me. 'I don't fancy waiting here forever, what about you? What if we headed for another part of the Altiplano?'

'Yeah, great idea. Let's do that.'

There was a bus just about to leave the station with Sacapulas written in large letters on the front. It was in the right general direction, so we hurried onto it.

Seated in one of the middle rows, crammed against each other, with four people to a seat meant to fit two, bundles and bulging wicker baskets under our feet, we both breathed a sigh of relief. At last, we were on the move. Through the window, I saw pine woods run past us, then deep ravines plunging through the brush into sunless valleys. We drove past dusty *comedores* with handwritten signs festooned across the doors. Whenever we stopped to drop off or pick up passengers, a crowd of children and young women besieged the bus, hawking roasted peanuts in paper cornets and sliced mangoes in clear plastic bags. In a matter of minutes, the cargo was hoisted up onto the roof and tied up with thick ropes that whipped the flanks of the bus with loud thuds. Then, with a crank of gears, we leaped forward. The hawkers ran along with us, reaching up towards the forest of arms that leaned from the windows to complete the last purchases in haste. At great speed, the bus climbed higher and higher on its way to the Altiplano, jolting us unceremoniously over the hard metal seats.

'*Un pueblo de mierda!*' some of the passengers said of Sacapulas. 'It's a shithole, bang in the middle of the driest region of Guatemala.'

'In summer, everything burns and turns to dust: the fields, the riverbeds, the trees. The sunlight is blinding.'

'There is no damned work in Sacapulas,' said others.

Now, however, it was the rainy season and, as the bus dropped us off, Sacapulas didn't seem to be such an inferno. It stood in a lush green valley on the banks of a fast-flowing yellow river. The first impression was that of a quiet slumbering village built around a square dominated by an immense oak tree. Around it, rose a church, a military post, the only hotel and sprawling houses. Everything was still and drowsy.

We walked into the church; it was dusty, unkempt, more like a warehouse than a place of worship. It stored dozens of life-size wooden statues of saints, most of them chipped, many dressed in a variety of fabrics. They stood there stacked along the side walls, facing the empty pews: lugubrious Christs bleeding on wooden crosses, crudely sculpted weeping Madonnas, demure-looking Saint Lucias offering up their gouged-out eyes on tin plates. Besides us, nothing stirred, only silence and specks of dust spiralling in the sunlight that filtered into the nave through the wide-open door.

On the other side of the square stood the military post. From a wooden turret where a couple of soldiers stood cradling their guns hung a large sign in Spanish. As I translated each word painstakingly – *Only those who fight... have the right to... win* and *only those who win have the right... to live* – I cringed at the thought of all the cruelties committed behind those walls.

One of the soldiers noticed us standing under the sign, and leaned over the parapet. He shouted something that neither of us could hear, but the way he shooed us off with the rib of his gun was unmistakable and, anxious not to annoy him, we hurried away.

No one sat under the tree in the square. A few people scurried along the cobbled streets like shadows and slid away furtively through a mesh of dirt lanes.

We agreed to leave the place as soon as possible.

There were no outbound buses, so we went and booked a room in the hotel. It was spartan. Two sagging cots flanked the wall lengthwise; in place of glass panels, chicken wire netting screened the two small windows; a naked bulb dangled low from the ceiling, shedding beams of glaring light. When we asked to have a shower, we were told there was no running water in the hotel.

'But there's a river nearby, el Río Negro.' The melancholic-looking Ladino who sat in the smoky reception room nodded towards the door. 'Just follow the Indios. You can't get lost.'

With our towels, we ventured along the path he'd indicated and soon we reached the riverbank. Here, we laboured over stones, boulders, tree roots, and as we went around a sharp bend, we came to a hot spring. Amid clouds of steam rising from the water, a large crowd of men and women of all ages sat by the river in various stages of undress. Some were bare-chested, some wore oversized white pants and unclipped bras, others were stark naked. The men kept to themselves, in a separate place. Each squatted in their private pools of hot river water, lathering themselves or simply soaking. Cortes, huipiles and other garments were gathered in bundles on top of the surrounding boulders.

Martin and I parted and went to look for a suitable bathing place. It gradually got darker and, having found a water pool sheltered by a bulky rock, I stripped off and sank into it. The water was hot, soothing, slightly sulphuric. All the dust of the day gone, washed off by the water, my whole body felt relaxed and free. I sat there thinking of nothing, just enjoying the magic play of light and shadow and the sense of well-being that spread through me. In time, among the clouds of steam, I could no longer make out people, only indistinct shapes.

I looked around for Martin. And there he was, standing out a full head taller than the other men. Travelling with him had been so very easy. And now we were here, naked, bathing just a few hundred feet apart.

Half an hour later, clean, dried and once again dressed, we retraced our steps in pitch darkness. As I walked in a haze following the vague forms ahead of me, I felt the touch of a hand on my bottom. I turned with a surprised smile, thinking it was Martin, but the hand belonged to a Mayan man behind me, who feigned innocence and scuttled hastily into the shadows.

When we reached the hotel, we were exhausted. Fully clothed, we slid under our thin blankets and immediately fell asleep.

During the night, as the temperature dropped, I tossed and turned in my sleep, unable to get warm. Then, for the second time that day, I felt the light touch of somebody's hand on me. And this time *it was* Martin's. He surrendered his own blanket, placing it gently over me. In the dark, he pulled a quilted sleeping bag out of his rucksack. He unrolled it and slipped into it very quietly; then he was asleep.

*

In the morning, we stood outside the village, along the main road that led to Nebaj, once again waiting. Just like before, there was no bus due for the next three days, so the only way out of Sacapulas was to hitchhike. The problem was, there were no cars. We stood there, hoping. An hour went by, then two, then three. Still nothing.

There, on the road, time was suspended.

'Martin, what is it that brought you here?'

'Well, it's hard to say exactly… It wasn't just one thing, more like a whole bunch of things. I guess it goes back to when I was little. I told you, didn't I, that my dad was Cuban and my mother Polish. There in San Diego I'd always felt different from the other kids. They'd tease me and call me *"the Chicano boy"*…'

'And that made you feel bad?'

'If it had stopped at that…' He shifted awkwardly. 'I am a Chicano man and proud to be one. But who wouldn't feel bad about being called a *wet back,* a *wop*, sometimes even a *kike*? I tell you, children can be truly horrible. And so, I always looked at the world from the outside, and whenever I could, I rebelled. As a teenager, I was part of a gang. The only thing I cared for was what my *pandilla* thought of me. I dropped out of high school and was stoned most of the time. My parents were worried sick. They tried everything with me, the harsh and the soft, with no other result but to make me despise them even more, my old man especially. He was law-abiding and a hard worker, and because of that I treated him like the biggest imbecile on earth. Poor guy! I'm certainly not proud of it, but that's what I was like. At least we get along now.'

As he spoke, I watched a whole range of emotions flash across his tanned face. It was hard to picture him as a rebellious teenager, or as a tough gang member lording it over the streets. His voice was too melodious, too modulated; it seemed better suited to expressing calm and sensible thoughts rather than the festering anger he was describing.

'Eventually, I grew out of it. By some miracle, I managed to get the grades and go to college. That's when I threw myself into student politics. I supported the causes of all minorities, went on all the marches and joined all the sit-ins. Then I met Amalia, whose parents were from El Salvador. We decided to hitchhike all the way from San Diego to Uluazapa, where her grandparents live. It took us a couple of months, but when we got there, we split up. So, we went our separate ways. She headed south to Costa Rica and me, I'm on my way to Zipolite, in Oaxaca, where I'll be working in an orphanage. I guess I'll be searching once again for some non-existent roots.' He laughed, with a touch of self-mockery.

'What about you, Monica?' He looked at me with open curiosity. 'What are your plans? In Panajachel, you said this place fascinated you and that you wanted to do something worthwhile. And now?'

I looked at the ribbon of gravel road that twisted down and up the crest of the hill, still hopelessly empty.

'It's a long story.' I sighed. I wished I could have painted a flattering picture of myself, of someone brave and committed, a *Pasionaria* come to fight a just cause. I wanted to impress him. But, after Suzanne – no individualistic foolhardiness for her, she was the real thing, like him, *truly* committed – I knew I'd come a long way down the list of people worthy of his respect.

'To tell you the whole truth,' I braced myself, 'I'm here because I've been dumped.'

'That makes two of us.' He laughed. 'Being dumped sucks!'

'*Meglio soli che male accompagnati*, as my mum often says. It's Italian, like her, and it means "Better alone than in bad company". It makes a lot of sense, doesn't it? Besides, being single has given me the freedom to be here. You see, I've always wanted to come, but he, Richard, wasn't interested. And now, here I am, finally.'

'So, you've come to lick your wounds.'

'Yes, that, and the fact that this is an exciting place. Take Nicaragua, I mean there's a full-blown revolution going on there. Now, I'm here on holiday and I want to see everything...'

'And so, what do you make of this place then?'

'Beautiful, no doubt, but... I confess, I'm a little disappointed with the people. I don't mean the Latinos, the white people in the cities, who couldn't be kinder, but the Mayans... However hard I try to make contact, I seem to be erased from their gaze. I'm right in front of them, and they don't see me. It's like I don't exist.'

'After four hundred years of brutal colonisation, what do you expect? The red carpet?' The smile he gave me made up for the harshness of his words.

He was right, of course. Why should I expect anything but mistrust? Hadn't I studied their history? I felt guilty about the sheer insensitivity of what I'd just said. But all the same, I couldn't silence that longing of mine to be liked, to be accepted, to be included.

'I guess I'm comparing them to other people who've been colonised but are not so withdrawn, so unfriendly,' I tried to explain. 'Take the people in the Caribbean. They were slaves for hundreds of years, but they're open, approachable, very laid-back. They play great music, they dance and laugh.'

'So, Monica, admit it,' he teased me, 'you're a girl who just wants to have fun. Let me guess. Your plane to Acapulco was hijacked and now you're here.'

I laughed, giving him a friendly push.

Just then, two vehicles appeared chugging up the hill, a pick-up truck followed at a short distance by a second van. A few minutes later, they reached the stretch of the road where we stood frantically waving and, amid thick clouds of dust, they stopped.

'*Muchísimas gracias!*' Martin and I jumped into the back of the first vehicle, settling down under its awning on a side bench where two Ladino men in jeans, cotton shirts and bomber jackets were already sitting.

'*Buenos días!*' Martin's wide moustachioed smile did the rounds of the van as the engine started.

'Been waiting long?' asked the older guy, a thin and wiry man with short grey hair and an ebullient manner.

'The whole morning. You were the first people to drive by.'

'You're lucky then! This route is not very popular. Sometimes people have to wait days.' His laughter boomed loud and clear over the noise of the engine.

Half a dozen fat jute sacks cluttered the floor between us. The man caught me looking at them.

'Fertilizer,' he explained. 'Manuel here has to deliver them to the farmers in Nebaj. Not an easy job, eh, *compadre?*' He turned to the younger guy, who just nodded. 'Four months ago, the guerrilla ambushed a pick-up van like this one and stole the entire cargo. That's why now we're travelling so close to the other car. It's safer.'

Martin and I shot each other a concerned glance. 'Hey! You two don't need to worry! Nothing has happened in a long time. All is quiet now.'

I gazed out of the back of the van at Sacapulas becoming smaller and smaller until it disappeared behind the ridge of the steep mountains that we were now climbing at reasonable speed.

'And you, what are you two doing here? Are you journalists?'

'No, why?' The question took me by surprise. 'Do you get many journalists around here?'

'Yes, with the excuse of the *aldeas modelos*, quite a few foreigners come to write about us. It seems we are famous!' He sneered.

I knew about these villages. The army had recently set them up to rehouse the displaced of the highlands – so they said. In reality, wanting to clear out the guerrillas from the area, in the last two years the soldiers had burnt down scores of Mayan hamlets. They'd pillaged, raped and killed most of the inhabitants, and then forced the survivors into tightly regimented camps.

'Are you from the Altiplano?' Martin asked good-humouredly, ignoring the man's sarcastic tone.

'No, I'm from the capital,' he replied, facing us squarely, 'but I've lived in Nebaj, preaching God's word, for the last four years. We get dozens of children coming into town every day with their harrowing stories. Some are lucky and have relatives to stay with, but the majority live on the streets. It's tragic, but it's always like that. It's always the people caught in the middle who lose out. It's the poor, the Indios, who always suffer.'

He was toeing the official line, which blamed the guerrillas for the killings and the sacking and razing of the villages. It was the version the government was keen to promote both nationally and abroad.

Next to me, Martin shifted uncomfortably and cleared his throat. 'But the guerrillas, I've heard they're Indios themselves. Aren't they?' he asked.

'Yes, there are a handful of poor peasants and soldiers gone over to the other side. But the hardcore are foreigners, all communists – from Cuba, Russia, no one knows for sure.'

Here we go again, the Cubans, the commies. I shuddered at the thought of the stamp on my passport.

By then we'd reached the edge of the plateau, and the van had begun to speed along a wider, less bumpy road.

'We'll be in Nebaj soon,' said the preacher. As if alerted to some unspoken danger, he lowered his voice by several decibels, and I had to strain my ears to catch his words over the rumbling noise of the engine.

'People work until they drop around here and stay forever poor, while the *latifundistas* get rich. Will things ever change? The guerrillas say they fight for the poor. But do they really? I tell my people – only the good Lord is on your side, have faith in Him. Only He can end your suffering.' From inside his jacket he pulled out a battered bible and gave the cover a mighty slap with the open palm of his hand. 'It's all in here.'

Avoiding each other's eyes, we just nodded.

We were now coming to the first houses of Nebaj. The place was just like any other village, except for its larger-than-usual display of military force. Wooden turrets and observation points with sentries and armoured vehicles rose at strategic corners. Here, heavily armed soldiers directed the traffic along certain routes and prohibited access to others.

Ahead of us, as I peeked from under the awning of our van, I made out half a dozen *indígenas* standing in line on the pavement, waiting.

My heart began to beat quickly.

It was a roadblock, yet again. A couple of soldiers were checking everyone's papers at gunpoint.

We slowed down, overtook the line of people, and stopped right in front of the two soldiers. From where I was sitting, I could see only one of them. He was Mayan – a short, thin man, his skin the colour of burnt sienna. His face betrayed no emotion. In silence, he examined the papers the driver had handed to him. Then he peered into the passenger compartment, squinting slightly as he inspected each of us, carefully. It took just one or two minutes, but during that time I dared not stir, just in case he singled me out. I read the same tension on everyone's face.

He waved us through.

'Life is dangerous in Nebaj,' the preacher went on, whispering, as we drove off. 'People keep their mouths shut, even children. They don't trust anyone, they're frightened, but who can blame them?'

He stared at us earnestly. I blushed, remembering the conversation I had with Martin earlier about the Mayans being unfriendly.

The van dropped us off at the end of a long, straight road.

'By the Lord's good grace, things will change,' said the preacher, shaking hands. 'Let's have faith.' He looked up to the sky.

We stood there waving until they'd gone.

*

Nebaj was cold and inhospitable. Precisely at three in the afternoon, a rainstorm swept through the town. A few hours later, the rain let up and turned to drizzle, then to a mist that lingered on in the liquid atmosphere. Drained of colour, the sky hung low over rows of squat single-storied buildings arranged along straight cobbled streets. A web of dirt alleys criss-crossed them and petered out into distant open fields. A few pedestrians hurried from one narrow pavement to the next, and then disappeared through archways into the town's patios and courtyards.

Built around one of these patios with rooms that opened onto a long porch, Las Tres Hermanitas was a family-run hotel for the rare visitor. Here, sitting at a small table just outside our room, Martin and I whiled away the rainy afternoon, reading.

He was studying the latest edition of the *Rough Guide to Guatemala*, and I was engrossed in a letter that, before leaving, I'd collected from the post office in Panajachel.

The bold and regular handwriting made me immediately feel nostalgic.

Cara Monica,

Today is the 15th of August, it's midday and I'm sitting at the kitchen table, which is set only for your dad. I'm on a diet, so today I'm skipping lunch. I really hope it works because I've begun to look like a big fat sausage, and none of my clothes fit me anymore.

Can you guess why I've put on so much weight? Yes, I'm trying to give up smoking, again. But this time, it's been two weeks and I'm determined. I already feel the benefits – I sleep better, my sense of smell has improved, even my skin looks smoother. But, sadly, I'm always famished. They say it's normal, that initially, when they quit, people put on a few kilos which later they easily lose. Is it true? Anyway, wish me luck. As for the rest, I'm afraid I have nothing good or interesting to tell you. Grandad has been poorly recently; something to do with his digestion, but his doctor doesn't seem to be worried. He's given him some supplements and prescribed lots of fresh air. Bianca, the upstairs neighbour, was run over by a car, last week. It happened near home, on the zebra crossing, and she's ok now, but since she had concussion, they kept her in hospital for four days. Zio Tulio has finally retired and let's hope he finds some new interest quickly, because without his job he seems to be falling apart. Your dad has the opposite problem; he's always working; there aren't enough hours in a day for him to do it all. He's well, at least he looks well, because, as you know, he never talks about how he feels.

That's all from me.

Monica tesoro, and you? You're the one with plenty of news, I'm sure. Why haven't you written? Where are you now? Still in that place with an unpronounceable name, Panaciana… something, or have you gone back to Nicaragua? In any case, why do you always choose the most dangerous places on earth, when there are so many other lovely countries you could visit where there's no war? Monica, please, don't keep me on tenterhooks. Drop us a line, give us a call. Just now I can only think of the worst. Your dad and I send you all our love. I'd ask him to add a few lines to this letter, but he's not around and I want to catch the post.

I miss you.

Mum

P.S. As I've already told you – but you've probably forgotten – next year in January, I'm going to retire, and I'll have plenty of time to do what I like. So, I was thinking, what if I came to visit you? Or would having Mum there cramp your style? I promise I won't get in your way. Let me know. All my love, tesoro.

It was the third or fourth time I had read my mum's letter, and each time, as I came to that P.S., I tried to imagine what she'd be like to travel with. I missed her too. I pictured her sleeping on hard beds, bathing in the streams, slumming it. Would she like Central America? What would she make of the people, of the Mayans? We often argued, I know, but still, I'd love to show her around and hear what she made of this place.

'Hey, Monica,' Martin interrupted my train of thought, 'remember when the priest in the van asked us if we were journalists?'

'Yes, he thought we were here to write about the model villages, didn't he?'

'Well, guess what. It says here that there's one at walking distance from Nebaj. It's called Acul. How do you fancy going there tomorrow?'

'Yes, why not? If the rain stops...'

I didn't really hold out much hope of that happening, but Martin was already planning our itinerary.

'It's really close, according to my guidebook—'

'*Con permiso.*' The curt interjection came from one of the three Ladino sisters the *hospedaje* was named after. She plonked a pot of piping hot coffee down in front of us, together with a tray piled high with homemade cakes. Her eyes avoided ours.

'*Muchas gracias, señora.*' Martin smiled broadly in an attempt at charming her. 'We were wondering how far Acul is from here. Could you maybe give us an idea?'

'It's near. An hour, an hour and a half, at most,' she replied curtly, as if better things were waiting for her elsewhere.

There was the sound of steps along the porch; the *hermanita* looked warily over her shoulders. More guests? Soldiers? But, no, it was a handful of Mayan women easing themselves awkwardly through the doorway, their huge cargos of homespun fabrics leaving barely enough space for each to enter. They came forward hesitantly, then stopped at some distance, unloaded their bundles and leaned against the pillars of the porch, smiling. '*Compre... Compre... Usted compre mi típica... son muy baratos...*' they chanted.

Our hostess approached them and talked to them quickly in Ixil. And suddenly, next to the brightness of the vendors' *huipiles* and their shiny plaits, her sternness faded, her face softened. Even the tight bun of grey hair seemed less grey, less tight, the dowdy Western clothes she wore less dowdy.

The conversation lasted a few minutes, then she disappeared down the porch, clearing the ground for the women to do their bartering.

'That always makes me feel bad.' Martin shifted uncomfortably, his hand reaching for his back pocket in an automatic gesture. 'Too bad I don't have cash for extras.'

I knew what he meant. It felt unfair to have money in my pocket when everyone around was so hard up. No way I'd buy all this handcraft, though.

There was an awkward silence, but the women quickly lost interest in selling their wares. They'd come to take shelter. Huddled together, they looked at every move we made with open curiosity. To my surprise, whenever our gaze met, they smiled. For once, they seemed to acknowledge I was there! At first, I thought it was because I was in the company of a man, no longer a strange young woman travelling on her own. But then, I began to wonder whether it had been *me*, who, until that moment, had failed to see *them* – the older woman with the lively eyes and bright red braiding, who covered her mouth to hide a missing tooth; the two thirty-somethings sharing a joke as they took turns drying each other's hair with their shawls; the three young girls who seemed happy just to stare.

No longer anonymous, no longer faceless, these people were living, breathing individuals; they were real people with their own stories. And they'd been there all along.

Outside, the rain pattered over the roof tiles and the cobblestones of the patio, blurring out the sharpness of all edges.

'This dampness really gets into your bones,' I complained. 'Water above, water underneath, water everywhere.'

I wore all the clothes I owned, layer upon layer, and I was still shivering.

'This is hardly the Altiplano I'd imagined.'

'Yeah.' Martin laughed. 'This is no Acapulco, for sure.'

I was about to carry on the banter when the Ladino sister approached our table once again.

'If you go to Acul, take this,' she said in a softened tone, putting a whole pile of brochures in front of us. 'A couple of gringos left these papers in the hotel last week. It's all in English. It might be useful.' And, as silently as she'd appeared, she left.

I was happy to let Martin do all the groundwork for the trip ahead and, as he began to sift through the papers, I buried myself in one of the paperbacks I carried in my rucksack.

A good hour later, he resurfaced, beaming.

'According to what I've read, the army are proud of their *aldeas* and only too happy when gringos like us go and look around. Besides, this one's really close. It's an opportunity not to be missed. Shall we go?'

I nodded.

After clearing the table, he laid out a crinkled map, wet and soggy around the edges, and flattened the creases with both palms.

'This is the Ixil Triangle. And here, to the left of Nebaj, this dotted circle is Acul.' My eyes followed his hand as it moved lightly across the map, indicating each place. The white half-moons of his nails stood out against the long, tanned fingers. 'If we go straight over these hills and keep heading east, we can't go wrong.'

It was dark now, and as I picked up the map to look at it more closely, from the end of the porch, the *hermanita* waved goodnight.

'*Buen viaje!*' she said, and disappeared down the corridor.

On the map, Acul did indeed look very near. The *hermanita* was right; it shouldn't take more than a couple of hours.

'A piece of cake,' said Martin.

*

Now we were hopelessly lost.

At first, the trail had been well trodden and easy to follow. It had taken us out of the village, over the hills across the narrow pass in between the steep flanks of the mountains. As we reached the other side, our plan to head east turned out to be impossible. The pall of grey clouds that hung low over the sky had blurred our sense of direction. Then, to our surprise, as the ridge of the pass fell away, a thick rainforest engulfed us in a dull sludge of darkness.

'Where's east then?' I shouted over to Martin, who trod cautiously through the underbrush a short distance ahead.

He stopped and threw both hands up in the air in frustration. 'No idea!' he yelled back. Then he plodded on, balancing over the slippery roots that stuck out underfoot, while ducking under the tangled creepers reaching down from the higher branches.

Covered in mouldering brown leaves, the path had initially coiled amid the trees, still visible, but soon it faded away, swallowed by the bracken and bramble and a thick tangle of thorny shrubs. Patches of colourless sky cleaved the thick foliage above our heads.

There was no point looking up anyway. It was the inclination underfoot that signalled our very gradual descent.

I made slow progress, concentrating on each step as I hummed a *marimba* tune I'd heard on the radio over breakfast. It comforted me. So did Martin's presence. Every now and then, I caught sight of his bright red anorak peeping out from behind the trees, and even when he seemed to have disappeared amid the foliage, I could still hear him tread ponderously through the rustling leaves and crackling twigs.

Although I'd scoffed at all the gadgets he carried in his rucksack, now I was more than glad that he thought of everything in advance. In fact, right now, I'd be truly delighted if, just like that, by magic, he pulled out a gleaming machete and started hacking at the vines.

Despite my desire to be self-reliant, I had to admit there were times when I was grateful to have Martin at my side.

While my body focussed on keeping balance, my mind flashed back to the young man that, earlier that morning, we'd found waiting by the cluster of adobe houses that marked the end of the village. As soon as he saw us, he came forward, hands deep in his pockets, the broad brim of his straw hat pushed low over his eyes.

'Going over to Acul? I'll take you. There are many dangers on the way, you know,' he said, keeping pace with us.

'*Muchas gracias, pero no*. We're used to mountain hiking. We'll be okay.' It was I who spoke for both of us in a firm voice, still walking. I was thinking of all the creeps I had to keep at bay as a woman travelling on her own, of all that unwelcome attention. Failing to read my mind, Martin glanced at me questioningly, but in the end, he nodded his assent, and we waved the man away.

At this, our would-be guide stopped in his tracks, saying nothing, but I had the feeling he stared long and hard at us until we were out of his view.

He'd be laughing now. Two smart-arse gringos, at the mercy of the Mayan gods.

'Damn!' Martin growled, barely fifty yards ahead of me. Climbing over some boulders, he'd lost his foothold and fallen into the brush.

When I reached him, I found him struggling to free his jeans from the thorns. One of his boots had come undone. The flap was hanging loose, and a squelchy mess of soil and leaves had collected around his ankle.

'These maps are too small scale, they're useless,' he complained. For once, he'd lost his air of bonhomie and, as he kneeled to clear the muck off his socks, he sounded impatient. 'We shouldn't have turned down that guy this morning. Think of all the hassle he'd have saved us. We'd be in Acul by now!'

I knew it was my fault and I felt guilty.

'Martin, sorry to—'

'*Alto*! Halt!' A man's voice cut me short.

We jumped, startled. The voice seemed to come from above. We strained our eyes and finally, a short distance high up in the trees, we made out a wooden structure camouflaged amid the foliage. Built in the shape of a quadrangle, it rose twenty feet above the ground on stilts, with a stepladder of knotted branches tied to the side. At the top, on a wooden platform, under a muddy green plastic sheet, two men in Western clothes and wide-brimmed straw hats waited, gripping their guns.

'*Párase*! *Stop!*' the voice called out again.

The order was superfluous, as we'd already come to a halt.

While one of the two men stood watch, the other clambered quickly to the ground. He jumped the last few rungs and, with long resolute strides, came over.

I thought I knew what was coming – a nerve-racking repetition of what happened at each roadblock. The fact that by now I'd learnt the ropes didn't seem to lessen the anxiety I felt – on the contrary.

As he got closer, I could see the surly expression on the man's face. He was a Ladino of average height, in his early thirties. He wore dark coloured overalls and heavy boots. Except for his conspicuous hat, he could have easily merged with the shadows and mossy trees. Was he a soldier, a *guerrillero*? Which side was he on?

The man stopped right in front of us. '*Adónde?*' he demanded in a hostile tone, as if he owned the forest and we were trespassers.

'*Acul!*' we shouted in unison, like soldiers going through a drill.

'That's where we want to go. But now *estamos perdido,* we're lost,' I explained, my Spanish faltering because of nerves. '*Está lejos?* Is it far?'

The man looked at us with mild surprise, as if he didn't expect a couple of rambling gringos to speak Spanish. He pointed at some rocks jutting out from beyond the observation point. '*Para allá,*' he said reluctantly. It's near. 'Why are you going to Acul?' he demanded to know.

'We've heard Acul welcomes foreign visitors, that the army's happy for us to see what they've achieved,' said Martin. He sounded convincing, but his eyes darted around anxiously.

'*Esperen aquí,*' the man barked, and marched off to confer with his companion perched on the platform.

Martin and I stood there, each lost in our own worries.

'Who do you think these guys are?' I whispered, breaking the silence.

'The *patrulla*, I guess. They're just ordinary guys, sort of security guards who keep an eye on who gets in and out of their village. We have nothing to worry about,' he said reassuringly, but his fists were clenched.

We watched the two men up in their turret talking animatedly, but the wind carried away their words.

At last, the man returned.

With knitted eyebrows and a scowl on his face, he stared first at Martin, then at me.

'*Cuidado!*' he warned us. 'There are many *guerrilleros por aquí.*' Gun clanking against his side, he walked deep into the foliage and in no time, he was gone.

'I was right,' said Martin. 'Those two were *patrulleros*. We were in luck.'

We got on our way, heading for the rocks the *patrullero* had indicated.

*

An hour later, we came to the end of the forest and, although the sky was as grey as in the morning, finally there was daylight and open grassland. After so much twilit greenery, it was exhilarating to see the entire valley spread out in front of us.

There, winding along the foot of the hills, was our trail. We followed it, relieved.

'Monica, that Cuban stamp of yours sucks, you know?' Martin said unexpectedly, an expression of concern on his face. 'Earlier, when the guy stopped us, I was really worried he might want to see our passports. And with that stamp on yours, we'd have been in deep shit, you bet. Tell me, why on earth didn't you ask the Cubans to stamp a separate piece of paper?'

'I didn't know I could,' I admitted sheepishly.

'You didn't know you could? C'mon, Monica, everyone knows! It's basic stuff. You'd have saved yourself, and me, a million awkward questions.'

I could see his point. Now that I was travelling with him, the stamp affected him as much as me. If I was stopped, he'd be stopped too.

We knew so little about our respective lives and yet we had no choice but to depend upon each other. I had complete confidence in him, and it saddened me to think he might not feel the same about me.

Since we'd left Panajachel together, I'd come to realise how hard it had been to travel alone. Now, in his company, I let go. It would be nice if our partnership could last a little longer.

I was lost in these thoughts when Acul appeared down below, sprawled over a valley that enveloped it like a cocoon.

The village looked just like in the photos on the pamphlets the *hermanita* had given us the night before, except that the sepia colour of the prints had given way to the lush green of the fields. From above, dozens of straight lines criss-crossed each other at right angles, forming a vast grid, as if drawn with a ruler.

As we got closer, the lines turned out to be no more than dirt tracks, each marked by a placard with the grand and lengthy name of some Guatemalan general on it.

We walked along one of them at random and right there, at the first corner, we came upon more *patrulleros*. Straight-legged, dusty boots firmly planted on the ground, the two men weighed us up from underneath the tilted visors of their baseball caps.

'*Buenas tardes*,' we greeted them, trying our best to be open and friendly.

'*Buenas*,' they replied curtly and, without questions, they watched us go by.

I'd expected Acul to be a labour camp where people had to work from dawn till night. Instead, although everyone seemed determined not to meet our eyes, the village felt far from oppressive. We walked past a brightly painted school; then, a little further, on the right, we came across a textile cooperative, and, just around the corner, a whitewashed health centre, brand new. Each place was clearly signposted in scarlet letters. People went about their business like anywhere else. I began to see why the army called this a "model village" and even welcomed foreign visitors. It was a showcase.

A sheaf of sunrays finally broke the clouds and cast fast-moving patches of light and shadow across the valley. It was much warmer and brighter now. We took off our sweaters, sat on a pocket handkerchief of lawn in front of the school and bit into our sandwiches.

At first, people ignored us. Then, a little girl walked past holding her mother's hand. She stopped and, eyes round with curiosity, turned to look at us. I waved to her. Taken by surprise, she waved back. Her mother whispered something to her and dragged her away, but a few seconds later, now at a safe distance, she also turned and, hiding a smile behind her shawl, openly stared at us for a few minutes. As she hurried away, half a dozen men appeared at the top end of the street. Emboldened by curiosity, they came over and stood around us.

A short, wiry guy with piercing eyes did the talking on behalf of everyone. He fired off a barrage of questions and then translated our answers into Ixil.

'Where are you from?' 'Are you journalists?' 'What do you think of Acul?' The questions became more detailed and pressing as the men, through their translator, asked us how much we earned, how much the ticket cost 'de allá para acá,' what crops were grown in our countries, what we exported, how we cultivated the land.

'Here, all work is done by hand,' said the spokesman with a mixture of stoicism and something akin to pride. His companions nodded and pointed at dozens of allotments clustered, at an impossible gradient, all the way up the flanks of the hills. 'A lot of machete work, you know. *Muy duro.*'

'And the *patrulleros?*' asked Martin, flashing his broad smile. 'Do they work the land too?'

'*Los patrulleros?*' The man gave Martin a puzzled look. '*Los patrulleros somos todos nosotros.* All men between fifteen and sixty-five must do patrol service, once every two weeks. That's the rule.' He looked stealthily around and lowered his voice. 'There are many rules here – like the military drills we do every Sunday. And not just the drills...'

He stared at us meaningfully, as if there was something else he meant to say. At the last minute, he seemed to change his mind. His sharp eyes darted around from face to face. Then, with a shrug, as if dismissing an unpleasant thought, he gestured at the surrounding hills, at the houses, at the lush valley glittering in the sun, and said:

'*Acul es muy alegre, verdad?* Yes, life is good here.'

It was mid-afternoon when we decided to trace our steps back to the *hospedaje.*

'Take this path,' the man recommended. 'It's shorter, and you won't have to go through the woods.'

The path took us through solitary valleys, up and down green hills, across gurgling streams. There were very few people about and they all kept well out of our way. Bent double under huge stacks of wood, the moment they saw us, they took off over the next hilltop, but when, hot on their heels, we got to it and looked down into the dip of the valley, they'd gone. The same happened when we approached any of the solitary farmhouses dotted along the way. Smoke rose from the backyards; piglets rooted around in the grass; giggles and laughter from children playing echoed in the air. Yet nobody was in sight – just lingering ghosts and muffled sounds.

'Someone was here just two minutes ago.' Martin sniffed the air like a bloodhound. Across the yard in a corner, a handful of embers smouldered on the blackened earth. 'They heard us coming and ran away.'

'They're hiding. They're afraid of us.'

It was clear our presence was causing much anxiety. I was mortified. How to convince these people we were no enemies, that we were totally on their side?

'Let's go, Monica. We'd better leave these people alone,' said Martin.

He was right. We hurried on our way.

The path wound itself past the farmhouse, past the piglets, and finally consigned us to the privacy of our thoughts. Now that the way back was clearly visible and easy to follow, my anxiety wore off, and I began to take in more of the surroundings.

At each step we took, the village turned gradually smaller until it became just a splatter of colour in the jungle, later a tiny dot, and then it finally disappeared, engulfed by the greenery. Now only the ragged mountains towered high up above our heads, dwarfing the entire valley.

'Look at those slopes. See how steep they are,' I said to Martin, pointing at the plots clinging stubbornly to the sides. 'How can those guys farm up there? How do they do it?'

'Yeah, what a tremendous effort, eh?' Martin said with a sympathetic nod. 'Those guys got me thinking about the summer job I did when I was at college. After a few backbreaking months of construction work, I was done for. Fit for nothing in the evenings but a beer and the game on TV. Still, compared to theirs, my life was easy.'

'Mine too. But, Martin, did Acul feel any different to you from the other villages? I've heard so many terrible things about this place, but, to me, it didn't seem so bad.'

'That's only on the outside. Think about it. People are stuck there, in that valley. Using the guerrilla as a pretext, the *patrulleros* make sure no one leaves. Their real job is to police the place. And, given that, at some point, everyone does patrol duties, they're in fact spying on each other. The army has quite ingeniously thought it all out.'

'I can't think what I would have done if I'd been forced to stay in my hometown, let alone a place like this. Slit my wrists, turned into a moron, blown the place up? Who knows...'

'Go on, tell me more.'

'There's nothing to tell.' Then, regretting my curtness, I added, 'Sorry, Martin, but what shall I tell you? About the boredom of growing up in northern Italy, in a small provincial town? You don't want to hear about that, I'm sure.'

But that's precisely what he wanted, he said.

'Is that why you went to England? Is England less boring than Italy? I find that hard to believe.'

Like most people who never lived there, Martin had a romantic view of Italy.

'Italy is not just pizza, pasta, *mandolini* and *vespas*.' I laughed. 'Believe me, it's not what you imagine. I wasn't happy in my hometown. My family, friends, everything was oppressive. I wanted to travel, see new places, meet new people. But no one took me seriously. They just laughed at me, called me a "dreamer", and invented imaginary dangers to put me off. They just didn't get it. So, as soon as I could, I showed them. I left.'

'Why choose England?'

'Chance, really – one of my dad's friends lived in Brighton and he got me a job in a pub. I loved it there. Even my acne cleared up. I decided to stay and go to college. I ended up at a university in Essex, in the middle of nowhere. But even then, England seemed to me more interesting than my hometown. The university itself was inspiring.'

'What was so special about it?'

'I was in the right place at the right time. It was great to be a student. At Essex, I discovered politics. So much was going on in those days: marches, sit-ins, rallies. There was no time to sweat over books. Besides, that's when I met Richard.'

He looked at me with open curiosity now.

'What was this guy like?' He sounded me out cautiously, aware he was treading on sensitive ground.

I stopped along the path and put on my sweater. I was stalling. How could I sum up four years of love, hurt and angst?

'He was exciting, daring,' I began. 'Everything felt more interesting when he was around.'

Martin looked at me, surprised. By now, the sun had disappeared behind a bank of clouds and a fine drizzle had begun to fall, making the woods on the hills look greener. He pulled up the hood of his anorak.

'For him, politics was everything. He was totally involved and even got himself thrown out of uni. We shared the same interests. But I soon realised there was another side to him. He was domineering and manipulative. He took the lead, but then left me to deal with the fall-out from his mad stunts. When the police came calling, he ran back to his folks and his middle-class life. Besides, he liked women and women liked him. So, one day, he just dumped me for somebody else.'

Martin looked at me with sympathy. 'You deserve better, Monica.' He gently squeezed my arm.

'I guess anyone deserves better. But, guess what, sometimes I miss him, the excitement, the fact there was never a dull moment when he was around. I get angry with myself for still feeling like that. Why can't I get him out of my system and get on with life? How could I fall for such a bastard?'

He said nothing, but I could see him thinking – *Get over it, c'mon. The guy's not worth it.*

The drizzle had turned to a downpour, and we got soaked. Ten minutes later, the sun came out again and dried us out. It continued like that – drizzle, sun, rain, sun, showers – intermittently, without either of us realising the hours were passing.

Then, within minutes, a thick cloud of darkness descended on us.

It was nightfall. There was no moon in the sky, no stars to guide us. The path gone, nothing to help us get our bearings, we stopped talking and focussed solely on our descent.

I knew the town had to be somewhere below, at the bottom of the hill, an hour away, according to what the men had told us. But we were like two blind pilgrims feeling our way with our feet and, whenever necessary, with our hands. We advanced cautiously, with frustrating slowness. Martin went first, as he could see in the dark much better than me. I followed at a short distance, stumbling, falling, and humming the same tune over and over, to keep my spirits up.

And the two men I'd seen walking ahead of us earlier, where

had they gone? They were clearly visible only minutes before the grey-blue afternoon had turned into pitch darkness. They'd vanished, but where to? A few lights danced and bobbed up and down several feet below – their torches? But even that flickering soon faded away.

We scrambled on, sliding over the bulk of invisible rocks, scraping our hands in the thorny underbrush as we tumbled downwards into the valley.

'How much further do you think it is?' I threw the question into the darkness at intervals.

'Not long. We're almost there,' Martin shouted back.

I knew he was lying. He didn't have a clue where we were or how long we'd be. But those calls and answers wove a comforting thread between us.

Then, at some point, I saw a light that, unlike those torches, did not dance in the darkness only to disappear, but remained solidly pinned against the blackness. Minutes later, another unblinking yellow eye began to glow further down the valley. Then, a whole cluster of them, arranged in a spiralling shape.

I said nothing, wanting to be sure. It was Martin who shouted first: 'Monica, look at that! Those are houses!'

We raced downhill with a clatter of loose rocks following our footsteps. In the diminishing darkness, the shadows and bulks that came towards us began to take shape.

Finally, we made out the roofs of the village. We turned towards each other, delighted. I threw myself into his arms, like at a great effusive party where everyone, happily drunk, embraces. He kissed me. I kissed him back.

That night, in the freezing *hospedaje*, Martin thought better of covering me with his own blanket. He walked over to me and slipped into my bed.

CHAPTER THREE

MONICA AND MARTIN

The following morning, we climbed into the back of the lorry that ferried the villagers to the Pacific coast. It was packed with men, women and children sitting on planks set out in rows across its width.

The cotton-picking season was about to start and field hands were needed. It was badly paid work, the *hermanita* had told us at the *hospedaje*, but, all the same, it was work, and people couldn't afford to turn it down. As for us, that lorry was the quickest way out of Nebaj.

I looked around. Perched on the improvised benches, feet dangling, the children held tight onto the adults' elbows, trying not to fall. Most people were half-asleep, eyes shut, heads bobbing. It was stuffy and hot. A musty, dank smell of sweat, damp clothes and rotten vegetables lingered in the air. Worst of all was the feeling of being trapped within the tall sides of the lorry, unable to catch even a glimpse of the landscape we drove through, except for a rectangle of clear sky that hung over us like a neon-lit ceiling. This is how cattle travel, I thought.

Jolted about by the careering vehicle, I began to panic. I couldn't breathe.

Martin took my hand and somehow managed to manoeuvre me past the tightly packed benches to the far corner where a mound of firewood was scattered on the floor.

'*Con permiso... Perdón... Disculpe...*' He sheepishly apologised to all.

I helped him stack one log over the other against the side of the lorry. I climbed on top and looked out over the edge. I gasped and not only for fresh air, but because right in front of me lay the whole range of the Cuchumatanes, a succession of bluish-green peaks, jagged crests plunging into deep valleys. They criss-crossed the horizon, turning gradually lighter until, far away in the distance, they blurred into a hazy halo and then merged with the pale blue sky.

Martin still held my hand. As we both clung onto the edge of the truck, I felt a wave of gratitude towards him. What would I have done without his help?

'Beautiful, isn't it?' he shouted above the noise of the engine, pointing his chin at the breathtaking view.

I squeezed his hand and he smiled at me.

We leaned forward, the wind ruffling our hair. We watched the dusty road meander amid the mountain ranges as we climbed higher and higher onto the edge of the plateau.

*

In the following days, we boarded one crowded bus after the other to reach our destination in the heart of the Altiplano, Todos Santos Cuchumatán.

By now, I'd heard quite a lot about the place and its people – 'The Todosanteños are proud, confident,' 'They don't take shit' and 'Their *trajes* are the best in Guatemala.'

It was all true. To begin with, everyone was much taller – 'the result of being better fed,' said Martin – and yes, their clothes were more colourful than anywhere else. The women had blue ribbons threaded into their jet black hair, and the men strutted about in their finery like peacocks. They sported some unusual footwear –

a cross between flip-flops and open-toed walking boots covering the heels – round straw hats, home-spun red collars and funky trousers with red and white stripes.

When we entered the only shop along the main road – the butcher's – and asked where we could buy a pair, the Ladino behind the counter shook his head.

'You won't find *típica* on sale in Todos Santos. We don't cater for tourists around here.' He was a mountain of a man and, as he spoke, he brandished a carving knife as threatening as his colossal arms. His smile was kind, though, almost indulgent, as if in front of him stood not two seasoned travellers but a couple of children in need of guidance.

Early the following morning, we woke to the hum of voices rising from the square, right below our hotel room.

When I pushed the wooden shutters open and let the fierce daylight in, streams of people were walking below our balcony, their heads just within arm's reach.

It was market day and, from the neighbouring hills, vendors and buyers had flocked into town and were now bartering, laughing and arguing over the price of the merchandise on display – sacks of potatoes, onions, coal, as well as shoes, Western clothes, working tools of every description.

We ran downstairs and joined the hustle and bustle, content for once to be inconspicuous – two solitary foreigners lost in a sea of black tresses and straw hats.

The fair could not have been timelier. A few days earlier, Martin had lost his Swiss Army knife and, after our recent hike to Acul, there were two large holes in the soles of my shoes that let in dirt and pebbles and, worse, rain and mud. The situation was critical.

The *feria* solved our problems: Martin found a penknife with a beautifully carved wooden handle and, from under a pile of plastic sandals and heavy-duty boots slung on a trestle table, I dug out just the perfect pair of trainers – size 4, lightweight, with a tiny pocket on the side hidden under a miniature Guatemalan flag, and, most importantly, dirt cheap.

'Running out of money?' Martin asked, when he saw me count the notes in my pouch with an absorbed air.

'Not quite,' I replied, blushing as always at the mention of money. 'But I have the whole summer to get through.'

I wasn't poor, certainly not by Guatemalan standards, but now, out on my own, with just my Nicaraguan salary to fall back on, my worries were real. I had to scrimp and save like most people here.

Around mid-morning, we grew tired of the people pressing in from all sides, the vendors shouting, the hubbub. We exchanged a glance and, strolling along a path that petered out into a grassy trail, we headed for the surrounding hills. They were deserted.

Buried in the tall grass of a secluded field, we made love.

It felt good to be there, naked, in the open, free, the smell of earth in my nostrils, the cool, soft grass under my body, the buzz of insects all around.

Afterwards, we lay on our backs, not saying a word.

All was quiet, except for the wind in the trees. No birds seemed to be nesting among those branches; no animals grazed in the fields.

Everything around glowed intensely green. Heavy rain must have fallen recently, making all the plants grow lush and bountiful. And yet, to me, nothing had substance, nothing seemed real. For a short moment, I lay there, suspended in my own bubble, watching the high winds sweep flocks of feathery clouds across the sky.

Then the world slowly came back. The vague echo from the *feria* drifted in from beyond the hills; a hidden stream flowed noisily; then the sound of a splash. There I was, back in the highlands of Guatemala.

'Monica,' Martin whispered by my side, 'I'm glad you came on this trip with me.'

'Me too.' I wasn't sure where this was going. Our time together would soon be up. But what if…

He picked up a blade of grass and ran it slowly over my shoulder, then down and along the inside of my outstretched arm.

'Monica, whaddaya say we walk the rest of the way instead of taking the bus? We could head north, towards the border. I could cross over to Mexico from there.'

I liked the plan. I'd often fantasised that one day I'd take off on foot, like a pilgrim. And, what's more, I'd be spending a few more days with Martin.

'Great,' I said, 'let's do it!'

'That's settled then,' he said, then he gazed affectionately at me. 'I like you, Monica. You're always ready for anything.'

I brushed some tiny leaves out of his hair.

'And I love being here with you,' I said, under my breath.

It did feel good. At first, I'd feared that sex might change our easy friendship. But, to my surprise, there were none of the battles of will I'd experienced with Richard. On the contrary, our time together was relaxing, joyful. What more could I wish for but to enjoy his company a little longer?

*

Next day, we set off on foot for San Antonio Huista, the last big centre before the Mexican border, where our paths were to diverge – mine back to my roaming across the Guatemalan mountains; his towards a new life waiting for him in Mexico, and new commitments.

It took us three days.

There were neither roads nor buses connecting the few Ladino villages scattered along the way, only dirt tracks that no one except for us seemed to be walking.

We rambled through emerald green valleys and over windswept hills where only the odd sheep was grazing. As we approached, they would turn, look at us suspiciously, then bleat and run away.

We drank the clear, ice-cold water from the mountain streams, and sitting on the rocks, we feasted on the avocado, garlic and peanut butter sandwiches Martin never seemed to run out of. Now and then we chatted, but mostly we were happy to walk side by side, taking in the fresh air, the views, the peacefulness.

The villages were a few hours' distance from each other. They were hamlets really – a few stone houses around a *plaza*, a granary, a corral for the sheep, sometimes a wooden stable. We came upon each quite suddenly and, as the path cut through their middle, we certainly didn't pass unobserved.

As we walked by, making a big show of smiling and waving, people mumbled a few grudging hellos and followed us with sidelong glances until we disappeared.

As Martin had rightly predicted, there were no *hospedajes* either.

At the end of each day, we had to face the problem of finding a bed for the night. We put the question to everyone we met and looked at them hopefully.

Only at the very last minute, when it was obvious that there was nowhere for us to stay, did some kindly soul – generally a woman – timidly come forward.

'You can sleep on my floor,' they would say, hesitantly, worried they might expose themselves to unknown danger. We did our best to reassure them.

Too tired to feel the sharp little stones digging into our backs through our thin bedding, in no time we'd fall asleep. At the crack of dawn, we'd be woken abruptly by a crowing rooster, and we'd be on our way.

We walked for hours, enjoying the physical exertion of the walk. At intervals, one of us would break the silence and begin to talk.

He told me about Zipolite, the place in Mexico he was heading for.

'In the language of the Zapotec Indians, it means "valley of the dead". It's a special place, very spiritual. The perfect site for Las Palmeras.'

'Oh, yes, the orphanage. What's it like?' I wanted to hear more.

He smiled at the thought. 'It's by the ocean on a beautiful stretch of coast. It's very wild around there – no villages, no farms.

And then you come to it, and suddenly you feel these vibes, this overwhelming energy...'

A gust of wind blew the hood of his anorak over his eyes. He stopped to fold it back over his nape, then he continued:

'There are fifteen children living in the orphanage, but twice as many go to the day school run by the volunteers. I've never seen more enthusiastic pupils. They're so affectionate, so loving that they make your heart melt. There's quite a bit of land too, an orchard, horses, people coming and going, a great atmosphere. Every decision is taken collectively, so each morning there's a meeting to plan the day ahead. Last year, on my way south, I spent a few days there, and the experience blew me away. It was like being part of a large commune made of people from everywhere – the States, France, Scandinavia...'

A commune. I must have pulled a face, because he hastened to say, 'I know you don't like hippies, but, really, Monica, these guys do amazing work. And they're deeply spiritual. Frank, the guy who founded Las Palmeras, died a couple of years ago, but everyone there still talks about him. A true force of nature, they say, a solid rock, a heart of gold. "Our guru", they call him. Pity I turned up too late and never met the man.'

A guru? A commune? The Valley of the Dead? A bunch of foreign do-gooders taking over an enchanted corner of the Mexican coast? It sounded suspiciously New Age to me. Where was the politics?

'What about the Mexicans? Do any of the local people work there?'

'Just a few. There's Jorge the driver, Maria in the kitchen, and two guys doing the cleaning. They get paid, unlike the others, and every night they go back home.'

In short, menial jobs for local people. I could just picture it. A garden of Eden, where a bunch of foreign hippies did their own thing.

But I was unfair. Those guys were doing good work. More than I could say about myself. Why was I so bent on rubbishing this place? Sour grapes? What was I trying to do? Persuade Martin he should stay with me instead of going to Las Palmeras? Pathetic.

'And the volunteers, what are they like?' I asked, forcing myself to sound more positive.

'Very much like me, same ideals, same goodwill. I'm sure we'll get along.'

An awkward silence followed. Could he sense my disappointment and the mounting jealousy at the thought that all that didn't include me?

The day was too nice and sparkling to let the sombre mood spoil it.

'I'm sure you will,' I said, finally.

We walked on, and I soon let go of my grudges, drawn into the soothing view of the rolling plains we were crossing, with those blue and verdigris peaks that both towered over us and cocooned us on every side.

*

Arriving in San Antonio Huista felt like being plunged back into an urban jungle of honking cars, revving motorbikes, horse-drawn carts rattling along the cobblestones, and hundreds of people, in *trajes*, in Western clothes, people talking, calling out to each other, arguing. Everywhere, there was movement – noise, chaotic energy – our last few days of rural seclusion now a distant memory.

We found a room in a *posada* with a "proper" bed, and then bought all kinds of comfort foods from the street vendors – ice cream, biscuits, *tacos*, a whole selection of sweet and salted titbits.

It was our last night together. Being on a tight budget and unable to afford the town's restaurants, we decided to have dinner in the privacy of our hotel room.

Wanting to create a romantic atmosphere, we laid out half a dozen candles around the room, draped some scarves artfully over the bed lamps and, finally, bought a quarter bottle of white rum to enhance the mood.

Then, sprawled on the double bed as if having a picnic in a grassy meadow, we gorged ourselves on our assorted provisions.

Martin poured his latest concoction into a couple of mugs. 'Here's a special cocktail I've made for us,' he said with an inscrutable smile, handing me one. 'We should call it *The Last Supper*.'

I thought about the word he just used: *last*, that is, final, terminal, no more suppers together ahead of us. My heart sank. I'd grown fond of this man. I was going to miss him, but I stared back bravely, pretending to be as chilled and detached as he seemed to be.

The rum mixed with the coke and the melted ice cream loosened us up, and words came easily.

'After being dumped,' Martin confessed awkwardly, 'I felt completely unsure of myself. I felt worthless. I thought no woman could possibly find me attractive.' He dismissed my exclamations of reassurance with laughter.

'Now I feel my confidence has come back. Partly it's because of this new job in Mexico. It's given me a new sense of purpose. But it's your doing too, Monica. You've been such a wonderful travelling companion.'

A travelling companion? Was that all? It hurt to hear such blandness. Despite all my efforts to be cool and uninvolved, I'd come to hope for more.

Propped up against the pillows, the moonlight falling through the window across his face, Martin watched me closely.

'What next, Monica? What are your plans?'

While walking on the Altiplano, I had spent much time and energy considering my immediate future. What I didn't know, though, at least not consciously, was that a hint of an idea had begun to take shape in my head. Now Martin's blunt question brought it to the surface and enabled me to flesh it out just a little and make it real.

'I don't really know, but one thing is sure – I won't go back to Nicaragua.'

I couldn't tell what had made up my mind. The sight of those wretched cotton pickers on the lorry? The *campesinos* forced to till the steep slopes around Acul? Martin's enthusiasm and commitment to his orphanage? Whatever the reason, it was now clear that teaching the middle classes of Managua didn't satisfy my need to be useful. I yearned for something new, something I could believe in.

'I guess I'll be looking for a more fulfilling job.'

'In a commune?' he teased me. He thought for a while, and for a moment, one last flicker of hope stirred within me. But then he said: 'I know just the place. It's in Guatemala City and could be right for you. It's run by a Jesuit. No, don't worry,' he promptly added at the expression of alarm that appeared on my face. 'It's not a religious institution or anything like that. This Swiss woman called Eva told me about it. I think she still works there. I'll give you her phone number, if you think it's a good idea.'

It was all the encouragement I needed. And, even if it wasn't what I hoped he'd suggest to me, I was definitely going to check the place out.

The candlelight cast long, soft shadows onto the peeling walls, making the ugly room look cosy. We talked, kissed, and stroked each other till early morning. Then, all candles spent, we fell asleep in each other's arms.

*

Early the following morning, we took the bus to San Pedro Nectar, where we would part. I would head back to Huehuetenango; Martin would carry on north to La Mesilla, where later that night he would cross the border.

The bus was crowded, so we climbed onto the roof and sat, huddled together, among sacks of potatoes and baskets of fruit and corn. A few more people made it onto the roof as well. They laughed and joked, dodging the branches that whipped their faces from the roadside. They didn't seem to notice us, and certainly didn't sense the shadow of our impending farewell. Why should they? Some chatted light-heartedly, others, heads bent, sat absorbed in their own concerns.

Martin's arms around me, I watched the countryside go by: muddy yellow rivers, green rolling hills, trails of puffy clouds spanning the sky, adobe hamlets, herds grazing in the fields, farmhands tilling dark patches of soil with rustic ploughs.

Wrapped up in my own emotions, I watched it all from a great distance, like a film.

Not even the pungent smell of thousands of onions wafting from the jute sacks around us or the cloying scent from the ripe pineapples could shake me out of my daydreams.

I had no romantic illusions about Martin, and it was doubtful he had any about me. We had made no plans together, so it was unlikely our paths would ever cross again. It had just been a holiday fling. And yet I felt sad and gloomy at the thought of saying goodbye to him.

As I savoured our last moments of closeness, the two hours' bus ride strangely began to feel a great deal longer. Time stretched.

Then, everything came to an end.

The bus driver stopped for lunch. We had a beer. Our goodbye was short and almost formal. We didn't look at each other. Martin kissed me on both cheeks and rapidly walked away towards his bus. I sat outside the café, at the only table. I did not move: I watched him stride over the scattered bundles, then climb the metal steps onto the bus. He did not turn to wave goodbye.

CHAPTER FOUR

HOTEL TRANQUILIDAD

Eight thirty: according to the guidebook, a bad time to arrive in this city. Danger lay in wait at every corner, said the book: pickpockets lurked in alleyways, muggers and rapists were ready to jump out of the shadows, not to mention the death squads raging through the town. The more I read, the more I panicked. I shut the book and tried to put my fears aside. Why should I let myself be intimidated by hearsay dangers? Still, as I walked the length of the narrow *calle*, I'd throw a cautious glance over my shoulder, just in case.

This was "Zona Uno", the district of Guatemala City with the highest concentration of guest houses and hotels, including the one Martin had recommended I go to. With darkness fast approaching, it was the place I headed for after the day-long bus ride from the freezing highlands to the sweltering hot southern plains.

Right ahead, jutting out from either side of the street, a blaze of neon lights and bright signposts closed in: Hotel Beaumont, El Colonial, Hospedaje Santander, Hotel La Verdad, Tienda y Comedor Marta. Typical of most neighbourhoods of the city centre, colonial buildings stood alongside modern high-rises;

colonnaded fronts of residential houses rose next to seedy hostelries.

With one last glance back up the street, I made my way to one of the end buildings, where a dusty car park opened up.

I stopped right in front of a nondescript door, looked up and read the bold blue letters printed above the entrance – four syllables that rolled off the tongue like a melody, conjuring up visions of lush pastures and blue skies: Hotel Tranquilidad. It was the place I was looking for.

I pushed the heavy door open and stepped inside.

The darkness swallowed me up, the tinkling of a bell echoing in the silence. At first, I saw only shadows. In time, I began to make out a rambling corridor. I followed it through into the belly of the building, where clearly daylight never reached. On a desk, in the corner, sat a table lamp, its old-rose shade dancing with sequins. Behind it, on the wall, a laminated sign read: *English spoken here.*

I stood there waiting, then pressed the old-fashioned bell, the only object on display over the satin table-cover. A few minutes later, the face of a young man peeped through from behind a door.

'*Buenas!*' He smiled broadly. '*Usted es de los Piss Cor?*'

Confronted with my blank stare, he pointed to a notice board hanging from the side wall. Scores of messages scribbled in bright blue ink were pinned under the heading US PEACE CORPS VOLUNTEERS.

I wasn't an American volunteer, no, but could I please have a room?

'*Ah, una aventurera, entonces.*' An adventurer, he called me. Was it a compliment or an insult? I wondered. I got the feeling that, in his books, it was certainly not the first. '*Sólo un momento,*' he said, giving me the once-over. Then, with a clinking of buckets and brooms, he hurried to finish his cleaning chores.

Back in the reception, he checked the hotel logbook.

'*Lo siento muchísimo*, only rooms on the ground floor,' he said with a lewd wink that gave the lie to his apologetic tone and made me feel uncomfortable.

I was given room number five, one of the front rooms, and sent off to have dinner so that the hotel staff could get on with the cleaning. 'It'll be ready before you're back,' the man assured me.

I paid up-front, left my heavy backpack at the reception, and once again I braved the streets.

Contrary to all expectations, I was relieved to find that the area felt relatively safe. I hurried past a few women standing in the dark doorways and got to my restaurant. Here, under a TV set screwed high up onto the wall above the tables, I polished off a plateful of *frijoles,* rice, fried eggs and tortillas, while an incomprehensible sitcom held the other customers in thrall. Guffaws of laughter drifted over to where I sat listlessly sipping at my beer.

What would Martin have made of this? I wondered. He would have found someone to chat with; he would have joined in; he would have got the joke. Where was he now? Most likely, in his orphanage. I missed him.

I thought about his good humour, his soft voice, the way he got on with people. I pictured him along one of the many paths we walked in the Altiplano: the beacon of his bright red anorak in front of me, the curiosity in his eyes when he turned towards me for a chat or a question. The thought of him made me smile.

I traced my way back to the hotel through darkness, feeling less alone, less frightened. I stepped through the front door with newly found confidence. Even the doorbell had a touch of audacity to it. As it rang across the hall, it acknowledged my change of mood.

'Número cinco.' I asked for my key, resolutely.

'Número cinco?' There was a different man now at reception. Less cocksure than the other one, a pinch more respectful, he was nonetheless adamant that no key for number five was in the wall cabinet where all the keys were kept.

They'd gone and let my room to someone else. Great! What now?

It was too late to go out into the darkness and look for another hotel. Besides, there was no guarantee I'd find anything as cheap.

I'd never been one to make a fuss over these things. As a child, I'd been terribly shy, and my mother had tried to cure me by sending me alone to the shop to buy my favourite comic, and even then, I'd chickened out. In my adult life, things had not changed substantially, but now the fear of being out there alone, at night, made me unexpectedly determined.

'You created the problem, so now, it's you who has to solve it,' I said. 'Find me another room.' I was the first one to be surprised at the firmness in my voice. Where had this alter ego come from? I wondered.

'Just wait a second,' said the receptionist in a conciliatory tone, and disappeared through a side door.

He returned two minutes later.

'No worries, it's all sorted,' he said. 'The first room to be vacant is yours. Just wait here.'

Momentarily relieved, I sat patiently in the small hall and watched the comings and goings.

A new frenzy seemed to take over the hotel. The doorbell rang every five minutes, and each time a man and a woman would be hurried into one of the front rooms. It dawned on me that this was a brothel. Why on earth had Martin suggested this place?

In between the insistent ringing, the hotel staff – the receptionists and a couple of cleaners – rushed frantically up and down the corridors, making and unmaking beds, mopping floors, piling dirty sheets and dustbin liners outside hurriedly vacated rooms.

Despite my predicament, I couldn't help watching it all with interest.

The clientele of the Hotel Tranquilidad was a fascinating mixture. Along the narrow corridor, a handful of young foreigners with colourful Guatemalan clothes and unkempt hair jostled with seedy-looking middle-aged men pressing mini-skirted local girls fast to their hips. To my horror, most of the girls were in their late teens, some of them younger.

'Oh, sorry!' *'Lo siento, perdón.'* 'After you.' 'Have a good night,' foreigners and locals said to each other politely.

Thanks to everyone's "discretion", the hotel seemed to tick along without a hitch.

Still, it was, quite clearly, the wrong time of the day to be checking in.

Both receptionists were now at the desk, talking between themselves. From time to time, they'd turn and sneer at me. As a woman travelling on her own, they treated me with the same contempt as the sex workers they checked in and out. Worse – I was beneath their contempt, for I wasn't bringing in extra customers.

Then a man on his own came in – a foreigner like me, an American.

'A room? Yes, sure. Number fifteen,' I heard one of the receptionists say to him. The guy was given the key and sent upstairs. It was plainly obvious he'd been given preferential treatment and allowed to jump in front of me, the single woman, the *aventurera*, as they called me.

I was furious. Had it been daytime, I'd have picked up my backpack and slammed the door behind me.

'He booked weeks ago,' said one of the receptionists, noticing my anger, but the glance of mockery he exchanged with his colleague was blatantly insulting and pushed me over the edge.

'Stop bullshitting me,' I yelled. 'I want my room, and I want it now!'

Swearing seemed to work. The two sprang to their feet and made busy with the register; they conferred with each other, turned back a few pages, forward a few pages more. Finally, they offered me another room.

'We need to clean it, though. It won't take long, don't worry. Half an hour at the most. Just sit in the lounge and relax.'

I grabbed my rucksack and followed them along the endless corridor into another hall. Soon the night seeped in, cold and windy, chilling me to the bone. I pulled some woollens out of my rucksack, then, sprawled out on a lumpy sofa, I dozed off.

I was outside a busy train station and I spotted Martin's anorak beaming like a red signal in the crowd. I called out his name. He turned, looked around, and when he saw me, he smiled. He looked strangely hesitant, though, almost clumsy. I ran towards him with open arms. Then, I realised he wasn't alone. 'Meet Joanna,' he said, pointing to the tall young woman who stood by his side. My heart sank.

She wore a long white dress and looked pale and ethereal, like a vestal virgin. Her blonde hair fell in long waves down to her waist; she stood next to him, upright, elegant, smiling at everyone. She wasn't just beautiful, she was stunning.

'Joanna works at Las Palmeras. She's one of the volunteers.' Martin looked at her, besotted, as if she were a cherished prize he'd won. 'She's on her gap year from Harvard.' He held his hand out and pulled her towards him. They kissed passionately. When they finally let go of each other and turned towards me, there right in front of me was not Martin, but my ex, Richard.

'How're you doing?' he said with a wink, and burst out laughing.

I woke with a start. I was shivering from the cold night air and looked at my watch. I'd been asleep for over an hour. And my room? What lame excuse would they try on me this time? Incensed and now deeply worried, I went back to the desk, ready for battle.

'Your room's not ready yet, sorry. This is a very busy night, you see,' said one of the receptionists. 'You must be patient.' Then, all the while exchanging amused looks with his colleague, he added, 'But if you don't want to wait, there's a solution, isn't there, Pedro?'

More grinning, more pantomime guffaws, and Pedro said: 'Yes, sure, you could go and share with the *viejito* of number twelve.'

'The old man is okay, you know. He won't try anything, believe me.'

They were now laughing openly in my face.

I was mortified, angry and very tired. Their systematic humiliation had gone on for too long. I made up my mind – even if it meant skipping a few meals, I'd splash out on a taxi and look for another hotel. I'd sleep at the airport, if necessary.

I let them carry on with their double act – the nudges, the winks and the innuendos. When they had run out of steam, I demanded my money back.

'But you haven't paid,' they protested in unison.

'What!' I roared, my shyness and restraint by now a distant memory. One after the other, doors began to open along the corridor. Tousled heads appeared, curious to know what the hubbub was about.

'That's it, I've had enough,' I said. 'I'll call the police.'

The threat together with the unwanted attention tempered our reactions. The guy who'd checked me in remembered that I'd paid him, and I calmed down.

The screaming had won me a room on the top floor, far from all the transactions going on downstairs.

I was taken up a jigsaw of staircases, across patios cluttered with potted plants, through a labyrinth of balconies and narrow corridors. We climbed higher and higher until we reached a small patio on the top floor. Over the parapet, the lights of the city shone brightly a long way below.

'*Aquí estamos, cuarto veintitrés.*' The man unlocked the only door along the patio. Tired and relieved, I carried my rucksack in.

As soon as I hit the pillow, I fell asleep.

*

The following morning, a flood of sunshine streaming in through the net curtains woke me up at dawn. I'd slept so well that, despite all my travelling and the previous night's adventure, I felt not only fully rested, but optimistic about life.

I looked around, taking in my surroundings.

I liked the room. It was basic, the furniture down to the bare essentials – a double bed with a chintz cover, a wooden bedside table the size of a napkin, an armchair with a sagging seat – but there were two huge windows that let in plenty of light and breeze and, of course, there was that patio outside, with its promise of absolute privacy.

I opened the door and, out there, I saw what I'd failed to notice in the darkness: a clapped-out wicker chair, a round table of solid stone, some brightly coloured shirts and pyjama trousers drying on a line between two walls. Scattered around the patio were lush tropical plants in terracotta pots: cacti with fleshy oval leaves, spiky bushes with flame red blossoms, miniature banana trees, coconut leaves shooting out of their dark casks as straight as swords. It was a suntrap where seedlings sprouted and grew overnight like a rampaging jungle.

I looked over the parapet. Where, the night before, a myriad of city lights had been twinkling six floors below, a web of terraced roofs and bustling streets spread out as far as the eye could see. It was quiet up here, the only sound being the muffled and distant echo of the early-morning traffic.

I sat at the table and basked in the sun, letting my mind wonder.

Yesterday, the guys at reception had called me "*aventurera*". Did they mean someone in search of thrills and excitement? Was that what I was? Was that how the Guatemalans saw me? Or, even worse, did they see me as someone taking a cheap holiday in somebody else's misery? That certainly wasn't my intention. On the contrary, I was seriously looking out for a cause to commit to, something that could absorb me entirely, something bigger than my own petty concerns. If I seemed to be drifting, well – it was because I hadn't found the right thing yet.

'C'mon,' I said to myself, loudly, 'stop whinging, and get a move on.'

All at once inspired, I got pen and paper from indoors. Back in my wonderful solarium, I wrote a resignation letter to my employers at Videonic in Managua.

It was short and to the point – the excuse most plausible. Something unexpected had happened at home, making it impossible for me to return to my teaching job after the summer holidays. Many apologies.

As I folded the letter into an envelope, I asked myself whether I was rushing into things. After all, although Videonic didn't pay me much, still, what it gave me was enough to live on, and since no other job was on the horizon, the most sensible thing would be to wait until I found one before resigning. But I was impatient, right now my morale was high, and writing the letter had felt so good. In any case, I told myself, I had the whole day to think it over before I plucked up enough courage to pop it into the post.

I sealed the envelope, put it into my pocket and left the hotel.

The morning was dry and crisp. The squat buildings, the shop fronts, the dusty streets – everything was awash with dazzling sunlight. The narrow pavements heaved with the relentless coming and going of people. It was hard to imagine now, in broad daylight, how last night I could have thought this place was dangerous.

My first plan of the day was to go and change some money. The night before, when paying for my hotel room, I'd used up my last *quetzals*. Now I urgently needed to dig into the precious dollar stash I kept in a belt around my waist. It was worrying to see how quickly I was going through it, but one good thing about the capital was, I'd been told, that the exchange rate offered by the local black market was better than anywhere else. So, armed with a city map, I set out for the old centre where, said my guidebook, most money changers hang out.

Ten minutes' walk from the Hotel Tranquilidad, I came to a wide *avenida* with battered buses and cars racing by. Along both sidewalks, rickety tables displayed a selection of trinkets: key-holders, plastic combs, bars of soap, anti-dandruff shampoo, Colgate toothpaste, all sizes of nail-cutters, you name it, they sold it. There was even a booming shoelace trade: a feast of brightly coloured strings on upright boards wedged between the stalls.

Feeling buoyant and full of hope, I threaded in and out of the hustle and bustle, dodging the obstacles, never pausing, until I stopped in my tracks at the sight in front of me.

The man sat at a street corner, propped up against the shiny glass of a shop window. He wore a pair of faded jeans, one leg cut back to accommodate a grossly swollen limb which was stretched across the pavement, blocking the way. A line of dark stitches ran along the length of the leg, bluish skin bursting at the seams of a badly infected wound, crimson flesh poking out between the stitches. The man, a young Ladino, extended his hand, addressing no one in particular. '*Unos centavos para comer, por favor!*' he chanted.

I came upon him so suddenly I almost stumbled over his monstrous leg. I winced with a mixture of pity and ill-concealed disgust, averted my eyes and darted across the road, dodging the cars and the buses.

But as I walked the streets, I kept on thinking about the man and his oozing wound. Why hadn't I stopped? As a tourist, I was like a millionaire to him. The feeling of guilt dogged me like my own shadow.

At last, I came to a beautiful Spanish colonial building with a clock tower. Around it a thriving money-changing market had established its headquarters.

Touts hung out in the alleys; they pressed from all sides, forcing passers-by to elbow their way through.

They were mostly women.

'*Tres por uno! Tres dólares por un quetzal!*' Shrill voices besieged me as I braved the crowd.

'How much, how much? *Cuánto quiere cambiar?*' The clamour matched that of the street vendors a few blocks away.

'*Aquí* we change everything: *dólares de los Estados, dólares canadienses, francos franceses... Usted diga.*' The crowd pressed against me.

It was total bedlam. A couple of women tugged at my elbow and pulled me by the arm, dragging me in opposite directions.

The heavily armed security guards around the building looked on indifferently as I was jostled and pulled about. They were there to protect the assets, the shops; people were not their concern.

I began to worry. What if, in the confusion, the women laid hands on me and snatched my money belt? Where could I escape? I looked around but there seemed to be nowhere to run.

Then, I met the eye of a young Ladino woman in a bright green dress. She stood at quite a distance but seemed to understand my silent plea. In response, she rushed over, set me free of the grasping hands and skilfully manoeuvred me out of the hubbub into a quiet corner.

'*Usted qué quiere cambiar? Dólares, verdad?* Come along with me, *pues.*' Her dress hugged her plump body and a gold star glittered on one of her front teeth.

Something about her – the star? That kind look she'd darted at me? – made me trust her straight away. Perhaps, more simply, it was the relief and the surge of gratitude I felt towards her for getting me out of that crowd. In any case, I obediently followed her along one of the back streets into a busy shopping mall.

In front of each shop window, she conferred with the guard on duty, checking the going rate. In the end, she decided for *tres por uno* – three *quetzals* for one US dollar – and took me into a store, right in the middle of the mall. Inside, clusters of people haggled with each other furiously, flicking through wads of notes.

We joined the long queue. At the end of it, a clerk sat in a booth, protected by a glass panel. 'How much?' he asked perfunctorily.

'Fifty.' I put the dollar bills through the slot in the glass. 'It's all in notes of five, I'm sorry.'

He looked up from the desk but didn't stop counting. The green bills flashed between his fingers like a pack of cards.

'*Aquí,*' he said curtly, and handed over two handwritten receipts, one for me, and one for my companion. '*Próximo!*' he cried out, gazing at the ceiling.

At the cash desk by the exit, we were given the money we were owed.

I stashed the hundred and forty-nine *quetzals* into my money belt, tied it around my waist, and then tucked my shirt over it into my trousers.

It was a fiddly operation that took its time. 'Better safe than sorry,' I remarked to my companion, turning towards the nearest wall to protect myself from indiscreet eyes. She gave me a blank look, fished a small string purse out of her cleavage and dropped a few coins into it.

'That's not much,' I let out, regretting my words immediately. Why would she care about what I thought? Despite my good intentions, everything I said sounded smug, arrogant. I blushed.

'*Sí, pues.*' As she spoke, there was none of the resentment I expected from her. 'Most of the commission goes to the agency bosses. Still, *gracias a Dios*, it's fifty *centavos* more than before.'

A quick nod, a brief smile, her gold star glinting, and off she went, lost in the crowd, in search of the next customer.

Relieved that the entire operation had come to an end without drama, I turned my attention to the next task on my list.

I walked to the nearest street corner, found a public phone and dialled the number Martin had jotted down for me on a piece of paper.

'*Aló? Diga,*' said a deep male voice the other end.

I asked for Eva and after a short wait a young friendly voice with a distinctive German lilt came on the line. She seemed delighted to hear about Martin and, yes, they did need volunteers at the centre. So why didn't I come for a visit the following afternoon?

'We're in Colonia Amparo, in the north of Guate,' she explained. 'It's hard to get to. You'll need to change two or three buses. But don't worry, come whenever you can. I'll be waiting for you.'

It was reassuring to hear this friendly voice at the other end of the line. It made me eager to get to the place and get started. As I put down the receiver, I smiled to myself, full of hope.

So, the time had come to decide. I patted the letter in my pocket – would I dare post it? There was no certainty I'd get the job, but, if I seriously wanted to change my life, I knew I had to burn my bridges. And so I dared.

I didn't have to go far to find a post office, as most public buildings seemed to be located within the same square mile.

It was an imposing colonial building with a wide arched door. Inside, in a large hall with a high vaulted ceiling, I joined a long queue of people. When my turn came, I bought a stamp and, with a knot in my stomach, handed my letter over the counter to be sent off. There, I'd done it. I'd sealed my destiny.

Out in the street, I felt light-headed, as if a heavy weight had lifted. I was about to go and celebrate with a drink, when I remembered with a pang the considerable – at least, for local standards – amount of money I had on me. Suddenly I felt more vulnerable than ever. The notes rustled against my waist awkwardly and I imagined everyone could hear the noise. Even if they couldn't, people were bound to notice the bulge around my midriff. I felt like a sitting duck and quickened my step, eager to reach the safety of the hotel.

As I walked away from the old centre, the confusion died down and I relaxed. It was a warm, clear evening. If I walked faster, I might even get back in time to climb to the top balcony and catch the last sunrays spread their crimson glow across the roof tops. What I craved, now, was an ice-cold beer –

A man suddenly sprang up in front of me. I stepped to one side, alarmed. Then I saw he was loaded down with samples of colourful *típica*.

'*Compre!*' He pursued me, blocking my escape.

He was a pedlar, an unusual sight in the capital, where most vendors sold their merchandise, however lacklustre, from makeshift stalls. He'd probably come by bus from Lake Atitlán for the day, wanting to beat the competition. And here I was, the punter he'd been looking for.

He unloaded his huge bundle on the pavement and set to work on me.

'*Mira aquí, mira este huipil. Bonito, verdad?* I also have beautiful homespun *cortes*. What about this red one? The colour suits you.' He unfolded lengths and lengths of deep red cotton, enshrouding me in it.

'*No, gracias.* There's nothing I want to buy.' All I could think about was sitting on that balcony, a beer in my hand, the sky ablaze all around.

He wouldn't have it. 'Wait. What about one of these *fajas*? Come on, be good, buy something for your friends *de allá*.' He unravelled a feast of hand-woven sashes, all long enough to circle my waist half a dozen times. I was dazzled by that triumph of colours. He saw the sparkle in my eyes, a glint of interest, he thought, and pressed on: '*Son muy bonitos, verdad*? Only ten *quetzals! Vaya, pues, cómprame uno!*'

'*No, gracias,*' I said firmly. I sprinted forward and gained the pavement ahead of him.

There was no way he could pick up his merchandise fast enough and run after me. I left him behind, looking disgruntled.

'*Eres mala gente. Mejor si no viniera,*' he grumbled.

I scurried away, trying to digest his hateful words. I wondered how many of the locals felt like this man – *Better if you lot, you nasty people, didn't come here.*

True, I wasn't contributing much to the economy. I hardly bought a thing. Also, I didn't want to be treated like a tourist or be mistaken for one. And now, without a job to cushion me, at least not for the moment, I was going to spend even less. In fact, from now on, only cheap hotels lay ahead of me – cheap restaurants, cheap means of transport, everything on the cheap. *Ba-ra-to*: the magic word that, with some luck, would allow me to hold out in Central America for months, or, quite possibly, even for years.

I quickened my step, and soon I was up on my private terrace, looking down onto the cobweb of streets that made up that chaotic city, all my thoughts and energy projected towards what the next day might bring.

CHAPTER FIVE

COLONIA AMPARO

The minivan I'd taken from the town centre broke down in the thick of the mid-morning traffic, leaving half a dozen of us stranded. I took two more buses, but when I got off at what I thought was my destination, Módulos de Esperanza was nowhere in sight. Had I got the bus numbers mixed up? But no, I'd followed Eva's directions to the letter. The place couldn't be far.

Determined to fight against a mounting feeling of despondency, I asked a passer-by if he knew the whereabouts of Padre Ramón's centre. He pointed vaguely up the road. 'Siga siempre recto,' he said, 'you can't miss it.'

I sighed with relief and set off along the dual carriageway, cautiously keeping to its dusty margin. Gushes of hot air took my breath away and swept me to the side each time a car or a lorry whooshed past.

On my right, I passed a compact area of squat modern buildings lined with busy pavements and tarred alleys. A hundred metres further, a crowded row of tumbledown shacks ran along the street, then sprawled fungus-like at the back, across the barren wasteland.

Built out of discarded planks and rusted metal, these shanties seemed to house the poorest of the poor. A ragged woman emptied a bucket of slops into a ditch, while, next to a pile of flat tyres, a man tinkered with a rusty engine. Behind him, searching for leftovers, a few mangy dogs snuffled between the shacks.

It struck me that several generations lived in these slums. Everyone was dirt poor, but this was not the same poverty I'd seen in the countryside, where the scenery was beautiful and people, if not exactly friendly, at least generally approachable. This was something meaner, nastier. There were no *trajes* here, no dazzling textiles. The few individuals who registered my presence looked at me with harsh, unsmiling faces. Resentment flickered in their eyes. 'What are *you* doing here?' they seemed to ask me, disapprovingly.

A troop of barefoot children burst out of nowhere. They were chasing each other in the dust, screaming and bubbling with laughter.

As I watched them, the cloud of misery that bore down over the place began to lift. Clearly, in the slums, people got on with life as in any other neighbourhood. Ignoring the bleakness of the setting, these children were enjoying the sunny day. They seemed happy. The dissonant note was me.

Ill at ease, I tried my best to walk by unnoticed, quickening my step and pointedly turning my gaze towards the steep hill that flanked the other side of the carriageway. Over there, protected by a gated entrance, the odd house pushed through the underbrush. There were no people in sight; no accusing eyes followed me around.

I pressed on.

The long walk, combined with the morning's transport misadventures, began to stir my appetite. It was lunchtime. It wouldn't do to arrive at Módulos de Esperanza famished – I had to eat something first.

A gravel path led me down into a vast low-roofed market, where I was enveloped by a haze of sun-filtered dust.

Up until then, all Guatemalan markets had been a triumph of colours and smells. I approached this one expecting more of the same. I imagined the slapping sound of the *tortillas*, the easy laughs of the stallholders, the welcoming smiles of the fellow shoppers. Instead, I was confronted by an atmosphere of sad neglect that mirrored the desolation of the surrounding shanties. Rubbish lay everywhere.

I stopped at a *comedor* that was called La Margarita, the Daisy, despite the fact nothing about it could even remotely recall a flower. Around a sooty kitchen area stood a few tables with long, straight benches screwed onto the earthen floor. The place was clean enough; but it gave the impression of being unloved. It was drained of colour; the plastic tabletops were off-white, and people's clothes dull shades of brown or grey. There were no flowers on the tables, just clouded glass jars of hot chillies that had long since lost their gloss.

A dozen customers, all men, sat in lines. Bent over their bowls, they ate in silence, while two Ladino women busied themselves around them.

I had the soup of the day, the ubiquitous *caldo de res* – the beef soup – ladled out of a blackened cauldron into a plastic bowl. It came with a couple of tortillas. To my surprise, it was delicious.

With a cup of chicory coffee in front of me, I lit my after-lunch cigarette and asked for directions to Padre Ramón's.

'Keep walking up the road,' said one of the two women. I couldn't help staring at the large wart above her upper lip. Her eyes caught mine and I flinched, embarrassed.

'It's five minutes away, at the most,' she continued, unperturbed. 'If you get lost, stop someone and ask.' Then, in a voice that was like melted butter, 'Everyone around here knows Padre Ramón.'

People, who until that moment had stared morosely at their plates as if into an abyss, suddenly came alive.

'Padre Ramón! *Es muy buena gente,*' exclaimed one. 'He paid for my mother's funeral.'

'*Sí, por cierto.* He's always ready to help out,' cried another.

'Remember when I was laid off? I went to him and "No problem," he said, "here's thirty *quetzals*".'

'Last year, he got me out of prison.'

'*Sí, pues,* he's an angel!'

An animated conversation drew in everyone around the tables.

I was glad to hear that they all liked and respected Padre Ramón. And if the cynic and lapsed Catholic inside me couldn't help thinking this priest sounded too good to be true, I also began to feel increasingly hopeful that he might turn out to be as nice to me as to these people – and offer me a job.

When I finally paid for my lunch and went back to the road, it was already mid-afternoon.

The "five minutes at the most" turned out to be well over half an hour. I began to think I'd gone past the centre.

I came to a derelict playground where a group of boys kicked a ball around the rusty swings and broken carousels amid clouds of dust. '*Hola, gringa!*' they screamed with excitement. I seemed to be the only diversion on offer in the *barrio*, that day.

I asked them again about the centre. '*Recto, recto!*' they replied in unison, delighted to be helpful. 'It's near.' Did anybody have a sense of distance around here?

I was hot and sweaty, and fed up with the long walk. I sat on a rock under a scraggy tree and took a couple of oranges out of my knapsack. In no time, the four boys came to stand in a semi-circle around me.

I offered each a piece of orange. We chatted.

I asked them about Colonia Amparo; what was it like to live here, did they like it? They all did, but '*Cuidado*,' said one, spreading his arms in a full circle. 'There are lots of bad people *aaaall* around.'

'See that kiosk over there in the corner? The police picked up a man from there last night,' said another.

'He was a killer,' said a third. 'He murdered people for money.'

'My dad knew him,' said another, boasting of the acquaintance as if the guy was a film star.

This confirmed what I'd heard about the marginal barrios. During the day, they were all squalor and poverty; at night-time, violence and death squads.

The boys decided to chaperone me. All the while chattering away about robbers and thieves, they walked me across the dual carriageway, then along a fast-disappearing sidewalk. Finally, they delivered me right in front of the iron gate of Módulos.

'*Adiós!... Qué le vaya bien!*' they shrieked enthusiastically, and they were gone.

*

There were no bells, no knockers. I pushed the gate open and climbed a long flight of steps.

On the hilltop sat a squat modern building with a spacious yard running along the front. Here, a man in a leather jacket crouched next to an ancient cross-country motorbike with a toolbox at his feet and a set of spanners scattered on the gravel. Behind him, a concrete driveway zig-zagged its way down the hill in sharp hairpin bends.

'*Buenos días,*' I said to the broad expanse of the man's shoulders.

He turned slowly, without the least surprise. '*Hola!*' His voice was deep, and his tone curt, off-hand, like someone who didn't want to be disturbed. He had dark curly hair, a full beard and a fierce moustache. A black smudge of grease stood out on his cheek like a gigantic comma.

I asked for Eva. He pointed to a wide-open door and told me she was somewhere in the house, working.

It didn't take long to find her. From inside one of the cubicles along the hall, I heard her distinct foreign accent. I sat on a wooden bench and waited.

'*Hasta pronto, Consuelo!*' A door opened and a heavily pregnant teenager stepped out. She looked at me with undisguised curiosity. I smiled at the girl and, craning my neck behind her, I waved through the gap at the woman standing by the desk.

'Hi! You must be Monica. I'm glad you've made it.'

She came forward and shook my hand with energy. She was tall, large boned, and wore her light brown hair in a loose ponytail. She seemed genuinely happy to see me.

On my part, I was delighted. 'So, you're a doctor?' I said, smiling broadly at her.

'Me, a doctor?' She looked at me, mildly surprised. Her light blue eyes were large and serious. 'No, I'm just a paramedic. I guess the white coat fools people. But, no, we have our own doctors. I only do routine checks. I do the blood pressure, I hand out the medicines, that kind of stuff,' she said, pointing at a desk piled with syringes, bottles and boxes of all shapes and sizes. 'Consuelo was my last appointment, so you've come at the right time.'

She took off her white coat and hung it behind the door. Underneath it, she was dressed in the sort of inconspicuous clothes – worn-out baggy trousers and ample T-shirt – that most locals wore in the capital.

'Let me show you around,' she said with enthusiasm, and led the way along the rambling corridor.

The centre was brand new and comprised a gynaecological clinic, a dental surgery and cubicles where people were treated for general complaints.

'The service is free but our doctors are volunteers, so they don't have much time. But if people went to the hospitals in the city, they'd have to take two or three buses. They may have to wait the whole day to be seen. That's if they're lucky. And when they do get to see someone, it may not even be a qualified doctor.'

We walked past an open door, and she nodded to a lanky man in a white coat. 'That's Doctor Romero, our dentist. And these are his patients. *Buenas!*' She smiled at the four men hunched on a bench along the wall. They were poorly dressed, emaciated. Each had taken off his hat and held it on his knees. They smiled timidly at us both.

'As you can see, Doctor Romero is busy… we'll do the introductions later. Now, let's go and look for Padre Ramón.' I followed her out of the building, struggling to keep up with her long strides.

There was a deep rumbling noise followed by the roar of an engine. We stepped into the yard just in time to see the man I'd spoken to earlier weave his way down the hill, astride his motorbike.

'Padre! Padre Ramón!' The growling of the Yamaha drowned out Eva's voice.

'He's gone.' She sighed.

So, *that* was the famous *padre*. What did I expect? In my mind, a *padre* was someone of gentle demeanour, with hands more suited to handling the chalice and the Eucharist than the salvaged parts of an old cross-country motorbike.

'Too bad you missed him.' Eva sighed.

'Isn't he supposed to interview me?' I asked anxiously.

'No. He delegates those things to us workers. Don't worry, we'll come to that later,' she said with a reassuring smile. 'I just wanted you to meet him because he could have told you everything there is to know about this place. It's his baby, after all.'

With admiration in her voice, she began to tell me about Padre Ramón.

'He never stops – he runs the centre, he lectures at two of the local universities, he even finds the time to write a weekly column for *La Tarde*. You must have come across some of these articles. His pen name is Víctor Pabsch.'

I shook my head, a little ashamed. I explained to Eva how I'd reluctantly given up reading the local newspapers, because I found it impossible to unravel the myriad twists and turns of the local party wrangling.

She looked a little crestfallen at this admission, so I quickly added:

'But everyone in town has great things to say about the *padre* and about this place.'

'It's all true. He's quite a guy: a thinker, a visionary. And he's not afraid to get his hands dirty.'

In the absence of the man himself, she took me to see the jewel in the crown of his collection: the old people's home.

The whitewashed two-storey building stood across the yard from the medical centre. It wasn't functioning to its full capacity yet. Of the thirty people it was built to house, only a third had taken up residence. They were all men, most of them well into their seventies. They had no family, no carers, no income.

Basking in the soft pink light of the late afternoon, three of them stood by the front door, chatting. Another one, wisps of snow-white hair framing his sun-baked face, sat alone at some distance, sharpening a machete while humming a tune.

A pleasant breeze rose from the valley, stirring the foliage and ruffling our hair.

'That's the visitors' area.' Eva pointed at half a dozen wooden tables topped with straw shades to the left of the house.

It had been planned in detail – the comfy chairs, the flowerbeds, the benches set out neatly on the manicured lawn. Even the picture-postcard sunset seemed choreographed. The place was pristine, ordered, the drabness and dispiriting chaos of the *barrio* hidden behind a grove of pine trees.

I wondered what it'd be like to work here, to be part of this mammoth battle against the misery of the encroaching shanties, to be another Eva doing a worthwhile job, to be another Martin. But, more to the point, what skills could I bring to such a place? Perhaps I could teach English as in Managua or, perhaps, help Eva. Anything they'd offer me, I'd be happy to do.

'Fancy a coffee?' said Eva.

We retraced our steps to the back of the main building where the staff – four paid workers, Eva and two other volunteers – lived in a long prefabricated bungalow.

I followed her down another endless corridor. 'Over there are the dormitories.' She pointed further to the left: 'That's Padre Ramón's office.' She showed me into a sparsely furnished kitchen-cum-living room. 'This is where we eat and socialise. No one's around right now, but the others will be here soon. They're great, you'll like them.'

While she busied herself around the gas stove, I glanced out of the open window and realised we were right on the edge of a deep ravine. Several feet below, at the bottom of a sheer drop, roared a torrent concealed by thick undergrowth. In front, amid the brush and the bramble, the flanks of the hill were strewn with all sorts of household trash, cardboard boxes, beat-up prams and a couple of old mattresses with rusty springs spiralling out in all directions. Among the miserable mounds of waste, I made out a couple of shirts draped on a washing line across the trees and, further down the valley, a rickety shelter put together with some planks – somebody's home.

Up on the Altiplano, Martin had told me gruesome stories about the *desaparecidos*, how at nightfall their mutilated bodies were thrown into the surrounding ravines and nearby ditches. How many had been dumped down here?

As I stood there, arms pillowed on the windowsill, staring into the valley, the boldness of Padre Ramón's choice of location was plain as day. Truckloads of rubbish were regularly emptied into this gorge. Among this waste, a few desperate people clung on to life and looked for things they could salvage, while many unlucky others found their burial place. Right in the middle of the worst dumping grounds of Guatemala Ciudad, Módulos de Esperanza rose like a challenge, and like a breath of hope. Yes, I concluded, I'd really like to be part of this.

'What did Martin tell you about us?' Eva interrupted my train of thought.

'He told me you're doing good work; and even though the place is run by a Jesuit, you don't need to be religious to work here. Because,' I paused, not sure how this would go down, 'to be honest, I'm not much of a churchgoer. What about you?'

'Me?' She looked at me, slightly amused, and then shook her head. 'I'm an atheist but I like the project. That's why I'm here.'

I breathed an inward sigh of relief. It felt safe to open up.

'I wasn't prepared for a biker-priest, you know?' I confided. 'Aren't Jesuits supposed to be intellectual, obsessed with theology, and very brainy? I sort of expected Padre Ramón to be like that – to go on spiritual retreats, that kind of stuff.'

She laughed and was about to say something, but just then a young man with long straight hair walked in. Eva introduced us. Federico was Argentinian and, like Eva, worked, without pay, as a volunteer.

'The locals get paid, we don't,' he said, pulling up a chair and helping himself to a cup of coffee. 'But we get board and lodging and as much coffee as we can drink.' Like Eva, he had that same earnestness, that same intensity. He looked at me appraisingly, weighing me up.

'Just think, Fede, Monica thought Padre Ramón was a hermit!' This idea was to them as bizarre as my struggling with the idea that a gruff biker was a man of the cloth. They both laughed at my naivety, but whereas Eva's teasing was gentle, almost indulgent, Federico's laugh had an edge to it.

'Things have changed since the fifteenth century, you know.' More laughter. 'But, as it happens, Padre Ramón does go on the occasional retreat, and I'm sure now and then he meditates.' He tilted back in his chair. 'But, what he does *here*,' he continued, eyes riveted on mine, 'couldn't be worldlier.'

'Yeah, he's definitely no mystic.' Eva's pale blue eyes gleamed in the half-light.

The sun was sinking lower in the sky, lengthening the shadows on the kitchen floor. A big wall clock showed it was a quarter to six.

Noticing my quick glance at the clock hands, Eva turned towards her colleague.

'Fede, Monica here hopes to come and work with us.' She leaned over and gave me an encouraging pat on the arm.

'Oh, yeah? And what can you do, Monica?' Fede asked, gazing at me searchingly. 'Can you give injections? Can you dress wounds?'

I shook my head.

'I hear you're a teacher,' he continued. 'Can you teach maths?'

For a moment, I considered blagging it and telling him I could. But I knew that, firstly, there was nothing I was more ignorant about than maths, and secondly, that, even if I tried, I'd be so useless at faking it that in no time I'd be found out. No two ways about it – I totally lacked the confidence to carry it off.

'Are you good at bookkeeping?' he asked next, staring at me with arched eyebrows.

I didn't seem to be good at anything that needed doing at Módulos. There was an awkward silence. Then, raising his open palms in the air as if to say, *Why on earth are you here then?*, he stood up and went over to the other side of the room.

While, with his back to us, he poured himself another mug of coffee, Eva smiled awkwardly at me.

Irritation grew inside me. Okay, there wasn't much I could do, but did this guy need to be quite so dismissive? He seemed to take some perverse pleasure in showing me up. After all, I was there, wasn't I? Didn't that prove my good intentions?

He put sugar in his coffee, stirred it, and returned to the table to continue the "grilling".

It seemed to me that the real problem for Federico wasn't so much what I could or couldn't do, but something more personal. Of course, he wasn't going to say it in so many words, at least not in front of the kindly Eva, but I could easily guess the real issue was he had me down as a "type", the foreign traveller, eager to experience some do-gooding self-fulfilment, but quick to bail out back to the comforts of home once the going got tough. From the start, as he eyed me up and down in a way that wasn't remotely sexual, I sensed he disapproved of me – the way I dressed, my big hair, the dreadlock I kept half-hidden behind my ear, my too brightly coloured clothes. To him, I was just another foreign hippy. It was payback time for my being so scathing of Pana's *viajeros*.

As he sat there with a contemptuous smile, his disapproval felt tangible. That both angered and intimidated me.

'I could teach English,' I managed to mumble.

'We already have someone doing that,' said Fede, sullenly. 'Jennifer's just signed a contract for the next two years. Can you wait till then?'

'Fede, I thought perhaps Monica could work with you,' Eva intervened conciliatorily. She turned towards me. 'Fede runs an after-school club for the local boys and teenagers. They love him, he's their hero.'

He stared at the ceiling, ignoring her.

'Monica could give you a hand with the boys, couldn't she?' Eva insisted. 'Aren't you always saying you need help?'

There was a long pause, when none of us seemed to know what to say, then Fede blurted out, 'Sorry, Monica, I know this isn't what you want to hear, but with no experience, you'd be more of a hindrance than a help.'

So there, he'd finally said it.

My face must have dropped at his point-blank refusal, making him feel a little sorry for me, because, when he continued, his tone had changed. He sounded much mellower now, as if he regretted his dismissive treatment of me.

'These kids are tough, they'd run a million circles around you, and anyone else, with no experience. You'd be exhausted after a week and no use to anyone.

'If you'd come earlier,' he carried on, 'I could have taken you to meet these kids. You'd have seen what I'm getting at.' There was no mistaking the genuine fervour in his voice when he talked about his work. 'But once you've proved yourself – and they have plenty of ways of putting you to the test – then you can do no wrong.'

I could imagine him getting down and dirty with the street kids, kicking around a football, acting as tough as them. But neither he nor, from what he was saying, the boys themselves would have any patience with a gringa do-gooder like me.

'We've another project in the pipeline,' said Eva, twisting the shiny bangle on her wrist over and over. She was doing her best to soothe my disappointment and diffuse the tension in the room. 'It's working with the victims of domestic violence. There's so much of it around here. Guys grow up thinking it's normal to hit their girlfriends. They always say, "What's wrong with that? That's what men do." When I hear this kind of talk, I feel like screaming. But…'

she paused and shook her head, looking sheepish, 'for that we need someone fully qualified, a social worker, someone with years of experience. Sorry, Monica!'

And then came the "thanks, but no thanks" bit that the whole afternoon had been leading up to.

'We appreciate your good intentions,' said Fede, 'but good intentions are not enough at Módulos. We need people with experience, lots of it.'

The fading light in the room blurred his expression, but was there the shadow of a smirk on his face?

'Thanks for showing me around anyway,' I said, trying hard to hide how cut up I was over their rejection. I glanced at the clock. 'I really must go.'

We stepped into the yard. Fede and Eva pointed out a dot in the far distance, a tin-roofed shelter, the bus stop I'd previously missed.

'Thank you, guys. This place is amazing,' I said as we parted. I genuinely admired Eva. As for Fede, there was no love lost between us. He barely nodded at me.

I walked slowly down the path Padre Ramón had driven along earlier.

From the brow of the hill, the centre commanded a vast view over the rolling plains, with their spread of makeshift dwellings, of half-built and never plastered concrete blocks, and heaps of rubbish everywhere. It was ugly and dangerous out there, and yet the scenery had some compelling beauty too. The sky glowed deep blue over the flat darkness of the hills. Electric lights flickered here and there across the plains. High up on the hill, the windows of the medical centre gleamed with the last blaze of daylight.

As I reached the end of the path, I turned and looked back. In the fast-dwindling light, I could see Módelos towering over the shanties. It was a gated community: either you were in or you were out.

I was out.

When I reached the bus stop, I waved once more to the two silhouettes on the hilltop; Eva's arm raised in the air, Fede already turning on his heel.

A second later, the bus pulled up and I jumped on.

*

Back in the hotel whose very name now mocked me – Tranquilidad, yeah, thanks – I felt so disheartened and vulnerable that, for a while, I didn't leave my room. Unemployed, with no place to go back to, and no travelling companion, I was beset by self-doubt and "what ifs".

I'd failed on all fronts – I didn't get the job, and even my brief romance with Martin had come to nothing. In short, I had become the kind of drifter I'd always been so contemptuous of.

I kept going over the details of my days together with Martin, which, after the bruising experience at Módulos, were bathed in a rosy glow. I mostly thought about those last few hours, when we'd held each other tight on the rooftop of the bus, without uttering a word. What if at the last moment Martin had rushed back, grabbed my hand and hoisted me onto the bus bound for Las Palmeras? This fanciful rerun of how things had gone was comforting. It lulled me into a woozy sleep.

During this time of self-imposed confinement, all I did was sleep, dream, listlessly read a paperback left behind, forgotten in the wardrobe by the previous guest, munch chocolate biscuits, read a little more and then mope again.

But even my sadness came to its natural end, and after three days of this, I woke up feeling ready to face the world.

I went and sat on the patio, and with my regained alertness, I looked afresh at my surroundings and began to notice a host of details.

Right across from my door, a flight of steps led over the concrete wall onto the roof and turned into a path that meandered from rooftop to rooftop, from one block to the next, like a hidden street wandering in and out of sight over the skyline. Up there, where the air was cleaner and fresher than at street level, I became aware of half a dozen people going about their chores.

On the nearest rooftop, a man was watering ranks of potted plants with a heavy canister, while two Mayan women, with long plaits dangling down their backs, hung their laundry on lines stretched between the roofs. Further along, a couple of men with a rickety ladder and old-fashioned tools mixed concrete and repaired a wall and, on a nearby terrace, a man in blue overalls raked coffee beans, drying them in the sun over a jute sack.

The morning was glorious. High-flying winds swept fluffy clouds across the deep blue sky, and, as peals of laughter soared in the air and reached me from across the roofs, all my worries and disappointment began to melt away. Nothing really mattered. Whatever the Fedes of this world thought of me, all around was light, bright, peaceful.

For the umpteenth time, I went over recent events and took stock of my situation. This time, I could see some of the advantages – I didn't have to go back to Managua to a job I didn't value. I was free to do whatever I chose. Most importantly, there was no need to follow in the footsteps of others, even if these "others" happened to be exceptional people, like Martin, Eva, or, bravest of all, Suzanne. I told myself that I should follow my own inclinations, pursue my own dreams. First and foremost, I should be myself.

I took a deep breath of fresh air, ready to meet the challenges that lay ahead.

In the last forty-eight hours, the way I felt about things had changed dramatically, including the way I felt about the hotel. Long forgotten was my rocky introduction to the place. Now, the Hotel Tranquilidad felt like the haven its name implied. I realised this had something to do with the fact that, except for a few Peace Corps volunteers on their way to and from the remote regions of Guatemala where they'd been posted, right now the majority of the hotel guests were tourists, mostly from the United States. Chastened by my recent rejection from Módulos, I'd become far less contemptuous of holidaymakers, people who were, overall, friendly and good-natured, with no pretentions to anything other than having fun. Right now, it felt good to have them around. Their North American twang echoed up and down the corridors and from behind closed doors. I never thought I'd say this, but yes, it felt reassuring to my ears. I smiled at the thought that theirs was the only *"English spoken here"*, as the sign claimed at reception.

I sat there, lost in thought, recalling Martin's soft accent, his laughter...

From the patio below, a conversation drifted up to where I was sitting.

Two Peace Corps guys were chatting. From the half sentences that carried over, I learnt that one had been entrusted with promoting tourism on the Pacific coast, and the other with the grand task of teaching kids how to pole vault somewhere in the north-east. Pathetic, I thought, and my attention flagged.

But when snippets of a completely new subject travelled up the stairs, I immediately cocked my ears.

'A reggae concert...' '...this weekend...' '...a couple of bands from Jamaica...'

I loved anything Jamaican; the music, the Rastafarians, everything. Proof of this unconditional love was the single dreadlock I'd lovingly groomed over the years, the one that, I suspected, had lost me credibility in Federico's eyes as a serious contender for the job in Módulos.

Emboldened by curiosity, I followed the voices down the stairs and came to a patio just like mine. Two clean-shaven men in their mid-twenties lay sprawled on deckchairs.

'Sorry, guys, but did I hear you mention a reggae concert?'

I'd caught them unawares. They looked at me suspiciously and, out of the corner of my eye, I saw one of them tucking something away, furtively, in the cup of his hand.

I must have looked reassuring, or at least innocuous, because in no time they relaxed and smiled at me.

'Yeah, that's right,' said, I assume, the pole vaulter – he was the taller, more athletic-looking one. With a giggle, he opened his palm and showed me the spliff he'd been hiding. 'We're not supposed to do drugs. It's against the rules.'

'Yeah, we gotta be careful,' explained the expert on tourism. 'Wouldn't do to have the folks back home thinking we were a couple of dope-heads instead of regular guys, just like them.' They giggled stupidly at each other.

'And the reggae concert?' I asked, wondering if I'd ever get a straight answer from these two.

'Oh, yeah, the concert. It's this weekend. In Livingston.' The pole vaulter took another toke on his spliff then held it at arm's length, 'Man! This stuff is sooo good.'

'Where?'

'Livingston.'

'Where's that?'

'On the Atlantic coast. Great place.'

'*Con mucho ambiente.*'

'Yeah, very… Caribbean. Great ganja.'

'Yeah! Don't forget the ganja,' said the other, giggling.

'Magic…'

They laughed knowingly and motioned to pass me their joint.

'Thanks, but I'll stick with this, guys,' I said, taking my battered Golden Virginia tin out of my pocket. It was the music I was interested in.

I sat down with them and made myself a roll-up.

'Tell me more,' I urged them.

*

Later that night, I packed my rucksack, and the following day at the crack of dawn, I found myself on yet another rickety old bus covering the 250 bumpy miles between me and the Atlantic coast.

PART TWO

CHAPTER SIX

LIVINGSTON

I arrived just after sunset, the sky still glowing, the first soothing shadows falling lazily from the hills.

There hadn't been much of a view during the boat trip. After leaving behind the sweltering heat of Puerto Barrios, the nearest port town, with its mosquito-infested market and its web of dusty alleys, I had seen nothing but water, the dark green depths of the Honduran sea over which large pelicans glided, hunting for fish. To my left, a shade lighter than the waves, an uninhabited green strip of coast. Then, suddenly, the ferry made a wide turn in the open sea, the engines were turned down to a deep-throated rumble, and slowly we moved towards a mysterious point on the shore. Soon, hills appeared in the distance, thatched roofs pushing through the engulfing tropical jungle, and we entered the wide, fast-flowing estuary of the Río Dulce. Squat wooden houses and ramshackle jetties straggled along the shallow ochre banks.

Only a mile to go and the sky hung on us more intensely blue by the minute, a hue of purple streaking the horizon to the open sea behind.

There on the boat, the two Peace Corps volunteers' gushing reviews of Livingston still echoed in my ears. But what had really fired my imagination and finally brought me here was reading in the *Rough Guide* that, there being no roads across the jungle, the village could only be reached by boat.

We drew closer to the coast and the scene lost its picture-postcard stillness. Amid the greenery there was movement, the sound of laughter and excitement, brightness… Closer and closer we came until the voices became clearer, and on the concrete landing I saw a sparse crowd of tall, strongly built people, most of them black: a cluster of teenagers chatting among themselves, a dozen large women fanning the flies away from round wicker baskets at their feet, and two or three old men sitting in wait on their rusty wheelbarrows.

The ferry soon reached the pier and we disembarked. The little port stirred into action: the teenagers called out to the passengers and laughed heartily; the old men vied with each other to load heavy baggage onto their wheelbarrows; the women hawkers uncovered their baskets and, with wide sweeps of their arms, touted their selection of sweet and savoury *tacos*.

'*Hola, gringa!*' A leggy boy appeared suddenly by my side. 'I show you Livingston, okay? *Cinco dólares, solamente!*' and he waved under my nose the stretched-out fingers of one hand.

Another slightly older boy cut in impatiently: '*Señorita, no le haga caso a éste, que no sabe nada…* I show you! *Yo, Marcos, soy* the best tourist guide in town. Four *dólares, vale?*'

Avoiding eye contact, I brushed off both their offers and marched on, but in no time, a man caught up with me. 'Hi, young lady! Coming on a boat trip along the Río Dulce?' He gestured at a group of people sitting on a boat moored nearby. 'Come on, come on board! Another three people and we'll be off… Only twenty *quetzals*. It's a good price! Just for you, *amiga*, because I like you…'

'Another time, later,' I mumbled and, as I hoisted my heavy rucksack onto my back, I smiled awkwardly at him. That – I soon discovered – was the wrong tactic, as the more I smiled, the more attention I seemed to attract. In the end, holding my head stubbornly down, I manoeuvred myself out of everybody's way and, amid the deafening noise, I walked up the hill on the lookout for a cheap hotel.

On my right, the Tucán had beautiful thatch-roofed verandas and a vast garden with an aviary where green, blue and red parakeets jostled against each other on their perches. Too expensive, I thought, and rapidly walked past it.

Beyond the two, three hundred metres of buzzing activity surrounding the port and the smart hotel, all sparkle suddenly fizzled out and the village slumbered in the waning heat of the last lazy sunrays.

Here, the road led past a row of dilapidated concrete buildings – cafés, sleazy bars, shabby little shops that, despite their rundown appearance, displayed lush tropical fruit and vegetables on makeshift stalls. To my relief, the bored-looking vendors behind them did not attempt to sell a thing to me as I passed; they seemed determined not to notice my presence, but it was clear that from beneath their lowered eyelids they were watching my every move. In an eerie silence, I ran the gauntlet of their hawk-eyed inspection and, feeling increasingly uneasy, I quickened my step.

Five short minutes later, I checked in at the Río Dulce, a light blue wooden hotel run by a rather brusque young woman who, setting aside all formalities, demanded to be paid in advance. The room I was shown was basic but gave onto a breezy balcony with a generous view of the street and the goings-on below.

'This will do me fine for the week I'll be here,' I said to the hotel keeper as she handed me the key.

'Just a week? Are you sure?' She looked at me knowingly and laughed. 'They all say that at the beginning, and then they end up staying for months.'

I took a quick shower and went out to explore.

Three, four hundred metres past the Río Dulce, the only paved road branched suddenly at a right angle. One of its arms sloped down to the seafront past quiet dwellings, the other took me in front of the Catholic church, the school, several bars, shops, a few restaurants, then, unexpectedly, it petered out in front of a muddy stream. Most people seemed to stop here, as if at a natural boundary, but a few braved the crossing over some unsteady planks.

I considered the slippery descent ahead of me, and the impenetrable forest across the stream. I thought back to when, as a timid eight-year-old, skis on my feet, I'd stared down what seemed an impossibly steep slope. Below, in the valley, my mother stood waving one of her skiing sticks. 'Come on, Monica, don't be afraid. You can do it!' she shouted, always encouraging me to go that extra length.

Overcoming my fear, I'd hurtled down the piste, elated by the rush of adrenaline that ran through me.

That memory, that same feeling of euphoria, now urged me on.

I crossed the stream.

Over the other side, on a steep and narrow flight of concrete steps sat a small group of old women. As I went to sit behind them in a corner, I said hello. They nodded back, their eyes briefly following me, but very soon, they lost interest and carried on chatting and laughing among themselves. Finally, they hoisted their baskets up on their shoulders and walked on. One of them vanished beyond a triangular archway that led to a vast field overgrown with shrubs; the others made their way into the jungle along a web of dirt tracks.

Sitting on the steps facing that deep green sea, I tried to imagine what lay ahead. There must be houses, farms, entire hamlets those women were heading for. There must be places buried in the vegetation where tourists wouldn't venture, and people lived their lives undisturbed. That's what I was looking for. But what if they resented my being there, snooping? Well, I'd never know until I tried. And so, rising to the challenge, I waited until I could no longer hear the women's voices and then randomly picked one of the paths.

For a while, there were only trees and knotted bramble, but five minutes into my walk, I realised that all around me the jungle was buzzing with human life. Camouflaged amid the greenery, houses rose up – one- or two-storey concrete buildings, wooden shacks topped with sheets of corrugated iron, huts made of bamboo reeds and roofs thatched with *manaca* leaves. Some tilted at an angle, decrepit, yet holding their ground like weather-beaten trees. And like wilful trees, the structures grew at random, either crammed tightly together, choked by the bracken and the bramble, or hovering solitary above vast and splendid views of the bay.

Here and there in the yards that opened in front of most of these dwellings, people carried out odd jobs: men sharpened machetes, women fried fish on open fires and children chased each other, getting in everybody's way. Voices came from all around, deep, loud, soft and raucous. A good deal of bantering marked every exchange, and frequent peals of laughter rang out while the same radio programme crackled noisily in the background.

No one was aware of my intrusion; people went about their chores without fuss, while, protected by the bushes, I enjoyed the rare privilege of observing everything in detail. After the intimidating stares I'd been subjected to along the main street, this newly found invisibility spared me from curiosity and suspicion, making me feel reassuringly safe.

The sound of an acoustic guitar drifted towards me, soon joined by a pleasant contralto voice. I recognized the lyric of *Blowing in the Wind*, the last thing I expected to hear in that remote corner of the jungle. I stretched my neck over the jasmine blossom growing along the right side of the path, momentarily inebriated by the sweet smell that rose from it.

In a dip, amid the tall grass, right outside a squat bamboo house, a white woman sat plucking the strings of a guitar. She was so intent on the chords that, for quite some time, she seemed not to realise she had a spectator. When she finally looked up and saw me poking out from behind the bushes, she smiled invitingly and called out in English, 'Hi, there! How are you? Come on, yes, come down…'

She rested the guitar against the door, then pointed to a steep path which, half concealed among the tall grass and the bramble, led to the house.

Slipping and sliding over the loose gravel, I descended the slope and reached the yard.

From close-up, the woman appeared to be in her late twenties, her skin translucent, the colour of golden-green olives. Her smile showed both on her lips and, below the arch of her thick dark eyebrows, in her lively chestnut eyes. Under the frame of a wide-brimmed straw hat, her brown hair was long and tangled and she wore a white and blue cotton print dress that hung loosely on her rounded figure down to her mid-calves. On her feet was a pair of red plastic flip-flops. Strong sturdy ankles gave her a solid appearance, rooting her firmly to the ground.

'I'm Mariangela,' she said warmly. 'Nice to meet you.'

'It's Monica. Good to meet you too.' I looked appreciatively around. 'I didn't expect to see any foreigners this far from town. This is great!' I gestured at the surrounding forest, at the bamboo house in front of me, at the thin strip of sea that peeped out from above the treeline.

'Yes, isn't it just wonderful?' Mariangela's voice was soft and infused with calmness, as if nothing was more important than to stand there, welcoming strangers with Bob Dylan's back catalogue. 'My sister and I got here from the lake two months ago. We like it so much better here. People are more relaxed, more open… We are Italian, from Naples, and, believe me, we've been to lots of lovely places, but this is by far the best.'

She herself was open and friendly, and there was something familiar about her. Maybe it was her Italian roots. Whatever it was, in her company I felt entirely at ease.

In her fluent, slightly accented English, she told me that together with her sister Giulia she rented part of the house from the Garifuna family next door. Only a thin wooden partition divided the two dwellings, but that was not a problem. 'Doña Marcela and I take it easy, you know… Any time I cook something special, I send a plate over her side. In turn, any titbits she makes she sends over to me. We do each other little favours, just like good neighbours. That's the way it should always be, don't you think?'

I agreed with her about helping "thy neighbour", but I couldn't bring myself to join in as she enthused over how nice the local people were. I found the place fascinating, but, so far, no one, except for her, had struck me as particularly open or friendly. It could just be my paranoia, but in the village they'd all seemed to barely tolerate my being there.

Mariangela looked at me quizzically, as if sensing my scepticism.

'It takes time to gain people's trust,' she said. 'But when they accept you, they treat you like family. Perhaps it's different in town, with people everywhere. But here, in the bush, we just have a handful of neighbours, and so there's no need to fight over things. There's no competition, no envy. Giulia and I just love it here. We couldn't wish for a better life.'

I turned and looked around. True, the setting was peaceful, idyllic even. A small outhouse rose to the right of the thatched hut.

'That's the kitchen,' she explained, before I had time to ask. 'With all that straw and wood, it's just too risky to cook indoors.'

'Any running water?' However much I scoured the surroundings for a well or a tap, I could see no sign of either.

'No, I'm afraid there isn't any. What we do is very simple. Every morning, Giulia and I go and collect a couple of buckets from the fountain by the docks. It's a bit far, but it's the best water you can get. People say that whoever drinks it will get spellbound and end up staying here forever.'

'Yes,' I said to her with a smile, recalling the words of the receptionist at the check-in desk. 'It must be nice to live in this place. There does seem to be something magical about it.'

She let out a light silvery laugh, then with solicitous curiosity she asked: 'And you, Monica, tell me, what brings you here?'

'I'm just travelling around,' I answered vaguely, not wanting to bore her with the details of my saga. 'In fact, I'm here for the reggae concert. It's tomorrow, isn't it?'

Mariangela looked surprised. 'They play a lot of reggae here, on the beach, but a concert… No, there's no concert planned, I'm sure, or I'd have heard about it. Sorry, Monica, whoever told you made a mistake.'

What? All those miles and *no concert*?

She saw the expression of disappointment on my face. 'Why – don't worry… Come and dance with us tonight! You'll have a great time, I promise! As good as any reggae concert, or even better, for sure!'

We hastily made our arrangements. Then, noticing how dark it had become, I said goodbye and quickly retraced my steps back to the hotel.

*

Back in town, night fell rapidly and, as the first lights came on inside the huts, it seemed that an air of peace and cosiness had descended on the village.

There was no traffic, no fumes. No cars, in fact. From my hotel balcony, high up on the third floor, I enjoyed an extensive view. A short distance from the paved road, in the back alleys, I could see people sitting on stools outside their huts, relishing the breeze. Some women chatted while plaiting each other's hair; a few men smoked, absorbed in their thoughts; swarms of shrieking children played games.

But the main street was where everything happened. There, people did their last-minute shopping, teenagers and couples took leisurely strolls in their best clothes. Along the pavements, a throng of street vendors sold fried fish, peeled oranges, sliced mangoes; a handful of children walked up and down with large bulrush baskets of *pan de coco*, golden coconut buns, still warm.

Although most people were black, there were many other races too: Mayan Indians, East Indians, *mestizos* and a few Chinese. The air resonated with a variety of languages, pitches and voices; the now familiar high-pitched strains of the Amerindians seamlessly mixed with the guttural deep tones of the Garifunas and their long unbroken sentences interspersed with French and Spanish words. It was a vibrant and pulsating world.

My attention was caught by a group of young black men coming from the port. They formed a compact line that took up well over two-thirds of the street, forcing anyone who came in the opposite direction to keep to its edges or awkwardly weave their way past them.

Protected by the latticed balcony railings, I gazed at them at leisure, undisturbed.

There were five of them, all working hard to look cool. And they succeeded, as they strutted forward with the same identical slouch. All very dark-skinned, they wore fashionable mid-calf trousers, printed T-shirts – one so short that it sexily revealed the man's belly button – and immaculately white trainers. Each sported a long dangling single earring and a hat.

The hats were as different as the five young men. There was a bright green baseball cap with the visor studiously turned to the side, a Rastafarian tam, a wide-brimmed straw hat tilted in a louche fashion to one side to frame the earring; the final two wore a silky scarf knotted pirate style at the back, and an electric blue fishing hat.

Feigning absolute indifference, the five young men stared hard, each keeping his eyes fixed in front of him, as if into an imaginary void. They'd got everyone's attention and they knew it. They puffed out their chests and, on intercepting the sideways glances many a pretty girl darted in their direction, they seemed to grow a few inches taller.

From time to time, they would all stop to meet an acquaintance or a friend, their cool machismo giving way to a profusion of wide smiles, white teeth flashing against the even blackness of their skin.

With each newcomer, they exchanged a complex ritual of handshakes: first, they grabbed each other's right forearm, then, after dragging the palm slowly downwards over each other's arms, they shook hands vigorously, and finally knocked fist on fist.

'*Qué tal la onda?*' was the greeting repeated over and over in loud deep voices that carried over to my balcony. 'How's the wave?' they said, likening life to a sea wave. How poetic.

Only a few minutes, the time to establish a quick connection, and off they went again to the next encounter a little further ahead, with the promise of '*Al rato*': I'll catch you later, until they had all disappeared down the street.

I observed all this from my balcony, replaying the scene later as I showered and changed, ready to face the night.

*

The place where Mariangela and I had agreed to meet was in the proximity of the most distinctive hotel in town, the African Place, a large concrete building that sprawled chaotically into a dip in the ground only feet away from the stream I had crossed earlier, just where the road came to an abrupt end.

With its crenellated turrets, Moorish windows, arched doors and Corinthian pillars, half-miniaturised medieval castle and half self-styled mosque, the African Place was the superbly kitsch landmark that, within hours of their arrival, visitors to Livingston would naturally gravitate towards. The main entrance came at the end of a portentous stone bridge that spanned a moat overgrown with banana plants and coconut trees. Given the ambitious grandeur of its design, it came as no surprise that the building itself was yet to be completed; a whole side of it, the most visible to those who came from town, had not yet been grouted or rendered, and the large unsightly bricks of the inner wall showed through. Two notice boards read *African Place* and *Café – Restaurant – Hotel* in large irregular capitals. The first, shaped like a shield, hung high up from one of the turrets; the latter had been nailed at eye level to the slanted trunk of a palm tree on the road before the bridge.

Right where the palm tree stood and the asphalt ended, a vaguely marked footpath descended steeply to the right over the grass towards the sea.

There, lounging on the grass or perched on a few boulders, was the gang of five I'd observed from my balcony a few hours earlier.

It was the exact spot where Mariangela and I had agreed to meet.

What on earth are they waiting for? I wondered, slowing down my pace, hoping that by the time I reached the path, Mariangela and her sister would have materialised. I hung back, looked pointedly at my watch, paced, checked my watch again, paced some more.

It was clear why the young men had chosen to loiter there; it was a kind of crossroads, and anyone wanting to go to the discotheques had to make their way down to the beach along that path. It was the perfect pick-up point. Showing the same insouciance with which they had earlier claimed the street, they now kept a tight check on "*la onda*", on anything and everything that happened on the beach.

As I got closer, affecting the same nonchalance, the guy with the exposed belly button sprang to his feet and, with a captivating smile, greeted me in Spanish. 'Hi, there! My name is Emilio, I'm from Livingston. And you, where are you from?'

'I'm Monica. I am from London.' Satisfied that, despite the nerves, my Spanish accent sounded reasonably natural. I let my eyes focus square and direct on the man's smiling face.

'Oh, what lovely green eyes!' The compliment was delivered with well-practised charm. 'Would you like to go dancing? I'll take you, if you want.'

My eyes were, and had always been, unmistakably brown, but before I had the chance of asking him jokingly if he was colour blind, all the others came forward and introduced themselves in such rapid succession that I immediately forgot who was who. There was a Tomás, an Oscar, or was it Norman? Then, Armando, and… Hector, was it? Or was it Esteban? But, whatever their names were, they were all very friendly, approachable, and within a matter of seconds had dispelled the initial impression of pretentiousness and bombastic self-importance.

'*Hola*, Monica!' Mariangela and her sister suddenly appeared.

Their silhouettes stood out against the artificial light shed by the lamppost in front of the African Place. They crossed the stream, dexterously balancing themselves over the narrow planks, then, as they reached the gravel, they quickened their steps. Mariangela came first, soft curves enveloped by her loose swirling dress; a few steps behind her came her sister Giulia, a slim young woman several inches taller than Mariangela, with long straight hair, a knee-length skirt and an elegant upright walk.

'*Hola*, Mariangela!'

'*Hola*, Giulia!'

'*Hola,* guys!'

'*Qué tal la onda?*' hollered each of them amicably, in turn. Hands, arms and fists criss-crossed each other like a quick domino game.

The greetings and the introductions over, without any discussion, as if acting on a plan made a long time before, we all made our way down the muddy slope, each of us girls chaperoned by a guy. Giulia walked with Tomás, the one with the sexiest walk; Mariangela with Hector, the self-styled pirate, with whom she plunged into deep conversation; and I… without much of a say in the matter, I found the charmer Emilio by my side.

Sensing my reticence, he asked with surprising candour, 'Tell me, Monica, are you by any chance one of those people who don't like black men?' I floundered. I'd never been challenged on the matter quite so bluntly. I spluttered some lame, over-eager words of reassurance, before realising that reassurance was the last thing he needed.

'Did you know that this village was built by us, by the Garifunas? The Indios, the Ladinos, all the other races came much later. The Garifunas came here not wanting to be enslaved. This became our refuge, our home. For us, there is no place like Labuga. Nowhere else life is as sweet as here.' He lifted his chest up in defiance and cried out, '*Ubafu lu Labuga*! Power to Labuga!'

His fiery speech brought a smile to my lips. I liked the way he claimed his roots. His pride made such a refreshing change from what I felt was the self-effacing submissiveness of the Mayans.

As far as the eye could see, the beach was fringed with palm trees, and bordered with a narrow corridor of dark humid shingle next to the shallow sea. On it we ambled, the three couples and, at some discreet distance, the two remaining guys, all heading for the discotheques from where the deep pulsating bass of reggae rhythms had just begun to reverberate.

The first disco we came to was in a large beach hut with a sloping thatched roof and cane reed walls. Five feet from the ground, the cane turned into openly woven trellis that let the night breeze through. Inside, in the dark, a few coarsely cut wooden tables and a long line of benches stood against the three walls; along the fourth, right at the end, behind the bar was a powerful sound system. From each corner two gigantic loudspeakers sent out booming waves of sound that filled the dance hall, then drifted out, reaching far in all directions, up and down the beach and up the hill into town.

A few couples swayed gently to the music in the middle of the concrete floor, and one or two people sat on high stools by the counter with their drinks. It was pleasant, but the guys looked at each other knowingly and agreed to try some other venue where, they said, there was bound to be more "*ambiente*".

The second discotheque was almost identical; the same wooden shack, the same thatched roof, the same powerful sound system. It had, however, the added advantage of being located just a handful of yards away from the shingle. In fact, the dance hall opened onto it as if onto an inner courtyard or a terrace, where people milled around with cans and bottles in their hands, enjoying the night breeze and the view of the shimmering sea.

Couples in particular seemed to appreciate this dark private space. Leaning against the wooden dories moored among the curved trunks of the coconut trees, each couple huddled together into a single shadow and talked in soft whispers, swathed in the anonymity of the dark.

'This is the Lugudi Barana, Monica.' Emilio explained that it meant "foot of the sea". I laughed at the wonderfully quaint expression.

'In Spanish, you would say "*la onda*", I guess.' He laughed a little self-consciously, suddenly looking much younger and, all the boastfulness gone, a little vulnerable. How old could he be? Possibly a good seven or eight years my junior.

As the music became louder, we all went to dance inside the shack.

They were playing old classics by Marley, Peter Tosh, Gregory Isaac, and the floor was full of couples dancing close to each other, swaying their hips slowly, engrossed in the pounding beat of the music and in the intimacy they shared. We joined in and soon each couple got separated from the others in the crowd.

I had always danced to reggae on my own and wasn't used to being led by a partner, but Emilio took charge of my body by the waist, squeezed it tight against his own, and moved me confidently across the floor, our legs firmly intertwined. In the meantime, he whispered softly into my ear.

At first, I resisted his amorous overtures. But what was that old adage? "When one door closes, another one opens"? Shouldn't I open this other door and seek solace in this man's arms? Wasn't this the best way to forget my recent failures, my humiliating rejection from Colonia Amparo, Martin, even my ex?

As *Stir it Up* played loudly, my body began to respond, and *what the hell,* I thought. The moment felt good. I let it happen.

He led me to a nearby cane boat shelter, his cousin's, he said. It was windowless, immersed in darkness; the only light coming through the slightly opened door framed a thin slice of moon intermittently concealed by thick banks of clouds running menacingly across the sky.

There, protected by this darkness, after fumbling with our clothes and bumping into this and that corner, we found a dory to climb into and, lying awkwardly on the wooden planks, we finally had sex.

For all his bravado and loud talking, Emilio turned out to be a rather clumsy lover. But the gently lapping waves and the distant soothing music provided what, for me, was the perfect backdrop to our romance.

Then, just as we were putting our clothes back on and getting ready to leave, the rain began. 'Ah! Here it goes!' said Emilio matter-of-factly. 'This time of year, it rains every night. For hours.' Indeed, what I saw through the door was not a downpour but a deluge. Large, thick drops pelted the sand, the sea, the palm trees, making everything around liquid. It was impossible to see further than a few steps ahead. Even the music was drowned out by the sound of the lashing rain. Everything seemed to stop and yield to the forces of nature.

For a long time, we stood there by the open door of the boat shelter, arms around each other, lost in our respective thoughts. The solitary place, the inner peace; despite the sound of the pouring rain, all thoughts and worries were suspended.

Well past midnight, the rain eased off, and Emilio and I walked back to the hotel along the beach. He took my hand and told me to jump over the puddles and the streams that here and there broke the continuity of the shingle. I took my slippery sandals off and strove not to stub my naked toes on the rocks and coconut husks scattered about the beach.

'Now… jump!' he said repeatedly, gripping my hand firmly and pulling me upwards over each obstacle. Each time, amid much laughing and giggling, I landed on a dry patch of sand.

At three in the morning, wet to the bones, we finally reached the hotel and kissed each other goodnight, while the town around us slept in a gossamer veil of rain.

*

Five hours later, streams of dazzling sunlight forced their way through the wooden shutters, shaking me out of sleep and into reality.

I got up, opened the door and, still yawning, made my way along the corridor to the bathroom. After splashing some water onto my face, I looked into the mirror and searched for the lovely pair of green eyes on which Emilio had complimented me.

I laughed out loud. It was hard to believe now, in broad

daylight, that I could have fallen for such a smooth talker. Yes, no doubt the man was physically attractive, but most of the previous night's magic had come from the place – the quiet sandy beach, the music, the swishing waves, the palm leaves stirring in the breeze, even that sudden deluge.

Today, along with all the puddles, romance had evaporated, and Emilio appeared for what he was – a young local man on the make, far too young, in fact, and cocky. What'd I been thinking?

I was just going to have to put last night behind me and hope I wouldn't bump into him in the street.

From the balcony, I looked down on to the streets with their usual buzz of vendors, passers-by and children. The scene was seething with life and energy, and I felt a surge of optimism and excitement at what lay ahead.

Now that I no longer had a job and was in no hurry to go anywhere, perhaps I could stay here a little longer…

As I leant against the banister, eyes shut against the midday sun, the heat on my skin felt good.

*

'Why not come and stay with us?' said Mariangela when, later that morning, we met on the main street.

The two Neapolitan sisters looked wonderfully bronzed and fresh in their flowing robes, their hair still wet.

'Yes, do come and be our guest. No need to pay us rent, just help out with the food, if you can,' said Giulia, adjusting the red hibiscus flower in her hair. 'The guys in town are only after one thing. You'll be better off staying with us.'

Had the sisters guessed about me and Emilio? If they had, they tactfully feigned ignorance. No probing questions, no comparing of notes with their own encounters that night. Just this very generous offer.

Or was it simply Livingston and its magic that made them so trusting and open towards me? Possibly. In any case, the two sisters were genuinely laid-back and carefree, not at all dissimilar in fact from the Panajachel crowd I'd been so scathing about just a couple of weeks earlier.

After my recent misadventures, the invitation flattered and touched me at the same time. What did I have to lose anyway? Nothing. On the contrary. With money worries looming large in my mind, their proposition came as the most fortuitous of gifts.

The following day, I moved in.

*

My new home was in the district of Nebagó, one of the northern *barrios*.

As I began to get my bearings, I discovered a short cut to it.

Crossing the muddy stream over a bridge of planks, I came to the flight of steps where, only a couple of days earlier, I'd sat, feeling very much like an outsider, and watched the two elderly women exchange jokes. Now, instead of turning right at the bottom of the steps, I climbed right up, walked under the triangular archway and came to a vast cemetery overgrown with shrubs. A narrow path meandered amid the tombstones that poked up, unkempt and disorderly, among the bramble and the tall brush. The sweet scent of jasmine blossom filled the air.

There was no clear boundary between the graveyard and the first houses of Nebagó. One ran into the other, the dead and the living sharing a laid-back proximity.

I'd soon find myself in someone's backyard, setting off a racket of barking dogs and cackling hens as I passed.

On the first day, a skinny mongrel with a vicious growl chased me, caught up with my open sandals and sank its little teeth into my heel. It was only a graze, but I learnt my lesson, and from then on, I made sure I carried a handy stone or two.

After winding around a good many thatched huts, the path petered out into the jungle and, finally, in a dip before the trees stretched out behind, there it was, the squat bamboo house for which I so much envied Mariangela when we first met – and now my home.

Inside, the house was as basic as Mariangela had described it to me. In fact, there wasn't much to it, except for the thatched roof of *manaca* leaves and the cool shelter it provided from both sun and rain. The earth floor of the courtyard continued uninterrupted into the hut, the only difference being that, indoors, we swept it thoroughly with a rudimentary broom that we then hung up on the back of the door.

The space was divided by flimsy cane reed walls into three sections. Mariangela's bedroom was occupied entirely by a metal-framed double bed with legs that lifted it three feet above the ground. Then there was the kitchen with a roughly cut wooden table covered with a flowery plastic top, three stools, a sideboard with some crockery and plastic glasses on display. The third and last section was a vast empty space festooned with hammocks that hung from the wooden beams. Giulia and I slept in this room, with our backpacks neatly stored in one corner. In the morning, we folded our hammocks into a tight loop, tied them high up onto the roof beams, and our bedroom would turn into a rather bare living room. That was all – simple, no frills, spartan.

Although she slept alone, Mariangela had hardly more privacy than Giulia and me. Whether good or bad, everything in our house had to be shared.

We did our cooking in the outhouse, over a mud stove. Here, Mariangela excelled herself.

'I've always wanted to live in the countryside,' she said, sitting back on her heels and blowing into a pile of twigs. In less than no time she would have a blazing fire going. She was a natural; you'd never guess she'd spent her entire life in a city.

I'd been warned about the water. To go and collect it, we walked the two and a half miles to the fountain at the harbour. Although we took turns, it was Mariangela, again, who showed a real aptitude for the task. While I struggled under the weight of the water buckets, she glided forward, upright and stately, long neck and chin up, the container firmly balanced on the crown of her head, arms swinging loosely by her sides. She sauntered like that – avoiding rocks, dogs, unforeseen obstacles – unruffled, all the way home. She'd watched carefully how Garifuna women carried all sorts of bundles on their heads and endeavoured to imitate them. Now, except for her skin colour, she could be taken for one of them.

Meanwhile, the rainy season was rapidly advancing with longer and more frequent downpours and streams of mud flooding the pathways.

At first, to keep dry, I walked along the edges or jumped from rock to rock. However hard I tried, I'd slip and end up in a puddle, so that my feet were always wet. Eventually, I figured out that wearing shoes made little sense. Shoes were not only very slippery but got muddy and had to be cleaned umpteen times a day. I took them off and stored them on a wooden shelf inside the house, where a green coat of mould began to spread over the leather, making them look like two growing plants.

I now walked barefoot everywhere. I loved the sensation of the earth under my feet. It made me feel close to nature, free.

I was doing my best at going native, except that, when I looked around, all "natives" were wearing shoes. However much it rained, every night they were down at the disco in their immaculately white canvas shoes. How could they wade through all that mud and keep so clean?

There was no bathroom in the house, nor was there a well, so I took to bathing daily in a stream.

Early in the morning, I'd stroll down the narrow valley to one of the shallow pools the stream formed as it meandered through the tall brush. I'd choose a secluded spot, strip naked, lather myself with soap and then dip in the fresh, cold water. A myriad of little fish gathered around me and nibbled at my skin. Five short minutes, then I'd hoist myself out onto the grassy edge. Stark naked, I'd dry out in the sun. It made me think of the Altiplano. This time, though, there was no Martin to share my thoughts with, but no gropers either, just a wonderful feeling of being in nature, all alone.

After this refreshing start to the day, I'd wander back, taking in the loud reggae music from the nearby houses, the jingles from the blasting radios, the sound of excited Garifuna voices arguing together – or were they joking? *Soon I'll be able to tell*, I hoped.

In the meantime, I observed everyone closely. Despite being just a village, the place contained a surprising variety of characters, of human types, of different races. It was a microcosm of the bigger world, a place where past and present mixed. In Labuga, Mayan and African ancestral traditions seemed to coexist peacefully with the latest Western fads.

Then, one day, I went into the Wangs' general store and in between a selection of engines for motorboats and fishing tackle, I found a shelf stacked with stationery and exercise books, the kind schoolchildren use for doing their homework. I bought several, and in them, I began to write down the stories that unfolded, other people's and my own.

*

One day, as I went to collect the water, I bumped into Jeff, the pole vaulter, one of the two Peace Corp volunteers I'd met in Guatemala City. He was coming right off the twelve o'clock ferry and, as we recognised each other, we stopped and said hello.

Our exchange was brief. 'See you later, on the beach,' I said vaguely, and off we went to our respective destinations.

Predictably, I met him again that night at the Lugudi Barana. The dance floor was taken up by twirling couples, and swelling fast with more and more arrivals, but he spotted me immediately in the crowd.

'Hi there! Good, eh? What did I tell ya?' he shouted. He looked happy, if slightly overwhelmed, or maybe just stoned, like before.

We swayed along with everybody else and tried to chat over the decibels.

'Hey, who's this guy you're with?' Right behind me, a familiar voice boomed into my ear and made me jump. It was Emilio. Amid the pushing and shoving of all those bodies, I'd failed to notice him as he approached.

'Remember, *mi amor*, you're mine,' he whispered into my ear, while pointedly ignoring my companion. And then he was gone, engulfed by the crowd.

I carried on dancing. I hadn't seen Emilio since that night in the boat shed, as I'd been keeping away from his usual hangouts, wanting to avoid the embarrassment of a meeting. He too seemed to be giving me the wide berth on the few occasions he'd seen me from a distance. It was inevitable, though, that in such a small place as Livingston, sooner or later, our paths would cross. What I felt now wasn't, as I expected, the embarrassment of having to face him, but anger at his words. I did my best to control it. I even managed to smile at Jeff, but inside I was boiling. How dare he! And the tone…

Ten minutes later, Emilio was back. '*Mi amor*, buy me a Coke, will you?' It was more a demand than a playful request.

I spent the rest of the night avoiding him.

That week, no more wide berths, everywhere I went, there was Emilio, besieging me with boastful claims and absurd demands. I tried to put him off, but no refusal could shake his conviction that he was "my man".

One afternoon, I sat in a field, in the shade of a palm tree, surrounded by my usual paraphernalia of pens, notebooks and a dozen hanks of multi-coloured threads. I was indulging my new passion for braiding wristbands, the way I'd seen Mayan women do.

The day was wonderful, and I was so pleased about that rare moment of privacy that, lost in my bubble, I began to hum a tune.

Just then, the silhouettes of two men came bumbling along the beach, laughing.

One of them was Emilio and, as I ducked into the grass trying to make myself invisible, out of the corner of my eye, I saw his head swivel in my direction. Shit! Too late! He must have seen me.

Some swishing through the grass, and two minutes later, '*Oh, mi amor,* that's where you're hiding!' he shouted and plonked himself down, right next to me, beckoning his friend Oscar to join him.

I mumbled a few ineffectual words, while trying to disentangle myself from the arm he'd wrapped around my shoulders. In vain.

The two men each carried a bottle of Venado, from which they took generous swigs. Ignoring my presence, they talked to each other loudly in Garifuna, except that, from time to time, Emilio would turn towards me.

'*Verdad, mi amor?*' he said over and over, each time planting a sloppy kiss on my cheek.

And each time I cringed, wishing he'd take his hands off me. But with no one else in sight along the beach, only the two of them and me, I felt vulnerable and weak, and angry with myself all over again for being so stupid as to have had a one-night stand with this guy. What if they both suddenly turned nasty? I had no choice but to humour them.

Then Emilio saw the wristbands.

'Here, Oscar, take this one,' he said, grabbing two of the brightest. 'My girlfriend here wants us to have them. Don't you, *mi amor?*' With mirthless laughter, he handed him a blue and orange wristband, and kept a purple and green one for himself.

'But… they're mine…' I mumbled in one feeble attempt to stand my ground.

'*Sí, pues,* but, *mi amor,* you want to be nice to me, don't you? I'm your boss, remember?' he replied, tying the band around his wrist.

A surge of anger tightened my throat.

You? My boss? I wanted to shout. *That'll be the day! Clear off, you bastard!*

But again, wary of the risk – two of them against me – I caught myself in time and didn't say a word. Seething with frustrated rage, a rictus smile on my face, I sat there, all the while wishing they'd choke on their next swig.

Half an hour later, having drunk their rum to the last drop, they swooned, keeled over into the long grass, and immediately fell into a drunken sleep.

I made my escape…

*

In a village as small as Livingston, news spreads like wildfire. Word of my encounter with Emilio and Oscar had got around.

The following day, as I sat outside the Lugudi Barana enjoying the breeze, I saw the silhouette of a man sauntering along the beach. He looked familiar and, as he drew closer, from his sexy swagger I recognised Tomás, the guy who, that night at the Lugudi Barana, had paired up with Giulia. Out of the five, he seemed the most mature.

As he reached my bench, he stopped and came to sit next to me.

For a while, he didn't say a word. We both stared at the tiny island in front of us where a single palm tree bent its fringed foliage over the sea.

'*Tienes que agarrar la onda de aquí.*' He broke the silence. "*La onda*", literally, the wave, as I knew, also meant the "vibe", the "flow". 'You must learn to go with the flow. Listen to me, Monica. Choose one man and stick to him.'

I gave him a puzzled look.

He pushed his baseball cap backwards and scratched his forehead. 'Yes, Monica,' he said sternly, '*te compromete demasiado.* You go from one guy to the next, like a butterfly. You raise hopes, and then you dash them. No wonder you get into trouble. Stop fooling around, Monica.'

So that's why he'd come to sit with me – to put me straight on how relations between men and women played out in Livingston.

'And you, who are you sticking to?' I said, jutting my chin out, defiantly.

He grinned at me, revealing a row of slightly prominent white teeth.

'A lovely Swiss girl.'

A few weeks earlier, before leaving the country, she'd taken him to Lake Atitlán, paid for the hotel, the bus trip, everything. 'A stroke of luck,' he said. 'Perhaps, one day, she'll invite me to Switzerland. That'd be good.'

'Are you in love?' I asked him.

'No, *I'm* not,' he seemed affronted by the very idea, 'but *she* is. And when "*a una mujer le agarra el amor para un hombre...*"'

'You're such an opportunist! Shame on you, Tomás! Where's your self-respect? Where's your dignity?'

'What's the problem? She loves me. She wants me there.'

'You don't care about her, do you?' In the face of his boastful indifference, I couldn't help but identify with the Swiss girl. 'You're just using her!'

'So what?' He shrugged his shoulders and, looking offended, he swaggered down the beach.

Later, as my anger ebbed away, I grudgingly pondered on Tomás' advice. There was some undeniable truth in it. Hadn't I already felt the consequences of having a fling with the first available man in Livingston? But instead of settling for one man, as Tomás recommended, I resolved to swear off all emotional entanglements for the duration of my stay.

CHAPTER SEVEN

UBAFU LU LABUGA

L ife was beginning to feel more comfortable. I was learning to pace myself along the local rhythms and tempos. One day, I took my watch off and stored it at the bottom of my backpack. It lay there, forgotten, as I learnt to tell the time by looking at the passage of the sun across the sky.

I began to explore the surroundings, going further afield each time.

Soon I became known as *"la pequeña exploradora"* and teased for the determination with which I walked about during the hottest hours of the day.

No one moved a muscle – not even the animals – except for me.

I went far and wide, and I realised that the harmonious melting pot I'd been so impressed with initially was in fact a reluctant collision of communities. An unwritten social order seemed to have apportioned separate parts of the village to each group.

The Mayans – locally called los Indios, or los Inditos – lived in the green hills around Labuga, some in remote farms buried deep into the jungle, others in a couple of hamlets that rose to the north by some waterfalls. They grew corn, rice, pineapple and beans. The women came into town and peddled *tamales* – maize pasties wrapped in banana leaves – *tortillas* and heaps of thick dark beans. Small and discreet, they sat along the main street, talking softly in *ketkchi*. When they had no more food to sell, they stood up – large pleated skirts undulating over thin calves, babies strapped firmly across their backs – and walked home.

The men came into town to sell firewood. They staggered under huge stacks of it, eyes down, flat backs parallel to the ground, a strap slung across the foreheads, like harnessed mules.

They hardly had any contact with the other town dwellers.

On Sunday, when entire Mayan families came into town for entertainment, only one of the men, the *pater familiae*, would climb the steps of a café or a restaurant and cross the threshold. He'd stand there by the entrance, hat in hand, waiting humbly to be noticed. When spoken to, in halting Spanish, he'd order one or two dishes to share with the whole family. Outside, the women unloaded their bundles and squatted on the ground, surrounded by silent children swathed in yards of fabric, despite the heat. They never sat indoors with the other customers. They ate outside, large families of two or three generations sprawled in the ditches, segregated, set apart.

The "Ladinised" Indians were vastly better off. They weren't racially different from the Mayans who lived on the outskirts, except that they were westernised both in clothes and manners.

'See that shop over there?' Tomás said to me one day, pointing at one of the many groceries that dotted the main street. 'Until yesterday, *el Indio* who now runs it owned just the clothes he stood in. He began by peddling a few bags of potatoes, later he bought a stall, then a shop. Look at him now. He owns the entire block.'

Ignoring our recent argument over the Swiss girl, Tomás had taken it upon himself to "educate" me not only about how I should behave with men but over all kinds of local matters. Despite his unconcealed prejudices and his patronising manner, he was a font of information.

'Damn Indios!' he complained. 'They're taking over all the *tiendas*. They work non-stop, and they make lots of money. But try and ask them for credit. "*I can't, I'm poor,*" they moan. Liars! They're bloody mean, that's what they are!'

Sometimes, my wanderings took me down to the docks and along the banks of the Río Dulce, where the "coolies", the East Indians, lived. There, along the pier, I walked past half a dozen large deep-sea trawlers, then, as the tarred road petered out into a web of sandy paths, I wove my way through a labyrinth of fishing nets stretched out amid the palm trees.

There were plenty of stores, cafés and restaurants around this *barrio*, but, the rare times I walked into one of them, I felt like an intruder; the women stared at me with suspicion, the men with impudence. Even the *ranchera* music that blasted from the bars struck me as being too sentimental or too brash. Unlike my beloved *reggae*, it seemed to distance me, to shut me out.

So much for the "magic" of Livingston. It was still there, I still *wanted* it to be there, but it was fleeting, fragile. Just when I thought it was within my sights, it vanished, erased by a hostile glance, a smirk, or an abrasive word, like in this *barrio*. Even so, I yearned to know more. I was curious.

The *mestizos*, or Ladinos, made up an oligarchy whose life revolved around the church, the school and the town hall. Sent from the capital to work as civil servants, they behaved like minor celebrities. Always perfectly turned out in pressed suits and well-shined shoes, they talked in loud voices, patronised the best restaurants and addressed everyone who wasn't white with the familiar "*tu*".

But the real big shots in town were the Wangs, an old Chinese family arrived several generations earlier via Belize. I made their acquaintance soon after my arrival, as theirs was the only local shop that changed dollars, at – I was to discover – scandalously inflated rates. Nothing moved without the consent of these two brothers. Tall and proud, they owned the local cinema, the biggest store, the only motorbikes. Often away on business, they stood aloof, too rich and "superior" to socialise within the village.

Then there were the likes of me and the Italian sisters, the visiting Westerners and the established ex-pats, a mix of Americans and Europeans.

But – Tomás insisted – it was the Garifunas who were the only "rightful settlers" in Labuga, having founded it almost two centuries before.

Although their thatched huts rose all around, their highest concentration was along the north coast, near the border with Belize. They were fishermen, but, unlike the East Indians who were organised in small cooperatives, the Garifunas went out to sea in small dugout canoes, alone. As their catch was enough for little more than personal consumption, they led a hand-to-mouth existence, with no savings, no capital. The women sold the fish along the main street from wicker baskets, the children *pan de coco* from door to door. Many had relatives in the United States, who regularly sent money home until, on retiring, they came back to Livingston, built two-storey brick houses and spent the rest of their lives by the sea, lost in nostalgic reveries about the "golden days" of Labuga.

The Garifunas had an undeniable forte: music.

Traditionally, music marked all the important events of their lives, from birth to death. The African drums featured prominently in this music, but so did the more typically Latin American strumming of guitars, and later, thanks to Bob Marley and his success worldwide, reggae was included in the local repertoire. The result was a fusion of harmonies and rhythms that thrived, thanks to their openness to most outside influences and trends.

When tourists began to appear on the scene, the Garifunas turned their musical ability into a source of income and transformed their old kiosks along the beach into discotheques. Just like the Lugudi Barana, these were no more than large squares of concrete flooring with sloping roofs of *manaca* leaves, and a bar in the corner. But at night, bathed in moonlight, with the breeze and the swishing of the waves, these places held out the promise of romance. Many foreigners passing through were spellbound – some by the laid-back atmosphere, some by the people – and ended up staying longer than they'd planned, just like me. How right the hotel keeper's predictions on that first day had turned out to be.

The Garifunas were easy-going, approachable and – for me, no minor detail – very good-looking; add to that, the pride in their roots, their seeming self-confidence.

'Not so long ago, everyone came here, everyone,' Tomás boasted. 'Big professors from America, big people from Europe coming with their tape recorders, talking to everyone, talking to the old folks. And then they went back to where they came from and wrote books about us.'

I looked at him inquisitively. Could Tomás have seen me scribbling away in my notebook? I made sure I did it discreetly, either early in the morning in the house when both Mariangela and Giulia were still asleep, or sometimes as I sat under a palm tree on the beach during the siesta, in the hottest hours of the day. No, I reassured myself, he was unlikely to have discovered my secret writing.

*

Ubafu lu Labuga read the slogan on some T-shirts that hung on display outside a shop. *Power to Livingston.* I remembered Emilio's saying in one of those moments when I was enamoured of all things Livingstonian.

I went in and bought one. It was bright yellow with a red disk hovering above a thicket of stylised palm trees.

That night, I wore it at the disco, happy to share in the local pride.

And so, this is how it went on. One day full of the magic of the place, the next day down to earth with a bump.

*

As I'd discovered on my very first night in Livingston, the main meeting place for all Garifunas, young and old, was the Lugudi Barana. There, at night, on the dance floor or just outside, in front of the sea, young couples flirted to the sound of reggae, salsa and *soca* beats.

From behind the bar – a shock of white hair near his temple, a corner of his mouth permanently raised in a knowing smile – Martino began the night by playing to his older customers laid-back reggae classics, low-key stuff. Outside, the waves swished in the darkness beyond the coconut trees and, on the shingle, clusters of young people stood about, chatting.

In time, they all drifted into the dance hall. Then, Martino put on some livelier soca and *salsa* rhythms that got everyone up on their feet.

Time was going by. It was now the end of September, and "the season of the rains" had reached its climax. Late at night, always at the same hour, dark clouds gathered over the coast and all hell broke loose. In vain, Martino turned up the volume on his giant stereo. The sound of the rain drowned the beat, but people stubbornly danced on.

The storm over, all those who'd been delayed by the rain walked in and filled the place with renewed energy. On the dance floor, scores of young bodies, some still wet, swerved, circled and pulsed with the beat.

The couples glided across the floor, as if one unit. A few dreadlocked men danced alone, with abandonment, absorbed in their own world.

In the thick of the crowd, squeezed in skin-tight shorts, a curvy blonde gave her best. She shook her bottom, flicked a long mane of bleached hair, striking one pose after the other.

'That's a man who likes a different *onda*,' someone told me as she came along the street one day. She had no hips to speak of, but what she had, oh, boy, could she sway them!

Men stood in the doorways. '*Hola, guapota!*' '*Qué tal, mi amor?*' they called out, amused.

Bibi brazenly sauntered by. She blew a kiss to one, flashed a seductive smile to the other. '*Hola, muchachos lindos!*' she cried in her falsetto. 'Hi, guys! You know you're all mine, don't you?'

Then she stopped right in front of the handsomest and hunkiest man of the group and gazed suggestively at his biceps. 'Yes, *mi amor,* you too.' All coy, she fluttered her eyelashes at him. 'All mine, *sí, pues*, down to the last macho.'

When the man reached out, laughing, she jumped back, with squeals of affected fear. 'You'd love that, wouldn't you?'

She walked off and waved one last time.

As I watched Bibi disappear around the corner, I felt sure that in Livingston, no one judged, no one condemned; Livingston was for everyone.

Like I say, one day full of the magic of the place, the next…

CHAPTER EIGHT

THE SEASON OF THE RAIN MAN

One night, on my way home from the Lugudi Barana, I got lost. It rained so hard, so relentlessly, that I gave up any attempt to stay dry. Ahead of me and on each side were overhanging walls of shrubbery. I walked in the middle of the path, struggling to see in the dim light, my bare feet splashing in the muddy water, by now resigned to taking a very long shower.

As I walked to where I thought my house might be, I saw a light flickering in the darkness. It was a torch and whoever was holding it was coming towards me.

Some steps forward and I made out the silhouette of a man – slim, not very tall, kitted out with a waterproof jacket, a pair of heavy-duty wellingtons, an umbrella and that precious torch he was now flashing into my face.

We came level and I inwardly gasped.

It was Emilio. A flashback to another rainy night when he'd guided me through pools and puddles – what was it about this man and rain? We hadn't bumped into each other since that not so rainy, not so romantic, day on the beach, when he'd been so obnoxious.

'*Adónde?*' he asked, glancing at me from underneath the brim of his rainhat.

'Home, but I lost the way.' I struggled to make myself heard over the rain. 'I live past the cemetery now, with Mariangela, her sister, and—' As if he didn't already know.

He cut me short. 'I'm going the same way. Come along.'

I followed him, trying to keep up with his strides. He didn't hold my hand, this time; he didn't help me jump over the puddles and pools.

A large thatched hut came into view and we ran to take shelter under its eaves.

'Let's stop here for a minute,' he said, without looking at me. Then he fumbled in his pockets, found a key and opened the front door.

'My house,' he mumbled, and ushered me in.

The room was full of framed pictures, dozens upon dozens of them, covering the four walls – photos of children in school uniform, couples posing in their Sunday best, some old guys looking stiffly into the lens, the same smiling woman – his mum? – with different babies in her arms. And there, between two windows, the man himself, Emilio – looking even younger than now, fourteen or fifteen, if that, his hair in cornrows like a girl, a pair of horn-rimmed eyeglasses.

'The rain will soon let up,' he said, pointing at a sofa still wrapped in sheets of plastic.

I sat on the very edge of it, a pool of water spreading at my feet.

He sat opposite and lit a cigarette. When had he started smoking? It didn't suit him.

The rain drummed loudly over the roof. I stared first at the pictures, then at the earthen floor, while the silence grew. It was unlike him to be so quiet. What had happened to all his boasting – to "I'm your boss", "*mi amor*", "buy me this", "buy me that"? In this unnerving silence, a knot of apprehension tightened in my chest.

'I won't find my way home unless you show me…' I said, trying to sound relaxed.

He jumped up, picked up his torch and led the way out of the house. At length, we came to a group of huts.

'Here you are.' He pointed at one of them, and rushed away.

It was the wrong house. I walked around in circles, not recognising anything. It was two or three in the morning, not the best time to knock on people's doors.

I had no other choice but to go back to Emilio's.

He opened the door. In his underwear.

'That wasn't Mariangela and Giulia's house,' I explained, 'the one they rent from Doña Marcela in Nebagó.'

'Ah, *that* Mariangela, the Italian girl! Why didn't you say so earlier? There are lots of Mariangelas in Livingston, you know.' Then, with the slightest hint of malice, he added, 'We're nowhere *near* Nebagó.'

I was relying on this man for help. He was my only hope of getting home.

'You know where the Italian sisters live, don't you?'

He looked at me strangely, weighing me up. 'Yes.'

'Can you take me there?'

He let me wait just long enough. 'Sure, but before that,' he riveted a pair of calculating eyes on mine and blurted out suggestively, '*antes, hagamos un rato el amor, eh, Monica?*'

Agree to a quick one or get lost – those were my options. I got up from the sofa and, as I stepped towards the door, I threw an angry '*Adiós*' over my shoulder.

He caught me on the threshold.

'Here, you'll need this,' he said, and handed me his torch. Then, grudgingly, he gave me a series of vague directions.

'Thanks,' I mumbled resentfully, and left.

*

The house I shared with the Italian sisters soon became a magnet for *la mara* – the gang of my early days in Livingston – and all their friends.

Three foreign women under the same roof, all three so approachable, so friendly. Visitors presented themselves at all hours.

'*Hola, amigas!*' one would cry, his smiling head poking through an open window, boyish, awkward, chancing his luck. '*Hola, qué tal la onda?*' would shout another, leaning cockily against the frame of the door, confident he would not be turned away.

Giulia and Mariangela welcomed everybody, the people they knew and those they didn't, people who introduced themselves as friends of friends of friends…

The two women gave time, money and food to whoever came around without ever expecting anything back. Above all, they had the enviable knack of being friendly while managing to keep their visitors at arm's length.

I felt uncomfortable with this open house policy, but I myself was a guest. I had no say. When the house got too crowded or some guest overstayed their welcome, I'd pick up one of my notebooks and leave in search of a quiet corner where I could write.

But in Livingston, finding a quiet corner had become almost impossible.

'Where are you from?' 'What do you do?' 'How long are you here for?' It was an endless refrain of questions, always the same, in the street, in the bars, in the restaurants, wherever. Our "foreignness" made us the centre of both wanted and unwanted attention.

'Newcomers must pay their dues in Labuga,' said Tomás. He made it sound reasonable, like a local tax we had to pay.

We paid it willingly, day after day – until the day we came back home to find that Mariangela's beloved guitar had vanished. The wall it usually hung on was empty. We searched the rest of the house and asked the neighbours, but no one had seen it.

We were spoilt for choice for possible culprits. Anyone of the so-called "*amigos*" could be now in the nearest bar seeing what he could get for it.

'*Qué mala onda!*' the guys said sympathetically, offering to try and locate the guitar. The thief himself was most probably among them, his exaggerated concern giving him away.

Even then, Mariangela and Giulia found no fault with the Livingsteños. They thought everything was perfect.

I was less forgiving. But while there were limits to my tolerance of the sisters' lifestyle and of how they saw things, at this point I was reluctant to move out of the house. I imagined Emilio jumping out from every bush and byway – it seemed safer to be amid this throng of eager *amigos*.

I spent my time fascinated, often dumbfounded, watching the lives of others. The rare times I found myself alone, I filled my notebooks with events, thoughts and impressions – all my other plans on hold.

Eventually, matters were taken out of my hands. Mariangela met Manu, a tall, athletic Garifuna with a winsome smile. Giulia met Daniel; good-looking, outgoing, charming.

It wasn't long before, after a spell of romantic courting, both women moved in with their respective lovers.

Alone in the house, I soon realised this place was too large and costly for just one person, and I began to look for other lodgings.

There was a small thatched hut for rent a couple of miles outside the village on the way to the waterfalls. It was in a bad state but close to the sea. It had two rooms, a veranda, a wonderful view of the bay. All for nine dollars a month. The downside: it had no running water, no electricity, an earthen floor. But there was a well behind the house for washing and a one-ring camping gas stove for cooking.

By the end of October, at the tail end of the rainy season, I moved in.

*

CHAPTER NINE

DEAR MUM...

Dear Mum,

Sorry for not writing earlier, but these last few weeks I've been busy moving house. Now I live in a barrio called Campo Amor, the Field of Love (!), in a quaint beach hut that I rent for next to nothing. The drawback is there's not a single shop nearby, everything has to be fetched from town, and so it took forever to get settled. What a nightmare!

Everyone along the beach knows me by now. They nod and wave as, for the umpteenth time in any single day, I trudge past them, stooped under tons of stuff – food, books, gallons of drinking water – you name it, and always a trusty umbrella under my arm, everything bulging out of my battered old rucksack. I expect they see me as yet another eccentric foreigner, one of the handful who live in this village.

Anyway, the good news is that with all this heat and all this trudging, I've lost a few pounds. I look healthier, very sunburnt, but definitely no more pasty-face, and no more inches to pinch. Come to think of it, wouldn't this be the ideal place for your diet?

I could go on ad nauseam about the time and energy it takes to get anything done in this place. A cup of tea means a three-mile walk to the fountain. Washing clothes takes up the best part of the day. Remember Mariangela, the Italian sister? Well, I told you, I'm not like her. I'm not the Girl-Guide type. I use up a whole box of matches to light a fire, and by the time I get it going, I'm all hot and bothered, and in a foul mood. And as for carrying things on my head, well, that's not going to happen. You'd laugh if you could see me lumbering my way back from the fountain, stumbling over a tree root and spilling most of the water I've just collected. You're probably nodding your head right now, saying this is exactly the way your daughter likes doing things, the hard way. But here, I have no choice. I trip over, dust myself off, gather up my buckets and tramp all the way back. Not that I'm complaining. Well, actually, yes, I AM complaining, this letter is reading like one long complaint, but you know what I mean, you know I like a challenge. And the good bit is that, at night, I'm so tired that as soon as my head hits the pillow, I'm out.

Despite all the problems I've mentioned, I love it here. You'll be happy to hear that this is the safest place I've been to in the whole country, in fact, in the whole of Central America. It couldn't be more peaceful, more laid-back, more tranquil.

Well, I've loads more to tell you about my new life, but I'll save it for another letter.

And now, tell me, how's Grandad? Is he feeling any better? What does the doctor say? And zio Tulio, has he come to terms with being an old-age pensioner?

Dear Mum, you make me out to be more forgetful than I am. Of course I remembered the date of your retirement. And yes, it would be nice if you came to visit. l must warn you, though, I don't know whether, come the spring, I'll still

*be here. Nothing seems settled in my life at present. But as
soon as I make up my mind, you'll be the first to know, I
promise.*

A big hug for now.
Monica x

P.S. Write soon and give my love to Dad.

*

LIVINGSTON, 23ᴿᴰ NOVEMBER

Dear Mum,

*It was great to get your letter so soon. I'm so pleased to
hear Grandad's health is stable and that you're still on a diet
and have stopped smoking this time, it seems, for good. Well
done!*

*As for me, the longer I stay, the more I like it here. But
let me try and give you a sense of my new place and of my
new life.*

*As I told you before, my beach hut is a long way from the
town centre, in the middle of beautiful green fields. I have
only a handful of neighbours.*

*There's Francisco, my landlord, but I never see him,
except for when I hand over the rent at the beginning of each
month. Then, there's Lara, who lives in a large thatched house
with windows and doors all facing the bay. With her, live
five children aged between two and twelve – see the enclosed
photos. Two are hers; the other three are her sister Silvia's. A
couple of years ago, Silvia decided to do what many women
do in this village and travelled to the States in search of work.
Now she's the distant breadwinner and Lara the head of a
boisterous household.*

*I've noticed it's quite common here for children to be
brought up by aunties, uncles, grandmothers, distant family*

members, sometimes even by total strangers. 'Este niño me lo regalaron,' people say of an unrelated child who lives with them. 'He's a present, a gift.' The arrangement seems to suit everyone.

What else can I tell you about my neighbours? About the adults, not much. When we meet, like civilised people, we say good morning, how are things, and in the same breath goodbye. The children, of course, are a different matter. They're very curious and on the slightest pretext they drop by.

They come as early as six, six thirty. On hearing Francisco's sow nuzzling the bamboo wall of my bedroom, I jump out of bed and swing the front door open. A handful of chickens totter in, necks twitching right and left. They're the local street sweepers. They peck at the stray rice grains and breadcrumbs half-hidden in the sand, and keep my floor clean.

When I finally shoo the chickens out and start on my breakfast, the children gallop in, and, guess what, they always want what I'm having.

I hope you like the photos. I love the one of them sitting close together on the grass, it's so them. Don't they look great? They love posing for the camera. No shyness, no hesitation. 'Take one of meeee, Monica.' 'No, meeee next.'

My favourite is Fin, the one in front, first on the left.

He gives me the most heartwarming welcome when I meet him along the path. 'Hola, Monica!' he shouts from a distance, and runs up to me, skipping through the field, his bouncy little body appearing and disappearing in the tall grass, his arms wide open. He has an unusually clear voice for a child of three. 'Chineame! Chineame!' he hollers, and looks up at me with big round eyes and a runny nose. He jumps around me on his bare feet. I pick him up and squeeze him tight. He feels smooth and pliable in my arms, like a piece of rubber.

The other children in the photo are Fin's cousins Mario and Dino, and his sister Manuelita. Look at the coffee-coloured doll she's holding. It looks just like a miniature of her.

The one smirking at the camera is Paco. He's the oldest of the boys, and Isabel, his sister – she's the one with the worldly-wise air now that she's started going to school.

The first time we met, Isabel wanted to borrow my lipstick. Poor kid, asking me of all people! I had to disappoint her. 'A little perfume?' she asked again, full of hope.

'No, sorry, I don't do perfume either.'

'WHAT?' She looked at me with a mixture of pity and disapproval. And that was that, the end of a beautiful friendship. She's ignored me ever since for failing to live up to her exacting standards of femininity. Except at breakfast time.

I'm going on and on about these children, I know. But I really like them. They're lovely little people, they do what they're told – most of the time – and the things they say! They crack me up. A breath of fresh air, I can't quite believe I'm saying this, but they're a joy to be with.

Yes, Mum, since I got here, my imagination has begun to run wild. Sometimes I picture myself settling down in this place and having children. Who with, I wonder, since I don't know any nice men. And yet, in my dreams, I see two little brats – a copy of Fin and Manuelita, only lighter – running around the place while I go about my business, and all around is peace and quiet, and friendly neighbours. Giulia and Mariangela say this is the best place in the world to raise a family. Perhaps they're right. But, oh, Mum, don't you worry, there's nobody in sight!

You ask me what I do with my time here. I bet you think I'm sunning myself and lazing around on the beach all day. No way, that's not what happens. As I told you, carrying out the smallest chore takes ages, and so I'm forever busy with the cooking, the cleaning, the washing... it's never-ending.

But there's something else I do, day in day out, regularly – writing. So far, I've filled a couple of exercise books with *whatever happens to me and to other people in the village. I usually write in longhand, but, a week ago, as I passed by the shop window of the Wangs, among the half million gadgets on display, I spotted an old Remington. It was battered, the letters F and J were scratched and faded, but, after replacing the ribbon, I tried it out and it worked. In the end, I bought it for 15 US dollars – yes, I had to pay for it in dollars, the Wangs are greedy – and now it sits here on my rickety old table. When I write, it makes a terrible clacking noise, but at last now I can copy out all my notes neatly, making it look so... "professional".*

I know, a typewriter is a little cumbersome to cart around, but the need to fix my memories of this place and to treasure them is so strong that typing it all out has become a necessity.

Dear Mum, in the last few weeks I've been thinking about your visit and, given that I'm likely to stay on in Livingston for quite a while, I asked around when it's the best time, weather-wise, for you to come. I was told that, if you want to avoid the monsoon, the best season is February to April. In any case, don't worry, whatever period you choose, it'll be fine by me.

All my love to you and Dad. Write soon.

Monica x

P.S. See the picture of my new home? It's basic but comfortable. There's a well at the back, but the water is only for washing, not for drinking. See the porch? I've hung a hammock under it, and early in the afternoon when it's very hot, I lie in it and take my siesta. The ocean is beyond those palm trees on the right and, especially at night, when it's extra quiet, I can hear it roaring. I wish you could see the tiny yellow butterflies flying everywhere now that the rains are over!

CHAPTER TEN

THE QUEEN OF HAPPY LAND

My life in Livingston felt like a dream, but I was to have a rude awakening. I was on a tourist visa and, at the end of my third month, I realised that, in order to stay longer, I had to trudge all the way to *Imigración* in Guatemala City and apply for an extension.

I made the day trip to the capital and, after queuing for a long hour, I was seen by a surly-looking officer in a sparsely furnished room. I expected a barrage of questions, but the man hardly looked up from his desk and perfunctorily stamped my passport, granting me two more months.

Two months felt like a lifetime, and as the memory of Martin and the pain of my rejection by Módulos faded away, I set out to enjoy the world about me, and did my best to capture it in words so that I would never forget it.

It was now the end of the rainy season and the heat was rapidly increasing.

The early hours of the morning were usually cool, but when the sun crawled higher and higher into the sky, there was no more breeze in the village, only that red-hot unblinking eye staring down at the thatched roofs and at the people slowly making their way through town.

Soon it was too hot even to walk. By noon, people had retreated to their homes, leaving a simmering stillness behind.

But come evening, when the sun finally plunged into the sea and long shadows fell from the darkening hills, the place awakened.

On the beach, a cool wind rose from the sea brushing the palm trees. In town, the first lights came on – the harsh electric lighting in the streets and shops, and the soft haloes of light in the candle-lit shacks.

I'd taken to strolling along the beach and into town at this hour. I walked slowly and stuck to the shadows, so that both my whiteness and my "foreignness" might pass unnoticed. I'd discovered that, for all my eagerness to be accepted as one of the locals, I was more comfortable being an observer. Like that first day in Livingston when, protected by the greenery, I'd ventured past the stream into the life of those faraway neighbourhoods, now, equally happy about my invisibility, I observed every detail from behind the scenes.

With the first darkness, a steady flow of people poured into the main street. Washed, perfumed and spruced up in freshly laundered clothes and polished footwear, men and women of all ages came out to see and to be seen.

Boys as young as thirteen strutted about just like the "Magnificent Five" I knew, the *mara*, while, sheathed in skin-tight clothes, the girls sneaked sidelong glances at them, then hid behind the screens of beads woven into their braids.

The pavements were lined with the same women vendors I saw in the morning on my way to the fountain. Solid-looking and impassive like the stone steps they sat on, they hollered, '*Pan de cocoooo! Pescado fritoooo! Naranjas! Fritaaaas!*' Unlike earlier in the day, business was thriving. Now drawing in a flurry of customers, their trays were quickly emptied.

And the sounds – the loud, deep-throated laughter of people greeting each other, the shrieks of children playing in the back streets, the barking of distant dogs, the pigs grunting and, of course, the music.

The night began on this mellow note.

Real nightlife started sometime later with yet another change of scene.

As the hawkers and the children turned in for the night, the streets became once again deserted and the action focussed around the bars.

At about ten, "Happy Land" opened. It was the most popular nightspot in town because it was right in the centre and didn't close until the small hours of the morning, when its customers had run out of money.

From behind the flapping red curtain came the sound of a popular Mexican ballad and of deep male voices, cursing and arguing.

I only caught fleeting glimpses of these men as I walked by – a cowboy hat on a hairy nape, a pair of jean-clad legs leaning against a stool, a Cuban-heeled boot tapping the floor in time to the music.

Waiting for their clients, a group of sex workers sat on the front steps, chatting.

By this time, most unaccompanied girls hanging around the bars were scanning the scene for likely customers.

'You see those two girls over there? The two in shiny pants leaning on the railing?' said Tomás one night when we bumped into each other right at the corner. 'They're my neighbours. During the day, they clean people's houses. But, at night, they pack their children off to bed and come here to earn a few extra *quetzals*.'

He turned and nodded at them.

'They do a quick one for a beer or the cost of a boat ticket to Barrios. Even for free, if they like you.' He winked at the two women and they cheerfully waved back.

In the drunken stupor of those late hours, the girls seemed to have a poor choice of clients.

But the undisputed queen of Happy Land was Ruby Jade.

Like one of those flowers that give out their intoxicating scent only in the darkness, she appeared on the front steps of Happy Land night after night, like clockwork, at eleven. She sat among a mixed crowd of grave old men and rowdy youngsters, excitable as fighting roosters. She was unperturbed, in fact amused by the drunken arguments flaring up right behind her, on the porch. She shrugged her shoulders at the commotion and grinned.

She sat there waiting, elbows on wide-spread knees, a few wisps of hair escaping from underneath her red beret jammed on her forehead. The crescent of a scar on her right cheek matched the curved edge of the hat, and her tight jeans emphasised her slinky figure.

Ruby Jade was no washerwoman or maid after a few extra dollars, but a real "pro". From these steps, she directed her nocturnal business with keen judgement, choosing her clients whenever she could. She was from Belize and didn't speak Spanish, only English and Garifuna, which restricted the range of her business to the local black men or to the "gringos", whom she seemed to prefer.

'Hi, friend!' she called out to me. 'How are things?'

I usually stopped for a chat. She was always brimming over with excitement.

"She's a woman,
she's a rude woman,
she's a true woman,
and she turns me on"

She sang in a low husky voice. It might have been the one-hit wonder of the year, but I was convinced she herself was the inspiration.

Together, we walked down the mud track to the discotheque. A tall, lanky gringo was on his way up the hill. He was young, fair, with a college-boy look.

'Oh, babe! Where have you been?' cried Ruby Jade, pouncing on him. Like an old friend, she slipped her arm under his and made him turn back. 'Let's go to the disco, babe,' she said with determination. The white "babe" was so surprised that he just followed her. Now she was in charge, and he slavishly succumbed to her charm.

Every night, Ruby Jade would turn up at the Lugudi Barana with a different man. 'My boyfriend,' she called each one of them. These men all looked alike: tall, solid, rugby player types, alone, on vacation. Fascinated by her exuberance, they ended up buying her one drink after another until she was drunk. Then, she'd laugh thunderously and dance her way through the crowd with sinuous movements of her pelvis, taking up the whole floor.

Then, one day, almost overnight, all of Ruby Jade's joyfulness seemed to vanish. I saw her pace the street, like a captive animal in a cage. 'Hey, girl,' she called out to me. 'What's up?'

'Can't stop today,' I replied. 'I'm in a hurry. Sorry!'

She looked offended.

'What's all this hurry for? What's so important? No use rushing in Labuga, don't you know? Once you get to the end of town, then what? No way out of here, remember?'

She laughed, but it struck me that deep down she wasn't joking, just trying to convince herself.

I knew she was homesick. Ever since I met her, Ruby Jade had been telling me she was going home "at the end of the week". Home was Punta Gorda, Pee Gee, the nearest port in Belize. There was a boat out from Livingston twice a week, but every week, she missed it. 'Next week,' she promised. 'I'll leave next week, you bet.' But she never did.

Then, one day, almost before I knew it, my two months' extension came to an end. There was nothing for it but to go to Belize.

I'd heard that even some of the ex-pats who owned the best hotels were on a tourist visa, like Jill – of the Hotel Flamingo – who strolled through town shading her pale complexion under a frilly white parasol, or Ezequiel, the African Place's owner, who rode his white horse along the main street, stiff and proud on his saddle like a twentieth-century *conquistador*. Every three months, they too had to renew their visa and make their way to Pee Gee.

At ten to nine, I boarded the ferry and, amid the excited crowd of passengers and swaying stacks of luggage clattering up the gangway, I found a seat at the rear. Most of the passengers were small traders going to Belize either to sell or to buy goods. Others were going to visit relatives who lived, like many Livingsteños, in the south of Belize. Then there were those like me, who just needed to leave for the requisite seventy-two hours – no hardship, really. But for the privileged few, wealthy ex-pats like Ezequiel and Jill, some well-aimed nods, winks and greasing of official palms got them back on the same boat and home before sundown.

On board, people were very excited. They talked, laughed and waved a thousand goodbyes to friends and relatives who'd come to the docks to see them off. From the women vendors who'd lined the pier, they bought scores of garishly coloured snacks, chicken drumsticks and portions of fish piled on top of tiny tortillas. They passed these snacks, dripping with sauce, to their travelling companions seated at the other end of the ferry. Although the journey took less than two hours, there was a general rush for food, as if people were afraid of never eating again. This was not a poor crowd. As they picked at the *chaomin* with delicate fingers, golden rings and silver bracelets flashed in the sun, and the women's gigantic solid gold earrings sparkled with each turn of the head.

In the crisp morning light, the passengers' clothes were an explosion of colour: flame red, marigold yellow, bright green, shocking pink and electric blue, set against the brown and black of their skin.

More and more people were boarding the launch; they carried heavy bags, bulky cases, bundles of footballs packed in large woven nets, and cardboard boxes tightly taped up. At last, the boat bulging at its seams, we were set to leave.

As we were about to move off the pier, the ropes uncoiling on the deck, there was some loud shrieking and one last passenger rushed on board. It was Ruby Jade.

From underneath the brim of her hat, she scanned the rows of passengers in search of a face she knew.

She soon found me, shouted out my name and pushed her way forward. Only then did I see the two heavy-set men following her. The boat engine had stopped as if some important last-minute cargo were about to be loaded. They came on board.

Ruby Jade reached my seat and squeezed herself in the narrow gap between me and the young man sitting to my right. He looked daggers at her, but she ignored his disapproving glances and resolutely turned her attention to me. Her two escorts were now looming over both of us.

'Ruby Jade Perry Castillo,' said one of them in a flat voice. 'You are being deported. You shall never again be allowed back into the Republic of Guatemala. *Entiendes?*'

Ruby Jade stared dumbly back at him, for the guy had said all that in Spanish and she hadn't understood a word.

'What's he saying?' she asked me in the pause that followed. I translated. She shrugged her shoulders, unconcerned, and laughed. 'Who are they to say? I'll get back all right, if I want, whatever they say. Yeah, trust me, one day I will,' she said. 'Even if I have to row all the way from Pee Gee.'

The immigration officer's monotonous voice matched the lack of expression on his face.

'You've overstayed your visa. You were given a two-week permit, and you've been here for seven months.'

Ruby Jade grinned and shrugged.

'What's this about permits, visas, immigration laws? I was born just over the other side of the bay. I speak Garifuna like everybody else.'

The two men left. As soon as they had stepped off the boat, the engine revved up with a deep growl and the muddy water churned underneath us. The people on the pier waved as we moved off into the deep waters of the Amatique Bay.

'Thank God that's over,' said Ruby Jade. 'Now, I can be truly excited about going home. Would you believe it, I haven't seen my daughter for the last seven months,' she cried, her big doe eyes full of tenderness. Then she burst into one of the gutsy peals of laughter she was famous for, and the man next to her invited her to 'keep quiet, *por favor!*'

Surprisingly, she took notice. Out of her red plastic handbag, her only baggage, she produced a slim book. It was a tacky pocket edition without a cover. With a deep frown, she eased into her seat and began to read.

I was surprised; reading didn't fit the image I had of Ruby Jade. But then, why shouldn't Ruby Jade spend a few hours reading like anybody else?

She appeared deeply absorbed, her eyes and the red petals of her nails laboriously travelling across the page.

Five minutes later, her serious face broke into fits of giggles. 'Look here!' she burst out, tapping the page repeatedly. She read out slowly, painstakingly, '*He wanted her... to suck... his... cock!*' She sniggered. 'Suck his cock! That's what it says here. Just look for yourself! And down here it says...'

At the top of her voice, she read out all the obscenities on the page. She repeated them over and over, each time a little louder, and then laughed raucously, as if she meant to entertain the entire boat.

My face started flushing hotter and redder. Whether or not they spoke English, I felt sure everyone on the ferry understood what she was saying, or at least had an inkling about the meaning of those words. I looked around for an excuse to disassociate myself from her, while I drew back to the edge of my seat. But Ruby Jade was relentless; she pursued me along the bench, nudging me with her elbow and addressing her remarks more and more pointedly at me – her new best friend.

Thankfully, within minutes, she had shut her book and tossed it into the capacious belly of her handbag. I sighed with relief. But Ruby Jade couldn't keep still. Staring at the blue line of the horizon, daydreaming, like most, was clearly not her forte, and soon she was looking around for new excitement. She stood up and walked down the gangway. Next thing, a plate of *chaomin* was thrust under my nose. 'Have some!' she insisted. She'd cadged it off an acquaintance she spotted eating, a few seats away from us.

After the snack, Ruby Jade fancied a cigarette; she simply slid it out of the hand of a total stranger with a wink. 'Here, have a smoke,' she said, passing the cigarette over to me.

I felt the eyes of all the passengers on us. We made such an unlikely pair; me, a white, pasty-faced shrinking violet, well, until this moment, I hadn't felt like one, but now arm in arm with this outrageous black sex bomb...

The sight of the Belizean shore looming suddenly ahead of us took me by surprise. As we got closer, the undulating range of blue hills flattened and disappeared under the broadness of the sky.

People started to get ready. Women slipped on their high-heeled shoes and smoothed the creases out of their dresses; men adjusted the angle of their hats, then slung their bags over their shoulders or dragged them across the floor towards the exit.

We soon reached the port and disembarked. The pier was even smaller and more basic than the one in Livingston. Beneath our feet, the sea peeped through the gaps between the wooden boards, each stripe a dazzling shade of turquoise blue.

Massively tall and very black, two Belizean officers stood at the checkpoint at the end of the pier. Chewing gum, they perfunctorily zipped and unzipped our bags. For once, Ruby Jade was silent and looked intimidated like everyone else.

The two of us carried so little luggage that we were soon through. We walked down the pier together. As we reached the shore, we separated. I turned right and headed for the nearest hotel, while Ruby Jade turned left and ran to her old house, skipping with joy at the prospect of seeing her daughter.

There was a British military base a few miles north of Punta Gorda. As we waved goodbye, I had no doubt that rowdy, rude, riotous Ruby Jade would soon find there a new supply of English-speaking *boyfriends*.

CHAPTER ELEVEN

'BIENVENIDA A TU PUEBLO'

My three days in Pee Gee went in a flash.

I stayed in a sleazy hotel close to the harbour, where I whiled away the hours chatting with some of the mostly American and French guests.

There, on the terrace of the hotel, we were soon joined by a couple of Belizean men, friends of the landlord.

With a fat joint doing the rounds of the coffee table, they told us about a naïve tourist being first set up by one of the local drug dealers and then handed over to the police.

'It cost him hundreds of Belizean dollars to stay out of jail,' said one.

'Yeah, it took him a lot of greasing of palms,' laughed the other, winking, as he took greedy puffs on the joint.

Only later, we discovered from the landlord they were themselves immigration officers at the port!

On my second day, I was sitting in a bar writing, when a tall black man crossed the street and came to stoop over my table.

'Lovely hairy legs you've got,' he said in a deep voice.

I looked down at the fuzz covering my legs. In the glaring

sunlight, it shone as bright as a golden fleece. For months, I'd neglected to shave, partly because I had bigger worries, and partly to make a point – wasn't the state of my legs nobody's business but my own? It hadn't seemed to bother Martin – or was he too gentlemanly to comment? It didn't deter Emilio either, or was he too much on the make that he'd overlook something like that?

'Know what they say about hairy women?'

Taken by surprise, I shook my head.

'Best in bed, that's what they say. Ain't it true?' he laughed, leering at me.

I blushed with embarrassment, and then got angry with myself for doing so. I brushed him away with a 'Cho!'

Everything people said or did during those three days filled me with a sense of discomfort. In Guatemala, there'd been plenty of roadblocks to set my nerves on edge. But I was mostly with Martin then. Was that it? Was this just another taste of what it's like to be a woman travelling on her own? Although generally low-key, here the danger felt more diffused, more pervasive, more personal. And, although I should have been used by now to people staring at me, I felt that in Pee Gee there was a different, almost threatening, edge to it. Or was it just my imagination?

When my seventy-two hours were up, I boarded the three o'clock ferry with relief.

Being the hottest hour of the day, it was the worst time to travel. The clammy afternoon sapped away all my energy. I sat with my back against the railings and edged myself under the boat awning, trying to take shelter from the unbearable glare of a sky white with mist and heat.

As we left the pier, a gusty wind brushed the dark green sea, curling it backwards in small foamless waves. Next to the boat, flocks of seagulls floated without moving their wings, leaning lightly upon the breeze.

Soon, the wind died out and the air became completely still. I could smell and taste the salt in it.

The ferry was as packed as a few days earlier. But this time there was no merchandise, only people who sat close together, some nodding off onto their neighbour's shoulder, others bent at awkward angles over a friend's lap. The women fanned themselves with their handkerchiefs or a corner of their pleated skirts, the men with their straw hats. Small children with open mouths and strands of limp hair stuck to their sweaty brows lolled in their sleep, cushioned against their mother's bosom.

The rumble of the engine matched the collective sluggishness of the boat.

As I sat in my own stupor, giving in to the drowsiness that made my limbs heavy as stone, my mind wandered.

I thought again of Martin, now in his orphanage. I thought of Suzanne risking her life to protect the *desaparecidos'* families, of Eva giving it all she got in *Módulos*. I even thought of the insufferable Fede playing superhero with his teenagers. These people were all doing wonderful work and I admired them greatly, and envied them, wishing I could be just like them.

But…

…I just wasn't as brave as they were.

There on the boat, I felt another crisis looming. What was I here for? What was I doing? Fede had been right about me. I lacked commitment. Had I got the job, I wouldn't have lasted long in *Módulos*. The reasons that had made me want to come to Central America – the wish to be good and help people, to do something worthwhile with my life – once again appeared hazy and confused. Like all those others I'd despised, the Brads and Breezes of this world, like them I was drifting, chancing my luck, bunking off adulthood.

Once more I was eaten up with wretched self-doubt.

Jolting me back to reality, the ferry made a wide arc over the open sea and entered the bay. Thrown into a frenzy by some passing shoal of fish, our following of seagulls grew restless; they whirled madly in all directions, then scattered, dived down to the sea, and finally nestled in the hollow of the waves, pecking at their scraps of prey.

It was almost six. In a matter of minutes, the tropical day would topple into night. The coast became hazy. Only the silhouettes of the palms stood out. The grey concrete slab of the harbour loomed larger and larger.

As we touched the pier with a thud and a grinding and scraping of metal, the lethargy of the port was shattered by the usual uproar of hawkers, porters, passengers, curious bystanders, people waiting for relatives and friends.

I thought back to when, four months earlier, I'd first set foot on that same pier. I'd been full of enthusiasm at the prospect of the alleged reggae concert, and also a little anxious, not knowing what to expect from a new place.

Now, everything felt easy. I knew what lay beyond the first three hundred metres of paved road; I knew there were discos on the beach; I knew some of the local characters. Even here, on the docks, the young woman who'd sold me some *pan de coco* that first morning was now waving at me with a smile. And wasn't that a nod I got from the old porter as he wheeled his pushcart right past me?

Within half an hour, I'd be back to the safety of my beach hut, my friendly neighbourhood, my laid-back existence. At last.

As I scanned the sea of faces crowding the harbour, I spotted a familiar grin – a white fan of protruding teeth, shaded by a baseball cap with the visor turned to one side. A new earring completed his look: a long white feather with its end threaded into a red bead.

'*Hola*, Monica.'

It was Tomás. He sauntered towards me and, as we engaged in the local ritual of elaborated handshakes, he intoned in his deep voice:

'*Bienvenida a tu pueblo*. Welcome home.'

CHAPTER TWELVE

NOCHE BUENA

Back in "my *pueblo*", life carried on just as before – laid-back and joyful. Every day brought something new and interesting, and, although things continued virtually the same, each night I went to bed with the feeling I'd learnt something important that day, something about the people and the place. Livingston was beginning to feel like home. Less magical, more ordinary, perhaps, but all the better for that.

The weeks went by and suddenly Christmas came knocking at the door.

'*Noche Buena... Noche Buena... Sí, pues, Noche Buena,*' wherever I went, amid the flood of impenetrable conversations in Garifuna or Kekchi, I overheard the same two words. My expectations rose.

Every day, the ferry brought more visitors – hippies, clean-cut young men on holiday from college, Ladino families from the capital – all there to see how well the Morenitos – the little dark people! that's what the Ladinos called the tall Garifunas – danced.

Along the pavements, the women vendors multiplied. Their fritters and fish patties quickly sold out and more were promptly delivered by a platoon of children whizzing about with their wicker baskets.

'*Qué alegre!*' The women clapped their hands at the prospect of the extra earnings.

At last, it was Christmas Eve – *Noche Buena*.

'Coming out with us tonight?' said Mariangela, appearing on my doorstep.

We met around midnight by the African Place – the two Italian sisters with Daniel and Manu, their boyfriends, and me, on my own.

When we reached the main road, the *fiesta* was in full swing. From the docks to the cemetery, a long row of stalls had sprung up on both pavements. Laid out on trestle tables or hanging from metal posts were dartboards, streamers, tombolas and rubber duck fishing games; and then prizes, lots of cheap prizes – soft toys, cups, jugs, plastic trumpets, fancy hair clips and red, green and yellow balloons.

We walked the streets and tried our luck. Then, loaded with our booty of cheap trinkets, we made our way down to the beach.

Outside the Lugudi Barana stood a battery of cooking pots on a trestle table. Enticed by the smell of roast chicken that wafted in our direction, we joined the queue.

'Only one piece?' said the woman vendor when my turn came. 'Where's your sweetheart?'

'Don't have one.' I lifted my shoulders to signal I didn't care.

'What! *Noche Buena* and you're alone?' She looked at me in disbelief. 'Go and look around, *pues!*' She winked at me and laughed.

I was about to tell her I liked my freedom, that I was happy like this. But she meant well. I just smiled and went to join the others under the palm trees.

An eerie crimson moon was rising out of the shimmering ocean.

'It looks much more impressive this side of the world, doesn't it?' said Mariangela, hypnotised by it.

And she was right – it did. The sight of it was stunning, but, as I watched it crawl higher and higher into the sky, the hawker's words played on my mind.

It was Christmas, a time for people to be with their loved ones. Was I really happy on my own? The woman got me thinking. To most people here, I must look like a lonely *gringa,* a curiosity, perhaps. But it was quite clear that not having a man by my side didn't win me their respect.

The music grew louder and jollier, making it impossible to keep still.

'C'mon, let's go in,' said Daniel, and we rose to our feet and danced our way into the hall.

I'd never seen the Lugudi Barana so packed. Entire families were there, all generations, the young and the old, including dozens of children running about the dance floor. Even the Mayan shop owners usually too busy to have a night out had turned up. They were all dressed to the nines – the women in taffeta frocks, chiffon belts, elaborate hairdos and a lot of makeup; the men in perfectly ironed trousers, impeccable shirts with starched collars, immaculate white socks and polished shoes. Here and there, looking conspicuous in their casual clothing, clusters of tourists and *capitalinos* bopped up and down and shook their stuff with abandon.

My eyes fell on a bench along the side, where everybody seemed to be looking.

Here, facing the dance floor, sat a white foreign couple – their appearance and clothing giving them away. She sat on his lap, wriggling her body against him, while he fondled her from behind.

'Why don't they take themselves to the nearest bedroom?' said an old man in an irritated voice. 'There are children here, families… C'mon, some respect!'

'That's gringos for you…'

'They come here and think they can do this in front of everyone. Like animals!' a woman with large hoop earrings complained loudly.

'Worse than animals!' said the man dancing with her. 'Animals have more shame than these two – they hide.'

Things got worse when Rasta Rooster, a self-styled Rastafarian from Pee Gee, a foreigner himself, sauntered in.

'Oh, no, not him,' I heard people say all around as he appeared. 'That good-for-nothing...'

Rasta Rooster had got off the ferry one day and never left. No one knew what he did or why he was here. Everyone knew, though, including me, that he "loved" women, especially foreign women. His favourite chat-up line went approximately like this: 'Hey, baby, come and live with me in the jungle. Yah, man, you'd look really beautiful with me there, in the Garden of Eden.'

This made most women laugh. But not even laughter deterred Rasta Rooster; on the contrary, it made him more persistent.

Tonight, he walked up to the couple and stopped right up close to the woman's chest. Then, ignoring her boyfriend, he brazenly started chatting her up.

While this threesome got a lot of attention, across the dance floor, by one of the exits, another two-people act was unfolding. A short foreign girl with spiky blonde hair repeatedly play-punched her young Garifuna male companion in the ribs.

'Hit me, come on, hit me!' She laughed, then quickly bounced back on the balls of her feet, like a featherweight boxer. He looked at her, puzzled, then, unconvinced, he punched her half-heartedly.

'*Púchica!* What's wrong with people tonight? First the horny woman on the man's lap, and now this straw-weight boxer.' Daniel laughed.

'Are you women all like that in Europe?' Manu teased the two sisters and me. 'Or is it just the full moon?'

This, I realised, was precisely what kept me enthralled, spellbound in Labuga. This overblown reality, this craziness, worked on me like a drug.

I thought of Martin joking about my being a girl who just wanted to have fun. Here I was, that girl.

On my way out of the hall for a breath of fresh air, I bumped into Tomás. He wore spotless white trainers, a happy grin on his face, and paraded an attractive white woman wrapped around his arm.

'Tomás,' I shouted over the noise, smiling at him knowingly, 'aren't you going to introduce me to your Swiss girlfriend?'

The thing was that – oops! – the girl wasn't Swiss. I realised my mistake from the glance of pure meanness Tomás darted in my direction. I should have known better than to embarrass him, and now it was too late.

He was quick to recover his cool.

'Monica,' he said, 'meet my Dutch girlfriend, Ella.'

Ella was tall and slim, with strawberry blonde hair. She seemed friendly. Tomás waited for us to exchange hellos, then stared coldly into my eyes. 'What about you, Monica? Where's your man?'

I shrugged my shoulders and, befuddled, opened my arms wide.

'Didn't I tell you to stick to one man?' He grinned as he savoured each moment of his sweet revenge. 'See what happens when you refuse to listen? You end up sad and lonely like tonight, see?'

'Me sad and lonely? *Cho!*' I brushed him off and went outside.

Everyone seemed determined to gang up on me tonight – first the hawker with her innuendos and now Tomás... Who next?

But, right there, in front of me, the ocean shimmered in the soft moonlight, and all around, the mellow reggae music merged with the lapping of the waves... Little by little, all my frustrations melted away.

Close by, the two Italian sisters snuggled up to their boyfriends.

I leaned back against the side of an upturned *cayuco* and buried my toes in the cool sand...

I thought of Martin, again, trying to imagine what he'd be doing at this precise moment. Would he be alone? Would he be thinking about me? Or would he have taken up with someone new, someone more "worthy"?

A commotion came from inside the hall. The music stopped and the lights came on, while, shoving and shouting, a stream of people surged out onto the beach.

Alarmed, we all rushed over to the windows and peeped through the lattice woodwork. Inside, nothing seemed to be wrong, except for an empty space near the bar.

'The beginning of a fight,' said Daniel, knowingly, 'but Martino, *el patrón,* is *buzo,* he's cut this one short.'

Giulia and I saw this as a perfect opportunity to get a round of drinks, and rushed to the bar. By the time we'd turned back from the counter with our beers, the hall was, once again, full of people.

'And those two?' Giulia nudged me in the ribs, pointing to the door. 'What the hell…'

Two soldiers stood to the right, guns across their chests, legs astride the doorway. A third had taken up position to the left, by the main entrance. They had blocked both exits and trapped us inside.

The neon lights came on and, from high up on the ceiling, glared down on us fiercely, making us squint. I shielded my eyes with the back of my hand and looked around. Everywhere I saw anxious faces. In the crowd, I caught sight of Tomás. He stood by the bar, a beer in his right hand, an arm around his girlfriend; he looked shaken, for once, and she appeared suddenly small as she cowered against him. Over the other side of the hall, flattened against one of the loudspeakers, stood Bibi, his face a grimacing mask of fear. Nearby, Rasta Rooster was no longer peeking down the foreign woman's décolletage. He looked around, completely bewildered, caught off-guard by the arrival of the soldiers.

I could feel the tightness in my throat as I struggled to keep calm.

An officer in green and brown uniform stormed in.

'Move! Move now!' he barked at people, waving his gun. '*Ándale, ándale, rápido!*' As he shouted, the officer – a Ladino with a thick dark moustache – strode from wall to wall, pushing the crowd against the sides. In a matter of minutes, he singlehandedly cleared the entire dance floor.

A deep silence descended on the room. Like everyone else, I stood there waiting, my guts all knotted, my heart pounding in my chest.

Guns at the ready, the three Mayan soldiers impassively began to search the men. They frisked them rapidly and in ten, fifteen minutes they'd done them all. To my relief, they didn't bother with the women. They left so quietly that I only realised they'd gone when the gap in the middle began to fill.

Afterwards, everyone began to talk loudly, all at the same time.

'How dare they come and play *macizo* with us, on *Noche Buena...*' said Manu, wiping the sweat off his forehead with a handkerchief.

'Yah, man. Pushing us about, bullying us...'

'Remember five, six years ago, when they came to round us up? They wanted to force us into the army. There was a wake in Labuga that night, and I went to hide under the coffin, covered in black sheets. That time, the soldiers didn't dare come into the *velorio*, and they never found me, ha ha!' Daniel laughed as he told the story to a small crowd gathered around him.

'Yeah, bro, they didn't catch me either. I ran into the hills...' said Manu.

'You two got away, you lucky bastards!' said a man with a scar across his cheek. 'I didn't. They picked me up right there, on the pier. I ended up in the district of Petén, up north, for two bloody years. No one there had ever seen a black man...'

'Bastards!'

'Bloody Indios!' people shouted.

At length, Martino turned on the strobe lights, then walked to the jukebox in the corner.

Out of the giant loudspeakers came the deep, prophetic biblical voice of Peter Tosh calling for justice and equal rights.

Still shaken, but determined to chase away the heavy mood, I took to the dance floor with all the others.

As I swayed to the mellow reggae, I thought of Rasta Rooster and his alleged corner of Paradise. Where was the happy oasis of peace and love he promised to all and sundry?

Not here, it seemed, not quite.

CHAPTER THIRTEEN

UN HOMBRE SENCILLO

'*Cuidado!*' called the man in a teasing voice.

With the help of a chunky stick, I was making my way down the hillside, cautiously. At the bottom, a muddy stream coasted the walls of the African Place and ran towards the sea.

Long before my time in Livingston, a concrete bridge had stood on this precise spot, linking the centre to the periphery. One rainy season, the bridge had collapsed, leaving a disarray of bricks in the muddy water and a few vehicles gathering rust outside the cemetery.

A makeshift bridge of planks had been put together – the very same I'd crossed the day of my arrival – and a team of local labourers had been employed to see to the construction work. But, as with any season, the rainy season came around again, and this time both slope and planks had become dangerously slippery. For people like me, owning no Wellingtons or proper shoes, the crossing was, to say the least, a challenge.

'*Sí, pues,* watch out!' the man repeated.

I looked up. He stood a few steps away from the other labourers and, leaning nonchalantly on the handle of his spade, he watched me inch my way down the hill.

He looked amused. Oh, yeah, what was so funny about a woman not wanting to fall into a pool of mud?

Had he seen the irritation in my eyes? For – and I swear I'm not making this up – in the time-honoured cliché of romantic fiction, it was indeed with one manly stride that he was there, tall and solid, next to me, offering me, so to speak, his hand.

'*Aquí, venga que te ayudo.*' He held my arm and helped me up the other side.

'*Muchas gracias,*' I said when, finally, I stood with both feet on firmer ground.

'*De nada.*'

He had a raucous, unexpectedly high-pitched laugh. The top half of his face was concealed under a large straw hat, but his smile was broad and peppered with a hint of mischief.

'Rafael Sócrates Melquior Gonzalez, *a la orden,*' he introduced himself, all in one breath, and, again, he laughed.

'*Mucho gusto.* Monica.' I smiled at him, won over by his gaiety and also, as he pushed the brim of his hat back, by his good looks.

In the days that followed, I bumped into him again, and again – first in front of the Wangs', then by the post office. Each time he greeted me with the warmth of a long-standing friend.

I responded with much the same enthusiasm. As well as handsome, he seemed very nice.

Then, one morning, as he walked past me, he whispered, '*Hey, ragazza,* you know what? One of these days, you'll be mine. I know it. *Sí, pues,*' and he looked at me brazenly.

I blushed. Against my better judgement, I was flattered. I was also slightly puzzled. Where did the word *ragazza* come from? Had he mistaken me for one of my erstwhile housemates? Did he know something about me already?

'Do you speak Italian?'

'*Poco, poco.* A few words. I've just been to Italy. What a beautiful place! And the women, wow! Gorgeous. Just like you.'

It was a cheesy pick-up line, I know, but he delivered it with such infectious mirth I couldn't help a smile.

A few days later, at lunchtime, I met him on his way back from the bridge. He was sauntering along the street in his working clothes – a pair of beach shorts caked with mud, a torn singlet and a pair of rubber boots torn around the toes. He had ropes of bulging muscles, testimony to a lifetime of heavy labour. His legs, by contrast, were thin and long with pronounced veins. He grinned at me from a distance.

'Come to my house, *ragazza*, and see how a *hombre sencillo* lives,' he said, coming to a stop in front of me.

Right there, a foot on the blade of his spade, and chin resting on the wooden handle, he recited all in one breath:

"Ten cuidado de las cosas de la Tierra
Haz algo. Corta leña. Labra la Tierra
Planta nopales. Planta magueys.
Tendrás que beber, que comer, que vestir.
Con eso estarás en pie. Serás verdadero.
Con eso andarás.
Con eso se hablará de ti, se te alabará
Con eso te darás a conocer." [1]

When he'd finished, he brushed a few stray dreadlocks off his brow and gazed at me.

'That's what the wise men say, and I live by it.'

Hmm, I thought, was this man for real? I kind of knew the answer.

The guy seemed to have the qualities that, against all common sense, I found so appealing in a man: a way with words, a certain amount of roguish swagger. In short, he was the type – Martin being the noticeable exception – I usually fell for. Given I'd been there and done that many times before, to my cost, it was best to keep away. But –

---

1   *Take care of the things of the Earth. Do something. Cut wood. Till the land. Plant prickly pears. Plant agave. The Earth will give you food, drink, shelter. It will sustain you. You'll be true to yourself. You'll be able to stand tall. You'll be spoken of, you'll be praised. You will be known.*

There was something else about this man that touched me – he seemed to be at one with Livingston, with its history and traditions; his whole being seemed to be rooted here. Or was I imagining things?

'Well then, you coming?' he said, flashing a disarming smile.

My curiosity was piqued, and so was my refusal to learn from previous mistakes.

'*Vale*,' I said, and followed him down the grassy trail, past a few old men who sat at the street corner, keeping an eye on the comings and goings, while pretending to be half-asleep.

We came to a small hut made of wood and bamboo cane. It stood a little distance from the path, wedged between a two-storied brick house and a bigger thatched hut.

Rafael unlocked the front door – and there I was, inside the *hombre sencillo*'s world.

Coming in from the glaring sunlight, at first there was only darkness. Then I began to make out a small but neat living space.

To the right of the door stood a wooden table, two stools, a reclining armchair and, lined up against the wall, a metal bed frame covered with a wicker mat. In a corner was a single burner gas stove; next to it, another table with a flowery red plastic top, and underneath it, two buckets of water. 'One for drinking, the other for washing,' he explained.

On the walls were rows of wooden shelves packed with books. This guy a reader? Impossible! – I laughed to myself. But then, on second thoughts, why not? Hadn't he just recited a beautiful poem? I stepped closer so I could read the spines of the books. Among the many volumes, I made out some familiar English titles: *Our Bodies, Ourselves*, read one cover. *The Well of Loneliness*, said another.

Aware of Rafael's presence right behind me – as he leaned against the door, arms folded and a grin on his face, his eyes following my own gaze here and there, studying my every reaction – I stifled a barrage of questions.

Pretending indifference, I quickly moved to the other shelves nearby, where dozens of empty rum bottles, rolls of toilet paper and penholders were haphazardly stacked. A large metal pot hung from one of the wooden beams, and a heavily pregnant white woman smiled contentedly from a life-size poster pasted over the back of the door.

'No bath, no toilet, no running water. Everything's natural around here,' he said, unlocking a door at the other end of the room.

He led me into a small yard separated from the neighbours by a fence of bamboo cane. 'Look at those,' he said, proudly pointing to a thick cluster of young banana shoots in the corner. 'I planted them two weeks ago. See how fast they grow. As the wise men say, the land is generous.'

Back inside, I began to make out more details. Two bamboo partitions separated the main room from an alcove with an in-built double bed. It was made of bamboo rods cut in half and had no mattress, just a yellow and brown sleeping bag thrown over it, two jaunty leopards leaping across its length. A mosquito net cascaded over the bed, and to the side, a tall set of bamboo shelves stored piles of neatly folded clothes.

Rafael made me a cup of coffee and offered me a plate of cold fried herring. Then, he stretched up to the wooden beam above his head, pulled down a red stripy hammock and tumbled into it. After drawing a chair close by for me, he reached out to a photo album lying on the nearest shelf and began to leaf through it.

'*Mi mujer*, Valeria,' he said, pointing at a young white woman with short curly hair smiling nervously at the camera.

I hid my surprise behind an equally nervous smile.

'And this,' he moved on to the next picture, 'this is Harüne, *mi hijo*. He looks just like me, doesn't he?' He did: the little mischievous face creased up just like his father's.

So, the man was married and had a child. Strangely, the double revelation didn't come as a disappointment; on the contrary, it gave me a sense of relief. It was the obstacle I badly needed so that I could keep in check any romantic feelings I may be tempted to have for him. A deterrent.

'And where are they now?'

'In Italy. Valeria doesn't like it here. She did at first, but…'

He gazed at the child in the photo with longing.

'Harüne will be two next month.' He sighed.

He turned the page and we came to a beefy middle-aged man in a checked shirt stretched tight around his belly. 'This is Giorgio, my father-in-law,' Rafael introduced him with a smile, 'a great guy!'

Pictures of Italian uncles, cousins, grannies, young and old relatives came next: group photos taken around lavishly decked dinner tables, glasses raised up in toasts, family gatherings indoors and outdoors with bluish hills in the distance. In one picture, a diminutive Rafael stood proud at the feet of the colossal statue of Michelangelo's *David*. The smile on his face was so wide that little could be seen except for two gleaming rows of teeth. After that, more monuments, more close-ups of Harüne, more friends, more family.

A long silence followed, until he broke it with his contagious laugh.

'Italy is wonderful, I know, but Labuga's my home and, however much money they offer me, this is where I belong.'

He peered at me out of the folds of the red canvas – dark slanted eyes, features chiselled out of dark mahogany, a full head of shoulder-length locks. His eyes held mine, caressingly, seductively, full of desire.

'Life's sweet, isn't it?' he said, grinning. 'Life's for living, don't you think?'

He stretched out a long arm towards me.

Was this a good idea? Noooo, most likely a terrible one, but did I care? At this moment? No. I was one with *el hombre sencillo* – life was, indeed, for living.

I held out my hand. He seized it and pulled me into his hammock.

*

We began to see each other regularly. I often went to his place. This being right in the centre, it gave me the perfect excuse to pop by on my way to the fountain or the shops. I often spent the night there with Rafael.

But what I liked best was when he came to see me in my hut on the beach at night.

CHAPTER FOURTEEN

LARUNI HATTI – 1

The night descends upon this corner of the earth with the rapidity of a spent match. It literally falls upon us within a ten-minute span, and each time it catches me by surprise.

I put down what I'm doing, go out and look at the sky. No, it isn't a cloud blotting the sun, nor an eclipse, but night itself.

In the dark, the huts next to mine are blurry, lonely shapes. They appear still and silent, like animals lying in wait under the trees.

A cool easterly wind rises from the mainland. The sound of the sea grows louder, and the waves roll closer to the shore. In the swampland behind my house, the frogs start croaking. In the distance, the dogs bark. All around, the night comes alive with the shrill tremor of forest insects. Fast-moving clouds sweep across the sky. In the vast darkness, a myriad of stars gleam. Then suddenly the moon slides out of the ocean and ascends silently above the shimmering waves. A liquid, yellow, perfectly round disc. It's a full moon tonight.

Moon is *hatti* in Garifuna. "*Laruni hatti*" means moonlight.

That's what Rafael calls me when, feeling romantic and tender, he comes to see me in my hut. There is no fixed pattern to his coming. At times, he turns up in the middle of the night; other times, at dawn. I hear stealthy steps on the grass outside. At times, I do not hear anything; I only feel a vague presence of something or someone approaching. Then the door rattles and he walks in. When I am fast asleep it's even better. The creaking of the door hinges wakes me up. I open my eyes wide, and he's already there, his big white smile right above me. Chiselled in ebony, his face draws closer, much closer, a little closer still, and then I feel the touch of his lips on mine, and the smoothness of his skin on mine.

'*Nanibugia ynga!*' he whispers into my ear. 'You are mine.' I hate to admit it, but he's right. Against my better judgement, I'm seduced by his silver tongue.

With one of his long arms, he reaches a corner of the mosquito net gathered in folds above our heads and pulls at it. The light organdie tumbles down in a white and fluffy cloud and covers us like a tent.

Rafael's lips are soft and fleshy; his kisses reach deep down into me. We make love slowly. Rafael puts all his physical sensation into words. Our love is "hot" and "sweet" and "*rico*", and the initial "r" rolls wetly against the ridge of his palate as he greedily sucks on his tongue. At times, he stops and studies each bit of me. 'Amazing, isn't it? Women's bodies are extraordinary. Everything's there, so perfect, so necessary, each part… All that roundness, that softness… wonderful!' And he slides into me with ease, closing his eyes, with a sly grin on his face.

I always thought Martin was a rather good lover, and so was Richard. But I realise now that lovemaking reaches new heights with Rafael. Perhaps it's because I know that my time with him is fleeting, and that frees me from both the expectations and the censure of my old world. I can be totally me, not someone else's idea of what I should be. Besides, I've never been with a man who seems to like women so intensely as him. It's a good feeling. Being loved by a man like this makes me love myself a little more.

Afterwards, we talk into the night. He tells me about his life.

His dad was a violent and moody man, and his mother ran away from home when he was only a child. She started a new life, had other children and, he says, "forgot all about me". He lived with his father until the man died from a stroke, and then with some relatives for whom he had to do all kinds of jobs to pay his keep. Still very young, he left school and moved to Guatemala City where he lived off his wits. He was in turn a shoeshine boy, a construction labourer, a handyman for some rich family, a potter in a ceramic firm.

'I liked being a potter, I was good at it, but one day they caught me smoking a joint in the toilet and they fired me. After that, I got bored with the capital and came back.' He shrugs off two and a half decades of hardship with a laugh.

Back in Livingston, he met Valeria, and they fell in love. They lived together for two years, and then she became pregnant. It was a very happy time, he says. But later, when the baby was born, things got complicated.

'She couldn't adapt to my simple lifestyle. She wanted comforts, money, expensive things. One evening, I came back from work and she was gone. Not a word, not a note, gone, just like that, in great secrecy. And she'd taken my son with her!'

Sparks of old anger flash in his dark brown eyes. A year later, she wrote to invite him to join her in Florence. He did go but lasted only three months there. When I first met him, he'd just come back.

'I couldn't stand depending on Valeria for all things. If I needed a packet of cigarettes, I had to ask her. Anything I fancied, a beer, a shot of rum, a Coke, I had to plead with her. That's no life, I tell you. I wanted to work, but there was no work for me there.'

He wants to know about me: why I travel, what I'm looking for, what it is I want from life. So, I tell him I want to see the world and understand it. I want to learn from life; I want to be independent and free. During our late-night talks, I consolidate this new persona that since I've come to Central America has emerged out of me; a confident, resilient self, for whom love is free and non-exclusive. The more I talk, the more real this new *me* feels. I'm brave, strong, and surely not jealous. How can I be jealous, determined as I am not to get hooked on any man, and certainly not one with a wife and child?

All sorts of topics come up in our all-night conversations. We even talk about death. I shock him when I tell him I want to be cremated.

'That's terrible!' he says, glaring at me like a grim and implacable Mayan god. 'That's the trouble with you Europeans. You have no respect. Me, I want to be buried deep down into the earth, so that, when I rot, I can once again turn into soil. Pineapple, coconut and cashew trees will grow out of it, together with cassava, rice and corn. People will eat from it and become strong and healthy. Because we are the earth, *mi amor*, and the earth is us.'

Presented this way, death sounds like a comfortable rest place in the dark, and the earth a welcoming second womb. There's no reason to be afraid.

Rafael breaks into my thoughts.

'*Mira!*' he says, opening the back door and flinging the condom he's just used in the tall grass. 'Here's yet another of my children ending up in a rubbish heap!' It is so melodramatic that I begin to laugh. But then he adds, 'Why don't you have a child, Monica? Isn't it time you became a mother?'

Until I came to Livingston, I never thought I'd want children. But this is the trouble with this place – it makes anything seem possible. Of course, I know this is not the right man, reminded as I am daily about how much he cares for his wife and child. And yet, on hearing those questions day in, day out, my resistance begins to crumble.

Perhaps Rafael is right, and life is simple. To say it in his words, 'We only need a plot of land for sustenance, somebody to love and who loves us, and then, in time, the blessing of one or more children.'

'*Comprensión, mi amor*, that's what I'm after,' he says when I ask him what he values most in this "simple" life he envisages for himself. *Comprensión*, understanding.

In the old days, I'd have laughed knowingly.

'Oh, yeah?' I'd have said, 'you mean that very special kind of one-way arrangement, whereby it's the woman who does most of the *comprensión?*'

But today, I'm another person. I say nothing of the sort; in fact, I suppress the seed of any negative thought within me.

Just now I feel alive and vibrant and I don't want to spoil things.

*

Rafael likes cooking and we often eat together. As I turn up for dinner one night, I find a young man at the table with us.

'Meet Jaime, my stepbrother,' says Rafael.

Jaime's just returned to Livingston after a long absence and he's staying in Rafael's house until he finds his bearings.

The two share the same mother but have a different father. Jaime's dad is a Ladino from Honduras and Jaime is lighter-skinned than Rafael, ten years younger and ten inches shorter. He is a handsome young man with clever eyes and an open smile. He seems to live in fear of his brother, who, in all fairness, barks at him order upon order at which poor Jaime jumps to his feet.

'That's how an older brother treats his younger siblings here. That's the Garifuna way,' I'm told, when I ask Rafael why he's so harsh with him.

In any case, Jaime accepts it and bends over backwards to please and fulfil his brother's slightest whim.

'Here's ten *len*, go to the corner shop and buy me two cigarettes.' 'Jaime! Go and get me a bucket of water. Now!' 'I need two eggs. Here's a fifty *centavos* piece. And don't forget, I want the twenty *centavos* change.'

'*Sí, hermano! Por supuesto, hermano!*' and Jaime runs to the corner shop, the fountain, the *tienda* on the main road. He calls him *hermano* but defers to Rafael as if to his commanding officer.

It follows: Jaime was in the Guatemalan army for the last two years, forcibly conscripted, like many of the young men around here, but now he says it's the best thing that ever happened to him. 'It made a man of me,' he boasts. He stands to attention and clicks his heels; it would be laughable if it weren't so sad, and so scary. I dread to think what else he got used to. Now, he's unemployed and lives off his brother. He sleeps in his house on the camp bed or in the hammock and does small errands for him in exchange – he also knows how to make himself scarce when the situation requires it. Every day he goes to the docks in the hope of picking up some odd job or other, perhaps with the tourists getting off the ferry, or with the yacht crowd mooring along the quays, where the East Indians live.

Most of the time, though, Jaime fools around with *la mara*. Like them, he pierces his earlobes, trades earrings and baseball caps, combs his hair this way or the other, styling himself to improve his *cool* looks. Being nineteen, he wants to have, he says, "a good life".

In the house, the two brothers make big claims about their respective wives.

'*Mi mujer* is only sixteen and she's this little.' Jaime indicates with the slant of his hand an invisible point in mid-air, roughly coming up to his chest. Given he's on the short side, this makes his "*mujer*" either a midget or a child. Anyway, this is how he sees her.

'I've a three-month-old baby, you know? *Yo los quiero mucho a los dos.*' His gaze blurs into distant reveries.

His *mujer* and child live with his in-laws in Zacapa, near Guatemala City. This gives Jaime the freedom to fool around with other girls here in Livingston, dance the night away on the beach and, at the same time, to boast that he's a good father.

'*Mi mujer* has beautiful blue eyes,' counterattacks Rafael. 'Also, *mi suegro* Giorgio loves me so much! In fact, they all love me so much over there in Firenze! They treat me like a prince.'

It is just like a "love contest", who loves or is loved more, who has the best *mujer* or family to boast about. In Rafael's case, it is his father-in-law who chalks up the most compliments.

'Every time I saw something in a shop window and said, "Oh, I like that, that's nice," he went straight in and bought it for me. And just before I left, he called me to one side. "Rafael, here, take this," he said, and bang on the table, he lay down three thousand dollars, one note after the other. A gift. For me? Rafael smiles at his brother, confident that nothing Jaime might say can match that.

I soon realise that whenever Rafael talks about his wife – and not a day passes without him mentioning her – he always strives to draw comparisons between the two of us. It seems to give him some secret pleasure. Sometimes I wonder whether he does it in retaliation for my claims to being free and independent. Does he mean to give me a taste of my own medicine, or perhaps teach me how it feels to be jealous?

Not that I am jealous, of course. I know full well that what I'm having is just a fling. I make no claims on him, and neither does he on me. We are just friends, as Rafael puts it, *amigos*. We are both free.

And so, even when he thinks I am stroppy or difficult or stubborn about something and says, 'Just like all European women. Just like my wife,' I shrug my shoulders and laugh it off.

And, oddly, that's when, almost in the same breath, he swears that he loves me, that I am the woman of his life.

CHAPTER FIFTEEN

JAIME

One evening, I decided to assess my finances. This was something I didn't do very often, as I rarely had to break into my stash. My life being frugal, I spent only a few *quetzals* a day. That night, though, something prompted me to check the clear plastic envelope that, except for when I washed or went to bed at night, I guarded in the left cup of my bra, snuggled close to my heart.

And, lo and behold, one of the long sides of the envelope had been slashed. Of the one hundred and thirty US dollars it contained originally, only a bundle of one-dollar bills were scrunched up between lists and old addresses jotted down on scraps of paper. I counted them; there were only ten left.

I felt betrayed, devastated, and also sick with worry. What now?

I soon realised that leaving behind those few notes was not an act of kindness, but a delay tactic meant to cover up the theft.

Given that I was so rarely parted from my improvised wallet, my list of suspects dwindled rapidly to two: Rafael and his brother Jaime. Could one of them have crept up to the bamboo shelf by the bed and slashed the envelope I'd left on top of it? In the last ten days, I'd been sleeping over at Rafael's enough times for that to be possible.

At first, I thought the most likely culprit had to be Rafael, because in the last week or so Jaime had been away in Puerto Barrios. But why on earth would Rafael need to steal from me? After all, his father-in-law had lavished three thousand dollars on him just a couple of months before. Had Rafael made it all up? Given our liaison, I was willing to do all sorts of somersaults in my mind so that I didn't have to doubt him.

The money could have been stolen earlier, in which case, Jaime would be the rogue. Yes, that's it, that must have been what happened. The explanation sounded plausible and made me feel happier. Above all, it saved my faith in Rafael from being shattered, and kept alive our friendship.

This was my frame of mind when, bracing myself, I confronted Rafael about the missing dollars.

'Oh, Monica,' he said, looking first surprised, and then hurt, 'you don't think it's me, do you?'

He then put forward a number of possible scenarios.

'You've probably dropped the money on the beach, or perhaps you bent over at the fountain and the note slid out of your bra… It's easily done.'

In which case, wouldn't I have dropped the lot? None of this sounded convincing.

When I dared mention Jaime, he looked truly offended.

'My brother? Are you accusing him too? He needs to be told what to do, I know, that's why I shout at him, but he's a good kid, really. I guarantee for him. And anyway, he wasn't even here…'

That put an end to our discussion, but certainly not to my suspicions.

Jaime failed to appear for almost a week. When he did, he told a very complicated story. He was stopped and detained by the police in Puerto Barrios until a document check confirmed he'd completed his military service and was in the clear.

He proudly showed me a framed certificate with *Soldado Jaime Gonzalez Melquior* printed in large letters under a picture of himself in khakis with shorn hair and puffed red eyes. He hung it on the wall above his bed, blathering on about the army, the discipline, his many years of service.

In the meantime, proud as a peacock, he preened himself in front of a tiny mirror, getting ready for a night out.

Now on his wrist there was a new watch. 'One thousand metres waterproof, automatic, with an inbuilt alarm. Listen to this,' he'd boast, pressing a tiny button that turned on a carillon.

I asked Tomás, always abreast of the goings-on in town, to keep an eye on Jaime. He told me that, besides the watch, Jaime was sporting brand-new sunglasses, a pair of fancy trainers, and that night on the beach he'd spent a flurry of *quetzals* on drinks.

Anger welled up inside me.

In the street, whenever he caught sight of me, Jaime called out my name from the far distance. 'Monica! Monica!' He sounded cocky, as if he had a hold over me. I felt affronted, as if each time, sniggering up his sleeve, he might be boasting. *So, you think you're so smart, with your college education and your superior air. I fooled you, didn't I?*

I tried to ignore him, but there was no way I could avoid him. For months now, Jaime had been sleeping on and off under Rafael's roof.

It was no use feeling bitter. There was no time for self-pity. I was stuck in Livingston with ten dollars to my name.

'Come and live with me,' said Rafael. 'That'll save you paying the rent.'

I was grateful for the offer, but, feeling too proud, as well as too fond of my own freedom, I turned it down.

In the meantime, I told Mariangela and Giulia about my worries, and through them, rumours spread among the local hippy community.

One day, a lanky *viajero* called Alessandro approached me in the street.

'I hear you've been robbed. Bad luck, eh? But I have an idea,' he said, fixing his unblinking blue eyes on me in earnest. Then, he lowered his voice to a whisper. 'What if l gave you half a kilo of grass to sell around the village? No need to give me a cut of the profit. Not yet. You can pay me later.'

Beyond a doubt, that wasn't me. I pictured myself languishing in jail within a week. I declined politely.

A more legitimate suggestion came from Señor Gutierrez, one of the old men who sat on the street corner where Rafael lived. I met him at the telephone exchange where I was queuing to call my bank. We got into conversation. He was friendly and sympathetic, and I found myself pouring out my heart to him. He heard me out patiently.

'Why don't you start working as a language teacher?' he suggested encouragingly. 'You could teach English to the locals and Spanish to the tourists.'

It wasn't a bad idea. Sure, I wouldn't get rich, but the tuition would tide me over while Barclays took its time over my SOS.

I bought a dozen blank postcards. On each, I sketched out a bright green palm tree and, beneath it, a Garifuna man with dreadlocks playing a drum.

Wanting to learn Spanish and English in a Caribbean setting? Come to Livingston and enjoy the ambience. Experienced bilingual tutor. Lesson tailored to your specific needs. Contact Monica.

I did the rounds of all the cafés and restaurants. Next to each menu, I pinned one of my bright cards.

*

Teaching Spanish turned out to be an excellent idea. I had plenty of students. Most were people who, on passing through Livingston, fell under its spell and just like me, ended up staying longer than they had intended.

Among them was a recently qualified Swiss engineer on a world tour with a high-flying career waiting for him in Zurich; a dashing man from Texas on his way to entertain the *señoritas* of the Playa de las Mujeres in Mexico; a Japanese girl who had financed her travelling addiction by sporadic waitressing in Tokyo; a self-proclaimed libertarian socialist from Manhattan who turned up one day on my doorstep with a guitar slung across his back.

'Will it be okay just to have one or two lessons?' he asked. 'My return flight is next week.' Six months on and he was still joining me, true to the promises of my initial flier, under the same palm tree with the sound of the ocean in the background.

Every morning, I moved table and chairs out of my hut and positioned them so that both my students and I could see the comings and goings on the beach. We couldn't hope for a better source of inspiration.

On my first day of teaching, Rafael appeared about lunchtime carrying a plastic box under his arm. When out of it came a pasta dish he'd cooked for me at home, I was touched.

He fed me like this for three subsequent days, and then he stopped. 'What happened?' I asked him, more curious than upset over this change of heart.

On the third day, on the way to my place, he'd run into a friend. He immediately tried to hide the Tupperware he carried, but the appetising smell wafting from it gave him away.

'She's got you under her thumb, hasn't she?' the man teased him, sniffing the air. 'What will she get you to do next, eh?'

And that was the end of Rafael's lunchtime offerings.

CHAPTER SIXTEEN

MAMA JO'S NEW HOME

Next door to Rafael's place, in barrio Barrique, is a large ramshackle house with a tall, pointed roof of *manaca* leaves. It towers over Rafael's quaint little hut.

At seventy-eight, Mama Jo, Rafael's aunt, lives in this house, alone. Every morning, she gets up at six, picks up a large heavy pot of *atol*, a dozen glasses, another pot full of rinsing water and readies herself for what looks like a precariously wobbly descent. She takes her first tentative step, then, slowly and with uncanny steadiness, makes her way down the path to the street corner.

Her calves are as thin as matchsticks and her knees jut out as if they belong to a different set of legs. Yet, driven along by sheer stubbornness, in time she reaches the low stone wall where, every morning, day in and day out, for the last twenty years, she's been sitting selling *atol*.

There, she unfolds a clean white tea towel, and arranges her pots and glasses over it in a neat line. Once satisfied that all is ready, she places a cushion as flat as a *tortilla* over the wall and cautiously settles her large buttocks on the same spot where, in the evening, the old men loiter, talking in quiet voices as they scan the street.

'*Compre! Compre!*' she hollers as I come around the corner, and thrusts a creamy glass of sweet fermented rice in my direction. 'Buy glass *atol*, daaaalin... Only twenty-five cents.'

She knows a little English from when, decades earlier, the United Fruit Company played God along these coasts.

Tracing a giant question mark in the air with her long, thin arm, she points her chin at me. She wants to know where I'm about to go. '*Para allá...*' I answer. Or: '*Para aquí...*' and I point in some vague direction.

'Aha!' She nods, satisfied with our exchange of pleasantries and, no longer interested, she turns away.

I do not know whether she really needs the money from her *atol* sales.

'She keeps her *pisto* stashed away,' says Rafael. 'She's rich, you know? But, God, is she mean! She never lets go of her money. Does she think she can take it to her grave with her?'

Whatever her reasons, Mama Jo spends entire mornings sitting on those crumbling steps. She makes a few *centavos* and watches the world go by.

At around eleven, she collects her empty pots. They clink together as she walks back home, each step as slow and determined as when she followed the path down at dawn.

As she walks, she grumbles. She moans at the arthritis that is crippling her, at the dogs fouling the path, at the children chasing each other and getting in her way, at Rafael, who won't cut her front lawn or give her any free gasoline.

There is a permanent scowl on her face. She's toothless and her sunken jaws make her look slightly grotesque and menacing, like somebody you would want to avoid. But the grey pigtails escaping out of her chequered headscarf and the brightly coloured folds of her Garifuna dress belie all the grimness in her. The local children understand these things intuitively, and they turn her into the butt of all their jokes.

'Mama Jo! Mama Jo! Come on, catch us!' They tease her, scampering around her like a cloud of locusts. 'Come and get us!

See if you can!'

'*Niños safados!*' Her shrill voice rises over their taunts. 'Stop it, you hear me? Come and give me a hand. Here, take these pots over to my house. Now.'

Her voice is quivery, but the tone commands. She demands obedience and the children hasten to do as they're told.

At the beginning of January, I notice there's something different in Mama Jo. She's grumbling a little less. I even hear her laugh a couple of times. It's a spiteful little laugh that rises from the shallow depths of her throat, but laughter it is, nonetheless. Mama Jo is excited, you can tell.

She calls me over to her improvised *atol* stand and beckons me to sit on the steps next to her. 'Javier, my brother from los Estados Unidos, soon come.'

With her wrinkled hands, she smoothes the pleats of her red and green striped skirt, then she throws her arms up in the air and starts counting the days on her bony fingers.

'He come soon. *Día* twenty-six. Twenty-six *es un viernes*, right? *Bien*, twenty-four, *miércoles*, twenty-five, *jueves. Sí, pues*, twenty-six, *viernes! Sí*, he coming *viernes*. Friday, *pues*.' She chuckles and slaps the sides of her hips.

'What month?' I ask. 'Mmm, *febrero*, February,' she replies after careful consideration. Plenty of time for Mama Jo to savour her excitement.

'My house is old,' she says. 'One of these days it fall on top of me and bury me.'

That's where her younger brother, Javier, comes in.

He lives in New York, and every two years he comes for a brief visit. This time though, he is planning to stay longer – two, three, perhaps even four months.

'When he comes, he'll build me a new house.' Mama Jo's muddy eyes gleam.

The deal has been sealed in a hurried exchange of letters and, now, she's waiting.

One night, shortly after our conversation, a big woodworminfested beam falls from the roof of her house. The crash startles the entire neighbourhood out of their sleep. They all get up and run out into the street. Everyone, except for Mama Jo, who, undisturbed by the commotion, dreams on till morning. When she wakes up and sees the massive piece of timber lying on the kitchen floor, she screams:

'I knew one day it would happen! I knew it!' She sounds sort of satisfied.

'Tío Javier's going to be here soon!' chants Rafael. In his eyes, there's the same flicker of hope as in Mama Jo's. *See if this time I can squeeze some money out of the old man. After all, I'm the only son of his dead brother, an orphan. He should be nice to me.*

Where money is concerned, Rafael, the orphan, lives in eternal hope. Every Friday morning, he goes down to the harbour to play the lottery at the Wangs'. He stakes his last few *quetzals* on numbers 29, his age; 32, that of his wife; 41 and 59, his lucky numbers. He's feverish with excitement the whole day. At dinnertime, he's back in the shop. A little crowd stands around the radio, fired by the same hope. Then, the deep baritone of the announcer calls out: 'The winning numbers are – 55. Yes, 55. And then – 38. I repeat, 38. Next – 60! Yes, 60. The last one is – 45! 45! So, once more, this week's lucky numbers are: 55, 38, 60 and 45. Someone's struck lucky out there!'

That someone is never Rafael. He curses his rotten luck. But the following Friday, he's there again, playing the same numbers.

I have never been tempted to gamble, but not wanting to dash Rafael's hopes, I keep my misgivings to myself.

'*Suerte.* Good luck! I hope you hit the jackpot,' I shout to Rafael as he sets off, full of hope, to the Wangs'.

'Tío Javier has a house in Barrios,' he tells me, 'a big house of concrete blocks, on three floors. He also owns a house here in Labuga. And of course, there's the one in New York. The old man's loaded. *Este mi tío's* even got more *pisto* than you, Monica.'

'Oh, really?' I laugh. I'd like to add that being robbed has left me with a mere ten dollars in my pocket, but again, I keep schtum.

Every other family in Livingston has a relative in New York, Chicago, or Los Angeles, who sends them money to build solid, if ugly, dwellings. People all talk the same about these relatives: they boast their wealth, swell up with pride, and bask in the reflected glory of their success.

'I bet he'll take me back with him this time,' Rafael says, full of hope, most probably trying to convince himself. 'Would I go? Of course I'd go! Oh, me, oh, boy! I'd run for it. Working here for nothing, all these hours, for what? For a handful of *quetzals*, pffh. You know me. You know that I'm a hard worker, but I want to see results, real money! Over there, *allá*, I'd get a good steady job, a nice house, a radio, a TV, a nice electric stove, everything, even an indoor bathroom, so that every morning, I can get up and step right under my shower. Oh, that's life, not like here. I bet my uncle will fix me up with a job. You'll see. And he'll get me a visa. That man knows these things, he knows everything. He's a crafty fox!' Rafael says, full of hope.

On the last Friday of February, just as Mama Jo predicted, the midday ferry arrives, disgorging its passengers onto the jetty with Tío Javier and Mama Jo's new house or, rather, the materials needed to build it.

The demolition of the rickety old house begins in haste. With a scattering of palm leaves and splinters flying everywhere, three hefty men pull the house apart. New wooden boards are shipped over from Puerto Barrios. The truck drives to the site and unloads them into neat stacks. With handsaws and hammers, the men begin to build the house. Rafael is one of them, and for a few mornings he wakes up, rolls out of his hammock, opens the door and gets down to work at the site of the house-to-be, two steps away from his.

Now and then, Tío Javier comes to inspect the works. His arrival is always heralded by a wave of salsa.

As the music grows deafening, he makes his appearance around the corner: a tall athletic man in his mid-sixties. He walks like a young man in his immaculately tailored clothes – a powerful ghetto blaster vibrating under his arm. Am I the only one who feels the need to stop her ears? But yes, I look around and see everyone's carrying on unperturbed as usual.

Like King Midas, Tío Javier glitters in the sun, a little gold splashed here and there all over him. He wears a gold watch, a gold chain, a few gold rings, a pair of gold-rimmed spectacles. A gold tooth sparkles in his mouth. His shoes are beautifully polished and give him an extra shiny touch. He wears a small round straw hat, perched upright on his head.

From under his puffy eyelids, his sharp eyes scan the place for any sign of poor workmanship. He notices everything, from a badly hinged door to a missing screw.

'Hello,' he says cheerfully to everybody, sending me a casual glance through Rafael's half-open door. *Here we go, another white woman;* the shadow of that thought seeming to pass quickly over his face.

He throws another sweeping glance at me, then takes off almost immediately with his entourage of adoring relatives and "best" friends. They all live in the reflection of his glamour. The music machine does the rest.

His nephews, nieces, close and distant relations treat him like a king, pandering to his every whim in exchange for gifts of beer, food, items of clothing, a little money here and there. Then perhaps, one day…

Rafael follows him around like the rest. For the occasion, he pulls out the most pliable side of his personality and carries his uncle's ghetto blaster on his shoulders, rejoicing at the privilege like a child.

'The old man wants me to go out with him tonight,' he tells me as he jumps to his feet to oblige.

It's funny to see Rafael behave just like Jaime. This time, it's he who is the younger, therefore subordinate, relation. The tables have turned and now he finds himself at the receiving end. He accepts it unreservedly, keeping his grudges to himself and, occasionally, sharing them out with his closest friends.

'Let's see if this time I can scrounge some *pisto* off the tight bastard,' he confides to me. And off he goes, smiling and joking with the "tight bastard", in the hope of some reward.

He staggers back in the evening with a scowl.

'The old man is *chafa, codo*. I've never met anyone as tight as him. Can you believe it? He spent two hundred *quetzals* tonight in the bar. He bought drinks for everyone, including the barmaids. And me? What did he give me? Guess? NOTHING. Not a single penny. His pockets are sewn up well and good for me. I'm his dead brother's only son, and what does he do for me? Sweet fuck all.'

But the following day, when Tío Javier wants to be taken to the latest *fiesta* on the beach, Rafael is there first, offering his services and his protection in the crowd. Later, back in his hut, he complains to me about how tight the "old bastard" is. The same as ever. It goes on and on.

Rafael's cussing over his uncle makes me uneasy, and so does all this public arguing and fighting over money. It seems that, in this place, all human interactions – friendship, companionship, and even love – are measured in *quetzals*. Everything is reduced to money. It shocks me, but fascinates me too, and I do my best to understand why people act like they do. It must be necessity that makes them so materialistic, pragmatic, and unromantic. For them, it's a matter of survival, I guess. As for me, I feel uncomfortable and different from everyone else here, quite different from the Italian sisters too, who never mention this sort of problem and seem to get along fine with everyone.

Meanwhile, the new wooden house is coming along with unusual speed. It stands there almost ready, its four walls of light-coloured wood, the internal support beams. Only the metal roof and the windows are missing. But soon, '*soon come,*' says Mama Jo. It's going to be a nice-looking cottage well worth the wait.

That's when all the trouble starts.

Having waited so long for her new home, Mama Jo is determined to have a whole new home. No half measures. She gets the men to discard all the boards from the old house, even those that are in good condition and could be used again. They lie there to one side, getting soaked through in the heavy afternoon rain.

'With that wood I'm going to build a latrine in the backyard,' Rafael quickly thinks. 'At long last, I'll have a toilet.'

The idea is good, but it happens to be miles away from what Mama Jo has already plotted. She wants to sell the wood and earn some extra cash, and she won't give up her plan, no, not over her dead body.

'Selfish, mean old bag!' Rafael rails at her.

'Lazy bum. Good-for-nothing!' she retorts.

The argument gets worse and more virulent each day, but neither of them is prepared to budge.

By this time, Rafael is no longer working on the house, busy as he is entertaining and living it up with the "tight bastard".

'Today I'm going to Puerto Barrios,' he announces to me one morning. 'The men need more material for the house, and my uncle has asked me to go and fetch it. I'll be back tonight with the last boat.' Then, 'Wait for me, *mi amor*,' he adds with a wink. 'For dinner, I'll make you the best fish soup you've ever had, I promise.'

He preens himself in his best clothes and leaves, euphoric.

Rafael is famous for his soup. He adds grated coconut to it, and some secret ingredient he hasn't so far told me about. In short, it's well worth waiting for. That night, full of anticipation, I make my way to the pier.

I watch the passengers get off the boat, lugging their bags and heavy bundles onto the quay; I watch them disembark, at length, all of them, to the last one. Then I watch the porters unload the cargo out of the hold. I wait a little longer, just in case… But there's no sign of Rafael. Nor does he get off the following ferry in the morning, or the one after that. He's gone, disappeared.

Three days later, I'm in my beach hut, writing my latest entry in my notebook, when he stumbles in through the front door.

'*Mami*,' he says, full of elation, 'give us a kiss!' His breath smells heavily of liquor and his lips touch mine vaguely and inconclusively, as if they did not quite know where they were or had been.

'I've made a big mistake, *mami*.' The expression on his face changes to serious, genuine contrition. 'This time, I've put my foot right in. I am an ass.'

He pauses to place another soppy kiss on me.

'Yes, *mami*, I did a stupid thing. You know the forty *quetzals* that mean old bastard gave me for the timber? It's all gone, I've spent it.'

'How?' I look at him in disbelief. 'Not on booze… Forty *quetzals?*'

'Yeah, that's what I did, I drank it. I did it out of spite. I hate the old woman. Selling all that wood instead of letting me build a latrine for us! *Chafa!* Shame on her.'

And off he goes to spend the last few notes – a long-legged, V-chested silhouette staggering drunkenly along the path.

Is there any way of stopping him? I wonder. I doubt it; he seems so determined to take revenge on his aunt. I leave him to it, resigned.

The following day, as I walk by, there's no visible activity going on at Mama Jo's. No building, no timber, no boards. The work has stopped. I go past the half-finished structure, down the alley to Rafael's hut. I call him. No answer. The door is open, though. I go in and sit at the table. Where's everyone?

An hour later, Rafael walks in and throws himself into his hammock.

'What's up?'

He responds with a smile and a vague gesture, indicating he's in no mood to talk. He lies there, rocking himself quietly, the stillness of the afternoon interrupted only by the creaking of the beams and the swishing of the hammock.

Swish… melancholic hang-over waves… swish… of the day after… swish …

Just then, Tío Javier bursts in. 'Where's the wood?' he shouts, snipping the fragile yarn of togetherness Rafael has most likely been weaving inside his head for the last few hours.

'And the forty *quetzals* I gave you? Where are they?' Tío Javier insists.

No answer comes from the hammock. Not a word. It rocks and rocks. No need to enquire further. Tío Javier leaves in a huff.

I should leave too. What am I doing here pandering to Rafael's every whim?

I'm at the door, about to push it open, when from the hammock comes a mellow voice.

'*Mi amor!*' he says, packing all the charm he's capable of into those two short words.

How can this be the same man who drank away his uncle's money, the man who cusses him whenever he can?

'*Mamacita linda!* Please come here!' he pleads.

I turn and look at him. That inviting, seductive gaze of his makes it so hard to say no to him.

I close the door and go to join him in the hammock.

*

A few days later, we're having dinner by the light of a hurricane lamp, when there's a heavy downpour. The lashing rain takes to hammering the leafy roof with such a vengeance that any attempt at conversation is vain.

A tall figure appears silhouetted in the doorframe.

'Damn rain! It's just caught me halfway home,' says Tío Javier, rushing in to take shelter. 'I'm soaked!'

As soon as he sees his uncle, Rafael jumps to his feet. Then, displaying all the contrition and deference he's capable of, he pulls out the comfiest chair he owns and rushes to serve him a bowl of fish soup and a plate heaped with rice.

Tío Javier stares blankly at him, ignores the chair, and comes to sit by my side. Whatever he's going to say next, clearly, he wants to make me complicit.

'What part of the States are you from?'

I tell him I'm not American nor have I ever been to the States. 'Oh, you are not American. Strange, you look American.'

I watch him handle a piece of juicy fish. He picks it up and turns it daintily with his fingertips, careful not to soil his hands with the fat. His rings and gold watch sparkle as he bends forward to study my face by the candle flame.

'I live in Brooklyn, New York,' he says.

'And you like it there?'

'It's a heavy, aggressive and brutal world,' he replies. 'There is so much violence everywhere.'

I look at him anew, waiting for more. He doesn't elaborate, merely pulls a face. At length, he continues.

'Soon I'll retire, and then I'll come back and live here, with my own people.'

After a pause, he adds, 'Tell me, do you know why the Americans are so worried about Russia?'

I shake my head, at a loss.

He continues: 'The government is spending so much on weapons, but what are these weapons for, if the ordinary man is afraid of walking the streets? It's the same all over. The people of any country are always last on the list. Why don't they create jobs for people so that instead of stealing they'll be able to earn an honest living for themselves? Tell me, do you know if in Russia one can walk the streets in peace, without the risk of being mugged or killed?'

He scoops up the last of the soup and looks around. Rafael dutifully leaps to his feet, ready with a bowl of clean water and a clean towel. He keeps on standing there to attention until the older man has finished drying his hands.

Without making eye contact, Tío Javier contemptuously hands the used towel back to him.

And with that, he leaves, muttering to himself about the new generation who can't be trusted.

Shortly after that visit, Rafael is reinstated among the throngs of his uncle's adoring fans. All is forgotten; case closed.

Mama Jo, though, is a different kettle of fish.

'You liar! You thief! That's what you are, a lousy thief! A good-for-nothing! How long can you hold down a job, eh? Come on, tell me! Two days? Three? You lazy bum! To make a living, it's much easier to steal, eh? You scum bag! You rogue!' She won't let up.

By the time she's finished, the entire neighbourhood knows about the missing timber, even strangers passing by, in fact, anyone who has the misfortune to linger long enough to hear her out.

Rafael closes up like a clam. He lets her rattle on, to her satisfaction. When she's finished, a cold war begins. Full of contempt, she turns away in a huff when he walks past. He growls a string of sarcastic abuse whenever she wobbles past his front door on her way to empty her chamber pot right there, at the back of his house.

The stand-off doesn't let up.

'We are like that. I won't talk to her, she won't talk to me. We are both hard and stubborn,' Rafael explains. 'But I'm here for her, and she knows it. If she's taken ill, I'm the one who'll look after her.'

On the first day of April, as I watch the comings and goings from next door, Mama Jo moves into her new home.

CHAPTER SEVENTEEN

THE CHUGU

I walked along the beach in the darkness, Mariangela, Manu and Giulia ahead of me. We threaded our way through rocks, logs and other debris scattered on the shingle. The inky ocean breathed in and out, its surface unbroken by the waves.

The clouds rolled back and a quarter moon appeared, casting a shimmering beam of light over the water and throwing the jungle into relief. All around was the high-pitched drone of the cicadas.

We walked in single file, silent, the sand hard and compact under our feet. Whenever a palm tree arched out towards the sea, we made a wide circle around it and splashed noisily in the surf.

In the half-light, I could make out the silhouette of Manu leading the way, hands in his pockets. Mariangela followed, barefoot, Panama hat firmly in place, sandals dangling from her knapsack. Having stopped to untangle her calf-length skirt from a thorny bush, Giulia lagged a few steps behind. I was last. I walked slowly, at some distance from the rest, breathing in the balmy night.

It was close to midnight, and we'd been walking for what felt like hours.

It was Rafael's idea that we should meet at the *chugu*. He'd left a few hours earlier with Tío Javier and his entourage. On his shoulders, he carried the old man's ghetto blaster. Half lackey, half bodyguard, he beamed with pride.

'A… *chugu*? What's that?' I'd asked him earlier.

'A three-day *fiesta* for our ancestors. Come and see, if you want to know more. This is the last night…' he said invitingly. And, as the sun plunged into the sea, he disappeared along the beach.

Later, I met Tomás and, dying to know more, I asked him about the *chugu* and whether he'd be there.

'Me, coming? No way, that's not my thing. All that mumbo jumbo, that voodoo stuff. Nah!' And then, with a hint of mockery, he added, 'But you guys should go. You're going to love it. All foreigners go crazy for that kind of shit.'

That was Tomás. As for me, I'd been dying to learn about that "kind of shit" since the day when, while swimming with Mariangela in the Río Quehueche we'd come around a bend, and on a knoll, half-hidden by a clump of trees, I'd caught a glimpse of some thatched huts in the far distance.

'That place is haunted,' said Mariangela, staring at the white-hot sky as she floated on her back. 'That's what they say in town. We've been told to keep away… Woooo! Spooky…' She laughed.

The warning made it seem, if anything, more alluring. My imagination began to run wild, and so did Mariangela's.

Then, out of the blue, this last-minute invitation.

I told Mariangela about it and she brought along Manu and Giulia.

And here we were, in the middle of the night, all wired up, walking between the ocean and the jungle.

The town was far away now. Even the most isolated dwellings of the fishermen, the furthest farms and boat sheds, were nowhere in sight.

'See that star to the left above those trees? Look down from it. There's a rock there, hanging over the sea. Can you see it?' Manu indicated a remote point along the coast that, however much we strained our eyes, the three of us couldn't see. 'Right there, behind that corner, there's Belize.'

'Is that where we're going?' Mariangela enquired, alarmed.

'*Claro que no.*' He laughed. 'Don't worry, we're almost there.' But he kept on walking.

A little further down the beach, he took a sharp turn into the jungle. In the moonlight, the path shone white and sandy for a few yards, then turned into a trail scattered with squelchy leaves and choked by overhanging trees. Despite the darkness, Manu stepped through the undergrowth, sure-footed, clearing the way.

All around us, the forest came alive – piercing shrieks, trills and shrills, squeaks and flutters and, far in the distance, deep grunts and growls. When Mariangela pulled a torch out of her knapsack and shone it on the trail in front of us, there was scurrying and scattering, a rustling of leaves. We followed each other closely and dared not look around.

Manu stopped and shushed us.

'Hear that?' he whispered.

We heard nothing but the noises of nocturnal creatures going about their lives. A little later, though, from a long way away, came the muffled pounding of some drums. As we walked on, the sound became louder, more persistent, until, in a crescendo, it turned into a paroxysm of drumbeats. Suddenly it stopped, and all we could hear was a distant muttering of voices, laughter and the faint strumming of a guitar.

Ahead of us, light glimmered through the trees.

Passing a thick clump of sycamores, we came to a clearing. At the edge of it, like sentries guarding an invisible gate, were two old men seated on tree stumps.

'*Hola, Manu! Hola, muchachas!*' They greeted us with rasping voices. '*Qué tal con ustedes? Cómo andan?*'

We walked into the open. There, in the soft amber light cast by dozens of kerosene lamps hanging from the trees, scores of people stood around in small clusters.

I recognised only a few faces, but everyone seemed to know us.

'Hi there,' a white-haired man shouted to me. 'You're Rafael's *nummari*. He's about somewhere. I was talking to him just minutes ago.'

Rafael's *nummari,* his woman. Here and now, the word had a pleasing ring to it. I didn't contradict him.

I looked around, trying to spot Rafael. Some of the men had been drinking, but no one was rowdy or boisterous, as when partying in town. There were no brawls, no shouting. People chatted amicably, at ease.

Four huts rose across the clearing: a large rectangular one with many doors and a *manaca* roof sloping down to the ground; an open storage area – a thatched roof on wooden posts, cluttered with boxes, crates and wicker baskets; a smoky kitchen, where, through an open window, I could see half a dozen women chopping, dicing and slicing vegetables, stirring huge pots and gutting fish. The fourth hut rose at a distance and was completely sealed off. Under its sloping eaves, a spider's web of string hammocks stretched around the four sides.

Most people there were women, mainly old or middle-aged. They wore headscarves tied into large knots at the nape, and their traditional frocks. But tonight, there was something different about them. I couldn't quite put my finger on it, but something was missing... It finally clicked. The usual vivid colours – the crimsons, emerald greens and turquoise blues of all Garifuna garments – were nowhere in sight. Everywhere I looked I saw dull shades of beige and grey, like in an old sepia film. Still, the atmosphere was festive, and everyone appeared relaxed.

'Hey, girls!' A few old men waved to us from behind a waist-high oil drum.

'Try this!' One of them approached us with a hollowed-out coconut shell filled to the brim with a clouded liquid. 'It's *leche de yuca*, manioc milk. It's homemade, it's good stuff.' He smacked his lips.

I took a cautious swig. It was smooth and sweet and tasted like coconut water. I handed it over to Mariangela and Giulia.

Within minutes, we looked at each other, eyes watering and throats on fire.

'Strong stuff eh?' A chorus of guffaws rose all around.

Nearby, a group of women had improvised an oven out of a large cylinder and a metal sheet; they were now piling hot cinders on top of it.

I recognised Armando's mother, one of our *mara* friends. She recognised us too.

'Great to see you, girls!' she said cheerfully. Then, she sighed. 'If only you'd convinced my son to come along too! But no, he thinks this has got nothing to do with him! The ancestors, the *chugu*, all rubbish, he says. The only thing he cares about is having fun, *pues*.'

Fun was precisely what people seemed to be having here. All around me, men and women flirted and parried each other's quick-fire repartee. The whole clearing echoed with their laughter.

I was disappointed. I'd hoped for something new, surprising, or something out of the ordinary, at least. Instead… this. Why on earth was everyone so secretive about this "*chugu*" thing, if it was, as it seemed, just a big family party?

There was Rafael. Astride a fallen trunk, he was chatting in tight Garifuna with a couple of old men. I watched him from a distance as he joked with them, totally at ease. He was so different from the Tomáses, the Armandos and the other young men I knew in Labuga. Whereas they spent most of their time daydreaming about the latest Nikes and the coolest rap lyrics, Rafael embraced tradition. 'A simple local man, that's what I am,' he said, 'an all-out *hombre sencillo*.' From the very first, that's what had made him so attractive to me, besides, of course, his looks.

'*Mi amor!*' He called me over. At his feet was Tío Javier's ghetto blaster playing some *soca* tune. 'The old man's gone to sleep.' He pointed to the hut festooned with hammocks. 'He's left me with this to look after, see?' He grinned and turned up the volume.

But just as his music soared to the sky, a roll of drums drowned it. Around us, the chatting died down, and people filed into the largest of the huts.

Good – at long last, something **was** about to happen.

The two sisters and I looked expectantly at each another and followed on. But, on the threshold, held back by something – a sense of awe, or, perhaps, people's ominous silence – we stopped and, feeling like trespassers, we stood hovering by the door.

About twenty women stood facing the three drummers, all men. As they began to play, the women arranged themselves in rows and, hand in hand, started singing and dancing – one step forward, another one back, then, an identical step to the side, shoulders loose and bodies swaying gently to the beat.

The other men kept to the sides, watching, except for one, an old guy in a trilby and a pair of mirrored sunglasses that, in the semi-darkness, had no use other than marking him out from the crowd. Tall and inscrutable, he stood next to the drummers with a gourd in his hands. From time to time, he shook it and the room filled with the sound of surf whooshing over a pebbly beach.

Slow and hypnotic, at first barely louder than a murmur, the singing weaved in and out of the beat. Now and then, a high-pitched voice would soar loud and clear over the drums, followed by an outburst of plaintive voices.

'They're singing about the island of St Vincent, our homeland,' Rafael whispered into my ear, 'about our ancestors sailing across the ocean and risking their lives to come here.'

At a nod from the old man, the musicians sprang to their feet. Then, drums slung over their shoulders, still playing, they followed him around the room.

'See that guy?' Rafael lifted his chin in the direction of the old man. 'He's our *bujey*, our go-between with our ancestors. He's very powerful. He can cure people or make them ill.'

The dancers followed the four men around the room, moving backwards, then forward, to the left, then to the right, always facing them.

The *bujey* finally stopped. He shook his gourd in an upward motion, while the three musicians hit the hell out of their drums.

'They're waking the spirits of the dead,' explained Rafael, under his breath, 'the *bujey* with the shaker, and the drummers with the drumbeat.'

A lapsed Catholic, I was sceptical about God, or in fact any religion, including the existence of a hereafter. But now I was in the middle of the jungle and the music played on, soporific and hypnotic. With my eyes closed and my mind empty, I started swaying to the rhythm of the song...

'See that?' Rafael's raised voice shook me out of my daze.

In the far corner, a woman was flailing her arms about and tearing off her headscarf. Grey plaits cascading over her shoulders, she twirled across the floor, bumping into the other dancers and disturbing the neatness of the rows.

'That's the ancestor taking hold of her!'

Each time the woman broke into a delirium of leaps and bounds, the men slapped the skins of their drums harder. Arms raised high above their heads, elbows spread out to the sides, they sped up their tempo, spurred by the vigour of her dance.

'Sometimes, the woman talks and acts like a man.' Rafael put on a deep voice and laughed. 'Some swear like drunken sailors or demand to smoke big, fat cigars. Once, a woman I knew knocked down two full bottles of Venado, and when she came around, *púchica!* She was as sober as a judge! It was the ancestor, his spirit, who'd drunk all the rum.'

Would I witness something as dramatic? But, no, luck was not on my side tonight – the spirits seemed determined to behave.

The excitement soon died down. The drummers returned to their original positions, the woman stopped leaping and, wiping the sweat off her forehead, she quietly re-joined her line. Five minutes later, when the music stopped, the *bujey* walked across the room, swinging a smoky can, and the air filled with the scent of wild herbs.

'Happy?' Rafael turned towards me with a boyish grin. 'Now you know all about us Garifunas, our songs, our ways...' His eyes sparkled with mischief.

'Hey, *nati*,' Manu called out to him, 'what about a drop of *leche de yuca*? C'mon, man, let's go and celebrate!' They left us there and went out, laughing.

After refreshments, and with the addition of a guitarist, the three drummers were now ready to play for fun.

'Come on, girls, time to dance!' We were dragged by the arms onto the dance floor by a group of women. We had no choice but to imitate their shuffling steps. Soon, as the music changed to an upbeat lively tempo, I found myself having as much fun as any night at the Lugudi Barana.

By two in the morning, most people were drunk. Some talked loudly, slurring their words, while others, arms wrapped around each other, swore oaths of eternal friendship, and others still staggered across the clearing, lips glued to their rum bottles.

'*Mi amor!*' Rafael called out to me in a garbled voice. He stood on unsteady legs by the hut festooned with hammocks. Most of them were now occupied by sleeping bodies, but in the end, we found an empty one, climbed into it and tossed and turned until we managed a snug fit between my shoulders and his arms, my legs and his back, my neck and his chest.

But sleep wouldn't come. I lay there, going over the night's events – the dancing ritual, that old woman... Could all that leaping be truly the work of a long-dead ancestor? Was she really in a trance or was she faking it? Did those people really believe a spirit had taken hold of her? Was it a case of collective self-delusion? It didn't matter anyway. The main thing was that it felt so good to be there. All night, people had been open and friendly, making me feel one of them, at last.

'*Muchas gracias, pues*,' I whispered to Rafael and, realising he was already fast asleep, I planted a kiss on his shoulder.

Tiredness crept over me, blurring all thoughts. Curled up in the hammock, I heard the ebb and flow of the music die away in the distance. My eyelids felt heavy, so heavy...

A sandy beach stretches out in front of me. I smell the ocean. I hear it breathing in and out. I walk into the water, on and on, until my feet no longer touch the bottom, then I begin to swim. The water is deep, bottle green, warm. I duck in and out; each stroke thrusts me forward, smooth and weightless like a jellyfish. Free.

But the sun disappears, and the water grows colder. It swells in large waves. It sucks me far out, away from the land. I'm scared. I swim against the tide now. The swell tosses me up and down, like a rag doll. Where's the sky? I only see leaden angry waters, roaring breakers, foaming and surging in every direction.

A dugout canoe with three men on board appears in the distance, its maroon sails billowing in the wind. I recognise the man with the shock of white hair, the one who, earlier, called me Rafael's *nummari*.

He's so close, now, that I can see his magnificent eyebrows, bushy and white against his sunburnt face… then, his features fade and in front of me there's my mother. She smiles at me.

I smile back and stretch out an arm to lift myself over the edge onto the boat. But a breaker hits me hard. I lose my grip and plunge into the swelling waters… I swim back to the boat but, damn it! The current pulls me away… *Mum!* I shout. *Wait for me!* But the sea drags me away, further and further…

Leaning precariously over the side of the canoe, my mother scans the waters in search of me, a look of terror on her face. *Aaargh!* she cries out…

I woke up with a start and realised the cry had come from me. Squeezed between Rafael's shoulders and the bamboo wall, my cheek pressed against the rough canvas, I was hot and sweaty, and tears streamed down my cheeks.

I struggled out of the hammock, leaving Rafael mumbling in his sleep.

I'd eaten nothing throughout the night and my stomach was rumbling. I headed for the kitchen looking for some food. But there was nothing left, not even a bread cake.

Resigned to go hungry, I was about to leave, when Armando's mother appeared at my side.

'You look rough, girl,' she said. 'This will do you good,' and she handed me a cup of chicory coffee.

It was very hot and with far too much sugar, but I drank it all in one gulp.

'How did you like the *chugu*?' she asked, her eyes bright with curiosity.

'Good, yeah, interesting…' I mumbled diffidently, reluctant to express my reservations. 'Not that I understood much…'

'What's there to understand?' She laughed. 'It's a *fiesta*, it's how we honour our ancestors. It took a whole year to organise this one. People have come from all over, from Belize and even from the States…'

I thought of Tío Javier, who had travelled from New York.

She continued: 'People from the same family all chip in with money, food, and their time… This way, the family grows stronger. The *chugu* reminds us Garifunas where we come from, who we are…'

I stood there, by the door, hanging on her every word as I gulped down one cup of syrupy coffee after the other. I found myself envying her. It must be nice to feel such a strong bond with your ancestors, to know your roots, to feel the thread of continuity that links the present with the past… Then, proud of your identity, just like Emilio, you could go around proclaiming '*Ubafu lu Labuga!*' to everyone.

The unease that had lingered in my head after the dream quickly faded.

All around, people were packing up. In the uncertain light of dawn, the grey slowly turned into the reds, the golden yellows, the greens and the magentas of the hammocks being folded, of the chequered tablecloths wrapped over the wicker baskets, of the trees and the flowers. As if by magic, the brightness of the entire palette reappeared. Everything shone bright in the first sunrays against the verdant lushness of the jungle.

People were nearly ready to go now. In the kitchen, the women finished tidying up, one last bottle of Venado doing the rounds as they laughed and patted each other on the back. The men did the heavier work around the clearing. Two long wooden boats had come to pick up the crates, the crockery, the pots and pans, and those who were either too tired or too old to walk. The others would have to make their own way back.

'You'd better go, *mi amor.*' Rafael appeared, stretching and yawning by my side. 'I want to be here for my uncle when he wakes up.'

I left him there, standing to attention, ghetto blaster at his feet, and I went to rejoin Manu and the two sisters. We set off along the beach, last in a long line.

It was seven in the morning and the sun shone scorching hot over the coast. To the left, gliding over the choppy waves, one of the rowing boats caught up with us. From a distance, I could make out the *bujey*'s trilby. The sun flashed across his mirrored glasses. Someone waved to us, and we waved back. The boat moved fast, much faster than us. It overtook us with the least effort and in no time, it was gone.

*

The next day, I go to the *pila*.

There are four sets of these wash basins in town. They are made of concrete and have roofs of corrugated iron supported at each corner by solid pillars.

The largest, and the most popular, is a stone's throw away from the pier, hidden behind some tall bushes of *carnavel* that are always in full bloom.

At the top end, there's a freshwater tap. It's the fountain Mariangela told me about the day we met. 'Drink from it, and you'll stay here forever,' she said. I take up the challenge, and this is where, despite the distance, I like to come and collect my drinking water.

The place is always busy because the women – Garifunas, Ladinas and coolies alike – not only come here to do their laundry and get their water but also to meet and chat.

Today is no exception – I join the queue waiting at the tap.

There are women of all ages, each at her basin, bashing and crushing and wringing and kneading rebellious clouds of sheets and tall piles of clothing. Most of them are big and strong, with plump, muscular arms and huge breasts that shake in the effort. After lathering each item, they scatter them, still soapy, over the nearby lawn and leave them in the sun to bleach. They joke and laugh but never stop working. It's early morning but it's already hot, and although their arms are deep in water, they're covered in sweat.

In the far corner, a big, tall woman in, at a guess, her mid-sixties suddenly strips down to her waist. Mesmerised, I watch her pour bowl after bowl of water over her matronly breasts. 'Hiuuuh!' she screams, delighted, and everyone laughs.

'So, you're Rafael's girlfriend.'

I turn to look at the woman behind me. I'm not a hundred per cent sure that she's the one who spoke. The woman is short and light-skinned, and she, alone in the crowd of women busy chatting with each other, smiles at me. I don't recognise her.

I pause. 'I'm his friend, yes,' and I smile back.

'You're friends with Manu and Daniel's women too, aren't you? The Italian sisters?'

I can't work out what she's after, but there's no mistaking the sarcasm in her voice.

'Yeah…' I hesitate. 'That's right. They're my friends.'

She laughs. A long pause follows, when neither of us, it seems, can think of what to say.

'I feel sorry for you white girls,' she blurts out at length, and all the while she smiles.

'These guys you go for,' she rolls her eyes, 'handsome *varones*, *pues*. They know a hundred different ways to flatter a woman. But…' she pauses for effect '…what a bunch of lazy bastards! Not a single day's honest work between them… I feel *so* sorry for you girls. None of us would want anything to do with them, however nice they look.'

Overwhelmed by the onslaught, I stare at her. At first, I wonder whether she means well. Might this be a friendly warning? It takes some time before my anger sets in.

What's she trying to say? My love life is none of her business. I'm tempted to have it out with her. But things get easily out of control in Labuga. Do I really want to make a scene? What's more, at the *pila*, in front of everyone? In my head, I can just picture the pair of us screaming like two fishwives as we pull at each other's hair.

Luckily, it's my turn at the tap. With an awkward smile, I go and busy myself with the bottles. When I leave, the woman is still standing there, her eyes on me, grinning.

PART
THREE

CHAPTER EIGHTEEN

THE ITALIAN SISTERS

MARIANGELA

On leaving the house in Nebagó, the Italian sisters and I had promised each other we'd regularly keep in touch. But then, partly because of the distance that separated us, and partly because each of us was caught up in a new life, new chores and a new relationship, we ended up meeting only every now and then.

However infrequent, those encounters were important to me.

When we met, the three of us compared notes, exchanged juicy details and learnt a lot about the village and the men we lived with.

The one sister I saw most frequently was Mariangela, as she lived the closer of the two.

We waited for each other on the beach, where the Quehueche ran into the ocean, and went for leisurely swims up its winding banks, covering each time longer stretches.

Wide and murky green, the river bent like an arm at the elbow around a thick wall of mangroves. The water was always warm. We plunged eagerly into the shallow estuary, then, with slow and drowsy breaststrokes, we swam against the current, careful to avoid the weeds and the silt that floated on the surface after the heavy rains. We did not dare to rest our feet on the slimy bottom but kept swimming until we were exhausted. After a bend in the river, as we reached a hill of bright green ferns to our right, we scrambled up the slippery bank, then up the hill. There, hidden by a clump of trees, on a knoll overlooking the arch of the bay, stood the three thatched huts that, not so long ago, had fired our imagination. We'd since discovered it was an old ceremonial site now fallen into disuse, and this we found even more intriguing.

The place was totally deserted. We took off our bathing suits and draped them over the bushes. Then, stark naked, we lay on the grass, closed our eyes and, without a thought for the ancestral spirits who might take offense at our nudity, we enjoyed the warmth of the sun on our skin.

'Here we are, safe and sound once again. No perilous encounters,' said Mariangela, relieved.

People always warned us against the sharks, *pirañas* and alligators that allegedly lived in the river. We shrugged our shoulders and laughed it off; yet, from the look of relief we always exchanged as we trudged ashore, I could tell that neither of us were immune to these local beliefs.

Mariangela lay on her back, legs bent, a hand caressing her belly.

'I'd be in my fifth month, if things had gone right,' she whispered.

I glanced at her flat stomach, and then quickly looked away.

After an eleven-week pregnancy, Mariangela had suffered a miscarriage and lost her child.

She took the loss with dignity, without complaining, seemingly getting over it quickly. But soon after that, she began to lose weight.

'That girl is not well,' people began to whisper. 'She was so lovely and chubby when she first arrived. She had nice round hips, big buttocks, sturdy legs… Look at her now! Does she eat enough?' And they blamed Manu for not looking after her properly.

Mariangela claimed to be happy with him. They'd set up home

in the bush, away from – they never tired of repeating – people's jealousy and prying eyes. It took them over an hour to get to the village, as they had to wade through the Quehueche, cross some swampy land and then follow the beach to its very end.

If their existence was basic, it was also completely free, and this seemed to suit Mariangela to a tee. Barefoot and in rags, she brandished her machete with the nonchalance of a Western woman using a vacuum cleaner or washing machine. Every day, she collected and chopped firewood, cleaned and filleted the fish, fried it on the open fire, washed piles of clothes in the river and then made elaborate Garifuna dishes for Manu. She even taught herself to make coconut oil and started a small production for local sale.

During her pregnancy, she'd slowed down, of course, and spent more time in her hammock chatting with friends. Later, when it became clear she wasn't expecting, she reverted to her old self with renewed energy. This time, she said, she was determined to reorganise not only her own life but also Manu's.

First, she got a canoe and some tackle for him to go fishing. Then, she bought the legal titles to the piece of land where they lived. It was a lovely plot by the ocean that bordered on one side the Quehueche, and, on the other, the property of a rich man from the capital who hardly ever came to stay.

Over these grounds, on a hillock, Manu and Mariangela began to build their new home. Together, they cut the cane, tied up the reeds and lined the roof beams with *manaca* leaves. Soon the hut was ready: a thatched bungalow on stilts, with a veranda for hanging hammocks and a perilous flight of wooden planks running up to it. The kitchen was below the upper floor, with chest-high cane partitions sheltering a rusty gas stove from the wind blowing in from the sea. Although the new home had as few comforts as the one before, it offered a splendid view over the bay and the most wonderful sunsets I'd ever seen.

'I never tire of watching the sky,' Mariangela said to me, shooing away a couple of chickens that had wandered in to peck at the crumbs of our lunch. 'Out here, with no people around, no other houses, nature feels so much closer.'

Despite her recent problems, it was the happiest I'd ever seen her.

*

I was about to leave my house one night when I heard Mariangela call out my name.

Although it wasn't pitch-black yet, it struck me as odd for her to be coming this way at that late hour.

In the gathering darkness, I could just make out her silhouette walking rapidly along the path, the white oval of her face framed by her tangled hair.

As she got closer, I saw she was crying; cheeks, mouth and eyes screwed up; a smudge across the ridge of her nose. She wore a skimpy yellow dress, no shoes. Her sturdy suntanned legs were covered with scratches; so were her arms that hung loose at her sides.

'What's the matter?'

Her crying was louder now. Putting an arm around her shoulders, I gently led her into my house, made her sit down, and gave her a glass of water.

'H... have... y...y... you seen him?' she stammered in between the sobs. 'He... he's gone to the police!'

'Who's gone to the police? Do you mean Manu?'

'Yes, Manu. Who else? Look at this.' She placed a muddy finger behind her upper front teeth. With horror, I saw them move back and forth, under the slight pressure.

'He hit me,' she sobbed.

'He did what?' It wasn't difficult to imagine other guys being violent, but sweet, gentle Manu of all people... 'What happened?'

Right in front of one of those spectacular sunsets, they had squabbled over something as trivial as the sugar supplies for the week.

'It's your turn to go into town.'

'No way, it's yours. I went last week.'

In no time, it seems, the disagreement had turned into a full-scale row. Manu had been drinking.

'I won't let you turn me into your slave. Oh, no, not in a million years!' he shouted.

'Oh, yeah! More like I'm *your* slave…'

'There was a glint of madness in his eyes and I got frightened.' She paused to rinse her mouth with a sip of water.

'I knew I had to leave, and quickly,' she continued, while staring with alarm at her bloodstained spittle. 'I rushed through the hut collecting my things and threw them into a wicker basket. But he kicked it over and with all his bulk he blocked the doorway. That's when I lost my head and made a big mistake.'

There was another pause and then her voice went down to a whisper.

'I keep a bundle of notes stashed among the leaves of the thatch roof. No one knows my hiding place, and certainly not Manu. It's a perfect safe. Tonight, in my state of panic, I forgot all precautions and just reached for it. He saw me, of course, and grabbed the money from me. "Give it back or I'll call the police," I threatened him. That made him even more furious. He knocked me to the ground and kicked me hard in the mouth. The bastard! I'll probably lose my teeth now and look old and haggard like so many women here.' She burst into tears again.

It shocked me to hear about all this violence. Money, once again, seemed to be the central issue in Labuga, reminding me of the time when my own hundred dollars had disappeared.

I tried to convince Mariangela to rest on my bed, but she refused.

'I must stop him before he does something crazy. As he pushed and kicked me along the beach, he kept shouting he'll go to the police before I do.'

'What for? To give himself in? C'mon, Mariangela, you know he won't.'

But it was no use. She wouldn't listen. In the end, we walked into town together.

Just then, looking radiant in a long purple skirt and her hair neatly combed into a bun, her sister came forward in the opposite direction.

From afar, she greeted us with a great flailing of arms, but, as she got closer, the smile vanished from her face.

'Why are you crying?' she asked, alarmed.

She heard the whole story without flinching, then examined Mariangela's teeth and howled: 'Where's the bastard? Where's he gone? Just wait until I lay hands on him. I'll kill him, I swear to God, *lo ammazzo!*'

In vain, Mariangela and I tried to restrain her. She stormed off towards the main road, screaming, one determined step after the other, the folds of her skirt fluttering around her hips.

As she reached the street corner, she seemed to have second thoughts. She turned around and walked back to where we stood.

'How much did he take?' she whispered.

'Everything!' Mariangela replied under her breath.

Giulia's eyes filled with panic. 'E-VE-RY-THING?' she echoed, astonished.

'Yes, every single one of the eight hundred dollars I'd hidden.' They stared at each other for a long time, eyes locked, in silence. Then, with renewed determination, Giulia retraced her steps.

'I'm sorry, Mariangela, but I'll have to go to the police. He can't hit you black and blue, rob you of all you have, and then get away with it. Not while I'm here. You are my sister, and I won't allow it. That's that.'

In the meantime, the street had come alive.

Like a stage, the centre of it remained empty, but at the sides a curious crowd had begun to gather. Electric waves of excitement ran through it as people waited patiently for the commotion about to start. Befuddled, they watched first one sister then the other as they exchanged loud, angry sentences in their foreign tongue. Standing by the doorways, feigning indifference, the shopkeepers and bartenders also observed the scene with their ears cocked. By a kiosk along one of the sides, a cluster of dreads sipped their beers; among them, Rafael and Daniel. They stood there, strangely quiet. They didn't even nod at Giulia when she strode past, or at Mariangela and me when we stopped nearby.

Mariangela didn't look at all happy about her sister's determination to "rescue" her.

'Why on earth does she want to meddle in my own business? Doesn't she have enough problems of her own? Please, go and stop her,' she begged me.

I left her there, angry and sore, and rushed up the street only to meet Giulia on her way back from the police.

'It was closed,' she said with disappointment. 'So, I may as well go and look for Manu instead. In the meantime, why don't you get Mariangela to rest?'

It was an impossible request and she knew it. I watched Giulia turn into one of the back streets, her skirt fluttering like a hoisted flag, her crown-like bun making her a few inches taller. She headed purposefully for some of the most renowned sleazy bars in town.

Half an hour later, she was back at the kiosk where everybody still held the same position: Mariangela, me, the crowd of curious men talking in whispers among themselves.

'I saw him all right,' said Giulia. 'When I asked him about the money, all he could say was, "*What money?*" Just now he is in no fit state to talk.'

She seemed resigned to put things off until another day, when suddenly, the man himself entered centre stage. Although senselessly drunk, he came forward with his usual elastic step, heels hardly touching the ground.

He stopped at the kiosk, ordered a beer and then, stooping over the counter, began to chat in Garifuna with the other men. For a while, we watched them laugh. Then Giulia plucked up courage and walked over to him.

She tapped him lightly on his shoulder and said a few words. At first, he ignored her, then he seemed to change his mind.

Deliberately, he took a sip of beer, turned around slowly and spat the mouthful into her face.

She came back, wiping herself clean. 'You saw that, didn't you? No joy.'

'My turn,' said Mariangela and, against our advice, she left her seat.

She called out his name. He moved away from the kiosk and took a few steps towards her. Now, they both stood in the middle of the street facing each other.

'C'mon, Manu, give me the money back,' she said in a measured voice.

He tilted his head to the side, his round eyes fixed on hers.

'You!' he shouted. He seemed about to say more but couldn't find the words. 'You!' he repeated, breathing noisily through his nose. Then he lifted a menacing finger above his head and wagged it at her repeatedly.

'Don't you touch my sister!' All of a sudden, Giulia appeared by Mariangela's side. 'Give her her money back,' she ordered. 'Now!'

'You stay out of it,' Manu warned her, and turned to face Mariangela.

But Giulia had no intention of leaving. The three stood there, exchanging threats. 'I'll call the police!' said one. 'Shut up, you!' said the other. 'I want my money, now!' said the third. They walked slowly in a circle, occasionally stepping out of it, to the left, to the right, then back again with great wagging of fingers and hands on hips. Giulia had kicked her plastic flip-flops to the side, as if expecting soon to need her feet.

Then, cool and casual, Daniel skirted the periphery of the circle and said in a conciliatory voice: 'Manu, why don't you give Mariangela her dollars and let her go her way?'

Reasonable as it sounded, among local men, the suggestion was tantamount to a declaration of war. Happy to have, at long last, a real enemy to fight against, Manu turned viciously on Daniel.

'What are you meddling in here for? Is that your woman I'm talking to?' His finger came dangerously close to the other man's nose.

'Hey, watch out! Wasn't it my woman you spat at?' Daniel retorted, pushing that insolent finger away from himself.

It all went suddenly crazy. The two men began to push each other. They shouted in Garifuna, spicing their threats with Spanish words. Then, they took a few steps backwards, readying themselves for a serious fight.

Giulia and Mariangela looked helpless and confused now, as they stood right in the middle of the improvised boxing ring. They tried to patch things up, going first to one man, then to the other with pacifying words. It was too late. They were forcibly moved out of the circle with no choice but to watch.

Now the people in the neighbourhood and the shopkeepers stood in their doorways and openly watched. No one seemed interested in calling off the fight. On the contrary, they gave appraising looks first at one man, then at the other, hedging their bets.

In the middle of the street, Daniel and Manu faced each other, fuelling their rage with outlandish accusations. Eyes glued on to each other, fists clenched, they walked around in circles. Then, they surged forward and took swipes at each other, in turn.

They were both tall, Manu slightly taller, Daniel more robust. The first was athletic; he moved fast and light on the balls of his feet, and when hit, he bounced away, quickly. The second had massive upper arms and legs and stood his ground like a bull. Although he moved slowly, when he launched forward, he struck very hard.

Daniel talked incessantly. At first, he ranted and raved about the insults he and his woman had suffered, but soon he changed his tune and made high-sounding claims about being the best, the undisputed supremo. Only a fool or an idiot, he said, would dare take him on.

Indeed, Daniel was stronger. We all watched, alarmed, as he landed a resounding blow on his opponent's jaw.

Manu was finished and, soon after, he left the ring. 'Just wait,' he howled, 'I'll get a machete and slice you up!' I saw blood on his brow as he went past me.

Daniel stood alone in the centre of the ring, the winner.

Giulia rushed up to him and with solicitous care examined the sores on his hands.

Mariangela…

Almost unnoticed to all, Mariangela walked down the path along which Manu had disappeared. I called her, but she did not stop or even turn around.

Later, through the grapevine, I heard that Manu got extremely drunk that night. His left eye, his jaw and one of his hands sore and swollen, he sought relief in beer. Propped up against the counter of Happy Land, he gulped it down, then, unable to control his anger, he smashed bottle after bottle against the floor. '*Otra!*' he bellowed, standing in a mess of broken glass and wasted beer.

In the end, remembering his threat, he borrowed a machete and rushed to Giulia and Daniel's place. There, in the yard, he attacked his rival. With a long stick, Daniel disarmed him and forced him to run away, again. People saw him in the darkness dodge the trees and the huts, light and stealthy like a cat. And – I heard – Giulia and Daniel barricaded themselves inside their house, just in case.

As for Mariangela, she was gone, vanished. No one had seen her. Horrible thoughts went through my mind. Had she been beaten to death? Was she lying somewhere in the jungle, unable to move and scream for help? As time went by, Giulia and I became increasingly concerned. Even Daniel urged us to go and look for her.

It'd started raining, though. For two whole days, it poured down relentlessly. The Quehueche had risen very high, its strong and turbulent currents making the crossing dangerous. But on the third day, we woke up to a splendid sunrise. The sky was transparent blue. Along the coastline, the palm trees, the huts, the *cayucos* moored on the beach, even the distant silhouettes of the fishermen were carved out clearly against the sky. Out at sea, the mountainous contour of Belize shone green and close, almost at hand. Everything was bright and dazzling, as if recently scrubbed with brush and soap.

Giulia and I decided to go and pay a visit to Manu. The last we'd seen of Mariangela, she'd been following him at a distance. Perhaps he knew her whereabouts or, at least, he might be able to give us some clues. We were anxious about meeting him, though. What if he was still angry, or still drunk? What if he began to abuse us? But we had no choice. The plan was to go and get him to tell us where to find Mariangela.

We walked along the sea, crossed the now-tamed river, and after coasting the beach for over half an hour, we finally reached the hut.

From behind the small palm grove that sheltered it, came a thin cloud of smoke. 'He's cooking,' I whispered.

'Manu! Manu!' we both hollered. Somebody moved in the kitchen area, under the stilts. We heard the swishing of light footsteps on the grass, then, framed between the cane partitions, Mariangela appeared.

She was wearing the same yellow dress she'd been wearing a few days earlier, hair loose over her shoulders, a smile. 'Hello! Come to the back. We're having lunch.'

Not a word about the fight, her bruises, her wobbly teeth, or the averted danger.

Relieved, but also astounded, we followed her behind the house. There, by the open fire, sat Manu, one of his arms folded across his chest, his hand swollen.

'*Qué onda?*' He smiled at us broadly.

Squatting by the fire over a sooty frying pan, Mariangela picked up a piece of fish, drained off the oil, then handed it to Manu.

'*Gracias, mi reina!*' he said with gratitude.

Neither Giulia nor I had the courage to mention the brawl or even our worries. We both tacitly agreed it was better to pretend indifference rather than put at risk the extraordinary reconciliation they seemed to have reached.

We just sat there, exchanging wary looks. Then, after a few lame excuses about some last-minute chores that – oh, dear me! – we seemed to have forgotten, we said goodbye to the reunited couple and left them there, to their rekindled love.

CHAPTER NINETEEN

GIULIA

Not that Giulia didn't have her own domestic problems – Daniel was no hero when it came to his own home arrangements.

When Giulia first met him, the two sisters and I shared the house in Nebagó, and so I could see how completely bowled over she was by this handsome guy smothering her with charm and showering her with extravagant compliments. In those early days, she was enthusiastic about just everything to do with Livingston, and, with his flamboyant seductiveness, Daniel was certainly no exception.

Giulia herself was an interesting character. Born, like her sister, in one of the most densely populated neighbourhoods of Naples – the infamous Spanish Quarters, where, before you visit, you're warned to hide your camera and take off your watch – just like her sister, she was a back-to-the-land type. She loved nature and valued the peace and quiet of the countryside above all.

'My sister and I are here to relax,' she said that day in early September, when we first met. 'We'll be off soon.'

Six months later, they were both still here.

'We're getting ready. We'll be gone by April, perhaps May – you know, when it gets warmer,' they now said to people when asked.

They claimed, just like me, that it'd been the place, at first, and not any particular man, that had hooked them.

This was especially true of Giulia. In her eyes, everything was beautiful; the village, the people, by which she didn't mean the Amerindians or the Chinese, and definitely not the Ladinos – "*a bunch of male chauvinists*", as she called them – but the Garifunas, whom she adored. She liked the free and easy way they brought up their children, how, from a very tender age, they were expected to help around the house; she loved, she said, "their sense of rhythm", their "athletic" bodies, even the festive way they celebrated death. For her, everything Garifuna expressed a healthier approach to life.

'Aren't these children just like any others?' I argued. 'When they want something, and start whining "*give me this, give me that*," "*regálame un len, regálame*," they're a pain, admit it. As for all Garifunas being good-looking, honestly, Giulia, just look around... Sure you see no ugly faces?'

'No way,' she insisted. 'These children are a hundred times more obedient. And the women – they are strong, direct; the men – handsome and uncomplicated, not like many of the Italian guys I know.'

'Please, Giulia,' I said, trying hard to restore some sense of objectivity, 'open your eyes. They're not so different. Can't you see how these guys lord it over their women? They revel in the usual "me Tarzan, you Jane" roles. What's so different? Tell me.'

'But it's natural,' she insisted. 'From time immemorial, man's place is at sea, woman's at home.' And that, for her, ended the argument.

For me... Well, I sounded sensible only in words. Deep down, my feelings about Livingston were as romantic as hers. For hours, I would carry on the debate within myself. Sometimes the "Giulia" part would dominate, and the no-nonsense, independent woman I liked to think I was would all but vanish.

No such inner conflict troubled my friend. She seemed to relish the routines of domestic life. Every morning, prim and proper, solemn, even, as if performing a ritual, she milled around town with her shopping basket. She made no secret of spending long hours by Daniel's side cleaning the fish or painting his boat. In my mind's eye, I could see her, at night, rocking herself contentedly in her hammock, waiting for him to come home, dinner ready on the table, long shadows cast by the light of the candle over the bamboo walls. Her new life was simple, romantic, and she fitted into it like a hand in a well-worn glove. Just another of my fanciful projections? Quite possibly. But what I knew was that she proudly referred to Daniel as *"mi hombre"* and, with matching pride, he called her *"mi mujer"*.

Aside from discovering her "true self", as she said, in Livingston, Giulia had developed a keen interest in natural remedies and herbs. Now, whenever we went for a walk among what to me was just bracken and bramble, she'd stop and point at some shrub.

'See that plant over there, the one with the oval-shaped dark green leaves? It's called *tres puntas*. The infusion you get from it is disgustingly bitter, but it contains quinine and it's good for fevers, cuts, bruises, rashes, in fact, for almost everything.'

'And this one,' she broke off a twig from another bush, 'is *yerba mate* or *yerba cáncer*. If you brew it and drink a cup of it every morning, it's guaranteed to regulate your blood pressure. And that clinging vine to your right, the one with the small white blossom, can you see it? That's *sorosil*. Shred it, boil it, and then add to it rosemary, orange peel, *guamúchil, anís,* camomile, a clove of garlic and there you have a most effective contraceptive. I've tried it and it works.'

I looked at her dubiously, so she pressed the point. 'C'mon, Monica, don't be so cynical. Remember Doña Marcela, our old neighbour? She's the one who taught me these things.' I raised an eyebrow. 'Yeah, there are plenty of quacks about, I know, but some of these people really know their stuff. We should trust them.'

Seeing I was unconvinced, she laughed. Then she picked a red blossom of *carnavel* and threaded it artfully behind her ear through her shiny dark hair.

'I wouldn't mess about with strange plants,' I tried to warn her. 'You could poison yourself, no kidding.'

She gazed pensively at the bush around us.

'Yeah, the line between remedy and poison is thin. Sure. That's why people are so suspicious around here, haven't you noticed? Even the best of friends, even people from the same family.

'Remember Doña Marcela's husband saying to her, *"Mi amor, what's in this soup? Poison?"* Afterwards, he'd roar with laughter, as if it was the biggest of jokes. But he really meant it, you could tell. And anyway, didn't he insist she ate from the same plate?'

Yes, I did remember. We lived so close to our next-door neighbours that nothing could pass unnoticed between us. At the time, the two of them sitting there spooning their soup out of the same bowl seemed to me just a charming scene of family life, full of intimacy and affection. But what if Giulia was right and the man was in fact doubting his wife? I thought of all the other couples I'd seen sharing their plates or bowls. Could they all be fearful of being poisoned?

'Don't worry about me.' Giulia smiled reassuringly. 'I'm very careful. I never try something unless I'm a hundred per cent sure.'

*

Giulia's *hombre* was an attractive *Rasta* who had been to Australia once. Being from Adelaide, his previous girlfriend – his *baby mother*, as he called her – wanted to set up home over there. Things had not worked out. Six months later, Daniel was back in Livingston.

If his relationship had been a failure, his time abroad had gained him status and prestige among his mates. He never lost the opportunity to show off by talking about his time away. I often saw him outside some bar, holding court in front of an impromptu but attentive crowd. He entertained them with a vast repertoire of wild descriptions of "*allá*".

'You should've seen the yacht I had over there,' he intoned, darting a pugilistic glance at anyone who dared raise so much as a quizzical eyebrow. 'A forty-footer, three sails, an eight-berth cabin, and a speed of one hundred knots…'

Back home, Rafael, who'd seen the photos, maintained it was no more than a ten-foot dingy that had seen better times.

'And the fire-spitting chrome-plated chopper he says he rode along the Great Ocean Way? Ha!' Rafael sneered contemptuously. 'A wheezing clapped-out old scooter...'

But Daniel loved the sound of his own stories. And so, he made everything he'd done, seen, or heard during his stay in Australia, bigger, louder, bluer, redder, in short vastly superior to anything Livingston had to offer.

'So, why did you come back, Daniel?' some brave listener would always ask.

Daniel would shrug his ox-like shoulders. His thundering would come to a halt. Then, smiling to himself, he would admit in a soft voice, 'I got bored. And anyway, there's no place like home.'

Being on the outside, it didn't take me long to figure out that, for all his charm and bluster, his sense of himself as a "man among men", Daniel was in fact an unexceptional *hombre*, with the same vulnerabilities, the same insecurities about his place in the world, as other men.

For Giulia, the realisation came much more gradually and only four or five weeks after she'd moved in with him.

At first, Daniel happily contained himself. He and Giulia lived through a sort of honeymoon when he'd comply with all her wishes, including spending several romantic nights together. But soon the urge to revert to his old ways burst forth. And, given that drink and "fighting talk" provided the necessary bulwark to self-doubt, at night-time Daniel took to going out and having *more* than a few *octavos* with his friends. He often got gloriously drunk.

Giulia wasn't at all pleased but convinced herself that it was in her power to reform him.

'Don't go to the bars, Daniel!' At first, she tried to charm him. 'Stay with me tonight! Let's go and dance, come on.'

He ignored her.

Then, she began to criticise his friends. 'How can you let those good-for-nothings decide your life! "*Come here, Daniel! Go there,*

Daniel*! Here, have another bottle of Venado, Daniel!"* And every time, you do as you are told, you silly man!' Daniel laughed at her impersonation, but as night came, he went out all the same.

Everything else having failed, the arguments started.

One morning, she stormed into the *comedor* where I was having coffee and came to sit with me. Camouflaged under a long strand of hair, it didn't take me long to notice her black eye.

'He hit me! The big man took it out on someone half his size. Damn bully! Coward!' she ranted, in a loud voice. 'He's just like all the others. A servant to cook and clean for him, that's what he wants. And my money. These men are all the same. They see a *gringa* and immediately they try and sponge off her.'

People sitting nearby couldn't help hearing her. An elderly woman who lived near our old house in Nebagó stood up, and on her way out, she came over.

'*Mi hija*, men are no good when they drink. They lose control. But, listen to me.' She stared at her with piercing eyes, her voice down to a whisper. 'There's something that can make him stop. There's an infusion… Come and see me, you know where I live.'

And she left us there, speechless.

I broke the silence first. 'Risky…' I stared at her questioningly.

'Yeah,' she replied with a strange smile, 'but he deserves it. Besides, wouldn't it be just great to make a fool out of that brute?'

On leaving the *comedor*, Giulia appeared to be in a much better mood.

*

Two days later, I was in a shop waiting to be served, when I heard her call me from the street.

'Monica, d'you have a moment?'

I went outside, and we started walking along the street.

'Guess what? I've done it!' She was beaming. 'See this?' She handed me a brown paper bag, discreetly. I opened it and, at the bottom, saw some reddish-brown powder that smelt just like tea.

'Earlier this morning, I gave Daniel some of this stuff to drink.'

I balked at the news, but in her eyes, there was so much excitement.

'After last night's binge, he woke up with a massive hangover. So, I offered to make him some tea, and I mixed it in.'

'And…?'

'And, nothing, he drank it and fell asleep. Ten minutes later, I left the house. That was about nine. But now… now I'm getting cold feet. Will you come and check him out with me?'

We turned left at the end of the road and cut through the backyards of several houses, before finally coming to Daniel's.

The door was shut, the way Giulia had left it.

We pushed it open and went in. There was no one. The windows were shut, and there, on the wooden table, was a cup – empty.

'Daniel, where are you?' Giulia called out, as pale as a sheet.

There was a slight movement outside, past the open kitchen area, at the back of the house, some gasping and panting.

We followed the noise and there, at the bottom of a shallow dip, Daniel was crouched in the grass, prodigiously throwing up.

Giulia rushed forward, kneeled by his side and placed a hand on his forehead to keep his locks out of the way. He was down to vomiting his bile.

'What did you put in that tea?' he cried out.

'What d'you mean?' she answered in an offended tone. 'Nothing! Chaw! Here I am, helping you, and you dare accuse me of… poisoning you! What a nasty mind you have!'

How well she acted the part of the outraged wife.

She fussed over him – brought him water, wiped the sweat off his forehead. I stood at a short distance, not knowing what I should do.

From behind his back, she quickly glanced at me and winked.

At this point, I made my excuses. 'Goodbye, Daniel. I see you're in good hands.'

*

That night, Rafael and I were sitting at the counter inside Happy Land when Daniel walked in.

'Oh boy! I've been so sick all day! No more booze for me, not for a while!' He slumped onto a chair, kind of washed out.

'Hey, c'mon, *nati*! Don't be such a chicken,' Rafael said to him, and then shouted to the barman, 'a beer for my friend here!'

Straight from the fridge, the bottle was frozen cold, with drops streaming down the glass. For a split second, Daniel hesitated. Then, he grabbed it; with his teeth, he flipped the metal top onto the counter and spilt a little beer onto the stained wooden floor of the bar.

'*Para los ancestros*,' his deep baritone boomed across the tables. '*Salud*!' Then, he knocked it back.

CHAPTER TWENTY

THE COMEDOR CALI

Halfway down the asphalted road that runs across the town from the docks, there are two small family restaurants. They stand close to each other, on the same side of the road. They belong to two sisters: Marga, the younger, is single; Carmen is married to Joaquín. All of them, Marga, Carmen, Joaquín and their numerous children, are Ladinos. They speak Spanish, dress in a Western fashion, and are the much-impoverished descendants of the *conquistadores*.

The two restaurants are always crowded, at mealtimes with customers, the rest of the day with children – some doing their homework, others absorbed in table games. Sitting in the doorway, I often see the same smiling teenager bounce one of the little ones on her knees.

There's no competition between the two restaurants. The clients themselves see to it. The customs officers, the policemen and the other petty bureaucrats all choose to patronise the Comedor Livingston run by Marga, whereas the "sleeping-bag" foreigners, the hippies and all the other shoe-string travellers prefer the Comedor Cali, because it's cheaper.

When I'm in town, the Comedor Cali is my favourite hangout.

I get there early in the morning, choose a table in the sun, and take a book out of my bag, or a pen and some writing paper. I sit there alone, waiting for Carmen or Joaquín to emerge from the back.

The place is small for a family of seven. The largest room is the dining room, where I sit for hours.

I count nine calendars hanging from the peeling walls, with pictures of kittens or white rabbits in the arms of sweet-looking little girls. Along the wall, to the left, stand two bulky refrigerators. They're old and battered, but in this heat they are worth their weight in gold. On top of one, there's a TV set; on top of the other, a cassette recorder and, next to it, left behind from several long-gone Christmases, a little plastic fir tree. Scattered around the room are three round tables and two rectangular ones with red and white checked tablecloths, several benches and a miscellaneous selection of old rickety chairs. The concrete floor is unswept, and trails of ants march through the crumbs.

Were it not for the warm welcome I invariably get from the family, I would gladly give this place a miss. But their friendliness is so genuine, so heartwarming, that I turn a blind eye to the dirt and the squalor. Anyway, by now, I don't really notice it.

Today, I'm particularly early and no one seems to be around, except for Tifón, an old mangy dog lazing in the sun under a stool. I go and sit by the open window and start reading.

The door between the two refrigerators opens and Carmen walks in.

Round and soft, in her late thirties, she has short, curly black hair, shiny eyes and, in line with the fashion of the day, a gold star glittering in the white enamel of a front tooth. With one hand, she wipes away the last shadow of sleep from her eyes; with the other, she buttons up her blouse. When she sees me, she smiles.

'*Buenos días*, Monica! Coffee?'

I follow her down the three steps that lead into the kitchen. Under a low roof of corrugated iron, the sooty, narrow room opens onto a grass yard. There's no door separating it from the dining room so that Carmen can keep an eye on people coming in.

I sit on the top step and watch her go through her well-practised routine. She feeds the old stove with firewood, lights the fire, fills an enamel pot with water from the pipe outside, places it over the hot metal plate to boil, stows a bowl of ground maize on a shelf ready to be kneaded later into *tortillas*, then, after clearing some space on a long marble surface cluttered with crockery, she sets about jointing a frozen chicken with surgical precision.

'*Cómo anda usted*? How are you today?' she asks me.

Out of the corner of my eye, I see a couple of plump turkeys hover by the door. A second later, they stalk determinedly across the kitchen floor.

'Chaw! Chaw!' Carmen shoos them away and pounds her feet on the concrete. The birds quickly back away, only to stroll in again a few seconds later, quiet but insistent, flashing their red wattles and twitching their tiny heads.

'*Muy bien*,' I blurt out. 'I got a letter from my mum. She says she'll come and visit.'

'*Qué bien!*' She offers me a cigarette from a new packet.

We light up. Even then she doesn't stop working. In one hand she holds a knife and in the other her cigarette.

'Who's coming?' The man's voice comes from somewhere behind.

I turn and look up and right there, slouching against the doorway, is Joaquín. He's tall, skinny, with pointed features and a tuft of straight black hair falling over his forehead. For someone who runs a restaurant, his stomach is surprisingly flat. He's been standing there for who knows how long. He's the other smoker in the family. As he speaks, a cigarette droops from the corner of his mouth.

'My mother. She didn't say when, but soon, I think.'

'*Qué bien!* Something to celebrate, then, eh, *cafetera*?' He always teases me about my coffee habit. Whenever he talks, his denture drops from his upper gum. Spellbound, I watch him mouth words that have a split second's delay on the movement of his jaw.

I go back to my table by the window. A few minutes later, nine-year-old Wendy brings me a cup of coffee, the china chattering in her unsteady little hands. The zip of her dress is halfway down and her hair is like a bird's nest, but her friends are waiting and she's in a hurry. She's about to fly into the street when Joaquín stops her: 'Wendy! What about the sugar?'

Without any "buts" or "what ifs" or "later", Wendy runs back into the kitchen, picks up a bowl with the word *"shugar"* printed on the lid and plonks it in front of me. Before anyone can stop her, she's out.

'Look at her, running around barefoot like an *India*.' In the kitchen, Carmen shakes her head.

'We'll make you a *tapado* when your mother comes, *pues*,' says Joaquín.

'What's that?'

'The best fish soup in the whole district, made with big river crabs, shells, the lot, and many types of fish, *róbalo*, *palometa*, shark, all stewed in coconut milk for hours. Then, with a bit of luck, we'll get a *tepezcuintle* and add it to the soup.'

'A tepe... what?'

'A *tepezcuintle*. It's a furry little animal, a bit like a cat or a fox, with bright red eyes and a big bushy tail, this big."' He points halfway down his calf. "It lives in the jungle, sleeps during the day and goes hunting at night. It tastes damned good in the *tapado*, but these days it's like the *quetzal*. People know they exist, but who's ever seen one?"

From across the room, his dark brown eyes twinkle. Is he pulling my leg? You never know with Joaquín. He stands the other side of the table, so thin that one day, I know I'll see him levitate above the floor just like a Catholic saint, a halo of cigarette smoke around his head and a billowing cloud of tobacco bearing him upwards.

I never eat here, I only drink coffee, but I know that neither Carmen nor Joaquín mind me sitting around. They like chatting with us foreigners, and we like them too. Many of us, women in particular, come to this place as if to a safe haven from the *mara,* the Tomáses, the Emilios, who instinctively give the place a wide birth. To us, Carmen is like an older sister we can depend on for advice.

'I'm glad for you, Monica,' she says, drying her hands on the front of her apron before she joins me at the table. 'It'll be nice for you to have your mother here, you know, someone from *allá,* at last, one of your own people.' She bends her head to one side and looks at me studiously.

'It's no good mixing with people who are so different from us. Different blood types don't mix.'

I look at her, disconcerted. What does she mean? How much does she know about my love life? I haven't told her a thing, but just like in the past with Emilio, nothing stays private around here.

'You don't believe me, do you? Just look at Mariangela. When she first got here, she was a lovely girl with nice round hips, nice skin. The picture of health, she was. And look at her now: half the size she used to be, hips gone, smile gone, as pale as a ghost.' A pause, and then she repeats what everyone says around here. 'It's all the fault of that guy she lives with, you know. He makes her work like a slave.'

Carmen gets heated during these discussions. She is as sweet and caring with us girls as she is hard on our Garifuna boyfriends.

'They only want you for your money,' she says. 'Then when they've got you under their thumb, they boss you about, beat you and run around with other women. Did I ever tell you about Valeria? No? Well, not so long ago, there was this Italian woman called Valeria. She lived with that Rasta guy, that good-for-nothing, what's his name? You know who I mean, don't you, Joaquín?'

'Yeah, his name's Rafael.'

'Yes, Rafael. Well, Valeria had a child with him. The little boy was lovely, so light-skinned, a real beauty, as pretty as a doll. The man was horrible to Valeria. He started saying the boy was not his son, that she'd slept with other men. And he beat her. She often came here and cried. Anyway, one day, she'd had enough, and decided to run away. Of course, she didn't tell him. She planned it in secret. She told him she'd take the baby to see a doctor in Guatemala City. Instead, she went straight to the airport and took the first flight home. From the airport, she wrote him a letter. When he got it, you should've seen him. He went wild. He ran after her, but it was too late, she'd already gone.'

Joaquín is staring at me as if waiting for me to say something. I stare back, struggling to hide the sick feeling in the pit of my stomach, a mixture of anxiety and disbelief. I bought into Rafael's version of events – that Valeria could not adjust to Labuga and had gone back to her fancy life in Italy. All this I'm hearing now must be a lie, malicious gossip, nasty rumours. People here love to embroider things. But what if it's true?

'Believe me, Monica,' says Carmen, 'these guys are nasty. They'd rather steal from people than do a scrap of work. Watch out.'

'*Tiburón! Carne de tiburón* for sale! Shark by the kilo!' At the door there's a Garifuna fish vendor with a large wicker basket on her head.

'*Hola*, Doña Marcia, *adelante!*' Carmen beckons her in.

The old woman lowers her basket onto the nearest table and removes the shiny banana leaves covering the fish. Carmen picks out four large chunks and half a dozen small pieces. They laugh and joke with each other, like good neighbours.

The sun is very hot now, my insides knotted. The smell of fish fills my lungs. I need to get out of here. Instead, I sit, in the masochistic hope that I'll hear more about Valeria and Rafael.

But nothing follows. Carmen and Joaquín get down to their daily chores.

I manage to finish my second cup of coffee and then I pay. Just then, the two young Mayan women who daily come to help Carmen in the restaurant turn up for work. One has a large flat face that masks her emotions; the other is small, vivacious and alert. They move carefully under the bulk of their pleated skirts and, as they pass me by, they glance timidly at me. They go into the kitchen, and without waiting for instructions, they take the maize dough down from the shelf and begin to flatten it into perfectly round tortillas. It's nearly lunchtime.

'*Adiós,* Carmen!' I shout.

'*Qué le vaya bien,* Monica!' says Carmen, waving goodbye.

I leave the *comedor,* followed by the sound of the women's fast-clapping palms. As I walk down the road, I hear them talk to each other in *ketkchi.* From time to time, they burst into a peel of laughter, then they lower their high-pitched voices and whisper secretively among themselves.

CHAPTER TWENTY-ONE

LOVE AND MONEY

Carmen and Joaquín's revelations swirling around in my head, I go over to Rafael's with half an idea of talking to him about what I've just heard. He's at work, of course, so I sit there and from the belly of my sack I pull out my notebook. Partly I need something to distract me, but mostly I know that writing will help me process what I've learnt, as well as get some control over my worst fears.

I've been writing for only a few minutes when Gabriel, a guy I've probably just seen once before hanging around Happy Land, knocks on the door.

'Where's *Mister Gam*?' he asks, *Mister Gam* being one of Rafael's many nicknames.

'Gone to work,' I reply, trying to remember who this tall and lanky man could be.

'Tell him Gabriel called.' Dark-skinned, with finely chiselled delicate features, he stands in the doorway, watching me without the shadow of a smile. The stillness of his gaze is disconcerting.

Then he takes a step indoors, as if he doesn't believe me and expects to find Rafael somewhere about the house. But he barely gives the house a glance. Instead, he hands me the joint he's smoking. It's the last thing I need, but I find myself taking it anyway. It's an automatic response, an act of civility, of politeness even – like when someone you meet for the first time holds out their hand and you shake it.

As I meet his stare, I read in it the flicker of curiosity, and something else too. Is it my imagination or is he daring me? He's certainly trying to size me up. Does he too know all about Rafael and Valeria?

I take a long and deep toke.

'Tell *Rafa* that Gabriel came by,' he says one last time as I hand him back the joint. He's out before I can thank him.

Two minutes later, I'm floating in mid-air, feet, legs, arms, my whole body no longer responding. The cane walls of the hut close in on me and then suddenly back away, in and out, repeatedly. I look down at my hand, still holding the pen I've been writing with. It lies there inert on the page, disconnected from me, hovering on the last word I've scribbled: *today.* All edges between me and the surrounding objects have become fuzzy, uncertain.

Somehow, I make it to the hammock in the middle of the room and slump into it, face upwards. I lie there, staring at the beams bearing down on me, unable to move a finger or think a single thought.

It's midday when I finally manage to snap out of my catatonic state. On uncertain legs, I walk out into the blinding sun, to the comforting buzz of street life.

I dislike the effect drugs have on me, and by now I'm wary of Gabriel. He seems all of a piece with the bad news about Rafael and Valeria. Besides, his cockiness makes me as queasy as his dope.

But it's most probably under the effect of Gabriel's *ganja* that, when Rafael returns later, I don't say a word and, my paranoia strangely leavened, I manage to greet him as if nothing has happened, as if all is as calm as before.

*

Weeks later, I was having my usual cup of coffee at the Comedor Cali, when one of the Garifuna *pan de coco* vendors came in, excitement shining on her face.

'At last, she's done it! Good old Mariana! Best thing she's ever done, *pues*!' the tall, busty woman told anyone around who cared to listen. She plonked her basket onto the nearest table, sat herself in front of it and, fanning herself slowly with the hem of her ample skirt, she continued:

'All that whoring, all that coming and going… She's had enough of him. So, guess what. This morning, outside her house in Campo Amor, she made a big pile of all his things and burnt them. The fire's still blazing as I speak. That'll teach him to run around with all those *gringas*!'

Mariana was Gabriel's wife and the mother of his two children, aged five and seven. "All those *gringas*" boiled down to just one – Clara, his new Spanish lover.

Clara had turned up in Livingston six months earlier and, within weeks of her arrival, had taken a fancy to Gabriel. Married or not, with or without children, he was the one. In town, they said she spared no effort until she won him over. But really, who could resist her and her husky Castilian voice? Before coming here, she'd worked as a flight attendant for Iberia Airlines, and that gave her a halo of glamour that none of the rest of us foreign girls had. Even in an old pair of jeans, she managed to look slick, sophisticated and… wealthy. Gabriel had been easy prey. She could give him the life he dreamt of, so he'd simply jumped at his good fortune. In no time at all, he'd moved in with her. Rumour had it she was soon to have his child.

I hardly knew or cared about Gabriel or Clara, but their story gave me a lot to think about. Everything seemed complicated at this point. Money, love, women and men, wealth and poverty, money – again. In the light of what I'd learnt about Rafael and Valeria, this pattern of events unsettled me. It was one thing to read in textbooks about the injustices of the world economy, to theorise about class differences, but another to experience them in real life. It began to feel all too close and personal. It was all too much.

I went and talked it over with Mariangela. No one was wiser on these matters, as, before he'd taken up with her, Manu too had been married. The youngest of his four children had only been ten months old when he'd left his wife for her. Now, every so often, sent by their mother, one or other of these children would turn up on their doorstep needing a *préstamo* of a few *quetzals*. Mariangela always gave them more than they asked for.

'Look at it this way,' she said to me calmly. 'I've deprived Manu's family of its breadwinner, so it's only fair that I should compensate for it.'

I could see her point. It was the moral thing to do. It was an arrangement that left everyone satisfied; the ex, the children, Manu, and even Mariangela. It made everyone happy.

Still, there was something in her logic that made me feel uncomfortable. I couldn't believe that love was so prosaic, that it could be counted in *quetzals*, in dollars, that it was concrete and measurable like any material thing.

'What about romance?' I insisted. Once again, I thought of Richard, my ex. "Soppy and sentimental", he would have called me, and then dismissed romance as a bourgeois invention, a layer of false consciousness that helped capitalism tick over.

'Romance?' said Mariangela. 'Of course there's a lot of romance between me and Manu. We spend many romantic nights in our beach hut by the ocean. We love each other. But people around here are poor. Think of it as child maintenance a man must pay by law after a divorce, the only difference being that, in this case, it's not Manu but me who dishes out the dough. But how could he, if he hasn't got a penny to his name?'

It made perfect sense except – money wasn't, after all, such an insignificant detail. However hard she pretended to believe she and Manu rose above it, not so long ago, she'd been beaten black and blue over her stash of dollars. Had she forgotten?

So, I stumbled through, contradicting myself again and again, still unable to reconcile myself to the crudity of these money-love transactions.

*

Would relationships work better when the woman, rather than the man, happened to be the local?

Take Alessandro and Ylenia.

Ylenia's family lived in a rambling concrete house at the back of Mama Jo's. I often bumped into her mother on my way to Rafael's. She was a handsome giant whose opinions – everyone said – had to be reckoned with. The men in her life had come and gone, leaving behind several half-siblings, each a different shade of black and brown. Ylenia was pitch-black, and stunningly beautiful.

Alessandro was the *viajero* who, after I'd been robbed, had approached me with the idea I could sell some grass for him around the village. He had singled out Ylenia among all the pretty local girls and courted her relentlessly until she'd gone to live with him.

'Does she really fancy him?' Mariangela, Giulia and I often wondered. We looked at each other doubtfully and laughed at the thought of long-haired, blue-eyed hippy Alessandro walking through the village like a prophet parting the waters, or a new Jesus Christ Superstar. 'He's totally up himself, isn't he?' But, in the end, we'd say resignedly, as if to placate some fiscal god, 'Who knows? The ways of love and money are endless…'

Alessandro was an artisan, he said. Once or twice, I'd seen him handle some pincers and twist some strips of metal into a ring, but I knew better than to believe that could be his only income.

One day, he went on a mysterious trip to Bogotá. A week later, back in Livingston, he stood at the bar boasting. 'You need balls for this line of work. Definitely not for the faint-hearted.' He said no more. He just smiled knowingly, flicked his wavy blond hair and let people speculate what "line of work" he was referring to.

Unsurprisingly, given they both inhabited the same druggy world on the margins of the law, Alessandro and Gabriel were close friends.

I was suspicious of both men and kept my distance, but I had to admit there was something redeeming about Alessandro, something that made me forget a good deal of the antipathy I felt for him – he adored Ylenia. The way he always praised her, the way his eyes filled with affection whenever he looked at her, the one thousand little attentions he showered on her; all that seemed genuine. This capacity for love was the best part of him. She responded with the same intensity of, perhaps not love, but certainly affection.

At long last, here was a "mixed" relationship, as Carmen would call it, that seemed to be working. I found it reassuring. It proved that, despite the many obstacles – so I reasoned – love across divides was possible. Or, at least, it was when genders were reversed.

*

'Have you heard the latest?' said Ramón, the shopkeeper, to one of his customers. With precise, automatic gestures, he took down a big leg of ham from the hook above his head, placed it on the meat slicer and turned the switch on. I cocked my ears.

'...an accident on la Cuesta de las Cañas ...the car's a complete write-off... no, only Gabriel... the poor guy's dead...' I caught random fragments of the story, all else drowned by the high-pitched screeching of the machine.

'Sí, pues, that pinche gringo Alessandro killed our Gabriel!' from the far corner thundered one of the fish vendors, the oldest and the loudest of the women whom I regularly met at the harbour.

Shocked by the news, I left without daring to ask questions. Just then, Mariangela was walking up the street with her shopping basket. She'd already heard about Gabriel.

'Such a tragedy!' she said with a sigh, and to my many pressing questions, she hardly had anything to say. 'All I know is that Alessandro was at the wheel, that something happened, and he lost control. Tonight, there's going to be a velorio at Polly's, Gabriel's sister. We must go.'

'Do you think we should? I mean, in their eyes, you and I are no different from Alessandro. We're all pinches gringos, just like him.'

'First and foremost, we're all human beings,' she retorted. 'We knew Gabriel, didn't we? So why shouldn't we go and pay our respects to his family?'

As soon as night fell, Mariangela, Giulia and I, each with our respective partners, made our way to the *velorio*.

None of the wakes I'd been to until that night had prepared me for the dark cloud of gloom and sadness that hung upon Polly's house. There was no music, no dancing, no singing – none of the usual merrymaking that is meant to ease the pain.

All around were strained faces.

The surly-looking men who sat outside the front door playing cards under a canopy of white canvas barely nodded at us as we passed by.

In the kitchen area, a cluster of women sat disconsolately around the stove, arms hanging loose on their laps, their whispering drowned by the sound of muffled crying coming from the back.

Polly was nowhere to be seen, but in the sparely furnished living room, under the crude metallic light of a naked bulb, a dignified old man sat stiffly on a high-backed chair. Behind him, a walking cane with a brass handle rested against the wall.

I recognised the *bujey* who'd overseen the *chugu* a few months earlier.

'Gabriel's dad,' whispered Rafael, and went to greet him.

From behind a pair of gold-rimmed dark glasses, the old man looked up and nodded silently, his thoughts as opaque as those lenses. Then, he turned away and gazed into the distance. He clearly wanted to grieve alone.

Murmuring our condolences, we left the room.

Out in the backyard, a group of men stood around, talking in whispers.

'Twenty-six, was he? Too young to die like this.'

'All because of that *gringo*… I hear he's in hospital. Might lose one of his legs.'

'Hope he does. If he's not stoned, he's drunk. On that day, probably both.'

'Too right,' said a man with a thick gold chain dangling on his chest. He leant forward and looked furtively around. 'I've heard their car was stashed with coke. Those two, him and Ylenia, bought it in Pana. Set to go to Mexico, they were.'

'Ylenia? He's got her roped in too?' a short, squat man interjected. 'Impossible! From such a good family!' He tutted and shook his head.

'Well, you know what they say. Those who lie down with dogs…'

'How did it happen?' said a man who hadn't spoken before.

'Gabriel and his woman were in the back. The other two were up front, off to get their visa, at least that's the story. All those hairpin bends between Pana and Guate! And he goes and loses control of the car. Like I say, drunk, stoned, probably both…'

'I hear it was the brakes, they stopped working…'

'And what about the other one, Gabriel's woman, the Spanish girl?'

'Couple of broken ribs, but she's okay. She didn't lose the child.'

'And the coke?'

'Your guess is as good as mine. Money and drugs? Gone.'

'You know what it's like…'

'That's… six, seven thousand dollars nicely tucked away in the pockets of the *guardia civil*. There you go.'

From the kitchen, one of the women walked out into the yard with half a dozen glasses of hot coffee on a tray.

'Hey, Marcia, c'mon. Tell us what Mariana's got to say about it,' said the man with the gold chain, helping himself to coffee.

'Being left like that with two small children… What'd you expect? She shrugged her shoulders, she did. Said it was divine justice.'

'Yeah? What I've heard is it's all her doing, that she put a curse on him.'

'Gabriel was no saint, we know,' Marcia said, collecting the empty glasses. 'But as for curses… No need for any of that. He had enough enemies.'

It went on like this, each picking up from where the other left off. No end of suspects, no end of wild stories, no end of speculation.

Then it was Rafael's turn.

'The car was being chased,' he said with authority, sounding as if he'd been there and seen it all with his own eyes. '*El cabrón de* Alessandro wouldn't give his mafia cronies their cut, so they went after him. It was him they wanted to kill, but poor Gabriel got in the way. They shot him by mistake.'

'But no one's ever mentioned bullets or firearms,' I pointed out.

'You really believe everything you hear?' Rafael laughed. 'The truth is, Gabriel died to protect Alessandro. The others don't back the story? Of course, they don't. Clara's in hospital. And Ylenia... She's Alessandro's woman, what d'you expect her to say? The money they lost? A lie, they've hidden it. Wait for the whole business to die down, and you'll see how quickly they'll get out of Livingston and go and live it up somewhere nice. Poor Gabriel, if he knew he died so that those two could have a ball...'

The hours went by and everything people said was spiked with resentment and bitterness. At midnight, heaps of fried rice, chicken and juicy beans were dished out, according to tradition, but not even that managed to lift the mood or clear the general animosity against Alessandro.

At the last hour, in one last attempt to liven up the scene, Daniel fetched over his ghetto blaster.

At first, with a dreamy smile and stray dreadlocks escaping from his tam, he sang to the music. Then, pacing up and down the yard, he launched into a passionate sermon about Jah Rastafari. Words tumbled from his lips, mellow and soothing. His deep voice filled the place, commanding attention. People gathered around him, listening with approving smiles.

Giulia came to stand near me.

'I don't want to be unkind,' she whispered into my ear, 'but you know what? I think that here, as always, a higher power decided the course of events. On the day of the accident, those four people met their karma. Think of it. Neither Ylenia nor the baby in Clara's belly got hurt, because they were innocent. Clara was obsessed with Gabriel, so she was fated to lose him. Gabriel was selfish. He didn't care about anybody else. So, he lost what he valued most: his life. Finally, Alessandro. His stinginess is his worst defect. What better punishment? What goes around comes around...'

I looked at Giulia's composed face. She was totally convinced.

Meanwhile Daniel held centre stage; his eyes shone, his locks shook, his gaze was hazy. He stood there in the middle of the yard, like an actor on stage under the dazzling light of the reflectors.

'It was Babylon that killed our brethren,' he boomed. 'Down with Babylon!'

'Ya, man! Down with Babylon!' The men around him nodded.

Spells, CIA, mafia, karma, Babylon… each of these explanations made sense to those who espoused them.

Me? I wasn't so worried about finding someone to blame or discovering what had really happened. What I wanted to know was whether the Livingsteños would ever forgive Alessandro for causing Gabriel's death. Would they ever accept him back into their village? More to the point, would any of us gringos enjoy the same unquestioning acceptance we had come to expect until now?

It was just gone one in the morning when Rafael and I said goodnight and left the *velorio*. Daniel's baritone followed us down the path for quite some time before it finally died out in the dark.

CHAPTER TWENTY-TWO

PAUL

NEW YORK, NEW YORK

'What Information? What truth? Lies, goddamn 24-carat lies, all the lies fit to print, and then some. That's our so-called free press. Lies, lies, money, money.' Paul, the anarchist, let steam off before, during and after our Spanish lessons.

Once a week, at the appointed time, he'd turn up at my place, all boyish eagerness, notebook, pencil and rubber; ready to learn. For him, Spanish was the language of revolution, of Fidel, of Che, of Sandino. I soon realised we shared a number of similar ideas and, over the weeks, what had begun as a simple teacher-pupil exchange turned into something more substantial – a source of support and friendship. Still, whenever I could, I liked to provoke him.

'Come on, Paul,' I taunted him, 'you miss New York and all the wonderful things it offers. Just a little bit? The films, the food, Greenwich Village, the art, the culture, the gigs, the air conditioning…'

'Yeah, sure, New York has that and a lot more. But the price you pay? Man! Great, if you fancy spending your life busting your balls in a cut-throat concrete jungle. Not worth a few scraps of your so-called "culture", trust me.' He reached out for his guitar.

'Livingston has all the culture I need. And no artsy-fartsy bullshit here, no big, bad boss breathing down my neck, just freedom, man, *libertad*! I just get up in the morning, put on my jeans and walk to the beach. That's where I get my fill of culture, my *educashun*.'

He hummed the last few words over the chords of his guitar.

Sometimes we had our lessons at his place, sitting on the veranda. He rented an old house of bamboo cane built in a secluded spot, on raised ground. The side facing the valley tilted forward at an angle, giving me the disquieting feeling that at any moment it might tumble down the hill. In front of us was a tall hedge of *carnavel*. Through its foliage and red blossoms, we watched, unseen, the people stroll along the road below, and further away, we could see the sprawling cemetery, its tombstones covered with overgrown bush. Opposite us, on the hilltop, a vast secular *ceiba* stretched out its roots and branches. We sat there, on a long wooden bench, drinking cup after cup of strong ginger tea. The view was breathtaking, but we were so wrapped up in our discussions, we would only give it the odd glance.

'They say work sets you free, don't they?' Paul said, fixing his pale blue eyes on me. 'Bullshit, man. You could train a monkey to do most work. Work distracts you from thinking, reading and learning from life. New York is just about work and money, hustle and bustle, and what for?'

'"*Steer clear of New York, oh, yeah*",' he sang. '"*Steer clear of the big bad rotten apple!*"'

'Better one hundred years of Livingston than one year of what they call the "civilised world",' he always said at the end of each tirade.

Pale and thin, he always wore the same pair of jeans, torn at the knees, a black T-shirt, espadrilles and his inseparable guitar. In all the time I knew him, I never understood whether he was a good musician or a bad one. He would strum complicated tunes of his own invention, but his music was always a little raw, unfinished. 'Work in progress,' he said.

A New Yorker by birth, he'd once rented a flat in East Harlem. 'That concrete hell-hole, that Babylon, that den of iniquity,' he ranted about it. And yet it was forever-present in his doom-laden ravings. He made it sound as if Hell and Paradise had come together there, and seemed both repelled and fascinated by it.

At our first lesson, he told me he'd worked as a courier.

'That was one hell of a radicalising experience.'

Tearing around the city from the down-town depot across the river, delivering his packages to "Wall Street assholes", "assorted shysters" and "big shots", had opened his eyes to all the city's ills.

'One minute I'd cycle past some poor bums panhandling for dimes, the next I'd be cruising behind some rich guy in his chauffeur-driven limo. When you get up close to those guys, jeez, the look they throw outta their tinted windows, like they own the world. "Don't fool with me, kid, if you know what's good for you." Man, I hated those guys.'

But, it turned out, there were things in Livingston he didn't like either.

'These guys are just like my neighbours in New York. So damned cool. Hi, *amigo*. What's up, *amigo*? You wanna little smoke, *amigo*? They're all after something, a beer, a quarter of *Venado*, cash. Me? I nod and walk right past.'

Apart from me, his teacher, Paul had only two friends: Walter and Zina.

Walter was his live-in landlord. Among the young Rastas who crowded the town, Walter stood out as a rare "bald head". He shaved his skull smooth like a billiard ball. In his early thirties, strong, fit, mild-mannered, he spoke Spanish hesitantly with a lisp, making up improbable long words.

'*Este aquí es Paul, mi masmejorisimo amigo! Qué! Más que amigo, pues... mi hermano!*' he vowed, patting his white brother's back.

Walter was the most down-and-out landlord I'd ever seen. He

was forever borrowing money from his *"hermano"* until one day they came to the agreement that Paul would never again pay him rent.

Then there was Zina, a petite young woman of Garifuna and Mayan descent. With her luscious black hair cascading over her back, her large doe eyes, her skin the colour of milky coffee, she held a slew of spellbound men in thrall, each ready to lay himself at her feet.

'I look at her and can't stop marvelling. She's so... so... so artificial!' At first, Paul feigned indifference, and when he wasn't doing that, he would mock her. He had a talent for imitating her mannerisms. He coyly batted his eyelashes and, with a flick of the wrist, flung an imaginary mass of bouncy curls onto his back. He deconstructed each little part of her; her languid eyes, her candyfloss smile, the self-consciousness with which she stood and moved. Aping her, he'd even perfected a camp sway of the hips. 'She's like a B-movie starlet. She's acting all the time. But, yeah, okay, she's cute,' he said in the end, admitting his own capitulation. 'But, man, does she know it!'

A few months later, as their relationship became stronger, he finally moved out of Walter's house and went to live with her. That marked the end of our lessons, as, thanks to Zina, his Spanish rapidly improved. We still met for chats, although more rarely.

After moving in with Zina, Paul appeared different, more subdued. Even his rants, when they came, were half-hearted affairs. Gone were his boastful certainties of a few weeks earlier; now he was besieged by doubt.

'What do you think she wants from me?' As he struggled to make sense of something so far beyond his grasp, his blue gaze revealed suspicion, fear, surprise, incredulity, and hopeful expectation, all mixed up together.

But, from what he himself told me, Zina didn't seem to want anything at all. She wasn't after his money; she always paid more than her fair share; she treated Paul to food and drinks; she regularly went to work at the stationery shop in the town centre. She lived her own life and made no demands on him. Perhaps that's what bothered him.

Zina lived five or six miles out of town, in the jungle. Most mornings, on my way back from the beach after buying fish, I caught sight of her as she went to work, always so neat, so perfectly turned out. How could she be so… "pristine", after trudging miles through the bush?

'She gets up at the crack of dawn,' Paul said to me. 'First, she puts on her makeup, then she irons her clothes, and finally she leaves for work. And guess what. She walks barefooted.' He laughed. 'At the first houses, she washes her feet in a stream, opens her handbag and *voilà*! Cinderella slips on her shiny high heels.

'That's Zina for you, always self-conscious, always dolled up. She says it's her boss that wants her to look pretty. Who's she trying to kid? I know her, she likes the attention.' I said nothing. How was this mismatched pair going to get along?

Recently, he'd lost some weight. He'd always been thin, but now a slow burning fever seemed to be consuming him.

'How do you like living out in the bush?' I asked him.

'I love it. It's wonderful to be so far from Babylon. The view is amazing. You should come and check it out. I'm sure you'll like it.'

He didn't have to say it twice. One sunny day, without forewarning, I made my way to his house.

Although the rainy season had ended, the track was still slushy. To avoid the mud, I had to leap from one grassy side to the other.

As the path slowly wound up the hills, the roofs of Livingston grew smaller and smaller, until they disappeared behind a stormy sea of foliage. l walked along the ridge of a hill and from there, to my right, I saw a glistening blue strip of ocean in the far distance. To my left, as far as the eye could see, the green mass of the jungle spread out in waves.

I descended into shallow viewless valleys, and then climbed up to the top of the hills. Finally, I came to the house. It stood on a clearing a little below path level, made of a medley of bamboo cane and palm leaves. Chickens pecked around the grassless yard and a few vicious-looking ducks splashed in the rain puddles.

As I approached the house, a pack of dogs rushed out towards me, growling and showing their sharp teeth.

'Quiet!' someone shouted. It was Paul, who appeared on the path, right behind me. Immediately, the mongrels stopped snarling.

'Good timing,' he said. 'I'm just back from the woods.'

Under the malevolent stare of the dogs, I followed him down the slope into the house.

It was dark inside. Dazzled by the sunlight, at first, I couldn't see a thing.

There wasn't much to see in any case. Flowery oilcloth curtains divided the hut into three rooms. I found myself right in the middle of what must have been the living room. A rickety old table stood to one side, with three old chairs. A kerosene lamp hung from a beam. From beneath two dishevelled armchairs, some rusty springs uncoiled onto the earthen floor.

On the armchair closest to the door sat a slight young man with tattered clothes and a mop of unkempt black hair. As we entered, he sprang to his feet. '*Hola!*' he greeted us, with the same broad smile as Zina's.

'This is Rogelio, Zina's brother.' Paul introduced us. Then he turned to the other chair. 'And that's Lili, she's…' He stopped halfway through his sentence and rushed forward.

There, in the darkness, lay a small angular bundle, twisted and crooked like the frame of a broken chair.

The girl was six or seven. She smiled at him, nodding excitedly, then surged forward, striving to stand up and run to him. But, however hard she tried, something jerked her back repeatedly onto her seat.

Paul brushed his hand over her black curly hair, laid a soft kiss over it, and then knelt at her feet. Two pieces of string kept the girl's ankles tightly fixed onto the crossbar of the chair. With infinite patience, he set her free.

Then he gently picked her up and carried her in his arms into the yard. Lili shrieked happily and, wobbling on her emaciated legs, she began to chase the ducks through the puddles.

'Lili *es muy traviesa*,' mumbled Rogelio, with averted eyes. 'Yes, you're a bad, bad girl, always up to mischief!' He turned to the little girl, waving a menacing index.

'What on earth has she done to deserve being tied up?' Paul asked him, angrily.

Rogelio told us the little girl had gone into the bedroom and, while playing with Zina's makeup, had knocked a bottle of expensive perfume off the table, spilling the lot onto the dirt floor.

'There!' said Paul bitterly. 'A woman who can hardly afford food for her daughter, and yet owns enough cosmetics to open up a beauty salon! You see what advertising comes to?'

We broke off some straight branches from a tree and went for a long trek through the woods.

The jungle was thick and mysterious. The only sounds came from us, trudging through the undergrowth, and from the birds that called each other high up in the trees.

We came to a stream and plunged our muddy feet into the water. We sat there for a long time in silence. Paul stared at his feet, at the pebbles, at the tree trunks, then turned his intense blue gaze on me.

'I'm in a pickle,' he said. 'I'm running out of money. Soon I'll have to leave and go back to New York. And I am wondering whether to ask Zina to come with me. I'd have to marry her, wouldn't I?'

He told me about his scruples and good intentions, about how he thought she'd be quick at learning the ropes and even grow to like the city. But would it work between them? They were so different.

'What excuse do I have not to take her with me? I can give her a chance to see something of the world, expand her horizons. Above all, she could work there and make enough money to give Lili proper care.'

He spoke intensely, with passion. He wanted my advice. I felt like asking him when the place he claimed to loathe so much had become the Promised Land, but it would have been cruel. I stood there, nodding in sympathy.

Around us, a light breeze stirred the treetops, the birds sang, and the stream chattered on in the peace of the afternoon.

Later, he walked me to the first houses of Livingston. There we parted. He walked away with long, fast steps. When I turned, he'd already vanished up the trail.

CHAPTER TWENTY-THREE

THE SEASON OF THE SECOND RAIN MAN

The rains began again. It was a full-scale deluge. It poured for hours, making it hard to go out at night.

Rafael stopped coming. He didn't like getting wet. Besides, now he had a job in town, which took up most of his time and energy.

Out there in my hut on the beach, next to the quiet canal and the little palm grove that rustled in the cool easterly wind, I began to feel lonely and sad.

Violent gusts swished over my thatched roof, ruffling the *manaca* leaves. The hut was ancient and every night there was a new disaster: a trickle of rain there by the window, a small flood seeping from underneath the back door. Finally, part of the roof gave way.

At night, I would lie in bed, wide awake, and listen to the rain beating down. Right above me, through a ten-inch gap, a strip of dark sky stared back at me as I looked up. Thick sheets of rain fell through the hole, digging deep grooves into the sand.

'What're you doing there, living all alone in that crumbling shack?' said Rafael. 'It's unhealthy. You'll catch your death. Come and live with me! What are you waiting for?'

I'd always liked my independence. Besides, Carmen and Joaquín's words to me were still echoing in my mind. But, in the end, unable to bear either the dampness or the loneliness of my existence on the beach, I decided to ignore all warnings. At the close of a week of relentless rain, I accepted Rafael's offer and moved in with him.

Barrio Barrique was two minutes away from the corner shop, five minutes from the town hall, and ten from the docks. Rafael was rightly proud of his house. As he often reminded me, the *hombre sencillo* had built it himself on a handkerchief of land squeezed between Mama Jo's thatched hut and a two-storied concrete building where three Garifuna sisters and their children lived. Dwarfed by the neighbours, his hut looked quaint, like something out of a storybook.

Through the shutters of our bedroom window, unseen, I watched the three sisters carry out their chores in their yard. They'd pound yam and plantains in tall wooden pestles, wash gaudy-coloured clothes in their own private *pila*, and now that the *camarones* season had started, they'd sit in a semi-circle on low stools, cleaning mountains of pink shrimps in huge plastic tubs. As they worked, they sang in Garifuna. 'They sing about love, death, long sea journeys,' Rafael told me.

The three women only stopped to scold their children or shoo away the chickens and the pigs. Sometimes they burst out laughing. 'Youhouh!' they howled.

At the back, there were more houses, clustered around the overgrown backyard that Rafael had shown me so proudly the first time I'd gone there.

At noon, from each house came the sizzling and crackling of fish or meat being fried. For a moment, the backyard stood quiet and empty. Then, Chachón appeared, his bulk filling the frame of his back door, his belly hanging like a pillow over the waist of his trousers. '*Buen provecho. Bon appetit*,' he wished all the neighbours, visible and invisible.

This was my neighbourhood, and these were my neighbours. At such close quarters, life had no secrets for anyone who lived here. Nothing could go unnoticed, whether it was a new love affair or a heated argument, the joy in the birth of a new baby or the outpouring of grief on someone's death.

And yet, I soon discovered that this public existence had its unspoken rules. When the first circles of soft yellow light shone in the darkness, a sense of privacy descended over each hut. People hushed their voices, radios stopped blaring out calypsos and, back from their outdoor games, the children were finally sent to bed.

*

There's a part of the day I always look forward to, the morning, when, woken by the crowing of the cockerels and the neighbours' blaring radios, Rafael and I jump out of bed.

First, we open the front door and, for a few minutes, bask in the sun. Then, Rafael picks up his straw hat, his tools, and goes to work, while I stroll, barefoot, to the harbour and then along the beach.

I'm on my way to buy the most prized commodity in the village: *uvi*, fish.

It's only seven when the first fishermen come back to the shore. They sell their catch fresh, alive, still wriggling on the bottom of their boats.

A group of women rush up to each new arrival with their baskets, elbow their way through the crowd, pick out the best fish and bargain fiercely over it. They buy in bulk and, later, in town, they sell on retail.

There's an unspoken rule about this trade. The Garifunas buy only from other Garifunas, the small fishermen who go out at sea in their own *cayucos*. The Indians – the coolies, as they call them here – do all their buying from the big trawlers owned by the *capitalinos* and manned by other coolies. That is the way each group looks after and supports their own – something entirely lost on me in those early days when I idealised Livingston as a paradise of equality and diversity.

The longer I stay, the more I realise that, like anywhere else, Livingston is a divided and complex community, full of the usual fears, prejudices and ethnic hierarchies.

'They're simple girls, used to life in the bush,' says Carmen of her two Mayan helpers. 'Without their chickens, their pigs, their hills, they're lost. You have to tell them everything, poor girls, they're like children!'

'*Indio zerote,*' complains Rafael when the Ladino of the corner shop ignores him.

'*Pinche moreno,*' the Ladino shouts back.

It goes on like this, a never-ending to and fro of racial insults. Carmen had said it clearly: whenever they can avoid it, people of different races do not mix. And as I look around the beach, here, on this stretch of shingle where I'm now standing, I'm suddenly aware that she was right. This is Garifuna territory, and at this moment, I'm the only white person here.

Everywhere I look, there's fish – *palometas, mojarras, dromas* – strung up together in tight bundles by the gills or piled up, loose, on top of each other, in large wicker baskets. When these are full, the women hoist them on their heads and parade proudly into town, erect and stately, as if it was not slimy fish they were carrying but bunches of scented flowers.

I never dare go up to the boats myself. I watch the women bargain from a distance. When they finish, I approach them.

'Fish! Good fish! One dollar a pound!' Marciana shouts in my direction. She's in her mid-fifties, tall and busty. She's standing in the water with her pleated skirt gathered up around her waist. She waves at me and says something in Garifuna that makes everybody laugh. She probably cracked a joke about me.

In the meantime, legs deep in water, trousers rolled up to their knees, the men cut and clean the larger fish on makeshift wooden tables. With long, shiny knives, they slash through the meat, discard scales, tails, fins, tear out the guts and throw all the waste into the sea. Finally, they sprinkle handfuls of salt over the white flesh.

Among them, there's Bibi, the drag queen I see partying wildly in the bars and discos at the other end of the beach, at night. Here, today, in shorts and a ragged T-shirt, he looks like all the other men. Except that, as I watch him handle the large chunks of fish with dexterity, my eyes travel to his nails; despite being short and chipped, they're painted a bright shade of red.

A cloud of pelicans hovers by the shore, waiting for leftovers. Every time the men discard something, they all move forward together, flapping their wings noisily and snapping their beaks. From time to time, a lucky few catch a chunk in mid-air and swallow it all in one go, before another bird can tear it away from them.

There are the times when a boat comes in with a *róbalo* or a *sábalo*. Then a curious crowd gathers around *"la bestia"*.

Standing over the large carcass, a sturdy man with a bushy beard and a baseball cap jabs away at it with a stick. The big round scales flick everywhere, paving the shingle with glistening flakes of mother-of-pearl.

By hitting the back of a huge knife with the stick, the man rapidly slices the fish into large chunks and sells them to the people around. For a moment, there's a fluttering of green notes around him. He collects them neatly in between each finger; then, he rolls them up into a bundle and stashes them into his pocket.

The sun is getting hotter now. People work faster, with more precision. They hardly lift their eyes from their knives, and yet they never stop exchanging jokes. Amid their laughter, the working hours fly.

Carrying the six fish I bought threaded on a reed, I walk back into town with a sense of achievement. Then, back in the hut, I begin to cook.

Since I moved in with Rafael, this is my life. I live like most of the women here: I cook for my man, I go to the fountain and wash his clothes and mine, and at night I wait by candlelight for him to come home from work or from some bar.

This is what, jokingly, I call my Geisha period. It feels as if I've stepped into somebody else's life. By comparison, Mariangela and Giulia are borderline feminists, never holding back if they feel "their man" has crossed a line. But I don't mind this "submissive" me; I like the novelty. I even feel gratified when, on his way home for lunch, Rafael starts calling me "*Mi amor!*" so loudly and from such a distance along the path that everyone in the neighbourhood can hear him.

And then one day – 'Will you marry me?' He throws the question at me like that, casually, as if it were a joke.

I don't say yes or no. I just look at him and smile. That seems to encourage him.

'*Monica, aquí, va a ser mi esposa,*' from then on, he introduces me to everyone around. Not just as his *nummari,* but his future legally sanctioned wife.

This new, submissive me is flattered and happy, like a child who's been promised a trip to Wonderland. But when I lapse back into my adult self, I'm aware of how preposterous the proposition sounds.

I go back and forth like this. One minute thinking, yes, if Mariangela and Giulia can do this, so can I. Then the doubts and the wild speculation. Is there a future for me and Rafael in Europe? Can I give him a better life than he has here? Would he adapt? He didn't the first time around, when he spent those three months in Italy with Valeria. But surely he's learnt a thing or two from that experience. Besides, this is me, not Valeria. But, more to the point, would I want him to adapt? Adapt to what? To the dullness of a regular nine-to-five existence? Haven't I spent most of my life running away from that very idea? That's why I've wound up here in the first place.

There've also been many warnings coming my way. Carmen at the Comedor Cali, the young woman at the fountain, they've all tried to tell me something about this man. Should I believe them?

Are their stories true? I'm aware the situation is far from ideal, but... But just now I'm happy to be living right here, with him, in the *barrio*, feeling at last fully part of it. Just now I don't want to think ahead, weigh the pros and cons, torture myself with big, painful questions. Why not let things run their course? Stripped to its bare bones, life can be simple.

CHAPTER TWENTY-FOUR

SATURDAY NIGHT FEVER

Working on the missing bridge during the rainy season was like Penelope's weaving. During daytime, the eight labourers slogged away in a pool of sweat and muddy water while they bolstered the banks of the stream. At night, large chunks of soil crumbled off the edges, and the torrential rain undid their work.

Every morning, in front of each new landslide, Rafael cursed furiously, first at the damned weather, then at the cheap materials. But above all, he cussed "that useless lot who sit on their fat asses" in the town hall.

'Starting work on the bridge now, in the middle of the rainy season? Damn fools! When was the last time they picked up a spade? They don't know the first thing about the building trade, and there they are, deciding everything. Those worthless *capitalinos* are in charge of everything. They live it up in Guatemala City, then come back and tell us what to do.' His outburst over, he would thrust his tattered straw hat low over his forehead and step into the torpid mud.

Five days a week he went on like this, no let-up in the rain, and no let-up in his impotent anger. Then, finally, it was payday.

Every Saturday, an indefinable sense of restlessness crept over the village. It started early in the morning and continued throughout the day. By evening, the air was buzzing.

At ten to five, the bridge workers dropped their shovels and gathered around the foreman.

'*Hombre,* why don't you cough up a few more *quetzals* this week, eh?' said one of the men.

'Yeah, *jefe,* come on. This bridge is bloody hard work,' said another.

'We did loads of overtime. We slogged through our lunch hour, didn't we, guys?' said a third.

The foreman cut them short: 'You lot, stop wasting my time.' He was a spindly, mean-looking Ladino and stared coldly at each of them. 'If you want a pay rise, go and talk to *el patrón* in Puerto Barrios.' End of discussion.

Every Saturday, as I made my way past the missing bridge to one or other of my language students, I heard these arguments. Sometimes I would stop under the arch of the cemetery and, half-hidden by the foliage, watch the men thrust the notes into their pockets and walk away, muttering, disgruntled. They complained loudly that the pay was miserable, that it wouldn't last them through to the end of the week. And yet the prospect of a work-free Sunday would soon boost their morale. The occasion called for celebration. They patted each other on the back and, roaring with laughter, they made a beeline for the nearest bar. They would get drunk as quickly as possible and then – depending on each man's taste and inclination – either stagger through town and keel over into a ditch until morning or start a brawl over some real or imagined offense against their manhood. On Saturdays, Livingston was like that – a scene straight out of a Spaghetti Western.

As for Rafael, first he liked to come back home. There, he stepped out of his mucky overalls, and then, standing naked in the backyard, he washed the grime off himself with buckets of soapy water. Finally, he slipped on the clothes he had brought back from Italy. He was a swanky dresser. His best was a pair of white and turquoise striped trousers, a matching shirt and waistcoat, and white leather shoes. He tucked his thick locks into a Tam hat banded with red, gold and green. Then, unable to keep still and in one place a moment longer, he went out on the town.

He would start the evening alone, drinking and smoking in a kind of frenzy. A few hours later, having satisfied his thirst for excitement, he came and joined me either at home or on the beach, at the Lugudi Barana.

*

SATURDAY 12TH MARCH

The night was peaceful. A breeze blew in from the sea, and the stars glittered. Sitting on an old dory, I watched a silver slice of moon rise slowly from behind the crest of the palm trees.

Belén, one of my Garifuna acquaintances, sat with me. I'd met her in town, and she'd followed me down the beach, chatting about the usual things – about not having any money, her husband over in Canada, the day's unbearable heat.

Belén was in her early thirties, tall and thin, with striking looks. She wasn't beautiful; she was too bony, with missing teeth and a mean expression on her face. And yet I couldn't take my eyes off her. She exuded charm, a captivating grace. She sauntered along the street, straight as a broomstick, several inches taller thanks to a small straw hat with a red ribbon perched on her head. Her sinewy arms swung rhythmically, and her piercing eyes met people's gazes full on. *You try and mess with me,* they said.

'Watch out, she's a *ratera,*' the *mara* warned me. 'She steals from people.' None of the locals seemed to like her. With them, she was sullen and uncommunicative. With us foreigners, though, she was all smiles. Her lips would part slowly, at an angle, over a wide front gap framed by a couple of golden teeth. Her grin was disarming, but in time, even the most gullible of foreigners wised up to the anger that flashed through her eyes.

She had a thick, husky voice, the voice of a woman who's been around.

'*Qué tal, amiga?*' that night, she called out to me from a distance. She was dressed up for the occasion – tight red and white stripy pants, a frilly shirt, huge hoop earrings and a golden chain.

'*Amiga! Necesito una ayuda para comprar un Venado!*' Direct, straightforward. No heartbreaking stories from Belén, no disabled husband or sick children, no beating about the bush. She wanted a quarter bottle of rum. Could I buy it for her?

I could, so she followed me down the beach into one of the bars.

Five minutes later, she was sitting quietly next to me, clutching her *cuarto*, now and then taking bold swigs from it.

Music blared out of the discotheque. It was the old reggae classics that Martino played at the beginning of each night – Bob Marley, Peter Tosh, Bunny Wailer. I stood up and traced a few steps on the sand. Then, unable to wait any longer, I left my *amiga* to her rum and went inside.

The hall was jam-packed with bodies shimmying and rocking to the beat. The odd soloist leapt and shook between the couples. I joined in and forgot all about Belén sitting on the beach outside, scanning the dark with her hawkish eyes.

As more and more people entered the hall, the dancing became more sensual and daring. Clad in shiny fabrics, the women's bodies shimmered as they swayed and wound themselves around the men. Emboldened, the men clasped them tight and pulled them closer against their hips.

I plunged into the crowd and the flood of music. After the deep booming of the reggae bass, came the echoing sound of a steel band, then the lilt of a calypso, and finally the relentless slapping of dozens of conga drums. I was engulfed by waves of sound.

I danced for hours, oblivious of everyone around. I was also oblivious of the absence of Rafael.

Then, suddenly, there he was at the far end of the hall. He danced a crouching dance of his own invention, all his energy compressed there where he stood, his eyes fixed on to the ground, half closed. He stepped to the right then to the left, his spindly legs always returning to the same spot, an enigmatic smile on his face. I knew that, for all his concentration, he was keeping a close eye on me and on the man I was dancing with.

Feigning indifference, I danced on with Armando. We struck one pose after another and laughed. With Rafael watching me from across the room, I was having to work hard to maintain my free and easy mood.

I kept an eye on him too and saw him dancing with a pretty, chubby girl. She had a beautiful oval face, bright slanted eyes and a dashing smile. She wove herself sensually around him.

A few minutes later, he sprang up right behind me. I turned to dance with him, but his steps did not match mine. Each wrapped in our own world, we danced to rhythms that played inside our heads and only we could hear. We did not need partners.

When he went to the bar, the pretty girl suddenly appeared by my side. With a smile, she grabbed me by the arms and pressed me tightly against her breast, then, dexterously, forced me to intertwine my legs with hers in one single interlocking wave. She was in charge of me. She made me turn right, and then left. She made me pirouette. At first, I felt stiff and clumsy, but gradually, I began to respond. When I finally performed to her satisfaction, she led me to the bar from where, slouched against the counter cluttered with empty bottles, Rafael watched us.

'My name is Sara,' said the girl, 'and this is Rafael, my *nati*, my half-brother.' In the Melquior family, all the siblings had different fathers, and none of them looked alike.

'I'd do anything for her,' said Rafael.

'Yeah, me too,' she answered.

Now that the identity of the beautiful woman was no longer a threat, I relaxed.

I danced until I was exhausted. Rafael and I drank and laughed and kissed and hugged. Pretty soon, we were drunk. Now Rafael looked even more impressive as he danced. He spread out his arms wide, with the power of a falcon in flight. Spellbound, I watched him smile to himself. What was he thinking? Only his body was here on the dance floor; the rest of him seemed far away, floating God knows where. He reminded me of the *bujey* at the *chugu*, the shaman who turned out to be Gabriel's dad. As he shook the incense around the room, the old man had seemed distant and unapproachable. Perhaps, just like the *bujey* that night, Rafael was now in a trance. Mesmerised by him, I danced and danced.

At the Lugudi Barana, the night came to an end. We were the last revellers to leave. But we wanted more – more music, more fun, more of everything, so we walked along the beach and went into all the bars that were still open. In each one, we became a little happier, livelier, drunker. It was three in the morning when we decided to pay our last visit to Brizas del Mar.

The place opened only on Saturdays when a Garifuna band performed to a bunch of *aficionados*. It was a strictly Garifuna hangout and even that night, despite the late hour, the dark green barn was packed.

The band played *punta*, a medley of repetitive African rhythms and guitar-based ballads. Until then, I'd never heard music like this, nor had I seen these guys in any of the other venues. They were mostly old, and sat in clusters at rectangular wooden tables, on benches screwed to the floor. They drank bootleg rum and talked Garifuna in loud voices. On a dais in a corner, stood a battered jukebox – silent. The music came from a long, narrow gallery running high up along one side of the hall. Perched on it, dark faces receding into deeper darkness, sat the musicians: two drummers, a guitarist, a shaker player, a vocalist. The sixth guy was blowing on a conch shell that emitted a long and sad solitary note, like the distant horn of a departing ship. People in the audience knew all the lyrics and sang along. Then, one after the other, they took to the dance floor. With complex shuffling steps, they moved across it, first the women, coquettishly, with slow rotating movements of the hips, then, more jerkily, the men.

Were I sober, I would have felt like an intruder in such a place. But I was very drunk and, although I thought I saw sly glances, the quick turn of cold shoulders, and sensed a touch of mild hostility in the air, I chose to ignore it. I walked into the hall with absolute confidence, as if by right I belonged there.

In the dim light, I made out a few familiar faces: a couple of girls from Happy Land entertaining a passing British sailor; the man with silvery hair who at the *chugu* had called me Rafael's *nummari*, the one in my dream. He was having a break from playing in the balcony, and when he saw us, he waved his rum bottle in the air. A happy drunk, I waved back.

At the other side of the room, I caught sight of Belén. She saw me too and marched over.

'Call Rafael for me, will you?' There was an unmistakable ring of hostility in her voice, but I was so blissfully happy that it washed over me. Like a chirpy carrier pigeon, I flew obediently right over to Rafael and delivered her message.

Immediately, he walked over to Belén and the two started an animated discussion in Garifuna. In a daze, I stood there and watched them mouth incomprehensible angry-sounding words, each underlined by frenzied gestures.

Something snapped, and suddenly all those words turned into an outburst of rage.

The two pounced on each other and people jumped out of the way. Inside the makeshift ring that formed around them, Rafael cursed and shouted, flailing his arms right in front of Belén's face, and spinning around, out of control. She shouted too, but there was a pleading note in her voice. Her long, thin arms looked very fragile next to his muscles. She fended off the blows, but neither retaliated nor retreated. She took a few steps backwards, to the left and to the right, ducking his blows.

Around me, the world spun. I had to do something.

Suddenly I found myself hugging Belén by her waist.

'Leave my friend alone! Don't hit her!' I cried, wanting to defend her not just from Rafael but from an entire troupe of imaginary enemies gathered around.

Without knowing how I got there, I found myself crouched

behind a screen of fishing nets. Belén was by my side, whispering mysterious words in a soothing voice.

Then, I was catapulted right into the middle of the yard. I was still holding on to Belén when the ominous silhouette of Rafael appeared, brandishing a huge stick with both hands. He aimed it at us.

The heavy blow landed on Belén's back and pulled us apart. Belén recoiled but remained standing, upright.

In the confusion that followed, a one-legged man with crutches grabbed hold of me. I sank into his arms, finding comfort in the mellow sound of his voice.

I sobbed, powerless and frustrated.

Then I must have blacked out. All I remember of that part of the night was Rafael dragging me away from the one-legged man, and me scrambling behind him up the steep path to his home.

Sometime later, I vomited up my guts in Rafael's backyard. As I bent over on the grass retching, I felt a presence lurking in the dark.

When I looked up, there stood Belén.

'Come, quick,' she said. 'Pick up your things and come with me, now!'

'Tomorrow, Belén,' I pleaded. 'We'll talk tomorrow. Just now, let me be.'

To my surprise, she vanished.

I went inside and tumbled onto the bed, next to Rafael. Then I fell into a dark and heavy sleep that lasted well over twelve hours.

I woke up with a throbbing head, a foul taste in my mouth. All around were the smells, his and mine, of a misspent night. I struggled to make sense of what had happened. It had all spun around me so fast, so uncontrollably, with people shouting words I didn't understand, and then, on top of it, all that damned alcohol. Thinking of it made me dizzy.

The memory of Rafael's violent outburst against Belén suddenly came back to me and shocked me all over again. I needed an explanation. I asked him for his side of the story, if indeed he had one. I **needed** him to have one. What could ever justify so much brutality?

He turned his back on me.

'You don't know that woman. She's a menace. You stay out of her way. Now, do me a favour and leave me alone, I need to sleep.'

I got up and made myself some coffee, while he pulled the pillow over his head.

It was mid-afternoon when he put in an appearance. He went to the demijohn, poured himself a large glass of water, and drank it with big, noisy gulps. Then he came over and put an arm around me.

'What's gone on between you two?' I said. 'I need to know.'

'That woman is mad. Don't have anything to do with her. It's just a big fuss about nothing, okay? It'll blow over. Why do you care about her anyway?'

'I want to know. What could she have possibly done for you to hit her like that?'

'I just defended myself, didn't I? You don't know that woman. Years ago, we had a fling, and she never let me forget about it. *La zorra* won't give up. Yah, man, she's hooked on me. She's, like, totally obsessed. Anyway, that's all in the past. I never liked her. No one can tell me what to do. That woman loves fighting. You should have seen the size of the guys she picked fights with. She's afraid of nothing, that one. Once she stabbed a man and almost killed him.' He smiled wickedly at the shock on my face.

'Last night, you saw it yourself. She started it.' He lay down on the bed, burying his head under the pillow, again.

'Started what?' I insisted.

He sat up and looked at me defiantly.

'Okay, then. You want to know what your precious Belén thinks of you and your kind? You really do? So, here's what she said: "*What is it with you and these filthy gringas I always see you with*?" That's what she was going on about as she chased me all over the place. "*You're my man, you're my man,*" he said in a high-pitched voice. 'That's your Belén, that's your friend. And *la cabrona* thinks I belong to her.'

That evening, when Rafael checked his wallet, he flew into a rage. Except for one pitiful five-*quetzal* note, he'd blown his entire weekly pay.

'I'm an asshole! From now on, no more boozing for me, only spliff,' he promised himself. 'I'll stay here in my hammock and quietly smoke my *mota*.'

*

Monday came around again. The sun blazed down as usual, and Rafael and the other labourers were back at work on the missing bridge.

CHAPTER TWENTY-FIVE

CARA MONICA...

After that ill-fated Saturday, all I wanted was to forget the brawl. I told myself that it was Belén who had started it. "*La ratera*", as Rafael called her, brought all that rage upon herself.

That was how I squared Rafael's viciousness with the sensation of his soft, protective arms around me. That was how I soothed my conscience.

Would Rafael ever lash out at me as he'd done at Belén? Not in a million years, I told myself; that was just impossible.

Whenever I thought back to that night's events, everything was blurred. I was too drunk, and the world spun too fast for me to make sense of things. At least that's what I tried to tell myself, over and over, until I began to believe it.

What's lunch going to be today? Chicken or fish? That was the question I now asked myself each morning – all other, and bigger, questions left unasked, for if I asked them, I knew what the answer would be.

Instead, I threw myself, perversely, into my "wifely" chores, going either to the beach to stock up on *palometas* or *róbalo*, or to the corner shop, where Ramón, the Ladino storekeeper, handed over the counter, wrapped in a paper bundle, the two chicken quarters he'd weighed for me.

'*Hoy te rayaste!* Discounted price today, aren't you lucky?' he said spiritedly, thrusting into his pocket the three q*uetzal* notes I gave him.

Every day, before I went back to Rafael's hut and started cooking, I popped into the post office, just to see if there were any letters waiting for me.

I'd throw a questioning look across the room at the Ladino woman behind the desk, who immediately recognised me. Usually, she stared back and shook her head ruefully, saving me the long queue.

But today she nodded and smiled, and, when my turn came, the bundle she handed over the counter was bulkier than I ever hoped.

*

TREVISO, 8TH MARCH

Cara Monica,

I've just come back from your grandad's funeral. Two weeks ago, he took a turn for the worse and was admitted to hospital. He died eight days later, but until now I couldn't face writing.

We all knew he wasn't well, but his decline was so sudden, so rapid that it came as a surprise. And so did the cause of his death. Guess what? Il nonno suffered from cirrhosis of the liver, that is, he drank too much. There I was, so worried about my smoking, my diet, your father, your Uncle Tulio, that I missed out on what was really going on with Grandad. A man who, after having half of his stomach removed all those years ago, always diluted his wine with water; a man who, when out with his friends, emptied his drink in the nearest flowerpot or umbrella rack to pretend he could hold his alcohol. What mattered to him was being with his friends and paying his round. As he aged, his circle got smaller, and I guess it became harder to get away with his tricks. He got into the habit of drinking sherry, Baileys, any liqueur that left a sweet aftertaste in his mouth. He started drinking at home. Now I know how many bottles he went through. I blame the doctor. How could he have failed to notice? All those tests for what? In fact, I think we all failed him. If we'd kept a closer eye on him and his habits, he'd still be here with us, alive!

I suppose the good thing was he didn't suffer much or for very long. When in hospital, he had a few bouts of colic, then, just a few days later, he could no longer keep his food down.

Miranda and I took turns at his bedside. She did the nights and I did the days. Armando arrived from Melbourne on Wednesday. Thank God he made it in time.

Around midday, Granddad said to me in a calm voice, 'I won't see the morning.'

'Playing doctor, are you?' I laughed. 'Making your own diagnosis?'

We bet ten thousand liras and shook hands on that. The joke seemed to make him happy.

Around four, four thirty in the morning, he passed away. At two, he waved goodbye first to me and then to Miranda. Then he lost consciousness. He ranted and raved about some village fair. 'Let's not move from here,' he said, 'this is a good place. Go and tell Miranda...'

At some point, to give him some relief, Miranda and I put our arms underneath him and propped him up. He smiled; you know that smile of his. 'It feels good to sit here on this bed of cyclamens...' That was the last thing he said.

Later, he raised his arm to make the sign of the cross, but I had to help him because he was so weak. His eyes were misty; his breathing was calm. He died like that, peacefully.

Monica tesoro, that's all my news.

And now I must ask you about yourself. Has the money from your bank arrived yet? I expect it will take much longer than usual, given that Livingston is so out of the way.

Dear Monica, both your dad and I are very worried. You never call, and we get a letter once in a blue moon. You say there are no roads, only a ferry, and the post takes ages. Yes, okay, but why on earth are you staying in such a godforsaken place? What if we need to contact you in an emergency? Do you ever think of that? And anyway, how much longer are you going to be in Guatemala?

I've also been thinking about the dates of my visit. Presumably you'll be staying in Livingston for the next two or three months, so how would you feel if I came around mid-May? Just me, on my own. Your dad has refused point-blank. 'It's her duty to come and see her parents, not the other way around,' he said. And, you know him, he won't change his mind.

Tesoro, please call me when you get this letter, so we can talk about it. In the meantime, Dad and I send all our love.

I miss you.

Mum

*

SHEFFIELD, 2ND MARCH 1987

Hi Monica,

Hope you're having an amazing time in Guatemala.

There's loads of letters waiting for you here. Most are just the usual bumph, but one looks major important. So, I'm forwarding it to you. Hope it reaches you before you move on.

Well, that's it. It would be good to know when you get this.

Cheers!

Keith

*

Barclays Bank PLC

Consumer Finance
PO Box 362, Manchester, M60 3PN
Telephone: LO-CALL 0845 3000442, Fax: 0845 3000552

Credit Card Number: 4667 6233 1929 3332

Miss M.L Florimonte
29 Hunterhouse Rd
Sheffield S9 1NP
Date of Notice: 30/03/1987
Issued in accordance with Sections 76(1) and 98(1) of the
Consumer Credit Act 1974

Important – you should read this carefully

Dear Miss Florimonte

We are writing to remind you that you have missed payments due under your credit card agreement.

This notice relates to the following payments:

20/10/1986 minimum payment due	*£278.00*
28/10/1986 minimum payment due	*£303.50*
You have made the following payment(s) towards the amounts requested above:	*£0.00*
Amount of payments outstanding for this arrears notice:	*£581.50*

The Bank hereby terminates your agreement, including an overdraft or reserve facilities, with effect from 20/03/1987 and makes demand for full and immediate repayment of the balance on the account (currently £ 397.75) with effect from that date. In the meantime, no further drawings on the account will be permitted. Daily interest charges of £0.50 will accrue from the above date until full payment is made.

If you do not settle the balance on your account, the Bank may transfer the debt to one of its recovery units or agents with a view to taking further action. Additionally, it is the Bank's intention to register details of the account with credit reference agencies.

This may seriously affect your ability to obtain credit.

If you have difficulty in paying any sum owing under the agreement, you can apply to the court which may make an order allowing you or any surety more time.

If you are not sure what to do, you should get help as soon as possible. For example, you should contact a solicitor, your local Trading Standards Department or your nearest Citizens' Advice Bureau.

Yours sincerely,

James S

Director

Barclays Consumer Finance Managers

*

And so, like buses, you wait for ages for a letter, and three turn up at once.

PART
FOUR

CHAPTER TWENTY-SIX

TALKING CRICKETS

"Dài retta a me, disse il grillo a Pinocchio, ritorna a casa."

LA AURORA INTERNATIONAL AIRPORT, GUATEMALA CITY, 19TH MAY.

I lean against the banister and look down into the arrival lounge. The plane from Amsterdam has yet to land, so the hall is empty, except for three Ladinos in sage green overalls clanking their mops and buckets across the floor. From my lookout at the furthest end of the visitors' gallery, I can see as far back as the set of doors through which the arriving passengers will soon burst forth. Around me, groups of relatives sit waiting, while swarms of children chase each other in their Sunday best. Not a single Mayan or black person among us; only those of European descent.

As I breathe in the collective excitement floating, almost tangible, in the sunlit vaults, a stentorian voice announces on the intercom: '*El vuelo 234 de Lufthansa acaba de aterizar.*'

Ten minutes later, the first passengers trickle in through the doors, then a thicker crowd, and finally a flood of people behind trolleys piled high with baggage. They look up to the balcony from where friends and family call out their names. They wave and shout to each other, brimming with happiness. The relatives hurry down into the hall to meet the arrivals and throw their arms around them.

There she is, wearing a sky-blue anorak, jeans with the hems rolled up, sunglasses perched on the crown of her head and a pair of brand-new trainers. They're so white, they sparkle. She marches on, suitcase in tow, a leather bag across her shoulders. She scans the hall at eye level, unaware of the balcony above.

'Mum!' I cry out from the top of the stairs. She looks up and finally sees me. Smiling, she drags her suitcase bumping across the floor towards me.

'*Tesoro*! How wonderful to see you, at last!' She hugs me tightly. 'You know, Monica, I've come to take you home.'

Here she is, on the warpath, already. I take a deep breath, trying hard to keep my irritation in check.

With a wry smile, I take the suitcase from her and, wheeling it briskly around all obstacles, I lead her through the sliding doors into the blazing sun. There's a line of taxis parked along the pavement, with heaps of luggage and clusters of people fussing around them. We get into the first one available.

'You certainly won't get lost with those on, eh, Mum?' I point at her feet. She laughs and we both slump back onto the seat. She looks tired, that initial combative energy now gone from her. I congratulate myself for not getting into conflict as soon as she got here.

Our taxi leaves La Aurora Airport, and we career along the dual carriageway, watching the verdant hills rolling past us through the windows.

*

Our time together starts like this. We tiptoe around each other carefully, always on guard.

'You look well, Monica,' she says with a conciliatory smile. 'I like your tan, and your sun-bleached hair. Very nice! That length really suits you.' After the effusive outburst at the airport, she's now working hard at being nice to me.

On my part, I act like the most scrupulous of hosts. In the days that follow, I take her around the baroque monasteries, the convents, the churches. We go to the museums and admire the stucco porches. I tell her what I know about the history of this country, about its culture. I do my best to pass on my enthusiasm for this place. As for my private life, I keep it strictly to myself.

'Everything's so green around here!' she says, looking at the hills. 'Mind you, it's nowhere near as hot as I expected. I wish I'd listened to Miranda and packed those extra jumpers...'

From La Aurora we come straight here, to Antigua, the ancient capital, a colonial Spanish town with a baroque church at every corner and a crown of volcanoes towering over us.

Our hotel couldn't be more different from my old hangout, the Tranquilidad, in Guatemala City. It's on a sleepy cobbled street, a stone's throw from the main square. Through an iron gate, which is always wide open except at night, we come to a patio full of exotic plants where we have breakfast. A long veranda paved with terracotta tiles runs around the sides. The furniture – benches, chairs, tables and chests of drawers – is chunky and solid, made of heavy oak. Our room is on the second floor and fitted with comforts I've forgotten all about, including – at my mother's insistence – our own private bathroom.

What my mother likes best is the local craft market.

'Look at these blouses, Monica! And the runners over there... wonderful, aren't they?' She weaves her way between the stalls, pointing at fabrics so bright they glow against the muted blue of the sky.

She's already stocked up on presents to take home: some green and purple wristbands for Doretta's children, a couple of cloth dolls in local costume for Miranda's collection, a hand-woven blouse for her knitting friend Mirella.

'It's a bargain!' she says every time.

Quick at seizing the opportunity, the vendors gather around her, insistent and hard to shake off.

She's surprisingly good at haggling with them, considering she doesn't even speak their language.

'*Tre quetzals*,' she starts, counting on her fingers and flailing her hands in the air. It's a continuous to and fro between her and the hawkers, a melodious sing-song of numbers, until they agree on a price. When she doesn't want something, 'NO!' she cries out, and that "O" projects rotund and final from her mouth. There's no winning her over, no tiring her out. She firmly stands her ground until, one by one, resignedly, the vendors slip away.

At each purchase, I cringe, trying my best to hide my embarrassment, but it shows on my face, I know. After all, she's known me since the day she brought me into this world; for her, I'm like an open book.

What a load of useless trinkets! I can't help thinking, and I hurry her away.

'Why, Monica, what's the matter?' she says, 'what's all this haste for? Do we have to meet someone or be somewhere? No, we don't. So? Come on, relax!'

She's right. We have all the time in the world. Still, something about her irks me deeply. Maybe it's all the "touristy" things she's bent on doing. Yes, that's what it is – being with her makes me feel just like the tourist that from day one I've tried so hard not to be.

Ultimately, there's no denying that's what we both are. But the thing with her is she's so unashamed about it.

'Of course, I **am** a tourist,' she admits happily. Then, she flashes a mocking smile at me. 'A tourist in a pair of white sneakers, aren't I?'

Next, we'll be going to Lake Atitlán, where I'd like to show her the villages named after the twelve apostles.

She'll have bought all her presents by then and so, hopefully, I'll be able to relax.

*

Here we are in Gringolandia, once again, in Panajachel. I'm irritated by the vendors' pushiness, their touting and peddling right up to the front steps of the hotel. While I hate all this, my mother doesn't seem to mind.

'What do you expect?' she says. 'That's how they make a living.'

We go for a walk outside the village, in the hills.

To the right of our path in the distance, two Mayan labourers toil away, bent over a field.

'Look! They're using a wooden plough,' she says as she stops to stare at them. 'Incredible! It's just like home in the olden days, just like the *contadini* of our valleys.'

She goes on to tell me about when, as a child, she spent the summer in her grandmother's farm in the Brenta Valley. From dawn to dusk, men and women of all ages bent over the land ploughing, sowing, weeding and carrying firewood on their backs.

'They worked till they dropped, just like these people,' she says with heartfelt compassion. 'The land belonged to some distant *padrone*. Once in a blue moon, he would turn up. I can't remember him, but what I do remember as if it was now is how everyone stood there, in front of him, humble, resigned, in silence, down to the smallest child. The men held their hats in their hands, eyes lowered, as if he wasn't just a man, but an evil god.'

I like listening to her. Her stories transport me back to times so hard to imagine that they take on the spellbinding quality of fairy tales. In a strange way, she reminds me of Martin. Yes, Martin, from what feels like a lifetime ago.

Despite their differences, their way of seeing the world is similar and stands at odds with mine.

To me, everything in this country appears exotic and beautiful, and it fascinates me precisely because of how different it is from all I know. My mother – just like Martin – looks at the same scenery, at the same people and, lo and behold, all she perceives are the things they share.

Neither of us is right or wrong, and reality equally escapes us. There's no doubt, though, that her way is more empathic. She truly feels for these people, the Mayans, the poor *campesinos*, noticing things I don't usually see, unless I'm in the company of someone, like her or Martin, who makes me look again and think twice.

'Look at the onions in that basket!' she says, as we weave our way between the market stalls. 'Amazing! There, see that tall pile of cauliflowers? Round, perfect, not a bruise on them. Just like a painting. And the size of those courgettes! They're more like pumpkins, aren't they?' She takes a deep breath. 'It's a crime people should live in poverty when the land is so rich.'

Her attention always zooms in on the downtrodden – the two Mayan labourers with pickaxes breaking a block of granite twice their size; the tiny boy skidding and slipping barefoot along a muddy hillside as, single-handed, he rounds up a flock of sheep; the frail old man on the dusty path in front of us, legs crippled by arthritis, tottering under a huge stack of firewood. In this respect, she certainly isn't the stereotypical tourist. For her, these are not charming tableaux to be "captured" with a click of her camera, but snippets of a life she identifies with.

I admire that side of her.

There is one thing, though, that I positively hate about travelling with my mother, and that's being her guest. She insists on paying for both of us. Of course, I know that if she didn't, I couldn't afford half of these luxuries – the private bathroom, the eating out in trendy restaurants and, God forbid, certainly not the plane fares to Tikal, where she wants to go next. Still, whenever she digs into her purse, I cower.

I think of Rafael and what he could do with the *quetzals* she blows on silly souvenirs. He'd buy the fishing net he's been raving about, or perhaps get the council to rig up a water pipe right outside his front door. *Unless he drank it,* says a little voice in my head, which I resolutely hush.

She tells me she wants to know how I live. Because of that, I see no reason to change my habits or my travelling routine for her. On her part, over this last week we've spent together, she's become more easy-going, more relaxed. Or, perhaps it's me who has mellowed. Whatever the reason, as time goes by, I find myself enjoying her company more and more.

Tonight, we are sitting in the same restaurant where some time ago I had dinner with Martin. The place brings up memories from that night when I stood in awe of Martin's friend, Suzanne, and vied with her for his attention. So much has happened since, that when I look back, I see a different Monica.

After a meal of seafood, stuffed peppers and fried plantains, we are both nursing a brandy while gazing across the lake. A group of young Americans play their acoustic guitars the other side of the terrace. All else is still.

We stare across the water into the darkness. Across the lake, a cluster of lights hangs in mid-air like a sprinkle of stars.

'One of the apostles' villages,' I tell her. 'San Pedro, I think.'

We sit in comfortable silence and stare out at the lake, at the lights, at the night sky. The scent of jasmine wafts towards our table, making me light-headed. Bells chime in the distance. Muffled laughter drifts from somewhere behind the trees, while a husky male voice draws out each syllable of Dylan's mournful *Knocking on Heaven's Door*.

I take a photo out of my bag and lay it on the table in front of her.

'This is Rafael,' I say with no introduction.

She flinches. Then, she examines the picture carefully in the half-light. She turns to me, frowning.

'Monica, I wonder... What is it you want from life?'

I'm speechless. What on earth could I say? That I do not know myself what I'm here for, that I'm in love with this rogue of a man, that what began like a game is now turning into something serious, something binding, and not in a good way?

I end up saying none of this. I simply study her face, trying to read the emotions moving across it swiftly and equally swiftly being hidden away.

From his photo, Rafael smiles on seductively – a black Rudolph Valentino in a singlet, oozing charm from every pore.

What is it she objects to – his blackness?

'I've nothing against this man, Monica,' she says as if reading my thoughts. She hands the photo back to me. 'I haven't even met him. I just wonder what you'd have in common.'

There's a long pause interrupted by laughter from the far end of the terrace. The Americans are about to leave. They noisily collect their duffel bags and knapsacks, sling their guitars over their shoulders and, as they reach the exit, they turn towards us.

'Adiós!' 'So long!' 'Buenas noches!' they shout and wave to us.

Foreigners are very nice to each other in Panajachel. They act as if we were all the best of friends. Yet another of the long list of things that irritate me about this place.

'We have more in common than you might think,'" I say with a sneer. "But you'll meet him soon and you can judge for yourself."

An engine rumbles through the darkness and sends short sharp waves slapping against the planks of the jetty. It's gone eleven and the breeze from the lake has turned chilly.

With a shiver, my mother wraps herself up in the woollen shawl she bought in the market earlier today.

We call for the bill, we pay, and walk back to our hotel in silence along the empty streets, our footsteps resounding loudly over the cobblestones.

*

We arrived in Livingston on a Thursday. The ferry stopped just long enough for us to walk down the gangplank onto the pier and for twenty or so new passengers to get on board. Then, with a grinding of chains and rumbling of engines, it cast off again towards Belize.

From the moment we set foot on the quay, everything seemed to conspire against us.

The dry season was at its peak. The burnt ochre fields cried out for rain, but no hope of any until the end of June, if we were lucky. The Siete Altares, the local waterfalls so popular with both tourists and locals, had dried out almost completely and lost their appeal. The water of the few remaining pools was stagnant and strewn with dead leaves, over which swarmed clouds of mosquitoes. The worst discovery of all was the well behind my house. The drought had reduced it to an inch or two of murky water.

'My place,' I said to my mother, when at the end of our hour-long walk, we came to my beach hut. Since I hadn't stopped paying rent on it, officially, it was still my home and I was proud of it, despite the dried-out surroundings.

I read disbelief in her eyes, a sense of being at a loss. 'But, Monica…' she hesitated, 'this is a garden shed, not a home!'

'It's functional,' I retorted. 'It protects me from rain and heat. What more would I want?'

But, clearly, what she saw was just a lopsided shack about to collapse. Inside, her gaze ran straight to the caved-in portion of the roof and the handkerchief of sky that peeped through the woven branches.

She asked me about spiders, mosquitoes and creepy-crawlies.

'You might catch something, Monica – malaria, dengue fever, or some other tropical disease. Doesn't that worry you?'

I laughed and shrugged my shoulders, deciding there and then I wouldn't tell her about the night when, in pitch darkness, I sat on what I thought was a loose spring off my bed. As I switched on my torch, a black shape with a swaying tail scuttled over the earthen floor and out of the door. A scorpion. That time, I did worry. I rushed all the way to the Lugudi Barana and ordered a fizzy lemonade. Nothing much happened, thank God. Over the next couple of hours, I just sat there, on a bench by the sea, my tongue feeling thick and swollen inside my mouth. Come midnight, I was back to normal and ready to go home.

No, that wasn't the kind of story I could ever tell my mother.

But, scorpions or not, there was no way that my mother would accept to lodge there, with me.

In the end, she checked into the Hotel Caribe. From the outside, it looked more like a hospital or a prison than a hotel, but it was conveniently central and, most importantly, there was running water in all the rooms.

A whole day went by with no sign of Rafael. He wasn't at home, and at work no one knew where he'd gone. I felt ambivalent. I was eager to get the introductions over and done with, and yet his absence came as a relief.

Then, on the second night after our arrival, he walked into the restaurant where my mother and I were having dinner.

He stood there, in front of us, in a pair of knee-length beach shorts and a red singlet. He carried two bulky demijohns of drinking water, looking for all the world as if he'd just bumped into two of his friends from Happy Land rather than his girlfriend and her mother.

Unperturbed, my mother smiled at him and pointed to a chair, while I sat there, a drumstick in my greasy fingers, butterflies in my stomach, gaping.

'Do you care for a cold beer?'

He shook his head, smiling. '*No, gracias, estoy de paso.* I only came in because I saw you from the street. I've just been to the fountain and must hurry home *con mis baldes.*' He pointed to the containers.

He casually turned to me. 'Tonight, there's a *velorio* in Nebagó. Why don't you take your mother there? She might like it. She'll learn something about Labuga.'

I wasn't sure my mum would fancy going to one of the local wakes, but who knows, he could be right, she might really like it.

'When you finish here, *pues,* come to my house and we can go together.'

I looked at my mother and she seemed keen.

'Great, Rafael. We'll be there in half an hour.'

He strode out of the restaurant, demijohns swinging at his side, and left us there at the table picking over our roast chicken, each absorbed in our own thoughts.

*

We walked along the grass path that, cutting through people's yards, meandered in and out of the thatched houses. Two young women sat in their doorways, chatting. When they saw us, they stopped in mid-sentence. They recognised me and gave me a smile, but looked my mother up and down, brazenly.

'*Buenas!*' they hollered in the end, and, no longer interested, they resumed their conversation.

I turned sharp left into the narrow alley that led to Rafael's. Away from the streetlights, the trail petered out into the darkness.

I could hear my mother stumble behind me. 'Careful, watch your step,' I warned her.

The door was ajar. I knocked lightly on the top shutter.

'Come on in!' said Rafael, in a raucous voice.

With a cautious but intrigued expression on her face, my mother followed me inside.

At first, all was dark and blurry, but soon the dim light cast by the hurricane lamp hanging from the ceiling lit up the familiar contours of the room. The shelves lined with books, the central wooden beam, the bamboo reeds of the nearby wall; everything was swathed in a soft, soothing light.

Right below the lamp sat Rafael, hunched over the table, a notebook opened in front of him and a biro in his right hand. At close quarters, he appeared to be jotting down numbers. He was so absorbed in his calculations that he only looked up at the last moment and then gestured vaguely towards the armchairs.

'I'll be with you in just a minute,' he said, and went back to his notebook.

I went and sat by the window, while my mother slid gingerly into the reclining chair nearest to the door. I watched her grip the armrests to stop herself from sinking deep into it. But, like a cocoon, the armchair hugged her in from all sides. In the end, she let go of herself and leaned back. I could see her sharp eyes scouring the darkness past the halo of the light.

I'd give anything to know what she was thinking, but, for once, her face was like a mask.

Rafael kept us waiting while he scribbled away. He bent over his notebook studiously as if tackling business that couldn't be delayed. I knew full well that for him the alphabet was a challenge, so, clearly, this was all just a show for my mother's benefit. He wanted to impress upon her he was a serious and busy man.

Finally, he put his biro down, snapped his notebook shut, and we headed out of the house.

We took a path to the left and headed up the hill, silently. Five minutes into our walk, there was a faint rumble, like a thunderstorm approaching or horses galloping in the distance. The further we walked, the louder and more insistent the sound became, until in a crescendo it rose into a booming roll of drums.

Now and then, I'd turn to check on my mother.

'Wait till I tell people at home I've gone and partied at a funeral,' she whispered under her breath. 'They'll say I'm crazy.'

I'm doing this just because of you, Monica. That's what she meant.

We followed the music and finally came to a group of houses huddled close together. They sat at the end of the tarred road, in a shallow valley crowned by a clump of banana trees. There, the *velorio* was in full swing.

Outside a wattle and daub house, a few old men sat at a trestle table under a canopy, playing a game of cards. Women in checked dresses walked in and out of the house carrying steaming bowls of food.

'Rafael, *nati!*' they called out. They nodded at me and my mother.

Rafael took us around the back where a crowd stood in a circle around two drummers. In the middle, boys and girls took turns dancing.

The atmosphere was festive. The two young musicians slapped away at their drums and the others sang along in hoarse voices; everyone talked loudly and laughed.

My mother and I kept at a distance, with Rafael towering over us like a mean-looking bodyguard.

At the far end of the circle stood Mama Jo, her stripy blue and white dress swaying to the rhythm; her small, bright eyes scouring the crowd. She spotted us and, on unsteady legs, she walked over.

'*Qué bien! Qué bien!*' she burbled through her missing teeth as I did the introductions. She grasped the hand my mum had stretched out to her and, holding it in the vice of her arthritic fingers, she gave her the once-over. My mum smiled at her nervously.

'*Piacere,*' she greeted her, then, having finally managed to free herself from the old woman's grip, she stepped back and turned towards me. In the meantime, one of the fish vendors who often sat at the street corner near Rafael's place left the circle and came to join Mama Jo and Rafael. The three of them stood right behind us, talking in Garifuna. Out of the corner of my eye, I could see the two women stare openly at my mother, at her clothes, at her necklaces, at her rings. They weighed her up. Then they nodded and patted Rafael on the back, laughing.

I could only guess what was being said. 'So, your *nummari*'s mother's come to check out her future son-in-law, eh, *nati*? Lucky you!'

Then the music turned to a soft purr. A tall, busty middle-aged woman in a figure-hugging red dress took to the floor. Totally self-absorbed, she shuffled into the circle from the far corner, one short step after the other, large fleshy hips rippling with the beat. When she reached centre stage, she stopped. The musicians stopped too. They rested their hands on top of the drums, and sat waiting. All eyes were fixed on her.

The woman stared back defiantly and, starting from the far right, she held the gaze of each spectator for a long moment before moving on to the next person along the line. Some gazed back; some laughed nervously; others looked away, embarrassed. When she'd finally gone through the whole circle, the woman swivelled round and faced the drummers. At this, as if at a signal, they started slapping their drums so hard they had to stand, and the woman broke into a wild dance.

The way she moved was bold and sensual. She gyrated her hips, shimmied her torso and pounded the earth with her bare feet. How could such a bulky body look so weightless, so agile and supple, as if floating in mid-air?

The music carried her away, each slap on the taut skin of the drums turning into a ripple of the woman's body. Possessed by the same rhythm, the people in the circle urged her on, clapping and singing.

'I'm glad it isn't me they're partying over.' A voice broke the spell – my mother's.

I turned to her and saw her staring at the dancing woman with narrowed eyes, her face burning, her mouth hanging open in disbelief. She stood there, transfixed just like all the others, but there was an expression of horrified aversion on her face.

'Could you please take me back?' she asked me at the first break in the music. 'My head throbs. I'm exhausted. It feels as if I've been dancing all night with that woman, right there, in the middle. Sorry, Monica, this is all too much for me.'

I walked her back to the hotel and, right on the doorstep, I bade her goodnight, struggling hard to hide my disappointment.

How could I even imagine my mum would feel the same as me about the dancing, the place, the people? It was all wishful thinking.

As I turned and closed the hotel gate behind me, I realised we'd forgotten to say goodnight to Rafael.

I knew he'd take offence at being ignored by my mother, but frankly I thought it might be better like this. For sure, he'd have read the uneasiness on her face, her disapproval. She'd never been tactful, but tonight she looked so overwhelmed, so wiped out, that I doubt she'd even want to try and hide her feelings.

The night was hot and sultry, and instead of going back to the *velorio*, I headed back to Rafael's. As I lay on top of the bed sheets waiting for him, my mind raced back to the woman in red, to her fearless staring and the powerful hold she had over the crowd. So many formidable Garifuna women seemed to be living in Labuga.

The night's drumming still echoed in my ears, together with the collective singing and the loud clapping. In my mind, I could still hear Rafael's voice, his laughter, as he talked to people, while glancing sideways at my mother.

I felt myself grow drowsier, wearier, and in no time, I was asleep.

*

In the days that followed, I found myself constantly running up and down the beach. Rafael and my mother lived at the opposite ends of town, and therefore, in an attempt to keep them both happy, I walked back and forth, from one to the other, several times a day. Despite my efforts, though, I always ended up displeasing one of them, usually my mother. The problem was that, whatever time we decided to meet, I was late. Why that should be, I really didn't know. It baffled me. I thought of myself as punctual. But in those days, however hard I tried, I arrived puffed out, guilt-ridden, really apologetic – and invariably between an hour and an hour and a half late.

My excuses were all plausible and partly true. My house chores were terribly time-consuming. One day, I told my mother that I had to go and collect drinking water from the well; another day, that I'd walked several miles to do the shopping, then, at the last minute, had realised I'd run out of paraffin oil and had to get it from the only supplier at the other side of town.

And then, of course, the weather conspired against me. In the month of June, the heat was formidable. It hit you like a crashing wave, and it certainly slowed anybody down, even the hardiest. At times, when I got to my mother's, my clothes all wet and my hair dripping, it looked as if I'd just stepped out of the shower, but it was only sweat.

Each time, I was totally repentant. I promised I'd be punctual as from the next day. And then, come the next day, I was late, again.

At first, my mum accepted my apologies unquestioningly; the second time, she complained good-humouredly; the third, she vented her frustration with some force, until, by the end, she was beside herself with anger. 'What time do you call this?' she shouted. 'You said three and it's half past five!'

I tried to appease her, but she wouldn't hear me.

I was caught between two people who both demanded a lot of me – my energy, my love, my undivided loyalties. Being here for just a short visit, my mother expected, quite reasonably, that I'd spend a good chunk of my time with her. Rafael – well, he simply wanted to assert his hold over me. They both persisted in ignoring each other and yet, behind the scenes, they fought relentlessly through me.

Rafael used all kinds of tactics to make me late for my mother.

'*Mi amor*, come and give me a hand with this letter, be good,' he would plead. Or: 'Come and lie with me for five minutes,' and he would peep seductively at me over the edge of his red hammock.

When everything else failed, he latched onto the smallest excuse to start an argument. He knew full well that I found it hard to leave in the middle of an argument, without first making it up with him and clearing the air.

As for my mother, she'd decided she had no time for him.

The turning point was an incident that took place the day after the *velorio*. Rafael offered to make some rice and peas for us. It was delicious. We ate, chatted, and for once all was well between us. But then, when lunch was over, Rafael stood up and slumped into his red hammock.

'*Mi amor*! *Cariño!*' he called me over, and then, ignoring my mother still sitting at the table, he pulled me into the deep folds of his hanging bed.

Without a word, my mother got up and left.

I saw her at the hotel later, when I went to try and smooth things over.

'That was so rude, Monica!' she said, still seething. 'Smooching like that in front of me. He did it on purpose, of course, wanting to embarrass me. As if he could… Above all, he wanted to show me he's got you under his thumb. But you, Monica, how could you be so… thoughtless! Why do you always do what he wants? Haven't you got a mind of your own?'

I was taken aback. I knew I'd done her wrong, but I never thought this episode could make her quite so angry. I sheepishly apologised.

My mother began to call Rafael the "hammock man". She meant someone who preferred lying in the horizontal position over getting onto his feet and doing some work, but there was also the sub-text of my own collusion with Rafael's baiting of her.

The next day, as I was about to leave his house and go to my mother's, the hammock man took his revenge.

'Rafael,' I said to him, 'would you mind keeping an eye on my house when my mother and I go to Belize next week? I don't want people to break in.'

He looked at me quizzically, so I added: 'What if I gave you ten *quetzals*?'

At this, the hammock shook and swayed, and then a string of abuse burst out.

'Ten *quetzals*? Phew! *Mujer tan cutre!* I'm not your servant, you know.' He went on calling me names, some of which I understood; *codo*, a miser, and some I'd never heard before. '*Mañana*, I'm going to look for a younger and richer woman,' he concluded. 'You and your *ruca fea*, you can both go *a la verga!*'

So, my mum was an ugly old hag and I a tight bastard. That hurt.

I stood up, went to the door and, without a word, I hurried out. This time, I felt no need for a peaceful settlement, or for closure. I only wanted to get away as quickly as possible and to be alone.

From the hammock came a surprised: 'Monica! Monica!'

I didn't care.

He followed me into the street.

'*Perdona!*' he said with the most charming smile.

I left him there, on the path, dumbfounded as, deeply offended, I went my way.

That night, when I got to the hotel, for once I was bang on time.

*

'Thank God, I've got some earplugs to help me sleep tonight,' said my mother as the music started.

The bar in front of El Caribe was blasting its usual repertoire of wailing Mexican *rancheras* – a fanfare of brass instruments accompanied by tearful singing and melancholy guitars.

I never liked this part of town, but the restaurant of the hotel where we were sitting was very handy; besides, my mum loved the *camarones a la plancha* they made there.

Shuttered and silent during the day, the bar came alive – just our luck – at nine thirty, ten at night. As the doors opened, people from all over the harbour, men mostly, began to drift in. From our table, we got a full view of them as, at first, they stood around, holding their beers, heads up, eyes fixed on a small TV set mounted high up on the wall. They were so intent on watching the latest episode of some *telenovela* that, except for the odd outburst of laughter or comment shouted across the room, all was quiet for the next hour. But soon the *telenovela* ended, and the music blasted out.

'It goes on like this till early morning,' said my mother, drowning her sorrows in a glass of ice-cold beer. 'Usually, I sleep through the noise, but then, at three or whenever they close, the rattle of the shutters being slammed down jumps me awake.'

Poor Mum. It must be such an ordeal for her – all this dancing and wild partying, the loud noise, the drunks, that… and discovering her daughter is in love with a man like Rafael.

'If you like, tomorrow, we'll find you a quieter hotel.'

'No need.' With a swipe of her hand, she simultaneously dismissed the idea and brushed the crumbs off the table. After a weighty pause, she stared pointedly at me. 'That's not what keeps me awake at night,' she said.

She'd been trying to have this conversation since that first day at the airport. Until now, I'd managed to avoid it, either by sidetracking her or by lapsing into a surly silence.

But the other day she caught me unawares. I was sitting on the beach, musing at the sight of two small children playing with their makeshift toys, small treasures they'd found lying on the shingle – a few pieces of wood swept in by the tide and the dried-out cask of a coconut.

'Would you like one of your own?' From somewhere behind me came the voice of my mother.

'You mean, a child? Well, this feels like the right place,' I let out, lowering my guard.

'Really?' she blurted out in a defiant, most combative tone. 'You do realise, don't you, that if you had a child with this man, you'd have to bring it up on your own?'

At the time, I managed to diffuse the tension by turning away towards the sea. I stood there, controlling my breathing, tight-lipped.

But now, sitting face-to-face across the table, there seemed to be no way to stem the flow of rebukes and accusations my mother was about to unleash. It was like a flood, an avalanche.

'This guy has you well and truly wrapped around his little finger, hasn't he? You're spellbound, Monica. But why? What's so special about him?'

And she told me how stubborn and contrary I'd always been since childhood, how I always got my own way. And now, here I was, bending over backwards to please this man. She couldn't work out why.

'Is it because he calls you *mi amor, cariño, mi corazón*? Is that what you need to hear? True, he lavishes hugs and kisses on you, and in front of everyone, don't I know?' She gave out a wry laugh. 'But are these signs of real love, of genuine affection? I wonder. Remember, Monica, words don't cost a thing...'

I kept silent, overwhelmed by her outburst. In any case, she didn't seem to expect an answer.

'He fusses over you as he would over a cute little animal... a pet,' she continued. She didn't seem to care that her words might hurt or insult me. 'Come on, Monica, you can't be serious! This is just an infatuation. It'll come to an end, the sooner the better. If only I could knock some sense into you…'

Angry shouting rose from the bar. A brawl had broken out among the men, and the noise drowned out my mother's words. It blew over as quickly as it had started, leaving everyone laughing and fooling around again.

'And another thing, Monica,' she started again, relentlessly, 'what have you got in common with this man? He acts like a child, and gets on best with people half his age, with teenagers and children. Whenever we discuss politics or anything serious, or when we ask him about Guatemala, he doesn't have a clue. He mumbles, he scratches his forehead.'

Yes, that was it. Had I presented her with Martin, his honesty, his clear sense of duty and purpose, there wouldn't be an issue, she'd be all for it…

'I don't blame him,' she continued after a pause. 'He's not informed, he's not educated. Life for him is about practicalities, about how to make ends meet. But it's you, Monica, that puzzles me. How can you seriously consider setting up home with him?'

By this stage, we were the only people left in the restaurant. We had finished eating a long time ago and our plates were empty. I poured the last of the beer into our glasses. There was nothing I could say. I just sat there.

My mother looked tired now. The tirade had taken up all her energy. She glanced at me sheepishly, as if to say, *I hope you forgive me, but it had to be said, it's for your own good.*

I felt very tired too, totally washed out, in fact, exhausted. I felt like I'd been climbing a mountain for hours, not sitting comfortably in a restaurant.

Impossible to ignore my mother's warnings. She was not one to mince her words. But however observant and clear-sighted she might be, I felt put upon by her and with my whole being I wanted to resist her.

After a long pause, I finally spoke.

'But he can change…'

Hadn't Martin changed from gang member to model guy? But, just like Richard, Rafael's bad-boy credentials were precisely what attracted me… not the kind of thing you could tell your mum.

She looked me in the eye, lips curved into a thin smile.

'People do change, yes, but only if **they** want to…' she said quietly.

We paid the bill and parted with a tired-out hug.

"'*Llorando y sufriendo… ahogado en mis penas… me estoy muriendo*," the male singer wailed from the jukebox on the other side of the street.

And for once, as I set off home, I took in all that "crying and suffering, the drowning in one's sorrow, and finally the dying from a broken heart" of the *ranchera* song, and let the sadness of those weeping guitars soothe my own.

*

My mother and I spent ten days in Livingston together and yet apart. What separated us was not so much the physical distance between her place and mine, but the emotional gap that, as time went by, seemed to grow wider.

When the day of our departure for Belize finally came, I was strangely relieved and, each for different reasons, so were Rafael and my mother. We all needed a change and, although my previous trip to Pee Gee hadn't been easy, I was looking forward to seeing the rest of the country and especially what my mother would make of it.

In the end, Rafael had agreed to look after my mother's luggage during our absence, and so, the day before leaving, I wheeled her bulky suitcase to his place and left it in a corner, standing upright. Then, early on Thursday morning, both carrying a small knapsack on our backs, my mother and I boarded the local ferry and set off for Punta Gorda.

Full of expectations, that first night, we rode through the mangroves of Placencia, hot air blowing on our faces, the motorboat skimming over the water in pitch darkness. Then the engine stopped, and we dropped anchor in a cove. Our hotel was at the end of a grassy path on a hillock. After a seamless sleep, that morning, as we came out onto the veranda, the long arch of the coast spread out in front of us – miles of sandy beach fringed by windswept palm trees.

Further on, the *cayos* with their evocative names: Cayo Pelican, Cayo Coco Plum, Cayo *Cangrejo* (Crab Key), Cayo Calabash, Cayo *Espanto* (Fear Key), Rendezvous Key.

At Laughing Bird, the midday sun is blinding. The powdery white sand sticks onto our legs like flour as we explore the beach. We find a gigantic pink shell polished by the waves, and two lace fans of coral – one black, the other white – swept in by the tide. A little distance from the shore, floating on the turquoise waters, is the boat that's taken us here. The skipper whiles his time away fishing. By the time we leave, he has a bucket full of red snappers. Except for the waves lapping on the shingle, all is quiet. Apart from us, there isn't a soul around.

Later, on another key, we come upon a bamboo hut with a wooden sign nailed above the door. It reads *The Lucky Fish Diner* in large, uneven red letters.

'I have twelve orders before you, ladies.' A woman in white apron and headdress leans out of the kitchen window and smiles. 'Come back in an hour and a half.' Just like that – firm, final.

And precisely one and a half hours later, under the thatched roof of the veranda, the same woman sees us to a table laid with a red and white checked cloth. Our feet sink in the soft sand of the floor as, encircled by mouth-watering whiffs of pungent lemon and fragrant rosemary, she places in front of us a large platter of the local delicacy, sea turtle meat.

In the absence of Rafael, my mother and I rediscover the pleasures of each other's company. We always find something to laugh about, often at the expense of our fellow travellers – like the American woman in our hotel in Placencia who stares at everything and everyone with an expression of pure ecstasy, as if in a trance. Is she high on something or does she really inhabit the best of all possible worlds? We nickname her "*la romantica*". Or the gangly British man in khaki Bermuda shorts with dozens of bulging pockets, laced up army boots and a safari helmet. One morning, we spot him on the veranda of our B&B. He's too busy gazing at the world through the viewer of his camera to even notice us having breakfast next to him. Dr Livingston-I-presume, we promptly mock him.

With these supercilious little jokes, we re-establish not only the similarity of our sense of humour but mother and daughter solidarity.

We both want to see as much as we can of this country, so we decide to leave the sleepy *cayos* behind and venture into the mainland.

The local transport turns out to be a nightmare of rickety old buses with broken suspension and punishing metal seats, just like those in Guatemala. Somehow, I thought that, having been a British colony, Belize might have a better infrastructure than the neighbouring countries. After all, the colonisers needed to get from A to B just like anyone else. But no, here we are again, bouncing along bumpy tracks of red clay, coughing through rising clouds of dust, and then, at times, wherever the rivers have overflowed their banks, we even wade through pools of muddy water. Every ten miles or so, the jungle opens up into a large clearing with long lines of wooden shacks on stilts huddled around a lonely farmhouse. A rusty collection of tractors, diggers and trailers stands by the edges of the glade, ready to cut down more trees and clear out more of the jungle.

We reach Stann Creek – Dangriga to the Garifunas – halfway up the Atlantic coast.

The coach drops us off in the southern end of town, which is old and ramshackle. The only paved road leads over a stone bridge divided into three sections – a central part for cars, and at each side a narrow pavement.

Past the fast-flowing river, we come to the northern district and, suddenly, the town proper begins. There are school buildings, a fancy town hall, a few churches, a police station and even a couple of brand-new glass-fronted supermarkets. Everything seems to be in better shape on this side of town.

There are lots of people about – young and old. The old greet us with the polished manners of the British upper class. Six years have passed since independence, but it seems that for these older folk, Britain remains the mythical "mother country", the home of all things "decent" and "proper".

As for the young, the place seems far from being a nostalgic outpost of Empire. Boys and girls of all ages strut about, flirting and showing off, as cool and rebellious as any on Brixton High Street.

And should you feel nostalgic for British food, we soon discover that you can get cheddar cheese in all the supermarkets and slices of bread pudding from any of the street cafés.

Seventeen miles south of Dangriga, everything changes. Hopkins is a Garifuna fishing village and that's where we are headed next.

My mother's guidebook does not mention that there is no public transport, but soon we find out that, except for the odd providential lift from passing pick-ups, the only way to reach the village is on foot.

It takes us the best part of the day to get there, but we are rewarded by a couple of very friendly encounters, one with the sheriff, who tells us that local employment is virtually nil, and that young people in Hopkins either join the army or the police; then, as we sit on an upturned *cayuco* resting, two young men stop by for a chat. They're carrying a big bunch of coconuts. There and then, with a machete, they slash open a couple for us.

So, here we are, under a palm tree, drinking coconut water, chatting, a lovely little island equipped with its own palm tree in the blue sea right in front of us – what more could we want from life? It certainly compensates for all of the blisters on our feet.

Rafael is never far from my thoughts, and whenever something happens – a man suddenly stopped and searched by the police – I try and imagine what he would do or say. Would he silently and deferentially acquiesce, like this man does, or would he create a scene? Would he make a joke of the whole thing, with that big smile of his? Away from him, with no probing questions from my mother – she studiously avoids any mention of him – I see only the charm; the way he has with words, despite his lack of education, the pleasure he takes in rolling his tongue around certain words, savouring them like he would a delicious *tapado* or a *conch soup*. It's the same tongue that can inflict the most horrible verbal abuse. But here, I only think of his soft caresses and the sweet words that lull me into a state of drowsiness as effectively as if I were on drugs.

On our way back to the Hotel Riverside, we bump into more cops. They're after what they call a "bush doctor", a thief, who, supposedly, "is" lodging or "has" lodged there. The owner, a dignified middle-aged woman with lenses so thick that it's like being watched by an owl, is far from intimidated.

'No way, I'm not coming to the police station,' she shouts to the two burly policemen towering over her. 'I've put Yale locks everywhere. Now, it's your turn. Go and patrol the streets. Do your duty instead of coming here and wasting your time and mine.'

And she sends them off, slamming the door behind them. How brave!

Would Rafael be that brave? How would he fare in a place like this, with police everywhere, their guns visible in their holsters?

After dinner that night, we go and sit outside a little bar. We order a couple of beers and we get so involved in recalling the events of the day that we do not see the man approach us.

'Do you have a light?' His deep hoarse voice makes us jump. He's tall, dark-skinned, in his mid-forties.

I pull out my lighter. He thanks me profusely, slurring his words. Then he grabs a chair from another table and comes to sit with us. My mother and I exchange a weary look.

'Excuse me, but this is a private conversation—' I protest feebly.

He doesn't hear me. 'Leonardo Melquior *para servirla.*' He cuts me short.

'Melquior, did you say? I know another Melquior. Rafael Socrates Melquior Gonzales, from Livingston. Do you know him?'

'He's my nephew! His dad, Diomedes, God rest his soul, was my stepbrother!' He hugs us enthusiastically, breathing alcohol fumes all over us.

We end up buying him a bottle of rum and we sit there with him, sipping more beer.

Despite being drunk, Leonardo is a mine of information.

He tells us about the two parts of town, the Garifuna old settlement, in the south, where the houses are falling to pieces, and the northern modern district where the Creoles live.

'The Creoles have all the good jobs, while the Garifunas struggle. That's not right, it was us who settled here first! But the Creoles have always been the lackeys of the British. They hold all the power now and treat us with contempt.

'There are even plans to turn our Garifuna Settlement Day into Tourism Day. Can you imagine that?' His bloodshot eyes fill with tears. 'I welcome tourists, but our national day should not be touched. We are no leopards or monkeys that rich people should come and see on their adventure holidays.'

Then he complains about how children are no longer brought up speaking Garifuna.

'Yeah, we're losing our traditions, our handed-down recipes, our old ways. The women no longer grow cassava or cook with it. It takes too long, so they go to the supermarket. But if it's true that we are what we eat, well then, what does plastic tinned food make us?'

His speech is increasingly slurred, garbled, but he makes perfect sense.

'Things are tough here for us Garifunas. How can one survive on thirty-seven Belizean dollars per week? That's not life, I tell you.'

The booze has finally caught up with him, and now he begins to blather about all those *cabrones, pinche Inditos, los políticos de mierda de este país.*

When one of his mates passes by, Leonardo gets up from the chair and joins him. '*Ubafu lu garifuna*, power to the Garifunas,' he shouts in our direction, and he's off to another bar.

I remember how Ruby Jade, the Queen of Happy Land, was determined to remain in Livingston, how reluctant she was to return here, and now I begin to see why.

*

The week flashes by and, before we know it, here we are, back in Livingston.

My heart leaps with delight when, on the pier, leaning against a lamppost, arms crossed, I see Rafael waiting for us. He's wearing his good clothes; a blue string singlet, stripy trousers and a red, green and yellow tam. He spots us before we see him. He waves and smiles.

'*Mamacita linda!*' he shouts. '*Mi amor!*'

*

'Monica, come and have a look,' my mother said in a calm, collected voice.

For the last half an hour, we'd been chatting in her hotel room. Perched on the windowsill, I'd been watching her fumble around the suitcase I'd fetched back from Rafael's earlier.

Although we'd been back for three whole days, we'd forgotten all about it until that morning when, sore from so much walking, my mum's feet reminded her about the comfy pair of trainers she'd packed away.

I jumped down from the windowsill and walked over to where she was standing.

'See this?' She showed me a tiny piece of metal in the palm of her hand.

'What's that?'

'It's part of one of the zips of the suitcase. I undid the padlock and, as I pulled it, the tag broke off.'

I picked up the shiny object and turned it round and round, feeling its jagged edges with my fingertips. I looked at her, waiting to hear more.

'Monica, I'm not Samson. And this suitcase is brand new. So is the lock. It can't have snapped just like that. Someone must have tampered with it.'

The suitcase was lying on the bed. It was sturdy, with three compartments. The broken tag came from the zip in the middle section, the only one that – she said – for no reason she could now remember, she'd secured with a lock.

We examined the zip and the tag carefully. There was no doubt about it; someone had cut through it. Then, to make it look as if nothing had happened, they'd glued the two metal bits back together.

'Oh, that's what he meant...' I mumbled under my breath and, in response to her quizzical look, I continued. 'The night we came back from Belize, Rafael told me his house was no longer safe. Apparently, while we were away, some of his stuff had gone missing.'

'What stuff?'

'Nothing much. A pair of shorts, I think he said, his favourite T-shirt, some old rubber boots. He was vague about it. The suitcase was still there where I'd left it, so I didn't worry too much. But he warned me I shouldn't leave the key where we usually hide it. He thinks his neighbours are watching us.'

She stared at me long and hard, as if to say, *And you believe him?* Then, she carried on: 'It takes hours to saw through metal. Whoever did it wasn't at all worried about being caught out.'

I turned away from her and looked out of the window. I didn't want her to see the disappointment, the utter misery on my face. So far, I'd refused to face reality, but this time there was no way I could shy away from the harsh truth – among his other sins, Rafael was a petty crook. Probably, it was him who'd stolen the hundred dollars, perhaps in cahoots with his brother Jaime... My mother's voice interrupted my train of thought.

'No matter, there was nothing of value in that middle compartment, just some clothes, and a pair of shoes. Everything's still here. Whoever worked so hard over that padlock would have been terribly disappointed.' She spoke in a light and reassuring voice.

But however gently she tried to soften the blow, we both knew it was no use – "whoever worked so hard" could only be Rafael.

I flopped down onto the bed and she came to sit next to me. Suddenly I was filled with an uncontrollable wave of anger about everything – the situation, the village, the world.

'You'll be happy now, won't you?' I said, venting against her all the pent-up rage that, really, I wanted to direct at Rafael. 'You've finally proved your point.'

'Oh, Monica, don't say that! You're so... wrong!" she replied with a stricken look. 'I never wanted you to be unhappy or wished to dash your hopes. It hurts me as much as you, believe me.'

She sat next to me and put her arm around my shoulders. Then, she was back to practicalities.

'Please, Monica,' she warned me, 'whatever you do, don't say a word to Rafael. Pretend that all is fine, that we didn't notice. Because, if you do, if he knows you suspect him, you'll open yourself up to a lot of trouble. Once the trust goes, that's it. So, promise me, Monica, not a word about this.'

'Okay.' I nodded, staring at the floor.

She slipped on her white trainers, shut the suitcase, and we were out. We walked for hours, far from the village, into the hills.

CHAPTER TWENTY-SEVEN

LARUNI HATTI – 2

Sitting on a tree stump, I look down from the hilltop into the harbour.

The view is vast and far-reaching. Right below, through the shimmering foliage, I see the road and the patchwork of corrugated iron roofs extending over the "coolie" side of town. Beyond it, close to the shore, a sailing boat with a US flag hoisted on its mast rocks gently in the waters of the Río Dulce. The other side of the river, thick grey clouds loom over a succession of mountain ridges, layered in different shades of green and blue. To my left, past the *manaca* roof of the Hotel Tucán, the silver-grey expanse of the ocean blurs into the sky. A couple of ships cross the horizon, suspended in mid-air.

Sounds reach me from the street below – the scraping of shovels and the pounding of grit falling into the hold of a cargo ship; the laughing and chattering of the washerwomen at the *pila*; the croaking of a parrot.

'I heard your name repeated over and over,' my mother said to me one afternoon. 'I was curious,' she continued, 'so I went downstairs to look around, and along the corridor that led to the dining room of the hotel, in a corner, I saw a bright blue and orange parrot perched on a stand. But as for it saying "Monica", I was completely wrong. What it said was *mandioca,* manioc. It must have learnt that from a street vendor.'

I wonder if it is the same parrot I'm hearing now.

Down there, to the left, half-hidden by the trees, is the terrace of the Hotel Caribe, and by that huge sycamore, in the corner, on the second floor, the room where my mother stayed.

Nearly a week has gone by since I saw her off at the airport.

'*Tesoro,*' she said, looking me in the eye, 'don't let your need for affection get the better of you. Kisses and caresses are not always what they seem.' Then, as she brushed away some limp strands of hair from my brow, she added, with a smile, 'You'll do what you want in the end anyway. Just be careful.'

For a few minutes, we stood there staring at each other in silence, not the tense, nothing-much-to-say-to-each-other kind of silence, but that deep moment of mutual stillness that comes naturally to two people who know each other inside out.

At length, her flight was announced. Time for one last hug. At passport control, she paused, turned, waved, and was gone.

That same day, I headed back to Livingston.

'*Qué onda?* What's up?' Rafael looked surprised when, late that night, I appeared on his doorstep. 'I thought you'd never come back,' he confessed, dazzling me with his smile.

'Why wouldn't I?'

'Because you belong to your mother, that's why. You're part of her. I thought she'd take you back with her.'

He pulled me into his hammock. His long arms held me tight – they are the most expressive part of him; they can either envelope you tenderly or firmly keep you at bay.

The longer I know him, the harder it gets to gauge his mood.

But that night, I knew beyond doubt that he was delighted to see me. I snuggled up in his velvety embrace.

*

A honeymoon period followed. At six every night, Rafael came home from work, washed in the backyard – scooping cold water over himself from a plastic bucket – and then he would change into clean clothes. Later, he would fuss with the hurricane lamp, adjusting the wick and the flame, while I would lay the table and serve the food I'd cooked for us. Once everything was ready, we'd sit down at the table, just like so many other couples in the village at this time in the evening. Afterwards, Rafael would slump into the hammock and, exhausted, doze off.

Sitting on a three-legged stool, I watch him sleep. In the soft halo cast by the flickering flame, the texture of his skin is smooth and luminous. The top of his shoulders glitters in the semi-darkness, bright and glossy, like burnished copper.

My eyes dwell on each detail – the slanted eyelids, the wide goatee, the high cheekbones, and the fleshy flower of his lips.

There's an obstinate and proud expression on his face, even as he sleeps.

In the background, the deep pounding of drums from a *velorio* blends with some jaunty *soca* music travelling from somewhere along the beach. The sound is faint but constant and obsessive. It throbs through the village like a heartbeat.

Woken by the music, Rafael reaches out to me. Eagerly, I climb into the hammock.

We talk a lot in the semi-darkness; well, it's mainly he who talks, while I listen. He talks about love, about life, about our "understanding". Just like many months ago, when we first met, together with "*mi amor*", the word "*comprensión*" crops up time and again in his rambling monologues. He seems to love the sound of these words.

Snuggled up in the embrace of his arms, I listen to him as he unravels his dreams.

'If someone gave me a hundred and fifty *quetzals*, you know what I'd do? I'd buy some proper fishing tackle and make a fortune with the shrimp trade.' A light push of his arm sets the hammock into a steady swing. 'Even better, with a couple of thousand,' and he looks at me hopefully, 'I could buy a motorboat and set up a business. I'd go to Punta Gorda and make it big in the *ganja* trade.'

'And sooner or later end up in jail,' I blurt out. 'Are you sure you'd like that sort of life?'

'Would I like that sort of life? Me?' He sneers. 'My dear, I like anything and everything. But what I like best is to have my little house, with a cement floor, an indoor toilet, running water and electricity. If that's what it takes, so be it.' He stares blankly at the roof beams and, after a long pause, he continues: 'With the money, I'll build two houses, one for me and my woman, you, if you're still here, the other to rent out to the gringos. For that, I need, say, three hundred, three hundred and fifty *quetzals*. First, I'll buy two hundred blocks of cement, then plenty of wood for the roof, and then hundreds of *manaca* leaves. To carry all that back to Livingston, I'll need an engine of 110 *caballos* at least. *Púchica!* I can just see myself in the morning taking off for Puerto Barrios at the helm of my flashy motorboat!' His face lights up. 'Once I get there, I'll load the boat with as many goods as it can carry and then, like a flash of lightning, I'll sail back and sell everything around here. Another day, I might go to Belize instead, and buy my ten kilos of *mota* to sell by the ounce to the gringos. I'll make a packet, guaranteed.'

He smiles to himself, lost in his reveries. Then from the nearby stool he picks up one of the many flyers I brought back from Guatemala City. It advertises a restaurant that's just opened in Zona Uno and features a photo of a casserole dish of pasta with the caption *Fettuccine con mariscos* underneath. It's so colourful, so appetising, that I can almost smell the seafood.

'You can cook Italian, can't you?' he asks me suddenly. 'That's another idea I have – a restaurant that serves hot meals around the clock. I could make Garifuna and Guatemalan dishes and you'd be in charge of the Italian and Spanish cuisine. I bet it'd go down a bomb here in Labuga. And whenever business slacked, I'd go fishing or up in the hills to plant rice, cassava and corn on my allotment. Our land is rich. Nobody's ever starved around here.'

Like a volcano erupting, his mind throws up a bubbling flow of projects. The central theme is money – how to make it, how to save it, how to increase it. The "hammock man" stirs into action, if only within the confines of his dreams. He talks too much, he dreams too much, but, poor Rafael, he earns too little. All the same, his reveries have a richness of their own, and I can listen to him talk like this for hours, which, indeed, he does.

I do not say a word, but from the way he looks at me I realise that, while listening, I've let some of my scepticism show on my face. I'm doing my best to hide it now, but it's too late.

'You don't believe me, do you? You think I'm mad or incapable of doing all these things! You... you're such a downer. You pour cold water on everything! You're no good for me. And you know why? Because you're rotten selfish, that's why. With all the money you have, you could help me. But, oh, no, you won't!'

Now his arms reject me, their welcoming smoothness of minutes ago vanished. Now they tense and twitch with a barely restrained desire to hurt. These are the same arms that, one night on the beach, raised a huge stick up in the air and landed a mighty blow on Belén's shoulders. I've tried so hard not to think about it, to mis-remember it, but now...

'You're an impossible woman to live with.' His voice peaks. 'You'll never understand me, never! Selfish, that's what you are. If only I had Daniel's woman as my *nummari*, by now I'd be all set up like him. The other day, hear this, he wanted to buy a new dory and, after haggling long and hard over the price, it turns out he's two hundred *quetzals* short. "Just a minute," he says to the guy, and he runs home. Ten minutes later, he's back with the cash right in his hand. Not a *centavo* less. So, he paid the man and took possession of his new boat. See? Giulia isn't making such a fuss as you. She's there for Daniel, because he's her man and she loves him. She knows that one day she'll get her money back, in fact twice, three times as much. A few trips to Belize, a little bit of smuggling, and they'll make a packet. Together. Have you noticed how, these days, Daniel's pockets are always full of notes?

Yes, that girl is *buza*. She knows what's right for her man and for herself. Look at you instead. Yes, look at yourself. You'll never be able to understand me. Oh, no! You're not cut out for this kind of thing. Oh, no, not you. You… you just sit on your arse and what do you do? You just… write!' In his mouth, the word sounds vulgar and offensive.

So, his dreams are crumbling, and all because of me, the rich princess turned frog. He hates me because, as he sees it, I've deceived him. I'm not Giulia, I'm not Mariangela, I'm not helping him the way the two Italian sisters help their men.

I see – in the end, our relationship has turned out to be the same as all the others, plagued by the same squalid, nitty-gritty practicalities. He's right – I'll never be able to understand him. Our partnership is impossible. It's always been. I just didn't have the courage to admit it to myself, or, for that matter, to my mother. *When poverty knocks on the door,* she'd say, *love flies out the window,* and here, now, I feel the flap of its wings…

*

Like before, the undisputable competence of the two Italian sisters in these matters was not lost on me. I went and sought their advice.

'Every single guy in this bloody village drinks,' said Giulia, forgetting for once that in Livingston things were supposed to be perfect. 'How hard did I try to make Daniel stop boozing? Not even poison worked on him. The next day, he was back on the bottle, same as before, if not worse. Just a whistle from his mates and there he was at the Lugudi Barana, knocking them back, never mind me at home, waiting—'

'Yeah, you're right,' Mariangela cut her short, 'but can you blame him? It's not just him. It's the drinking culture of Labuga. Are our Neapolitan men so different? They all drink to prove they're big, strong machos. It's like a brotherhood of a sort.'

It was early morning and we sat at one of the round tables at the Comedor Cali, puffing at our respective rolled-up cigarettes, a cup of coffee in front of us, a pleasant breeze blowing through the wide-open windows.

'I hear you've been good to Daniel, that you've helped him,' I said tentatively to Giulia, remembering Rafael's words.

'Yeah, I've helped him all right,' she replied, looking disgruntled. 'Got him a boat, a fancy fishing net for shrimps, gave him fifty *quetzals* here, a hundred *quetzals* there... not that much, really, just a start..." She paused to take a drag on her roll-up. 'Then his friends came around. "Let's go out, Daniel, let's go to Happy Land for a couple of beers..." You can imagine what happened next. Sold the boat, the net's lying there in a heap... He blew it.'

'When they're drunk, they lose it. Try and beat some sense into their heads and they become animals. Touch their masculinity and they lash out,' Mariangela continued, raising her index to her upper lip in an automatic gesture. Luckily, she hadn't lost her front teeth.

'I'm so fed up with spending my nights at home, alone.' Giulia sighed loudly. Then she brightened up. 'When I think of my ex, in Naples, bringing me flowers, buying me presents...' The thought made her smile broadly. '...I truly had him wrapped around my little finger!'

'And gave you a split lip that time you refused to change your low-cut dress,' Mariangela interrupted her, waving her hands. 'Let's be honest, Giulia, take away the fancy trappings, your ex was just the same as all the rest.'

I listened to them, sad to hear all this but also relieved to learn they were just as vexed and disappointed with their men as I was with mine. They seemed less shocked, though, less surprised, as if their past experiences had somehow prepared them to deal with these situations, with these guys. That was the difference between us. Nothing and no one seemed to catch them unawares.

There were other differences too.

These erstwhile urbanites were happy to live in the middle of the countryside. They enjoyed raising chickens, planting vegetables and living according to the rhythms of nature and the sun. I could see they were both cut out for that kind of life. For them, Livingston had been the right choice, the big escape from the city, and Daniel and Manu, with all their flaws, two likely companions.

That just wasn't me.

However much I tried to fool myself, I was not the rural, back-to-the-land type, like the two sisters. Hadn't I landed on these shores by mistake, in pursuit of reggae? The place felt exciting, so did the people, especially Rafael. And if everything about him indicated danger, I guess it was precisely the risk-taking involved in this relationship that attracted me. With Rafael, there was that same buzz I'd felt with Richard. What was he going to do next? What mad scheme would he be hatching? With Richard, it would be variations on the theme of let's-kidnap-the-Vice-Chancellor-and-hold-him-hostage. Rafael's plans were more mundane, coming down, mainly, to owning his own home, to starting his small business. But it was the way he did go – or failed to go – about it that kept me enthralled.

Rafael was no preening rich boy playing at politics; he had to work hard for every quetzal. He wanted something better for himself. Why wouldn't he? He *deserved* it. But, as my mother had astutely figured out during her stay here, without education, without the usual connections, the man had little hope of living a life much above subsistence level. In time, his own understanding of this would make him resentful and bitter and drive him more and more to seek solace in the bottle. Hadn't his father-in-law, Giorgio, seen that? Wasn't his generosity, the money he'd lavished on Rafael, nothing more than a get-out-of-my-daughter-and-grandson's-life pay-off?

All my mother had tried to do – I now realised – was to open my eyes to this inevitable outcome. Aware herself of what it meant to be poor, she'd wanted to protect me, to spare me from a life of hardship.

But what if I could give this guy the help he needed, just as the Italian sisters did with their men, just give him a leg-up, a push in the right direction, maybe the fishing net he dreamt of, or the motorboat, then, perhaps…

Tomás had once put it very aptly – if we chose to live in Labuga, there were dues that we, as foreigners, had to pay.

The three of us sat there a little longer, half-expecting that sooner or later Carmen would join us and give us the benefit of her counselling. But she was busy in the outhouse at the back, preparing a *tapado* for a big party coming for lunch, while Tifón, the resident dog, had taken it upon himself to give her a hand and bark the turkeys out of the diner as they ventured in, greedy for crumbs.

The morning breeze soon subsided, telling us it was time to go and get things done.

At length, we stood up, paid for our coffees and kissed each other goodbye, with the promise of keeping in touch.

*

After that conversation, determined to re-establish the peace with Rafael on the heels of our latest argument, I doubled my efforts to patch things up. I cooked, I washed, I cleaned, I did my best to live up to his ideal of *comprensión*. I worked even harder to be less contemptuous of his plans, his dreams. To no avail – we drifted further and further apart.

Every night, after dinner, Rafael quickly changed and went out. I never knew where. When I asked, I'd get a shrug of the shoulders and a vague 'Just out.'

'Do I ask you where you go, Monica?' he would then say. 'We're free, remember?'

I was left behind alone, in the hut, lighting one candle after the other while I devoured all the books on his shelves, one by one. Sometimes, I'd listlessly make an entry in my notebook, only to cross it out later, when, going over it, I realised how completely hopeless and desperate I sounded.

Why don't I leave him? I asked myself every night. But there I was, refusing to believe this dream world of mine was crumbling, all the while flogging the proverbial dead horse. It felt like a battle of wills – I, striving to change him, and he, resisting my efforts. Or maybe he was right, and I just wasn't trying as hard as the two Italian sisters.

Rafael would come home much later, well past midnight, my last candle long since expired. He undressed, took out a mangy teddy bear, a toy that had belonged to his child, and staring at it with syrupy tenderness, fell into a seemingly contented sleep. I curled up the other side of the bed, on the edge, shivering with cold and loneliness.

One Saturday night, as I sat reading by candlelight as usual, I heard his plastic flip-flops shuffle across the grass. He pushed the door open and, 'Get ready, *mi amor*,' he announced, bubbling with enthusiasm as in the old days. 'We are going to the beach. Me and you. Together.'

His speech was slurred from drinking, but the invitation was genuine, and it made me feel suddenly lighter, almost excited. I got ready. When was the last time we'd gone out dancing, just me and him?

'Put the *pan de coco* into the bread bin, please,' I said to him casually as I slipped into a dress, and pointed at some bread rolls lying on the kitchen table.

He grabbed the rolls and flung them into the bin, slamming the lid down. 'You don't need to tell me what to do, you know?' he shouted. The violence in his voice felt like a knife stabbing at my brief moment of happiness. I let out a cry of surprise.

'When have I ever left the house without first covering or putting the food away? When? Just tell me. You… you never change. You're impossible. All the time spoiling things. You don't understand me and never will!'

He slung himself into the hammock and said with hatred: 'You can go out by yourself. I don't feel like it any longer.'

I stood there, tongue-tied. What had I done? What was it all about? Where was all this fury coming from? Surely it was a mistake or a bad dream. I went up to the hammock and bent over him, stretching my arms in an attempt to embrace him.

'Don't touch me!' he growled. His mouth took on a sour turn, his eyes dark and blurry. But I was too shocked or too naive – how quickly the image of Belén had faded – to see the warning signals that flashed over his face.

I bent lower over him and tried to kiss him.

His slap echoed inside my head and burnt my cheek. I found myself lying on the earthen floor, flat on my back, my eyes in line with his long, thin legs.

He leapt out of the hammock, walked straight past me and went outside. I heard him talk with his cousin Augusto and with Simón, one of his friends. I peeped through the open door; the three stood there at the end of path, legs wide apart, arms folded across their chests.

I went up to them. 'Could any of you give me a cigarette, *por favor*?' I spoke with as much brazen levity as I could muster, topping it with an ingratiating smile.

Augusto averted his eyes, ignoring my presence; Simón flicked the ash off the tip of his cigarette and motioned to hand it over to me. 'Thanks—'

I was about to take it from him when Rafael intercepted it.

'Don't give her anything. She can buy her own,' he growled with a mad flicker in his eyes. He then crumbled the cigarette in his fist and hurled it away in little pieces.

'But, why?' I asked, unable to make sense of the events. 'Get out of my house!' he yelled. 'Get out, now!' His long arms flailed in the air like scissors.

'*Adiós, Rafa!*' '*Adiós!*' His two friends left quickly, as if they had seen sudden dark-grey clouds rumble with rain across the sky.

I walked back to the hut, but Rafael was already there barring the door from me.

'Let me in,' I pleaded. 'I'll just pick up my things and go, promise!'

'Go away! Who are you anyway? I don't know you. I'm the one who lives here. Alone!' His voice was as hard as metal.

With all my weight, I threw myself against him. But he was much bigger and stronger and did not budge. 'Let me in!' I kept on screaming. I was thinking of my notebooks and of my things stored on the shelves inside.

He swiped his right arm around. At first, I thought he was about to strike me, so I quickly jumped out of the way. But he stretched it upwards, reaching for something tucked away above the doorway, a few inches above his head. When he lowered it, he held a machete in his hand. The long, curved blade had been recently sharpened, so it glittered around the edges, even in the dark.

'Go away, I warn you...' His voice was calm now. A glint of something I could not quite define – was it amusement? was it cold anger? – flickered briefly in his eyes.

I gave myself no time to consider what it was. I quickly turned around and ran away.

*

Back in my old hut, I lay in bed, awake. I stared at the gap in the roof and through it I saw the stars. Thank God, it wasn't raining.

'You are free to come and go as you please,' I remembered Rafael saying to me once. 'One day, you'll just pack and go. But me... I was born and bred here. This is my home and my roots are here in Labuga. And so, whatever happens, I know, this is where I'll always live.'

In a few words, he'd summed up all that was wrong between us, the source of all tension. For him, I was yet another tourist, dipping in and out of his life. Just like Valeria before me, and who knows how many others. He knew that, by definition, tourists are always wealthy, and always passing through.

And what was he to me? I realised I'd never really allowed that thought to take root, not really.

I sighed. I couldn't sleep. I got up from my bed and opened the door.

It was a wonderful night.

The wind was warm; it stroked the foliage of the trees, lightly, with a hiss. The curved trunks stood out against a sky glittering with stars. Beyond the palm grove, overshadowed by a passing white cloud, was the round disc of the moon. Not quite full yet, nibbled away in one corner, peaceful, still.

All this beauty, so hard to square with the shock of that slap, of the humiliation of being abused in front of his friends.

What *did* I want from Rafael? Someone to share this... this kind of evening, no words, just two people so in tune with each other, and with this, that nothing needed to be said.

I sat on the doorstep. I had no clothes on and I felt that my nakedness matched the bareness of the moon.

'Larunihatti...' I whispered to the night. Not so long ago, that was my name.

The same moon looked down on me now. But how quickly things changed. One day, you felt loved; and the next, loneliness ate up your heart.

I sat there, moon-bathing, until I began to feel the chill in the air and little shivers ran down my back.

CHAPTER TWENTY-EIGHT

THE LONG GOODBYE

One and a half years had gone by since that day in late August when, running the gauntlet of people's stares, I'd first walked from the docks right into the heart of the ramshackle town.

So much had happened that it felt more like ten years. But now, suddenly, I knew it was time for me to leave.

I suppose I'd felt that way ever since that last terrible row with Rafael. The image of him standing there on guard before his house, the glistening machete in his hand, had stayed with me for a long time, till one day I forgave him. Yes, again.

My capitulation came after he followed me around for weeks, looking sheepish, and after a dozen remorseful messages he sent me through Daniel and Manu. When I finally relented and agreed to meet him, he apologised profusely and begged me to go back to him and start afresh. In the end, we came to an agreement: we would see each other in my own territory; from now on, he would have to come and see me at my house. After that – and after I had my roof finally repaired – things worked out much better between us, yet I knew deep down, and so did he, that my time here was up.

It wasn't a question of money; the small income I received from my language classes was sufficient for me to get by. It was something deeper: a kind of nostalgia for that other world which was slowly welling up. I missed the hustle and bustle of a large town, I missed going to the cinema or seeing a play, I missed reading the newspapers, I missed hearing the phone ring and wondering who was on the other end of the line. Above all, I missed having my old friends around, all of them loyal and steadfast, more loyal and steadfast than any of the friends I'd made here.

I felt strongly about Livingston, so why was it that I didn't seem to have a single genuine friend among the Livingsteños?

'You know what they say about you in town?' Tomás blurted out to me, one day.

'No idea. You tell me.'

In the last few months, the *mara* I'd befriended on my arrival had taken to walking past me without a word of greeting or a nod, just as if I were made of thin air. Even Tomás ignored me. That day was an exception. He'd literally bumped into me round a street corner and couldn't avoid saying hi.

At first, I thought the reason for their indifference was that, in their eyes, I was now a married woman, married to Rafael, that is. But there was more to it, it seemed.

'People say you are a spy and keep a file on everyone,' He laughed, but his laughter rang hollow.

So, that explained their silence, the hostile glances and the turning of heads.

My clicking away at my typewriter raised a lot of suspicion, I knew. Even Rafael had made some disparaging comments about my writing.

'I'm writing about Livingston,' I said to Tomás in my defence. 'Certainly, I'm not keeping files on anyone.'

'Why Livingston?'

'Why not? I live here.'

'Oh, well, whatever. For us, you're CIA.' Tomás sneered and, with a dismissive wave of his arm in my direction, he walked away.

I was on my tenth exercise book by now, each page covered tightly with my spidery handwriting. In time, I selected the best stories and typed them out. I guess it was my incessant clacking away at the keyboard that aroused people's suspicions. It wasn't so much that they really thought I was a spy. To them, I was just different, and that was enough to single me out and turn me into an "unknown element", the kind that isn't welcome. In a place where so few were literate, I could understand their wariness. I expected a little more, though, from Tomás and his mates who, as well as having basic schooling, certainly knew me better.

The encounter with Tomás marked a significant turning point. Afterwards, I felt a little sadder and lonelier. Not only could Rafael never be the man I wanted, but everybody around, the women, the Rastas, even the *mara,* now disapproved of me.

I'd tried so hard to blend in. Ever since I arrived, I'd lived the same way, eaten the same food, and worked like everyone else. I'd never flaunted either money or education. I genuinely felt that, if only I tried hard, I could become part of the community.

For I truly loved Livingston, in particular the throbbing liveliness I sensed all around. I also loved the setting – the lush greenness, the blue waters, the crimson moon, the dories moving slowly over the waves. I accepted everything, even many of the ugly, unappetising sides of life in the village, such as Daniel's drinking, Rafael's violent outbursts, or the women having to sell themselves for the price of a boat ride to Puerto Barrios. What mattered most to me at the time was that in Livingston I felt completely and utterly alive. It was my place in the world to have fun, as Martin had said to me teasingly all those months ago, until… it stopped being fun.

It was now hard to accept that not only did I not belong here, but I never would.

It didn't matter to anyone in Livingston that I shared the same poor conditions or that I strived to bridge the gap dividing us. I had opportunities, privileges, choices. They didn't. That was the nub of it. For them, I was inexplicably "playing" at poverty, and, when not doing that, writing about them – to what end? Who knew? But it couldn't be any good.

In those days, I began to think of my departure. A part of me resisted the idea; another, the more sensible, pushed ahead with plans. The cheapest way back to Europe was to fly from Belize City to London via the United States. So, one day, I went to the American Embassy in Guatemala Ciudad and applied for and was granted a visa, which was valid only until a certain date. That's how I went about it. I set the ball rolling and, although my heart wanted me to stop and reconsider, I had no choice, by that stage, but to follow it through.

I fixed the time of my departure for the 12th of February.

During those last few weeks, a feeling of tension soared.

I was apprehensive about changing my life so drastically. I knew I would miss Livingston; I would miss it like hell. I already did.

Sitting on a wall in the centre, quietly watching people while away the cool evening, I would often close my eyes and already see myself scurrying along endlessly long pavements, in the drizzle, grey and unsmiling people brushing past me, all immersed in indifferent silence, save for the hectic tapping of their footsteps on the tarmac and the unrelenting roar of the traffic.

Then I would open my eyes and, to my relief, I'd still be here – the voices calling out to each other, the drumbeat, and the chuckling all around.

How many times did I mourn Livingston even before I left it?

Each little moment of the day was highlighted by the feeling that I would soon be gone. I looked at some kids dancing, at the women carrying their baskets on their heads, proud and erect. That was the last time I saw it all. My heart felt heavy.

Each night, I said goodbye to Livingston. In the morning, I woke up thinking *This is your last Monday here*, or *This is your last Tuesday*. There was always some special "last time".

Till I became fidgety. Then I wanted time to fly.

At last, the day of the departure came. Somebody – a passer-by? Mariangela? – took a picture of me as I left the house that morning.

I've got it here, as I am writing: a light blue and pink stripy dress fixed around the waist with a cotton belt, a pair of weather-beaten trainers, a bulge around my stomach, my document pouch. With one hand I hold up an umbrella, a few broken spikes jutting out like antennae; with the other I'm clutching the strap of my backpack. I keep my eyes down as I smile at a puppy that seemed to have adopted me.

As I left the house and walked towards the docks, I saw Belén coming in the opposite direction. Wiry and upright, she walked slowly – for once without a hat – as she balanced a huge basket of laundry above her head, so perfectly still it seemed to have taken root. It was the first time I saw her engaged in these domestic chores.

'*Hola, amiga!*' she hollered in her raucous voice.

Ever since that infamous Saturday night at the beach, she'd kept her distance and, feeling wary and awkward, so had I – hence, the unexpected greeting caught me by surprise.

She noticed my backpack and, as she came level with me, she stopped.

'*Te vas?* Are you leaving?' she asked, seemingly with a glint in her eyes.

'This very moment. I'm off to catch the boat.'

She lowered her basket, and as she stretched her sinewy arms towards me, for a moment I feared she might be about to push me or start a fight.

'*Qué te vaya bien, amiga!* Farewell!' she said with a smile, the gold of her side teeth sparkling in the sun. Then, she bent over and squeezed me in a damp embrace.

I tried hard to guess what was behind this unexpected friendliness, that smile. What was she really thinking? But there seemed to be no hidden agenda, no hard feelings, no thoughts like *Hurray, at last she's off*. She'd come in peace with the sole purpose of bidding me such a warm and forgiving goodbye. Suddenly I felt guilty – guilty for being suspicious of her now, but mostly for failing to side with her against Rafael that night.

As we parted, a pungent smell of bleach followed her up the street.

Down at the docks, a crowd of people had already gathered, street vendors, visitors, but mostly merchants who were going to Punta Gorda on business for the day. Now that I was finally leaving, I wished I could be away as quickly as possible. But, as the gates that cordoned off the pier were still locked, I had no option other than to sit to one side and wait. I lit a cigarette.

I thought about the people who'd come to wish me farewell, the night before.

'When the weather gets warmer, I'll be off too,' Mariangela said, predictably. And, as we hugged one last time, Paul also mumbled something about being the next one to pack and go. Giulia couldn't come but Mariangela handed me her sister's farewell gift. The card on it read: *This infusion is meant to keep you company on your way back. Lots of love. P.S. planning to leave Labuga soon.* Everyone seemed set to leave.

Everyone, except those who couldn't.

'Why am I the one who always gets left behind?' Rafael said self-pityingly, as we laid in bed, his back to me.

That morning, I'd left him there, asleep, or pretending to be.

The gates of the docks were finally opened. I stubbed out my cigarette and I went on board.

Five minutes later, with a revving of the engine, the ferry moved off the concrete landing.

I stood by the railings and watched the thatch-roofed huts become gradually smaller, until they became one with the hills. Soon, the palm-fringed coastline began to grow thinner and thinner, sandwiched in between the converging blue expanse of sea and sky. Then, at the end, there was only blueness; blueness in front, blueness behind, deep, intensive blueness all around.

AFTERWORD

lthough the years I spent in Central America marked my life forever, determining some of my future choices, twenty-five years went by before, in the summer of 2013, I finally plucked up the courage to revisit the old places.

I found a different world.

In Guatemala, the end of the thirty-six-year war had brought about some positive changes. Q'eqchi', and other languages spoken by the largest and more influential Mayan ethnicities, was now officially recognised, and so, it seemed, were the Amerindian traditions and culture.

Museums dedicated to the Mayans had sprouted all over Guatemala City – the Museum of Archaeology and Ethnology, the Popol Vuh, the Museo Ixchel del Traje Indígena, to mention just a few. Here, exhibited in glass cases or along air-conditioned corridors, scores of straw mannequins sported the same *huipiles*, *cortes*, *fajas* and *morrales* that so many years before I'd seen worn in the streets.

The traditional *trajes* were still in use, but only a few were handwoven on the traditional backstrap looms; most were of a hybrid kind, of less intricate design, and made from cheaper synthetic fabrics. In short, they were now mostly mass-produced, mixing patterns from different regions in a hotchpotch of symbols and colours known as "modern fusion".

In Huehuetenango, I had an interesting chat with a local trade unionist.

'The war is over,' he told me when I enquired about the political situation, 'but things are, if anything, worse than before. Now that we are a "democracy", he spat out the word with contempt, 'we no longer make the news. The ILO, the human rights organisations, the international community, they all seem to have lost interest in us. It is as if, once the peace agreements were signed, they thought that everything was fine with us and we no longer needed their support.'

He went on to explain that, although both the unions and the rights of the Mayans were recognised, the economy was in pieces. 'Nothing has substantially changed with the peace treaty. The poverty is still appalling.' He concluded: 'Things are even more tragic than when we were at war.'

People, he said, were forced to live off their wits and invent their own jobs or do anything that brought in an income. Their activities varied from selling shoelaces at street corners to running food stalls along the pavements. Periodically, under the pretext that these stalls were a blight on the neighbourhood, troupes of security guards were sent by the council to storm the city centre and clear them all away.

Only a minority of Guatemalans were in secure employment. This, together with a tax system that benefitted the very rich, made for an impoverished society with services and state provisions cut to the bare minimum. And so, hospitals resembled lazarettos; schools had to make do without books, teachers and classrooms; and people were obliged to work into their old age or become beggars.

No wonder organised crime, drug trafficking and the black market were thriving.

The capital itself had many no-go areas. The few days I spent there, I heard so many gruesome tales of violence that, feeling unsafe, I hardly ventured out into those same streets I'd walked confidently twenty-five years earlier.

I hurried over to the Atlantic coast, to my beloved Livingston.

My heart was pounding as I got off the ferry and began to look around.

The village had expanded and now had not just one but several asphalted roads. Many of the old landmarks had disappeared, like the Comedor Cali and the Lugudi Barana, but a score of guest houses and rustic chalets for rent had sprouted along the beach. The African Place was still there, with its crenellated turrets and its tiles – now under new management.

Two big surprises were in store for me. A solid bridge had been built over the Río Quehueche, making the crossing possible in all weather conditions; and a wooden fence with a sturdy gate blocked the entrance to the waterfalls. On it, a sign in scarlet letters read: *Veinticinco quetzals la entrada por persona por día* – a steep entry fee for a beauty spot that, during my time there, had been free of charge.

'When I lived here in the eighties, you didn't have to pay to walk up to the Siete Altares,' I complained to the burly Garifuna who now owned the land, the chalet, the budding resort beyond the gate and, of course, the seven waterfalls. How had he managed to buy all that? I wondered. I always thought it was communal land.

He smiled at me charmingly. 'Lucky you! You got to know Livingston in its golden days. I lived in Chicago then!' He winked and gave me a thirty per cent discount.

As I walked back to town along the beach, I heard stealthy steps right behind me, and a thin old man appeared at my side.

'*Qué buena onda verte!*' he said and, as he smiled, I recognised the lively round eyes of Manu, former partner of Mariangela, the Italian sister.

He seemed genuinely happy to see me and, his being the first familiar face I saw, in that moment of recognition, I was pleased to see him too. Was this really the man who'd almost knocked Mariangela's teeth out? He looked so much frailer now, and shorter. Despite the memory of that shocking episode, I couldn't help feeling sorry for him.

We walked all the way into town together, exchanging news. Mariangela had long since returned to Naples, where she ran a small bed and breakfast business, and we'd often met when I travelled to Italy to visit my parents. She rarely talked about Manu and her time in Livingston.

'We Garifunas are a minority now.' He swept his thin arm all around to embrace the bottle-green ocean, the windswept fronds of the palm trees, the distant roofs of houses buried among the greenery. He sighed. 'Our children speak only Spanish now, very few learn Garifuna. We're losing our language, our identity, everything… People are leaving.'

Just what Leonardo, Rafael's uncle, had complained about all those years ago, when my mother and I met him in Stann Creek.

Manu and I stopped for a beer and, at the end of our conversation, he took me to one side and whispered into my ear, 'Can you spare me a few *quetzals* so that I can eat? Or a few dollars, whatever you have… *Una ayuda, pues…*'

With this first encounter, I decided I wouldn't go and look up any of my old friends. The thought of a similar meeting with Rafael, in particular, scared me. I worried that I might find him, just like Manu, a shadow of his former self. Not wanting to be disappointed, and unsure of his reaction to seeing me, I preferred to remember him as dashing and charming as he'd been in the old days. So, without enquiring about him or his whereabouts, I boarded the first ferry out of Labuga.

*

This last visit to Central America was relatively brief but made a strong impact on me. It prompted me to go back to my journals and revisit the places, the people and the feelings of those moments in all their unalloyed immediacy. So, back in Britain, I dug out my copious notes, the ones that according to Tomás had earned me the soubriquet of CIA operative, and began to write about those earlier times.

The exercise of narrating my experiences in Latin America forced me, here in the present, to dig deep into my young self and take stock of my past thoughts and actions.

Not an easy task, I knew, but I started this second journey full of confidence, wanting to impress my readers with how brave and adventurous I'd been. Gradually, as I went deeper into the past and into the details of some of the events, I could not escape the dark side of the experiences and stories I was relating.

Friends who read the first draft challenged me on what struck them as my "indifference" to many of the incidents I recounted, and to the brutal repression of the Mayans by the military. I witnessed this so often that, at the time, I barely raised an eyebrow and, without realising, took it for granted.

And so, painstakingly, I began to take stock. I tried to understand the reasons that had made me so complacent and unresponsive, not least in the face of the episodes of domestic abuse I witnessed, and of which I was myself a victim.

It's hard for me, as it is for many women, to come to terms with the extent of violence against our gender. The social bias against women is so profoundly ingrained that we tend to internalise it. This, I realised, was precisely what I had done in the context of my relationship with Rafael, and in my response to the violence against some of the women I knew in Livingston – Belén, Giulia and Mariangela.

Like so many women who pride themselves on their independence and strength, I'd always thought of myself as perfectly capable of standing up for my rights, and yet, by failing to take sides with my own gender and react with the outrage demanded by the circumstances, I had colluded with the culture of silence and victim blaming. In Livingston, I had accepted this violence wholesale – as those around me seemed to do – and even thought of it as part and parcel of the exotic image I had of the place, adding covert racism to my complicity and complacency.

*

What of the real people on whom my characters are based?

As Monica did, I continue to struggle with my relationship to money, my own, what I do with it, what others do with it, and especially what to do about others' lack of it. I haven't quite come to terms with all this yet, but possibly the most valuable lesson I've learnt so far is that, if we want to live like equals, there needs to be a very drastic shift in the way wealth is distributed worldwide.

Of Martin, I heard nothing more since the day we parted, except for a letter I found waiting for me on my return to Britain all those years ago. After some general news and a few anecdotes about his new life in Las Palmeras, he informed me that he was going steady with a girl he'd met there, herself an American volunteer. From what he said, she sounded just like the girl in the dream I had in Hotel Tranquilidad as I dozed off on a sofa, waiting for a room. *Come and visit us at the orphanage, whenever*, he said at the end of his letter. *A big hug for now, the best of luck.* I didn't take up the offer, and we soon lost touch.

My mother returned from Livingston full of concern for the situation she found me in. Needless to say, she was immensely relieved when I called her from Gatwick Airport, and told her I was safe home. The travelling bug seemed to have got hold of her in Guatemala and, in the years to come, she travelled to many distant places, full of curiosity and eagerness to understand the world.

Thanks to social media and the advent of smartphones, Rafael found my profile on Facebook and now we are in contact with each other. He doesn't drink anymore, he says, and, judging from the posts on his wall, he has indeed replaced the solace of the bottle with that of religion. But, going by the requests for "*una pequeña ayuda*" he sends me periodically, his life in Livingston is still a struggle. It seems he was right about being the one who is forever left behind.

Giulia returned to Italy a few months after I'd gone. Putting to good use everything she'd learnt about herbs in Livingston, she became a competent herbalist. I've heard she lives somewhere in the countryside near Perugia, close to nature, as she always wanted.

And what of her sister?

One day, back in Italy, in my parents' kitchen, the TV humming in the background, a couple of familiar images flickered across the screen. The first was the smiling face of Mariangela, a portrait picture of her taken some years before; the second was the footage of her brother being arrested for her murder. I dropped onto a chair in front of the TV. She'd been stabbed to death. At first, her brother had pretended innocence, but, under police interrogation, in the end, he confessed. I was in shock. Could that be the same brother who, on my visits to see my friend in Naples, had cooked for us and chatted amiably at the dinner table? That model of congenial "normality" turned out to be the same guy who would later explain to the police that he'd been driven to take his sister's life because she had "humiliated him" in front of his friends.

*

Years have gone by, but, still now, I often think about Livingston and the people I met there, especially Mariangela.

Her story was an eye-opener, if only in retrospect. The fact that she survived domestic abuse in those far-off lands only to fall victim to the same kind of violence in her own country, in her own home, seems to me very revealing. Beyond the exotic allure, it shows the existence of strong connections and similarities between distant parts of the world; it also proves that sometimes you need to go full circle before you can recognise what has always been right there, in front of you.

And so, it is to Mariangela, and to all the Mariangelas – the women everywhere, regardless of class, race, or culture, who have been abused, attacked, and even lost their lives simply because they are women – that I dedicate this book.

ACKNOWLEDGEMENTS

I started this project a long time ago and many people have supported me at different stages over the years. During the various writing courses I attended between 2010 and 2015 – at City Lit, Spread the Word, the Groucho Club, and the BBC – I was inspired by wonderful teachers and fascinating fellow students. I'd like to thank them all for their encouragement and for giving me many useful suggestions and ideas. Among the tutors, I'd like to thank Maggie Hamand, Shaun Levin, Eva Lewin, Mary Flanagan, Nicholas Murray, and especially Anna Owen, for her wonderful editing; among the students, the incomparable Rahila, super woman Eadie Heyderman, and kindly and insightful Lucy Shuttleworth.

My present writing group has also been invaluable in motivating me. Many thanks to both Lucy Shuttleworth and Ruth Herd. Our regular Friday meetings have kept me going even through the most difficult days.

Besides the aforementioned list of writing gurus and companions, I'd like to thank two people to whom I feel especially indebted: Barbara Flater who spent the summer of 1989 helping me draft the skeleton of what is now Livingston Unfound; and my lifetime friend Maureen McWilliams, who never tired of reading version upon version of the novel. I am very grateful to her for her invaluable suggestions, for offering her insights and above all for challenging me constructively, whenever unconscious biases and prejudices transpired from my writing. In short, I want to thank her for being my 'Talking Cricket' and helping me grow together with the story.

Many thanks also to others who advised me in their field of expertise – Gaby Weisz, Chris Holland from UCL Library Services, Mara Fongaro, Mauro Gonzo, Soledad Zarate, Pam Marshall, Louise Gilchrist, and all those friends who read the manuscript at different stages, and supported my writing efforts with their encouragement and generous enthusiasm.

As for the lyric on page 127, every reasonable effort has been made to trace its copyright holders. Having found no digital reference for it, I have come to the conclusion that either the song was written before online computer records started or was created by the character singing it in the novel. In the unlikely event that the rightful owner has been overlooked, the publishers will be pleased to rectify the situation at the first opportunity.

Finally, I'd like to thank the Book Guild team – Jeremy Thompson, Rosie Lowe, Philippa Iliffe, and the cover designer Jack Wedgbury, who, through a single image, has managed to convey so powerfully the overall mood of the story.